BARBARA DELINSKY

AN
ACCIDENTAL
WOMAN

A NOVEL

Simon & Schuster

New York   London   Toronto   Sydney   Singapore

SIMON & SCHUSTER
Rockefeller Center
1230 Avenue of the Americas
New York, NY 10020

SIMON & SCHUSTER and colophon are registered trademarks
of Simon & Schuster, Inc.

For information about special discounts for bulk purchases,
please contact Simon & Schuster Special Sales:
1-800-456-6798 or business@simonandschuster.com

Manufactured in the United States of America

10   9   8   7   6   5   4   3   2   1

Library of Congress Cataloging-in-Publication Data is available.

ISBN 0-7432-0470-0

ACKNOWLEDGMENTS

My books would not emerge healthy and hardy without the help of many people. In the case of *An Accidental Woman,* I begin by thanking my agent, Amy Berkower, not only for the title but for her constant support, understanding, and enthusiasm. I also thank my editors, Michael Korda and Chuck Adams. This book was a complex one; I always knew that it would work, though I didn't always know how. I thank Michael and Chuck for their patience in enduring months of silence on my end, and for their trust that I would, indeed, get all the pieces of the pie in place.

An Accidental Woman deals with two issues about which I knew precious little, and though I did book research and Internet research, the firsthand information I received from two sources was crucial. Jean O'Leary was wonderful, sharing her time and expertise with regard to lower-spine injuries and life in a wheelchair. Likewise, Betty Ann Lockhart was generous, knowing, and imaginative as she guided me through the mechanics and the crises of maple syrup production. Both of these women "got it" when it came to my plot needs, for which I thank them profusely. If there are technical errors in this book, the fault is mine alone. *An Accidental Woman* is meant to be neither a manual on paraplegia nor one on maple syrup production. I've had to take what Jean and Betty Ann gave me and work it into my plot. I like to think that any technical errors I made in the process have more to do with poetic license than ignorance.

I'm a cat person, as many of you know. I often incorporate cats into my plots, because I do know what it's like to have a cat in the house—which isn't to say that I know everything about cats. One of the things I *don't* know is part of *An Accidental Woman*. Instrumental in my getting this part right were the wonderful contributors to the bulletin board of the Best Friends Pet Sanctuary. Their response to my query was heartrending. I thank them, right along with the Sanctuary for the wonderful work that it does. My thanks, also, to myriad others who answered my questions on smaller matters. You all know who you are. Please know how much I appreciate your help—as I do, always, appreciate the help of my assistant. My thanks to Wendy Page for keeping my professional life in order so that I can focus on my writing.

As always, I thank my children—Eric and Jodi, Andrew, Jeremy, and Sherrie, listed in the order of their birth. Whether local or long-distance, they are the mainstay of my life. And Steve? He was there for me again. Not only did he feed me legal information, but, bless him, he sat over not one dinner but *two* and felt the emotion of my plot as I described the closing scenes to him. Tears in his eyes? A writer—a woman—a wife—couldn't ask for a better endorsement.

Finally, I thank all of you readers. I'm not sure I would have ever tackled this story if it hadn't been for your urging, yet writing this story has been an extraordinarily gratifying experience for me. We hear lots nowadays about the mass market, the economics of publishing, the bottom line. For me, the bottom line has been and always will be my readers. My thanks to each and every one of you.

AN ACCIDENTAL WOMAN

Chapter One

Within seconds of coming awake, Micah Smith felt a chill at the back of his neck that had nothing to do with the cold air seeping in through the window cracked open by his side of the bed. It was barely dawn. He didn't have to glance past Heather's body toward the nightstand clock to know that, but could see it in the purpling that preceded daylight when February snows covered the forest floor.

The purpling seemed deeper this morning, but that wasn't what caused his alarm. Nor was it any sound from the girls' room that caused him to hold his breath. They would sleep for another hour, he knew, and if not sleep, then stay in bed until they heard Heather or him up and about.

No. What held him totally still, eyes on that inch of open window, was the sound that came from beyond. Even in winter, the woods were filled with live things, but what he heard now was neither deer, nor owl, nor snowshoe rabbit. It was a car, moving very slowly down the snow-crusted drive toward the small house that Micah had built for his family.

Get out of bed, cried a silent voice, but he remained inert. Barely breathing, he listened. Not one car. Two. They inched their way closer, then stopped. Their engines went still.

Do something, cried that silent voice, more urgent now, and he thought of the rifle that was mounted high above the front door, out of reach of the girls. But he couldn't move—couldn't *move*—other than to turn his head toward Heather. She continued to sleep, oblivious to what he heard, unaware of the thoughts that held him there against her warmth.

As he watched the swirl of her long dark hair touched by a generous dusting of silver, he heard the stealthy click of car doors—one, then a second. He imagined that there might be even more doors opening silently, carefully guided by hands trained in covert operations.

A patch of Heather's pale shoulder showed through the tangle of her hair. He would have touched it if he hadn't feared waking her, but he didn't want that. Once she was awake, once she heard what he heard, once this moment ended, their lives would be changed. He didn't know how he knew that, but he did. A part of him had been waiting for this moment, fearing it for four years—and it wasn't just a superstition, the idea that because one woman had left him, this one would, too. Heather wasn't like anyone else; she was unique.

The footsteps coming toward the house were careful, making only the occasional crunch on the snow, but a lifetime of living in the New Hampshire woods had trained Micah's ear well. The house was being surrounded. He figured that his rifle wouldn't do much good against the five or six people that he guessed were outside. Nor did he figure gunpower was called for. The people out there weren't intent on violence. And what was happening was inevitable.

A soft knock came at the front door, a sound he might have missed if he'd been asleep. It had begun. He quickly slipped from under the thick down with a grace that belied his height and firm build. Silently he pulled on jeans and left the bedroom. In seconds, he was down the hall and through the living room. Not bothering with a light, he pulled the door open before another knock came, though Pete Duffy's hand was already raised.

Pete was second in command to Lake Henry's police chief William Jacobs, and was a friend of Micah's, which was certainly why he'd been chosen to come. The authorities would want things kept calm. Having Pete there, a man Micah trusted, would help on that score, though the look of regret on the man's face did nothing to ease Micah's sense of dread as his eyes moved past his friend to a second man who stood just behind him on the front porch. Micah didn't know this man, or the two women who were with him. All three wore jeans and identical blue jackets that Micah knew must have law enforcement initials on the back.

"We need Heather," Pete said in an apologetic whisper, with only the smallest jut of his chin toward the threesome with him. "They have a warrant."

Micah swallowed. A warrant was serious. "For what?"

The man with Pete extended both hands. One held paperwork, the other his ID. "Jim Mooney. FBI. I have a warrant for the arrest of Heather Malone on charges of flight to avoid prosecution."

Micah considered the man's words. There were serious charges and not-so-serious charges. He had always known that Heather hid her past. During those times when he had wondered what might have caused her secretiveness, involvement with the law had been worst-case scenario. Now he could only pray that the charges against her were of the not-so-serious kind, though he feared those wouldn't have brought the FBI to his doorstep at dawn.

"Prosecution for what?" he asked the agent.

"Murder."

A sharp breath escaped Micah—oddly, he felt relief. If murder was the charge, then there surely was a mistake. "That's impossible. Heather's incapable of murder."

"Maybe as Heather Malone. But we have evidence that her real name is Lisa Matlock, and that fifteen years ago she killed a man in California."

"Heather's never been in California."

"Lisa has," the agent informed him. "She grew up there. She was there until fifteen years ago, when she deliberately ran a man down with her car. She disappeared right afterward. Your Heather arrived in Lake Henry fourteen years ago and worked as a short-order cook, just like Lisa did in California in the two years before she left. Heather's face is identical to Lisa's, right down to the gray eyes and the scar at the corner of the mouth."

"There are millions of women with gray eyes," Micah said, suddenly aware of cold air on his bare chest, "and that scar came from a car accident." The words were barely out when he realized what he'd said. But the agent absolved him.

"Not this one. She escaped this accident unscathed, but the man she ran down died—a man she tried to extort minutes before she ran him down."

"Extort." Micah snorted, more convinced than ever that a mistake had been made. "Not Heather. I don't care what name she uses. She's gentle. She's kind. She'd die herself before she'd kill someone."

The agent was unfazed. "If that's true, it'll come out in a trial. For now, I need her to come out here. Either you bring her to us, or we go in."

"You can't do that," Micah said, straightening his six-foot-four frame. "This is my house."

"We have it surrounded, so if she's trying to slip out the back, she'll be caught."

Pete scowled at the agent. "I told you, Mooney. There won't be any trouble." The look he turned on Micah was pleading. "The law's on their side. We've got no choice."

Still Micah argued. "Eyes and a scar. What kind of proof's that?"

"We have prints," said the agent.

Micah studied the man. "Fingerprints?"

"Handwriting."

Micah read enough to know a little about the law. "That's not conclusive."

"I'd say you're biased."

"Same the fuck with you."

Pete stepped between the two men. Slowly and deliberately he told Micah, "They have a warrant. That gives them the right to take her. Don't rile them, Micah."

A low light suddenly came on behind him, a lamp near the spot where the living room met the hall. Heather stood there. She had slipped on a robe and held the lapels shut with one hand while with the other she steadied herself against the wall. As she looked at the people beyond the door, her eyes grew wider. Micah turned to look at her. Those eyes weren't just any gray; they were irridescent. From the start, way back, they had made Micah's insides jingle, and they did it again now, holding his in a silent plea.

Responding, he held up a hand to stop the two female agents who started forward, and, instead, went to Heather himself. Slipping his fingers into the hair at her nape, shaping his hand to hold her head, he searched her eyes for a sign of knowledge or guilt. All he saw was fear.

"They say you're someone else," he whispered. "They must be wrong, but they need you to go with them."

"Where?" she asked with barely a sound.

That wasn't the first question Micah would have asked if he had been in her shoes. He'd have wanted to know who they thought he was and why he needed to go with them. If Heather was truly in the dark as to why they were there, she would have wanted to know that.

But she was a practical sort, far more so than he.

"I don't know," he murmured. "Maybe to Willie Jake's office." He glanced over his shoulder at Pete. "They just want to question her?"

Before Pete could answer, the two women approached. "We need to book her," one told him before turning to Heather. "If you want to dress, we'll go with you."

Heather's eyes flew from one woman's face to the other, then to Micah's. She put a hand on his chest, burying it in the hair there as she always did in moments of passion, anchoring her then against abandon, anchoring her now against the terror that had seized her.

"*I'll* take her to dress," he said, but one of the agents was already grasping her arm and reciting her Miranda rights, as Micah had heard done dozens of times on television dramas. The moment would have been terrifyingly real even without Heather's eyes clinging to his.

Frantic to help her, desperate to do something, but realistic enough to know he was hamstrung, Micah glanced back at Pete. "Someone's gonna answer for this. It's wrong."

Pete came forward as the two female agents ushered Heather down the hall. "I told them that. So'd Willie Jake. He spent most of last night trying to talk some sense into them, but they have the warrant, Micah. It's legal. There's nothing we can do."

Micah turned back to Heather, but she had disappeared into the bedroom. When he turned to go after her, Mooney caught his arm. "You have to stay here. She's under arrest."

"Daddy?" came a soft voice from even farther down the hall.

"Oh God," Micah murmured and turned in alarm. It was Melissa, his seven-year-old daughter. In a voice that was as normal as he could make it, what with a growing panic, he said, "Go back to bed, Missy. Too early to get up."

But Missy, by far the more curious and bold of his two girls, padded toward him in her long pink nightgown. Her hair was as dark as his—and as thick and long as Heather's—but wildly curly. "Why's Pete here?" she asked, slipping a hand into Micah's, but looking at Mooney. "Who's he?"

Micah shot a frantic glance at Pete. "Uh, he works with Pete sometimes. They have to ask Heather some questions."

"What questions?"

"Just some . . . things."

"Now?"

"In a little while."

She looked up at him. "When the sun comes up?" That would make sense to her. It was what Heather had taught the girls when they'd been toddlers and had awakened Micah and her at ungodly hours.

"Yes."

Her eyes grew mischievous. "I'll bet she's still asleep. Can I go tickle her?"

"No." He tightened his hold on her hand. "She's already awake. She's getting dressed. I want you to go back to bed. Make sure your sister sleeps a little longer."

"She's awake. She's just scared to come out."

Micah knew it wasn't as simple as Star being scared or shy. He had long since accepted that the five-year-old possessed an odd adult insight. Star would know that something was desperately wrong. Her fear would be real.

"Then go back in and play with her. That'll make her feel better."

Missy smiled and released his hand. In the few seconds it took for her to step back and flatten herself to the wall, her expression turned defiant.

"Missy," Micah warned, waving her back down the hall, but before she could refuse, Heather emerged from the bedroom with the two female agents. She was dressed in jeans and a heavy sweater, the sheer bulk of which made her look lost. Her expression mirrored that. When she caught sight of Missy, she stopped short. Her eyes met Micah's for a single, alarmed second before returning to the child.

Missy was looking at the two agents. "Who're *they?*"

Micah said, "More friends of Pete's. Go on back in with Star, Missy. I need you to help."

Missy stayed pressed against the wall.

Heather knelt by her side. "Daddy's right, sweetie," she said in a gentle voice. "Go in with Star. She needs you."

Defiance gone, replaced by worry, Missy slipped an arm around Heather's shoulder. "Where are you going?"

"Into town."

"When'll you be back?"

"A little later."

"Are you sure?"

"Yes."

"Do you promise?"

Waiting for the answer himself—hanging his future on it much as the child was—Micah saw Heather swallow. But that was the only beat she missed. In the same soft voice, she said, "I'll do my best to be here when you get home from school."

"Do you *promise?*" Missy repeated.

"Yes," Heather whispered. As she straightened, she pressed a kiss to the child's head. She closed her eyes, and a look of anguish crossed her face. Micah imagined that she held the kiss a beat longer than she might have. Sure enough, as she came toward him, her eyes were filled with tears. When she was as close as she could be, she whispered, "Call Cassie."

Cassie Byrnes was one of Heather's closest friends, and she was a lawyer.

Micah took her hands, only to find that the sleeves of the bulky sweater concealed handcuffs nearly as cold as her skin. Furious, he turned on Pete, who raised a brow in warning and nodded toward Missy.

"Call Cassie," Heather repeated—which was certainly the right thing to say, certainly the *practical* thing to say, though not what Micah wanted to hear from her. He wanted her to profess utter confusion, to insist that a mistake had been made, to protest her innocence, even to cry and loudly declare that she had never in her life heard the name Lisa Matlock—all of which might well be the case, Micah told himself. But yes, Heather was a practical woman, and yes, given the circumstances, especially with the legality of the arrest warrant as vouched for by Pete, cooperating was the only thing to do.

Still, the handcuffs offended him. A small person like Heather didn't have a chance in hell of overpowering these three agents, plus however many were outside, even with both hands free. Not that his Heather would think of fighting. In the four years that they'd been together, he had never seen her lash out in anger at anything.

When the two female agents ushered her toward the door, he followed closely. "Where are you taking her?"

Mooney stepped in his path as the agents whisked Heather outside. "Concord. She'll go before a magistrate there this morning. She needs an attorney."

Go before a magistrate. Micah's eyes flew to Pete, who said, "They have to return the fugitive flight warrant."

"Is she being charged with murder?"

"No. Not charged with anything yet. They return the warrant and ask for extradition. Heather can choose to waive an extradition hearing and go back with them, or she can fight it. They can't take her back—can't charge her with murder or anything else—until they make a solid enough case that the charges are legit."

Micah wanted to know the how, why, and where of everything Pete was talking about, but he had more immediate questions, and Mooney was leaving. Following the agent out the door, he trotted barefoot down the steps, oblivious to the crusted ice on the wood planks, the snow on the drive, and the subfreezing air on his near-naked body. "I'm coming with you," he announced—a totally *un*practical thing to say, since he couldn't take the girls with him and they couldn't possibly stay here alone, but his words were driven by emotion, not logic.

Mooney ignored him and kept on going.

Pete became the practical one. "Not wise to do that right now."

Eyes on Heather, Micah watched her vanish into the back of a dark van, the vehicle farthest from the house. At the same time, two other men materialized from the woods and slid into the van.

Micah began to run. "I want to go with her."

Pete ran alongside him. "They won't let you. You'd be better going down later with Cassie. Let these guys go without a fuss now. Get them out of here before the sun's up. There's less of a spectacle that way."

Micah hadn't begun to think beyond the moment. Looking now, he saw that the sky had indeed begun to brighten. Pete had a point. But when the deputy pulled at Micah's arm and tried to steer him back to the cabin, Micah tugged free and ran on. He stopped at the closed door of the van, bent down, and flattened a hand on the window. His eyes met Heather's just as Mooney started the engine, and short of running along-side until the van gained enough speed to leave him behind, he had no choice but to stay. Straightening, he stared at the head that was turned and looking back at him. He held that gaze until the van rounded a bend and disappeared down the forest drive.

She was gone.

Suddenly, he felt cold inside and out. Turning fast, he started back to-ward the house. Of the two cars he'd heard earlier, only Pete's Lake Henry cruiser was left.

"Some friend you are," he muttered as he stormed past the deputy.

"Hell, Micah, what could we do?" Pete cried, following him. "They had the warrant for her arrest."

"You could have said it was wrong. You could've said they made a mis-take."

"We *did*. But, Christ, they're FBI. It was already a federal issue. What could we do?"

"Call us. Warn us."

"How would that've helped? Would you have run off, like you were guilty of something? This was the only way, Micah."

Micah took the front steps in twos, energized by anger.

"Look at it this way," Pete said. "They have to *prove* she is who they say. You think anyone here's going to say she's someone else? No way. So they're going to have to dig up other people. That'll take some time, don't you think?"

What Micah thought was that *any* amount of time he was separated from Heather was bad. He wanted her with him, and not just for the girls' sake. He had come to depend on her gentleness, her sureness, and—yes—her practicality. He was a nuts-and-bolts guy who sometimes was so focused on the small details that he didn't see the larger picture. Heather did. She was his helpmate when it came to being human. She was also his partner when it came to maple sugaring, and the season was about to start.

But she wasn't here. And he did need to see the larger picture. In this instance, that meant calling Cassie.

Striding into the house, he shut the door before Pete could follow, then promptly forgot about Cassie. Missy stood in the middle of the living room looking crushed, and though there was no sign of Star, Micah was sure she was near. He looked around the living room, behind and under the sofa, the chairs, the large square coffee table that he had built at Heather's direction, but it wasn't until he looked behind him at the bookshelves flanking the front door that he spotted her. She was on the bottom shelf, tucked in beside a stack of *National Geographic* magazines that were a stark yellow against the pale green of her nightie. Her knees were drawn up and held close by her small arms. Her hair, dark like his but long, straight, and fine, lay over her shoulders like a shawl. Her eyes were woefully sad and knowing, and they were watching him.

His heart lurched. It wasn't that he had stronger feelings for Star, just that he worried more. She was a more serious child than Melissa. And introverted. Whereas Missy said what she thought, Star was quieter. She had been an infant when her mother had left—"left" being the word he used in place of "skidded off the road, went down a ravine, and burned up in the cab of her truck." He knew that Star couldn't possibly remember Marcy, still he was convinced that she sensed the loss. Heather was wonderful with Star. Heather was wonderful with both of his girls. And now Heather had left, too.

Hunkering down, he caught up the child. Her arms and legs went around him as he straightened.

Not knowing where to begin, he simply said, "Everything's okay, baby," as he carried her down the hall to the room the girls shared. He set her on her bed. Like Missy's, it was a mess of gingham sheets, pillow, and down—Missy's pink, Star's green—all of which, again, was Heather's doing. "And everything's *going* to be okay. But you can help me out now, baby. I need you and your sister to get dressed while I make some calls. Then we'll have breakfast together."

"We won't wait for Momma," the child said in a sure little voice.

"No. She'll have breakfast in town."

"What'll she eat?"

He thought for a minute. "Eggs? Waffles? If we eat the same thing, it'll be like she's with us. What do you think?"

"Maybe."

"Oatmeal," Missy announced from close by. "Oatmeal's her favorite. She'd be having that. But I can only eat it if it has lots of maple sugar on it."

"Well, we have lots of maple sugar, so we're golden. Help your sister dress?" Micah said and, with a return of the urgency he had felt when the FBI van disappeared with Heather inside, he headed for the kitchen. Halfway there, he did an about-face and went back down the hall, this time to the room opposite the girls'. He had added this room soon after Heather moved in, hoping it would be for a child they would have together, but they'd been too busy, it seemed, growing the girls, growing the business. The floor of the room was covered with the dollhouse village he'd made for the girls and which they had arranged during a recent spate of snowy days. He had to step over the town hall and the library to reach the closet, then had to push spare clothes aside to get to the shelves built in behind.

The knapsack was on a shelf out of reach of the girls and far to the right, well hidden by clothes and boxes of Christmas decorations that had only recently been taken down. A drab brown thing, the knapsack was small and worn. Micah didn't know whether it had belonged to Heather herself or to someone else. To his knowledge, it was the only relic she had of her pre–Lake Henry days.

He pulled the knapsack from the shelf and shifted the boxes on either side to fill the space. Tucking the sack under his arm—and refusing to consider what was inside—he went through the kitchen to the back hall.

Jackets of various sizes hung from hooks at all heights, as did hats, lanterns, picks, and shovels, as well as a coil of plastic tubing that Micah was repairing. An assortment of footwear was lined against the wall, crowded in by the snowshoes that they'd been using each day when they trekked up the hill to the sugarbush to clear away winter litter and to check the mainline for damage in anticipation of sugaring time.

But he wasn't going to the sugarbush now. Stepping into the largest boots in the pile, he pulled on a jacket and stuffed the knapsack inside. For good measure, lest anyone be watching from the woods, he grabbed the plastic tubing and went out, down the back steps and over the well-packed snow on an oft-trodden path. The sugarhouse stood several hundred feet up the hill from the house. It was a long stone building with a large cupola atop, through which steam from the evaporator escaped when the sap was being boiled down.

Nothing escaped it now. There was no sweet scent, no air of anticipation. The sugarhouse and woods alike were cold and still.

Feeling only dread, Micah slipped inside and shut the door behind him. He went through the main room, past yards of stainless steel equipment, into the newly finished addition that still smelled of fresh lumber. This room was part kitchen, with a huge stove, rows of cabinets and shelves, and worktables for making candy from syrup, and part office, with Heather's computer on a desk and file cabinets nearby. Along an unoccupied wall of the kitchen half of the room, Micah set the tubing on a pile of other repaired coils.

Returning to the main room, he went to the far end where sugar wood was stacked high and deep. The wood here was a fraction of what he would use when the season began. The rest lay outside, beyond the large double doors that opened to allow an iron flatcar to bring wood in from outside along rails embedded in the floor. Back by those doors, at the rear end of the inside stack, he pulled off three logs at a time. When he found one with a significant curve, he tucked the tattered bag into the pile, put that log back, then the rest. Brushing his hands off on his jacket, he left the shed.

Back in the kitchen, he called Cassie Byrnes.

*   *   *

Cassie rarely slept late. Five hours a night was all she needed, which was a blessing. She would never be able to do what she did without those extra usable hours. Add on the fact that her husband and their three children were all *excellent* sleepers, and she could regularly count on the late night and early morning hours for work.

This particular morning, she was doing town business. With the annual election newly done, she had been renamed chairman of the Lake Henry Committee for the fifth year in a row—which should have been shocking, since she was a woman and barely thirty-six, in both regards distinctly different from the older men who had traditionally run the town. But times had begun to change, and Cassie was a major doer. A lifelong resident who was articulate and effective, she was also on the correct side of the environmental issues that were the Committee's major concern. Most often, these had to do with the loons that arrived each April, nested, and raised their young well into November. They were gone for the winter now, flown east to fish blissfully in unfrozen seacoast waters, unaware that Cassie's current concern dealt not only with them, but with humans as well. There were many in town who, fearing for the integrity of the lake, wanted to add security in the form of three police officers, one cruiser, and the appropriate testing equipment to steadily monitor the condition of the lake. Unfortunately, these additions cost money. Cassie was currently trying to determine exactly how much, so that the strongest case could be made for increasing the real estate tax at Town Meeting in late March.

The telephone rang. Eyes flying to the clock, she caught up the receiver. It was six-thirty in the morning. This was no pleasure call.

"This is Cassie," she said quietly.

The voice on the other end was low and tight. "It's Micah. They arrested Heather. We need your help."

Cassie drew a blank. The words "Heather" and "arrest" were not compatible. "What are you talking about? Who arrested her?"

"The FBI. They say she has a whole other identity and that she killed someone before she moved here. Flight to avoid prosecution—that's what they're charging her with. Then there's murder. And extortion. They handcuffed her, Cassie. Handcuffed her. And Pete was with them, saying the whole thing was legal."

Cassie remained numb for a minute. Heather Malone was her friend. They had been together the day before, barely twelve hours ago. Heather was the last person in town whom Cassie would have thought ever to be in trouble with the law. But Micah's distress couldn't be ignored, particularly if the local police were involved.

Setting aside her personal thoughts along with the work she'd been doing, she reached for her briefcase. "It may be legal, but that doesn't mean the allegations are true. I know Heather." She was on her feet, turning off the desk light. "Where have they taken her?"

"Concord, I think. They said there'd be a hearing this morning."

"Not until I'm there to represent her," Cassie declared with a certain indignation. "Let me find out for sure where she is, then you and I will take a ride. Pick me up in fifteen minutes?"

"Yup."

* * *

Fifteen minutes didn't give Micah much time to get his life in order. He and Heather had been a family long enough that he hadn't had to worry about who would take care of the girls before and after school. Thinking about his predicament now, he could conjure up only one name, one face for the job. Of all of the people whom he and Heather called friends, this was the one he trusted most.

Chapter Two

Poppy Blake had been awake for some time, lying on her side facing the wall of windows. Anyone looking in would have thought she was watching dawn creep over the lake, because it was surely a breathtaking sight. Snow lay pristine over ice eighteen inches thick. Tall hemlocks and pines formed a shadowed skyscape on the islands that dotted the lake and the east shore beyond. As day arrived, a swath of brightening light climbed behind their limbs, allowing for the weakest, most delicate shards of pale yellow light to filter through. During any other season, with maples, beeches, and birch in leaf, the light would have been blocked. In winter, though, when sun was most needed, it positively twinkled.

Poppy saw none of it. Her mind was miles away, in a dream place where one could erase mistakes of the past and start fresh. In that place, she wasn't lying in bed alone. Nor was her house on one level, or the room that might have held children filled instead with equipment necessary to keep her upper body strong and her lower from atrophy. Nor, in her dream place, was there a wheelchair by the bed.

Poppy's legs didn't work. They hadn't since a snowmobile accident twelve years before. In those twelve years, she had learned everything there was to know about life as a paraplegic—the most important lesson being that she couldn't turn back the clock and undo things. Only by accepting them could she lead a satisfying life.

Still, there were times when she dreamed. This morning the fantasy involved a man she had seen only a handful of times. He was five foot ten, had red hair, blue eyes, and a sexy baritone that she had heard many

more times than she'd seen the man in the flesh. He called her regularly—or used to, until she put him off one time too many. But what
choice did she have? She couldn't keep up with him from a wheelchair.
Apparently he had come to agree. He hadn't called in a month.

The phone on her bed stand rang now—a single line, far removed
from the complex system in the other room that Poppy used for business.
She ran a telephone answering service for Lake Henry and the neighboring towns, and sat for much of the day before a large bank of buttons,
directing calls from one place to the next, taking messages for the townsfolk, chatting with callers, passing on information. The phone on the bed
stand was her personal line, and while family and friends frequently used
it, they never called this early. It was barely seven in the morning. That
was cause for alarm.

In the seconds that it took to push pillows aside, turn herself over, and
reach the receiver, she had horrid visions of her mother being ill. But the
number illuminated on the handset wasn't from Florida, where Maida
was spending January, February, and March. It was a local number.
Heather's.

"Hey?" she said, half greeting, half asking, wondering why her friend
would be calling so early when they'd been together just the night before.
But Heather wasn't on the other end. The voice was urgent and deep.

"It's Micah. There's trouble." His next words blurred—made no sense
to her at all—until he said, "I need someone to get the girls to school.
Can you do it? I'm worried about Star."

Poppy pictured the little girl with long, silky hair framing pale skin and
deep-set dark eyes. She loved both of Micah's girls, but Star had always
been the one to tug at her heart. "Of course I can do it," she told him, confused, "but Heather isn't someone else. What are you talking about?"

"I'm not talking about anything. It's the FBI that's saying it."

"*Killed* someone? I don't think so. We've been friends since she first
came to town. She went through my accident with me, and she couldn't
have been more selfless or giving or understanding. Or comforting or
helpful. Heather couldn't kill anyone if she tried."

"That's what I said, but I don't count. I'll be there in five minutes,
okay?"

"I'll be at the door."

And she was. Poppy was a minimalist. She didn't bother with fancy clothes or makeup, rarely had, even before the accident. Rebels didn't primp and preen as their mothers might have them do. At the time, defying Maida in that way had given her great joy. Now, it wasn't rebellion that kept her from fussing, but pragmatism. A quick trip to the bathroom, where everything was perfectly situated for wheelchair access, and a cursory washing up was all she allowed herself this morning. What time she spent was in layering up her legs and pulling on sheepskin boots, so that her feet didn't chill without her knowing it.

On the porch, draped in a heavy parka, she combed her pixie-short hair with her fingers as she watched the headlights of Micah's truck approach. The road was narrow but paved, the latter being one of the concessions that Poppy had made when, soon after the accident, her parents had carved off a wedge of their own land to build her a house. She had put her foot down on having a direct link to their place, needing what small semblance of independence she could retain, and had opted instead for the longer road out to the street. Paving it meant less of a risk in foul weather. Indeed, the most recent snow, fallen three days before, had been plowed aside, leaving patches of bare pavement that had been neatly sanded. This morning even those patches wore a sheen of ice.

The ramp from the porch was built with the most shallow of declines, and even then, it had heat coils underneath that enabled Poppy to glide down without fear of skidding. Doing that now, she was at the side of the pickup when it stopped.

Micah was out in an instant. He was tall and solid, hatless as he often was, though his dark hair was thick and worn longer than even the country norm, so Poppy figured it kept his head warm. He wore faded jeans, work boots, and a plaid wool jacket that flapped open exposing a thermal shirt as he loped around to the passenger's side and lifted both girls out. Each wore brightly colored parkas and carried small backpacks.

"There's lunch in the packs," he told Poppy. "Heather made sandwiches last night. She always does it the night before . . . always . . . prepared." His voice trailed off and he looked suddenly stricken, as though what had once been innocent, even praiseworthy, was no longer so.

The implication, of course, was that Heather had been expecting something like this to happen—which Poppy couldn't believe was true. So she urged Micah on with the hitch of her chin toward the road. "You go on. Get this straightened out." She took the backpack that Missy was already passing to her as the older child moved behind the wheelchair to push. Then she held out an arm to Star, who stood braced against Micah looking forlorn. Poppy had to pat her lap before the child came forward.

"I appreciate this," Micah murmured. For a moment, he looked at the girls in a startled way that said he was only then beginning to think about consequences.

"They're okay," Poppy assured him. He looked at them a second longer, before returning to the truck. Poppy had Star on her lap by the time the truck was gone, at which point she declared, "Well, we passed *that* baton smoothly enough."

"What's a baton?" Missy asked.

"It's a thing that kinda looks like a rolled-up magazine. They use them in relay races, where one person runs his part of the race and hands the baton to another person, who then runs the next part. Push me up, Missy." She worked the wheel with one hand and held Star with the other, leaning around to peer at the smaller child. "Did you guys have breakfast?"

"We were gonna, then we didn't have time," Missy answered from behind.

"Daddy forgot," Star said.

"Daddy has lots on his mind," Poppy said, "but I have only you, and besides, you love my kitchen." She tightened her arm around Star as they rode up the ramp, entered the house, and headed straight for that kitchen. Everything in it was lower and more accessible than in a standard kitchen, from counters and cabinets, to sink and stove, to lazy Susans everywhere. For Poppy, these things were a necessity. The girls saw them as play.

Poppy was dying to know more about Heather, because the situation was bizarre. But she couldn't ask the children. Nonchalance was the way to go here.

So she acted as if nothing were unusual as she popped waffles into the toaster, and as she buttered them and doused them with syrup from the maple crop Micah had produced the spring before, she chatted with the girls about school, about snow, about upcoming Ice Days. Missy chatted back. Star remained quiet, close by Poppy's side.

"Doin' okay?" Poppy softly asked the little one from time to time, always getting a nod in return, albeit a solemn one. It didn't take a genius to know that the child was worried about Heather.

She'll be fine, Poppy wanted to say. *She'll be back. This is all a mistake. Your dad will take care of everything.*

But she didn't say a thing, because she didn't *know* a thing. And that irked her. She prided herself on being the pulse of Lake Henry, but she hadn't seen this one coming. She wondered if anyone had.

The more she wondered, the more annoyed she grew, because her thoughts moved beyond the simple fact of an arrest. She was adamant in believing that Heather was innocent of what they said. But someone had fingered her. With virtually anyone else, Poppy might have wondered if one ornery Lake Henryite had resented her easy acceptance by the others, but this was Heather. *Everyone* liked Heather. Even more, they liked Micah, who, though marginally reclusive, was a native, one of their own from the get-go. Heather would have been protected if for no other reason than that she was part of Micah's life.

Poppy particularly doubted that the betrayal had been internal, because there had been so many opportunities for others. Three months ago, Lake Henry had been the center of a news event that had focused on Poppy's own sister, and the media had been all over town. Poppy would put money on the fact that someone from that faction was responsible for this sudden upheaval.

But she couldn't say that to the girls, either. So, calmly, she washed syrup off their hands and mouths, helped them back into their parkas and pulled on her own. Back outside again, she let them ride the lift with her up into the brand-new Blazer that her mother had insisted on buying her before the onset of winter. It was poppy red and had been adapted for her needs; once the three of them were inside, she patiently pointed to buttons and let the girls retract the equipment. Focusing solely on them, she made sure they were belted in, drove them to school, and gave them big hugs before sending them off.

The instant they disappeared inside, she was on her cell phone calling John Kipling. Though born and raised in Lake Henry, John had spent most of his adulthood in exile. Given that he had left town at the age of fifteen—and that he was ten years older than Poppy—she had been too young to know him then. They had become friends only in the three years since his return. As of nearly six weeks ago, they were even related. On New Year's Day, John had married Poppy's sister Lily.

But Poppy wasn't calling him either as a friend or a brother-in-law. She was calling because he was the editor of the local newspaper, and she had an ax to grind.

Since it was barely eight-thirty in the morning, she tried him at the little lakeside cottage that Lily had inherited from their grandmother, Celia St. Marie. The cottage was smaller than John's a bit farther down the shore, but it had a history. So John had moved in, and they would be putting on a sizable addition once sugaring season was done. Micah was slated to do the work, which gave John an even greater incentive to help figure out what had happened to Micah's significant other.

No one answered the phone. Poppy guessed that John was either having breakfast at Charlie's Café or already at work.

She passed Charlie's first. It was a cheery sight with snow capping the red clapboards of both the general store and adjacent café. The wide brick chimney exhaled a curl of smoke, and a smell tinged with bacon and birch wafted into the Blazer.

She exchanged waves with the three men chatting out front, their breath puffing white against their dark wool jackets as they huddled into upturned collars, but she saw no sign of John's Tahoe. Less than a minute later, she spotted it down past the post office, at the yellow Victorian that stood near the edge of the pristine expanse of snow on the lake. That yellow Victorian housed the newspaper office.

Had it been summer—or spring or fall—she might have pulled in and talked with John face-to-face near the willows. But this was winter, and winter made maneuvering in and out of the Blazer over icy paths, much less unshoveled ground, harder to do. Besides, she wanted to get home to her phone lines. So she simply punched in the *Lake News* number as she drove past.

"Kipling, here," John answered in the distracted voice that said he was buried in the *Wall Street Journal, New York Times,* or *Washington Post.*

"It's Poppy," she said and jumped right in. "Do you know what's going on?"

"Hey, sweetie." His voice lightened instantly. "No. What's going on?"

"You haven't heard any news?"

"Uh, we slept late," he said a mite sheepishly. "Just got in, actually."

Poppy felt a twinge of envy imagining the why of Lily and him sleeping late. It didn't help her mood any. "And you haven't had any calls?" she asked tartly.

"You'd know that better than me."

"John."

"No. No calls yet." He was cautious now. "Tell me what I missed."

"Heather," Poppy announced, letting loose with her disgust at the situation in general and the need to place blame in particular. "You missed Heather." She gave him the basics, then said, "I'm wondering how something like that could happen in a free society, because Heather is *the* last person I would ever accuse of anything, much less false identity and murder. But someone did. So I'm driving along here," now on the road that circled the lake, with no other cars in sight, just tons of snow, scads of naked trees, and plenty of questions, "and I'm thinking about who the canary could be. No one in town would snitch on Heather, because everyone here loves her, and even if they didn't, they love Micah, and even if they *didn't*, they wouldn't betray one of us for fear of reprisal from the rest. So I'm thinking it has to be one of the bozos who was in town last fall during the whole mess that gave Lily her unwanted fifteen minutes of fame, and those guys are *your* friends—"

"They are not," John broke in, "but hold on, back up. *What* happened to Heather?"

Slowing when a deer darted across the road ahead, Poppy watched its white tail twitch as it leapt gracefully over a snowbank and loped off through the trees. "She was arrested by the FBI. I don't know much more.

Micah dropped the girls here in a rush and went to get Cassie. They were going off after the Feds. I don't know where—"

"To Concord. The Feds go to federal court, and the nearest one is in Concord."

Poppy drove on at full speed again, both hands tight on the wheel, though the road was beautifully plowed. "Federal court." She tried out the words. "Heather in federal court. Doesn't work for me."

"That's because you assume she's innocent."

"Well, don't you? Think back to every single interaction you've ever had with her. Did she ever sound like she was concealing a dark past?"

"No, but that's because I don't take her for a pathological liar. If she were one, though, chances are she could fool people. You'd be amazed at how convincing a pathological liar can be."

Poppy bristled. "Heather is totally honest. People trust her. Ask Charlie. He knows how to spot the good ones. It took him less than a year to get Heather out of the kitchen and into managing the restaurant. Hell, Kip, she's the one he leaves in charge when he and Annette go away with the kids—and, technically, she isn't even working for him anymore! Would he do that if she was dishonest?" She edged the Blazer to the right when an old station wagon approached. It was the postmaster, Nathaniel Roy, on his way to work. Nat was a bespectacled seventy-five, but he was sharp enough to know Poppy's Blazer and would have been agile enough to flick his headlights if he wanted her to stop. The fact that he simply waved and drove on told her that he hadn't heard about Heather, either.

"Poppy, you're preaching to the choir," John said. "I agree with you. But it's not like we've known her all her life."

"We haven't known you, either," Poppy pointed out. "Or Lily. Both of you spent years away."

"But we were both born here."

"And you'd condemn Heather because she wasn't?"

"Poppy, Poppy," John pleaded, "I'm not condemning her. I'm just making the same point that other people are going to make."

Poppy wanted to argue, but she knew he was right. "Fine then, let's move on. Can you make some calls? Find out where she is? Try to keep a lid on things? I don't want history repeating itself. Lily was hit with false charges, and the result was two lost jobs, an abandoned apartment in Boston, and a media circus."

"The result of which," John noted, "was that she fell in love with me."

"But Heather already loves Micah," Poppy reminded him sweetly. "She already loves the girls. She doesn't need a crisis to bring her to her senses. Honestly, why would someone do this to her? I cannot imagine she has a single enemy in town—and while you're asking questions, I want to know who *thought* he recognized her. In the process of clearing Lily's name last October, you humiliated several rather powerful media guys. Think there's a chance that one of them is seeking revenge?"

"They wouldn't dare."

Poppy gave a shallow laugh. "All three of them are still working."

"Yeah, but in lesser jobs and under closer watch, and there's still me. They know I'd have no qualms about pointing the finger at them if they tried to point it at someone here without cause."

"Well, someone did point a finger. While you're in Concord, see if you can find out who. You're an investigative reporter. Being nosy is what you do best."

"Yeah, well, in this situation, it could backfire. You want to keep this contained? Restraint is the way to go. Ask too many questions, and people start thinking you have something to hide. So let's concentrate on whatever's happening in Concord today. Let me make some calls. I'll get back to you when I hear something."

Poppy ended the call. Seconds later, she passed the stone wall that marked the entrance to Blake Orchards, her mother's pride and joy. The stones of the wall were waist-high lumps of snow, and the sign was draped with more of the fluffy white stuff. If she turned in and drove a half mile along the gravel road, between stubby apple trees that looked smaller than ever without leaves, she would reach her mother's house and a bit farther on, the cider house. Both were closed up for the winter.

Instead, she stayed on the main road as it climbed a hill and wound away from the lake for a bit, then back. Turning onto her own road, she followed it down to the lake. At the house, she quickly maneuvered her chair out of the Blazer and rolled inside to the console that held dozens of buttons. She was anxious for news. John wouldn't have called back so soon, but what she really wanted was a message from Micah.

*   *   *

Even slouched against the wall, Micah was taller than almost everyone else in the courthouse lobby, and a motley crew it was. Lawyers stood out from the rest in their suits, some of which had seen neater days. The people with them ranged in age from a pregnant young girl to a grizzled old man, and varied in dress from high school sloppy to rural casual, from Manchester stylish to Sanbornton woodsy to Claremont salt-of-the-earth. What all these people had in common was an air of unhappiness.

It was an emotion Micah shared with them. This was not where he wanted to be. He was supposed to be in the sugarbush with Heather, checking the mainline for last-minute damage. Yeah, he could do it alone, but he liked having Heather with him.

He had no choice, though. Cassie had told him to wait here, so he waited, his fists deep in the pockets of his flannel jacket, one booted foot flat to the wall, his eyes hooded, and his jaw clenched. He wanted to get Heather and get home. That was all. Get Heather, and get home.

After what seemed like an eternity standing there in that lobby, surrounded by the rumble of low conversation, Cassie strode down the hall from a room at the end. Long-legged, she was a standout in wool slacks and a blazer, a silk blouse and scarf, and a head full of curly blond hair, but the pickup of Micah's pulse had nothing to do with her good looks. He respected Cassie, but he wasn't drawn to her for anything but her legal expertise.

With Heather on his mind, he straightened.

Cassie didn't say anything when she reached him, simply indicated that he should follow her. Down another hall, they turned a corner. She knocked quietly on a door, the upper half of which was a milky glass, then turned the knob.

Micah expected to find Heather inside, but instead there were only an old, empty desk and a pair of battered metal chairs.

"Where is she?" he asked.

"Apparently still on her way," Cassie replied, putting her briefcase on the desk. "Here's the thing. There'll be a hearing in a little while. It isn't an indictment, per se, just a hearing in front of a magistrate during which the Feds return the warrant—the warrant in question being the one involving flight to avoid prosecution. Heather won't have to say anything."

She broke off when the door opened again.

Micah's insides lurched. Heather was there with a guard, who gestured her forward. She looked ghostly pale and even more terrified than she had been back at the house. Her silver eyes found his and held them, as though clinging for support.

At first he didn't move. There was a split second when he thought of the part of Heather's past he didn't know, the knapsack he had stashed away and the words that the federal agent had said. *We have evidence that her real name is Lisa Matlock, and that fifteen years ago she committed murder in California.* If Heather was hiding something like that from him, it would explain the fear in her eyes.

Then again, if she was innocent of the charges and feeling overwhelmed by something that was out of her grasp, her fear was justified.

He focused on that thought. She had no sooner stepped into the room when he crossed the floor, pulled her into his arms, and pressed her face to his chest. He didn't want to see those fear-filled eyes. But he could feel her trembling, which was nearly as upsetting. His Heather had always been calm and even-tempered. She had always been brave, as sure of herself as anyone could be who was a newcomer to a town as insular as Lake Henry.

He remembered thinking that about her the first time they'd met. It had been fall. With the syrup season long done, he was in carpenter mode. Charlie had hired him to install a wall of windows in the café to open it up to the birches. During the course of the job, he was in and out of the kitchen a dozen times a day. Heather was working there, first as a dishwasher, then helping prepare the food for cooking. She hadn't said much. To this day she wasn't a big talker—but neither was he. He remembered her being quiet, even shy, but self-assured. She had seemed comfortable with what she was doing, at peace, certainly not like a woman who was on the lam and had something to hide.

The guard stepped out into the hall and closed the door, leaving them alone with Cassie.

Micah said the first thing that came to mind, murmured against her hair. "Did you have breakfast?"

Heather shook her head against him and whispered, "They offered. I couldn't eat."

He held her tightly for another minute, then lowered his mouth to her ear. "Where'd this come from?"

She lifted a shoulder in a muted shrug.

"Did you tick off someone in town?"

Another headshake.

"Have you ever heard of that other woman?"

Heather started to cry. Micah didn't know if that meant she had or she hadn't, but he looked at Cassie in desperation. "She isn't that person. What do we do?"

Cassie had stayed on the far side of the small room, giving them these few seconds together. Now she came closer. She touched Heather's shoulder, the gesture of a friend, but didn't say anything. After a minute, she exerted the smallest pressure to make Heather look up.

"I need to ask this, honey," she said, "because I wouldn't be doing my job as a lawyer if I didn't. Are you Lisa Matlock?"

Heather's eyes were wet. "I'm Heather Malone."

"There," Micah said, annoyed. "You have it. What now?"

Cassie continued to study Heather's face. After what felt to Micah like an unnecessarily long time, which riled him all the more, she exhaled and looked at him. "Now we fight."

He set his annoyance aside. "How?"

"We go into that hearing in a little while and contest the proceedings. That's basically saying that Heather is innocent of the charges and that we will not waive extradition."

Heather made a frightened sound. Micah verbalized the source of her fear. "Extradition?"

"If we were to waive it," Cassie explained, "she would be immediately taken to California to answer the charges they've lodged."

"Would that be admitting she is Lisa Matlock?"

"No. It would be saying that we'll let the courts there prove that along with the other charges."

"Since she isn't Lisa Matlock, the charges don't apply."

"Right, but what I think and what you think and what she says is one thing. What the people in California think is apparently something else."

"Well, they're wrong. I want the charges dropped."

Cassie smiled sadly. "If it were as easy as that, I wouldn't have much work. Our system of criminal justice functions in roundabout ways."

"Innocent until proven guilty," Micah reminded her.

Cassie hesitated several seconds too long. "Not always," she said, shaking her head.

With those words, Micah had the awful fear that the trouble was just beginning.

*   *   *

Poppy had no calls to take for a while, which was typical of a Lake Henry morning in winter. During other seasons, when fine weather beckoned, people were out and about doing whatever tickled their fancy. Rainy days, snowy days, *cold* days tended to keep them at home. They were answering their own phones. They were reading the paper, cleaning up breakfast, stacking wood, hacking ice from the eaves, and if not that, they were starting to think about getting geared up to settle down to work in the easygoing way that Lake Henryites had.

She built the fire in the stone hearth to a blaze, made a pot of coffee, and sat back with a steaming mug of it to look at the lake, all the while wondering where Heather was, and what she was doing—and it wasn't just a nominal interest. Poppy had other friends she'd known longer than Heather, but Heather was the one she liked best. She felt closest to Heather, had from the first time they met. Poppy had been a sophomore at the state university, and Heather, who spent her work week inside at Charlie's, loved the great outdoors. Each weekend, a group of them went mountain climbing, and though Poppy had more in common with the college students in the bunch, Heather was the one she talked with the most.

Thinking back, Poppy realized that she had done most of the talking.

Heather was a good listener, and Poppy, who felt constrained by the town in general, and her family in particular, had needed to vent. Then Poppy's accident happened, and, through the nightmare of recovery, Heather had been there for her. She seemed to know what to do without being told. She didn't dole out pity or offer patronizing words of solace. Her underlying attitude was to accept what had happened and move on. That quiet approach had been a relief.

Poppy was thinking about that quietness—about listening rather than talking, and whether there had been a reason for it that went beyond Heather's basic nature—when a light blinked on the phone bank before her. Pushing that unsettling thought from her mind, she put on her headset, pressed the appropriate button, and said, "Lake Henry Library."

"Leila Higgins, please," said an unfamiliar woman.

"I'm sorry. The library doesn't open until noon on Wednesdays. Who's calling?"

"This is Aileen Miller. I'm with the *Washington Post*. I understand that Heather Malone worked at the library. I was looking for a comment from Ms. Higgins."

Poppy was dismayed, but not unprepared. When it came to handling the media, she had gone through trial by fire the fall before. Now she said, "Tell you what. If you give me your number, I'll pass it on to Ms. Higgins when the library opens."

"Who is this?"

"The answering service."

"Do you have a home number for Ms. Higgins?"

"Tell you *what*," Poppy offered sweetly. "Give me *your* home number, and I'll pass *that* on to Ms. Higgins."

There was a pause, then a magnanimous, "Oh, I don't want her having to pay. I'd be happy to call her."

"I'm sure you would," Poppy replied.

After another pause, Aileen Miller responded with resignation. "She can call me at work."

Poppy wrote down the woman's name and number, then disconnected the call and made one of her own.

"Police office," came a grumble on the other end.

"Willie Jake, it's me. What do you know about Heather?"

There was a pause, then a testy, "What do *you* know?"

"Only that she was arrested. How could you let that happen?"

"I didn't 'let' it happen," came the indignant reply. "I'm local. I can't control the Feds."

"Do they have evidence that Heather was someone else?"

"You know I can't tell you that. But would I have let them arrest her if they didn't?"

"What kind of evidence?"

There was a sigh. "I can't *tell* you that, lest I bias the case. But I'll tell you this—it was all circumstantial. A bunch of old photos of someone who might'a looked like Heather, reports of a scar, handwriting comparisons—all real iffy. But I say it again, these were Feds. I tried my best to change their minds, but in the end they did what they wanted to do. There's no messing with these guys when they set their minds to something, and when they have the paper to back it up . . ." He sputtered a drawn-out, "Whelllll . . ."

Poppy's private line blinked and John's number appeared. "Okay, Willie Jake. I get your point. Gotta run now." She ended the call and punched in the blinking button. "Any luck?"

"She's at the federal courthouse in Concord. A hearing's going on right now."

"What kind of hearing?"

"On the warrant. I don't know anything more. I got this from my buddy who covers the courthouse for the *Monitor.* He couldn't talk. He wanted to get into the hearing."

"Did you ask him to keep it quiet?"

"Oh yeah," John said, sounding dryly resigned. "He shot that idea down fast."

"Why? Heather's a nobody!"

"Well, the guy Lisa Matlock allegedly killed is a somebody. *Was* a somebody. His father was a United States senator from California at the time, earmarked for his party's vice presidential nomination, which he got three weeks after his son's death, in part thanks to the sympathy vote.

The ticket lost, and DiCenza didn't run for the Senate again, but he's still a force in the state, and he keeps the torch alive."

Poppy thought fast. "And you picture our Heather as the type who would mingle with political movers? I don't. She's too private, too shy, too down to earth. Sorry, John, but something doesn't jibe."

"Hey, I'm just telling you what my buddy told me. This was a high-profile case at the time. My guess is it'll get lots of attention now. I'm driving down there myself. Armand will want a story in the paper, and the best way to get it right is to see what's happening firsthand."

"Find out *why* it's happening," Poppy pleaded, "why it's happening to *Heather.*"

"I'll try. I'll call you when I get back."

Poppy didn't want to hold him up. If anyone would give Heather a fair shake, it was John. So she simply added, "Please," and disconnected the call.

Slipping off the headset, she took up her coffee and looked out at the lake. She tried to imagine what Heather was feeling—wondered if it was confusion or numbness or fear, or something else entirely. She tried to imagine Heather sitting in a cell in Concord, but couldn't give the image a face that fit. Heather always looked too . . . gentle. The scar did that. It was small, not more than half an inch long and curved gently upward from the corner of her mouth, the eternal optimist's smile.

Scars like that gave a person distinction. Many people had them.

Another button lit on the console, Poppy's private line again. This time, the number was that of Marianne Hersey's bookstore. Putting one end of the headset to her ear, she pressed the button. "Hey."

"What is going on?" Marianne asked. She was one of five women who had dinner at Poppy's every Tuesday. Formally, they were the Lake Henry Hospitality Committee. Informally, they were good friends sharing news, laughter, and gripes. Heather had been with them the evening before, as she was every week. "I just got to work and was sitting down with my coffee and doughnut, thinking that maybe I'd catch an author on the morning talk shows, and suddenly there's breaking news from Concord. Do you know what they're saying about Heather?"

"On television? Oh God. What are they saying?"

"That she deliberately ran down former Senator DiCenza's son, then fled from the scene of the accident and wasn't spotted again until a member of the cold case squad got a lead from someone who was here last fall. What do you know?"

"Not as much as you do. I'm going to go watch. I'll call you back." Poppy swiveled her chair, aimed the remote at the television, and turned on the set. No more than a second or two into channel surfing, she spotted a "Breaking News" banner. Since the story was just beginning, she suspected she had hit a different channel from the one Marianne had seen. This was not a good sign.

The reporter had barely begun to talk when Poppy's private line lit again.

"It's Sigrid," came the voice on the other end. "Are you watching this?" Sigrid Dunn was another of the Tuesday-night group. By day, she did large-loom weaving. The television was often on while she worked.

"Just tuned in," Poppy said.

"What *are* they talking about?"

"Let me listen." She raised the volume.

" . . . a major break in the investigation of the murder of Robert DiCenza fifteen years ago in Sacramento. DiCenza, who was twenty-five at the time, was run down as he was leaving a political fundraiser for his father, then a United States senator from that state. The car that hit him was driven by an eighteen-year-old named Lisa Matlock, whom, sources say, had threatened him earlier that evening. The FBI alleges that Lisa Matlock has been living in New Hampshire for the last fourteen years under the name Heather Malone. She was apprehended early this morning at her home in Lake Henry. She surrendered quietly and was transported to federal court here in Concord. A hearing has just concluded, during which Ms. Malone's lawyer formally contested the proceedings. That means that she will be fighting extradition. Since extradition is a state issue, the federal proceedings were dropped, and she has been turned over to the Office of the Attorney General of New Hampshire. She will be transported to the superior court in West Eames for a hearing there later today. This is Brian Anderson for Channel Nine, with breaking news in Concord."

"Do you remember hearing about this murder?" Poppy asked Sigrid.

"No, but fifteen years ago I was in the Peace Corps in Africa, so I wouldn't have seen the news. Is this *our* Heather they're talking about?" she asked in disbelief.

Poppy was just as befuddled. "Well, it's our Heather who's in custody, but it can't be our Heather who did that." She paused, thinking of the rapport she and Heather had, the sense that they felt things other people didn't. "Can it?"

"No. Absolutely not. We know Heather. I mean, we don't spend Tuesday nights talking about the weather. We talk about private things. We talk about *intimate* things. She couldn't hide something like that from us."

Poppy was trying to remember stories Heather had told about her childhood, but she could think of none. Heather was always more of a listener on Tuesday nights. She listened and asked questions—insightful questions that always got the others to talk more.

"We don't really know all that much about her," Poppy said quietly. "It's just that Heather's not a violent sort."

"It's just," Sigrid echoed archly, "that someone's up to no good. Someone in the press must have been pissed at us last fall. This is tit for tat."

"John says no."

"The news said that someone who was here last fall tipped off the cold case squad. Okay, so maybe John's right. Maybe it isn't revenge. But someone was looking at things he wasn't supposed to be looking at."

"Come on, Sigrid. They look at the crowd. Heather was in the crowd."

"Actually, not," Sigrid pointed out. "She wasn't milling around when the cameras were here. Missy had chicken pox. Remember?"

Now that she mentioned it, Poppy did remember. Heather hadn't ventured any farther from home that week than the pediatrician's office and the general store. Poppy herself had given Heather a blow-by-blow of all that she'd missed.

Except someone hadn't missed as much as Heather had. Someone had seen a face, imagined a similarity, and thrown a wonderful woman's life in limbo. Poppy wanted to know who that person was.

Chapter Three

Standing near the large leather sofa that dominated the living room in his New Jersey townhouse, Griffin Hughes held the phone to his ear. On the other end was Prentiss Hayden, once the most powerful member of the United States Senate, now in his eighties and retired to his farm in Virginia. Griffin was ghostwriting Hayden's biography and had run into a glitch.

"I don't want it mentioned," Hayden insisted.

"But it's part of your story," Griffin argued gently. One didn't argue any other way with a man of Hayden's age and accomplishments, much less with a man one respected greatly, as Griffin did this one. They simply disagreed on the extent of disclosure. "No one will think less of you for having had a child out of wedlock. You took full responsibility. You gave that child everything you gave the rest of your children. Do the others know about him?"

"In my family, yes, but the public doesn't. I'm not of your generation, Griffin. I can't rub this in the noses of my contemporaries, and that's who's going to read this book, y'know—old farts like me."

"You're wrong there, sir," Griffin cautioned. "There's a whole younger generation that wants to know how it was done—"

"Done in the good old days?" Hayden cut in. "Yes, well, we didn't talk about these things in the good old days. We talked about honorable debate and gentlemen's agreements. We were civil men. Why, I remember . . ."

Griffin listened to the memory, but he'd heard it before. Idly, he picked up the television remote, turned it in his hand, clicked on the set, but it was a minute of surfing before he caught something of interest. It was a breaking story from Concord, New Hampshire. Careful to offer Hayden a thoughtful "Uh-huh" at appropriate times, he listened to the news with growing interest, so much so that he must have missed one of those thoughtful "Uh-huh"s.

" . . . Griffin?" Hayden prompted.

"Yes, sir," Griffin replied.

"I thought I'd lost you. Damn cell phones aren't anywhere near as reliable as the regular kind."

"Can I call you back, Senator Hayden? Later today, maybe tomorrow?"

"Well, of course, but I don't want that issue mentioned. I won't be changing my mind."

"We'll talk tomorrow," Griffin said. He clicked off the phone and proceeded to stare at the television with a morbid fascination that held him glued even when he switched channels. Listening to one live report after another from Concord, he vacillated between disbelief and dismay. By the time the last of the clips ended, with Heather heading for the county seat at West Eames, and with promises of updates by reporters later that day, he was out-and-out furious.

Stabbing at the off button, he tossed the remote aside and snatched up the phone. He punched in his brother's number, and, while the phone rang on the other end, paced to the window and looked out over Princeton's main drag. He saw little of it today, though even in winter he had always thought the view had charm. His thoughts now were on Lake Henry. He hadn't been there in over a month.

Wondering if Randy—the *rat*—was in Lake Henry now, he waited only until his brother's answering machine picked up, then ended the call and punched in the cell phone number he had programmed into his phone. After a single ring, his brother's voice came through.

"Yo."

"Where are you?" Griffin asked without preamble.

"Right now? Three blocks from work."

Not Lake Henry, then. Washington, D.C. Griffin was grateful for that, but not enough to be defused. "I've been watching TV, this stuff about Heather Malone. I'm trying to figure out where it came from, and I don't like what's coming to mind. Tell me it wasn't you, Randy."

Randall Hughes, Griffin's senior by two years, sounded pleased with himself. "I'll give you a clue. I'm headed into the office for what will be the first of many interviews today."

"Tell me it wasn't you," Griffin repeated, tense and tight-jawed now, but if Randy sensed his anger, it didn't dampen his spirits.

"Damn right, it was me. Is this cool, or is this cool!"

"God *damn* it, Randy. That day in your office, I was thinking out loud. I remarked on a similarity. All I said was I had seen someone who *looked* a little like that picture on your wall. I never said it was her."

"That's right, and I picked it up from there," Randy said with pride. "This is unbelievable. I mean, her face has been starin' back at the occupant of this office for fifteen fuckin' years, and that's been me for the last fifteen months, and then my own brother gives me the tip. That's how it happens with cases like this. You pound the pavement all you want, but it's something totally unexpected that points you in the right direction."

"I didn't point you anywhere," Griffin insisted, wanting to erase the whole thing, certainly any possible role he had played in it himself. "All I said was that there was a resemblance. Know how many people look like *me* in this world? Or like *you*? When was the last time someone asked if you were related to Redford? Happened to me again last week. It's the jaw—that's all—the jaw that's square like his, so they ask, but it's an idle question. They don't honestly think we're related to the guy. Same with this thing. I just said the picture reminded me of a girl I saw. Did I even say it was in that town?"

"It didn't take a genius to figure it out. You'd just come from there. Every other word out of your mouth at the time had to do with that town."

That was because Griffin had come home enamored of Poppy Blake. Needing to tell someone about her, he hadn't even stopped in Princeton but had driven straight on to D.C. Randy and he, being the two youngest of the five Hughes brothers, had shared girl talk since they had been twelve and ten, respectively, and not once had Randy breathed a word of it to anyone else. Griffin had expected the same discretion now. He felt betrayed.

"You don't understand, Randy. These are good people. You can't do this to good people."

"Hey," Randy cautioned, suddenly sounding very much the law enforcement officer that he had always wanted to be. "I don't know what she's like now, but the law's the law. Fifteen years ago, that little lady took a walk. It's about time the Bureau caught up."

"With the wrong woman!" Griffin cried.

"No way, Red. Even if she'd had plastic surgery so we couldn't see the facial similarity—even if she'd had that little scar removed—we have her on the handwriting sample. It worked so well, I still can't believe it. I mean, I'm up there a couple weeks ago, and she's working at the little local library. I ask for a book; she doesn't have it; I ask if she'll write down the name of the nearest bookstore, and bingo! Matched right up to the writing sample we took from her high school files. We have her," he said with smoldering glee. "We have her cold."

"You asshole."

There was a pause, than an indignant, "What's wrong with you?"

"I'd never have said anything to you if I'd known you'd do this."

Randy sounded wounded. "Griffin, she killed a man!"

"Allegedly, and that's assuming she is this other woman. But did you have to use me to do it?"

"I didn't use you. You said something; it touched off something else in my mind; I followed through, did my research, investigated, went up to that little town, and nailed her—and what's it to you, anyway? You stopped going there. You lost interest."

It might have looked that way to Randy, but Griffin hadn't lost interest in Poppy. Not by a long shot. He had been intrigued since the first time he'd called Lake Henry wanting to do a story on her sister Lily, and Poppy had been the one to answer the police chief's phone. Spunk. That was the first thing he'd sensed in her. Right off the bat, she'd shown spunk.

I'm a freelance writer putting together a story on privacy for Vanity Fair, he'd said that day last September. *I'm focusing on what happens when privacy is violated—the side effects to the people involved. I thought that the Lily Blake situation would fit right in. Lake Henry is her hometown. It occurs to me that people there may have thoughts about what's happened to her.*

Damn right we do, Poppy had answered with feeling, and, that simply, he had felt refreshed. He liked her honesty. He liked her loyalty. The more obstinate she was, the more interested he became—and it wasn't just a game, the love of the chase that drove some freelance writers on. He had felt something melt inside when he had seen her for the first time in that wheelchair. The goddamned thing was lightweight, state of the art—and turquoise. Turquoise. That alone was as much of a statement of who she was as her short dark hair.

He'd had to cajole her before she agreed to let him take her to dinner, but they'd had an incredible time—had talked a steady stream for three straight hours.

At least, he thought they'd had an incredible time. But when he had wanted to arrange for a follow-up, she resisted. She let the machine answer when he called, and when he finally reached her, she said that he really needed someone else.

He knew what she was thinking. How not to? She had blurted it all out in the very first words she'd said to him face-to-face. *I can't run. I can't ski or hike. I can't work in the forest the way I was trained, because I can't get around in a chair on rutted dirt. I can't dance. I can't drive a car unless it's been specially adapted. I can't pick apples or work the cider press. I can't even stand in the shower.*

He understood that for twelve years she hadn't thought about those things. Now, with the interest he showed in her, she did, and she'd been taken by surprise. She needed time.

So he had given her that. He had dropped by later on the pretense of just passing through town, staying no more than a few hours, and every few weeks, he sent her a postcard from wherever he was. But he hadn't called in a month. That didn't mean he had been idle. He had gone to extremes, including a few under the table, to learn everything he could about Poppy.

One of the things he had known from the start was that she and

Heather Malone were best of friends. Heather had been on her way out of the general store that day when he and Poppy had come for lunch at the café. She hadn't stopped for more than a quick introduction to Griffin and a brief exchange with Poppy, but that exchange had been in the intimate tones of women who were close. Griffin was certain—beyond any reasonable doubt—that if Poppy found out that he was the one who had tipped off the cold case squad, she would never talk to him again.

"Is it her?" Randy asked.

Of course it was her.

"You said she didn't want a relationship," Randy argued. "If that's changed, you should've clued me in."

Griffin didn't know whether it had changed or not, but he wasn't saying that to Randy. He had his pride. He also had great hopes, which his brother could dash in an instant. So he said, "If you ever—*ever*—tell anyone that you got the lead on this case from me, you're a goner."

"Whoa. That's a threat."

"Coming from your brother, it sure is. I can make you mincemeat in this family. All I have to do is start talking about Cindy. You spend hours tracking down strangers, but you can't find your own sister?"

There was a second's silence, then a quiet, "Low blow, Griff."

"She's been gone for seven years now, put Mom in her grave, sent Dad out tomcatting, made family gatherings such a nightmare we don't bother much anymore."

"I wasn't the brother who got her hooked. That was James."

"So did we know?" Griffin asked aloud as he had so often silently. "Did we look the other way? Could we have stopped it?"

"Our family has ghosts. Most families do."

Griffin refused to reason the situation away. "Cindy's no ghost. She's alive out there somewhere. If you ever put in half the effort trying to find her that you've put into ruining a good woman's life, she'd be back in the fold."

"Hey," Randy suddenly said in a way that signaled a blow-off, "I'm driving into the garage under my building. No reception here. Talk later."

The phone went dead. Not that Griffin had more to say. He was thinking back on meeting Heather that day in October four months before. She had been concerned about one of her children and had medicine in her hand. The look on Poppy's face while they talked vouched for affection and respect. Poppy would never have a friend who was a killer.

*   *   *

Poppy was dying to be at the courthouse in West Eames. Like John, she wanted to see for herself what was going on. More than that, though, she wanted Heather to see her there and know that she cared. Same with the magistrate or judge or whoever was deciding Heather's fate. That person needed to know that Heather had friends who trusted and loved her.

But Poppy stayed in Lake Henry. For one thing, with Micah and Heather in West Eames, she needed to be close by for the girls. For another, though the courthouse was handicapped-accessible, she had no idea what the parking situation was with snow and ice thrown into the mix. For a third, a contingent of others from town were going there.

In addition to all that, she had work to do herself. By late morning, nearly all her phone lines had lit up. Some of the calls were from townsfolk wanting to confirm what had happened; these involved a simple repetition of facts on Poppy's part. Others were from the media, and Poppy knew all the right words to say. The challenge with those calls came in remaining patient and polite. With each additional call—each additional media outlet trying to sniff out dirt at Heather's expense—her civility was further tried.

Hardest of all, though, were calls like the one from Poppy's sister Rose, because they involved speculation, and speculation raised issues for which there weren't any answers.

"What if they keep her in jail?" Rose asked. "What will Micah do then?"

"They won't keep her in jail," Poppy replied. "She hasn't done anything."

"They can do it, Poppy. So what'll Micah do?"

"She'll be home."

"What if she isn't?"

"She'll be *home.*"

"What if they keep her for a while?"

"Please, Rose."

But Rose persisted. "Do you think Micah's worried?"

"Of course he's worried. He loves Heather."

"Forget love. Think about the girls. Who'll take care of them if Heather's in jail? Who'll help with sugaring?"

Poppy's stomach began to knot. It often did that when she talked with Rose, who was an alarmist of the first order. Rose was the youngest of the three sisters—the "Blake blooms," as they were known in town. Lily was the firstborn, typically introspective, sensitive, and focused. Poppy was the rebel, far more easygoing than the other two. And Rose? Rose was a clone of their mother, which meant that she saw the dark side of every issue.

Unfortunately, it was easier for Poppy to accept the fear of calamity in Maida, their mother, than it was to put up with it coming from Rose.

"Why are you fixated on this?" she asked now. "Heather will be *out*."

"I'm fixated on it," Rose returned, "because I know things you don't. Heather got all sorts of business ideas from Art"—Rose's husband, Art Winslow, whose family owned the local textile mill—"and she's put them to good use. New evaporator, new logo, new accounts. So here's Micah, who's just grown the business, thinking Heather would help, and suddenly she isn't there. The weatherman's forecasting sun. If the days start to warm, the sap could be flowing in two weeks. The timing of this is terrible."

"Rose."

"How did it happen?"

"I don't know," Poppy ground out and, ending the call, proceeded to worry about all of the points Rose had raised.

* * *

Griffin's mistake was in not packing up and hitting the road the instant his brother had hung up on him, because that led to an even greater mistake—he turned on the television again. Two seconds into channel surfing, he caught a news flash about the case. Two seconds after that, the anchor introduced a reporter who was on the scene, and Griffin was hard-pressed to look away.

"Lake Henry is refreshing," the reporter was saying. "In a day and age of complex lives often ruled by machines, the town is a throwback. With a population just over seventeen hundred, it is an old-fashioned kind of place where everyone knows everyone else and people protect their own. The town is situated on a lake of the same name in central New Hampshire, and this, folks, is the stuff of which getaway dreams are made. There's no making a wrong turn in a maze of avenues here; a single main street runs through the center of town and continues all the way around the lake. Uh, excuse me"—he thrust the mike toward a man who approached—"excuse me, could you tell us—"

The man walked by before the request was out.

Undaunted, the reporter resumed his narrative. "Behind me, you see the police station, the church, and the library. These three buildings hold all of the official business that is part and parcel of town life."

Griffin had been in each of the three buildings, and felt pleasure seeing them again. Each was made of wood and painted white with black shutters. The police station was low and long; the library was stately and tall; the church had a storied look, with a spire that stretched high into the tops of the trees.

"The town clerk and the registrar work out of the police station," the reporter explained. "The library rents its top floor to the Lake Henry Commission, and the basement of the church houses the historical society. The Commission, by the way, focuses on environmental issues, and since these are the top priority for the local folk, the Commission is the powerhouse of the town. When it comes to deciding other issues, Lake Henry is one of the last in the state to retain a town meeting form of government. Led by a duly-elected moderator, the townsfolk gather in the church for two nights every March to vote on issues of concern to the town for the upcoming year."

Griffin knew all this. Having grown up in Manhattan, though, he was as charmed hearing about these things now as he had been learning them last fall.

"The post office is that brick building across the street," the reporter said, and the camera zoomed in. "The yellow Victorian behind it is the local newspaper office. But if you want to experience the heart of this little town, you cross the street to my right." The camera shifted to a sprawl of crimson clapboard. "That is the general store, owned for generations by the Owens family. This is where townsfolk pick up groceries, medicines, newspapers, greeting cards, and gifts. Charlie Owens and his wife, Annette, run it now, helped in shifts by their five children, and they have expanded and changed it to keep up with the times. The café still serves breakfast all day, but the quiche on the menu is as likely to contain portabello mushrooms as cheddar cheese, the bread is homemade, thick, and filled with goodies like wheat germ and nuts, and the lunch sandwiches are served on baguettes with avocado slices and bean sprouts. Uh, excuse me?" He tried to snag another passerby, a woman this time. When she too walked on, he smiled at the camera without missing a beat. "Back at Charlie's, though, some things never change. The main part of the store centers around a woodstove, just as it did when Charlie Owens' grandfather had his little one-room shop. Townsfolk gravitate toward the chairs around that stove to talk about the weather and share the latest gossip. This is particularly true in winter," he added, pulling up his collar over cheeks that were already ruddy.

It was cold in New Hampshire, but that didn't discourage Griffin. He had initially seen Lake Henry in autumn, when the roadsides were awash with color and the air smelled of sweet cider. During his last trip there, it had snowed. As frustrated as he had been at making no progress with Poppy, he had loved that snow. Seeing it there on the ground now, he smiled.

The reporter went on with a billow of white breath. "I'm told that the weather here today is typical. But along with the chill in the air comes something else—the peace and splendor of winter in an out-of-the-way New England town. Standing here in Lake Henry is like standing in a Currier and Ives scene. Look around"—he demonstrated—"and you can still see Christmas lights and wreaths. The air is quiet and crisp. If there's a highway somewhere out there, you can't hear it. And the snow here is white, *still*, three days after falling. This is a rare treat for those of us who live in the city." He touched his earpiece, frowned briefly, then said, "I'm told we have something more now. While we await word from the superior court in West Eames on the fate of Heather Malone, we have a satellite hookup with Randall Hughes, the FBI agent who cracked the case. Back to you, Ann Marie."

Griffin's smile disappeared. Slowly, he straightened. Ann Marie was a beautiful woman, but his awareness of her had absolutely nothing to do with her looks and everything to do with his brother's appearance—live, vivid, *revealing*—on the screen. Horrified, he watched.

"For those of you just joining us," the anchor explained, "Randall Hughes is a member of the FBI's cold case squad. Agent Hughes, it's been fifteen years since Robert DiCenza was killed, and the FBI has been looking for Lisa Matlock ever since. You are being credited with finding her. Can you tell us how it happened?"

"I didn't find her myself," the agent modestly replied. "The apprehension of Heather Malone was the result of a unified effort by the FBI, the Office of the Attorney General of California, and the Lake Henry Police Department."

"What gives you reason to think that Heather Malone is Lisa Matlock?"

"I'm afraid I can't comment on that at this time."

"What led you to Lake Henry?"

"A tip. That's how most cases are solved."

"A *tip?*" Griffin shouted at the screen. "That was no tip! It was a *blunder*, which you *unconscionably* took advantage of!"

Calmly, Ann Marie said, "We understand that this tip came from a member of the press corps who was in Lake Henry last fall covering the scandal that involved a woman there and Cardinal Francis Rosetti of Boston. Is this true?"

Randy was a second longer in answering this one. He had the good grace to respond with a simple, "Yes."

"Is it safe to guess that a member of the press corps recognized her?"

"No." Again, a pause. "No, but a remark was made that led us to another investigation, and that investigation led to Ms. Malone."

Griffin simmered.

"What was that remark?" Ann Marie asked.

"I'm not free to comment on that at this time, either."

The anchor was unfazed. "Is it fair to say that if it hadn't been for the Rosetti scandal, the DiCenza case would still be unsolved?"

"No," Randy said promptly. "Something else would have come up. The past can only be hidden so long before bits of it start to leak. The government employs a cold case squad to be alert for those leaks and to track them down when they occur."

"Can you tell us how Heather Malone—Lisa Matlock, if the charges are correct—is alleged to have traveled from California to New Hampshire without being caught?"

"No. I cannot."

"We understand that she has been living with a widower named Micah Smith and taking care of his two young children."

"That is what the agency believes."

"Is Micah Smith considered to be an accomplice?"

"I can't comment on that."

"Have you been in touch with the DiCenza family?"

"I talked briefly with a representative of the family. They're pleased that there may be action in this case."

"Do you believe that Heather Malone will be returned to California to stand trial?"

"I believe that justice will prevail."

Sensing the interview was over, Griffin was trying to gauge the damage, when Ann Marie put on a perfunctory smile, said, "Thank you, Agent Hughes," and faced the camera again. "That's the latest word we have on this story. To repeat, we are waiting word from West Eames, New Hampshire, where a hearing is now under way to determine the immediate fate of Heather Malone . . ."

Griffin turned off the television and pushed a hand through his hair. Hughes was a common enough last name. If Poppy had been watching just now, she might not make the connection.

Wishful thinking, he thought sourly. Randy's hair was a deep auburn that could translate to brown in many lights, but there was the jaw they had in common. No getting around that square jaw. Put the name with the jaw and add the whole thing to the timing of Griffin's visits, and Poppy would know. She was quick. He had learned that from their phone calls during the mess involving her sister. She hadn't let him get away with a thing. For all he knew, she had already guessed he was the one who'd tipped off the law.

A fast phone call would tell him one way or the other—and a fast phone call was about all he had time for. He was behind in the Hayden biography. A deadline loomed. He had writing to do.

But he didn't want to find out what Poppy did or did not know in a phone call. Far better, he decided as he began pushing together the papers strewn on the coffee table, to drive on up and press his case in person.

*   *   *

Poppy missed the interview with Randall Hughes. She didn't hear the name, didn't see the face, because she was on the phone with her sister Lily at the time. Though Lily was two years older than she, Poppy was the protective one, because Lily had a painful stutter. It had been better lately, and in general, things were looking up for Lily. Not only was she in love, but, as she talked with Poppy now, she was driving back from Portsmouth, where she taught a class in music appreciation at a private high school. It was one of three such positions she'd won since losing two jobs in Boston the fall before. Adding her relationship with John to the picture, Lily had definitely come out ahead.

That didn't mean Poppy could stop feeling protective. Lily had been through a rough stretch. Now Heather's being in the news for no cause, much as Lily had been, was bound to affect her.

"It's like a rerun," Lily said through the static of a poor cell phone connection. "Heather is the only thing the local stations are talking about. I understand that I'm in New Hampshire and that this is New Hampshire news, but what facts do they have? I don't hear any, Poppy. Certainly none that make sense to those of us who know Heather. Has the press been calling?"

"Here? No. John was right. They know how we feel, so they're steering clear. Vivian Abbott called a little while ago." Vivian was the town clerk and had a view out the window of the Town Hall. "She said she could see two crews filming in town, but she said they were state, not national. Maybe national doesn't dare."

"Maybe they just haven't arrived yet," Lily said, sounding worried. "Have you talked with Micah?"

"He called during the lunch break. He said Cassie's trying to find out what evidence the government has, but they're making her file motions for everything, and motions take days. Heather's a wreck. *He's* a wreck."

"Do the girls know what's going on?"

"The school principal says no"—Poppy had talked with the man twice—"but that may change once the bell rings and the kids hit the streets. Hold on a sec, Lily. Someone's calling John." She punched in another button. *"Lake News."*

"It's Charlie," said a voice that was robust in its anger. "Kip's not there?"

"He's in Concord."

"Christ, I hope he's setting things straight with the folks there. Not five minutes ago, they were saying on television that Micah might be an accomplice."

"Accomplice!" Poppy cried. "Accomplice to *what?* There's no crime."

"Tell that to the Feds," Charlie said. "Better still, I will." He hung up.

Poppy returned to Lily, wisely not repeating what Charlie had said, because even without hearing this latest bad news, Lily was upset.

"If it hadn't been for last fall—"

"No, Lily," Poppy cut in. "Not your fault." Lily had been falsely accused of being romantically involved with a man of the cloth, and the whole thing had been turned into a national news story, thanks to one particularly unscrupulous reporter. "You had no control over that."

"Maybe not, but I can feel what Heather feels. Has Mom called?" she asked with barely a pause, which said that as improved as Lily's relationship was with Maida, Lily still felt an ingrained fear.

"Not yet."

"She will. She'll be freaked out. She left here after the wedding thinking the past was dead and buuu-uried." There was a pause, then a carefully controlled, "She'll worry that the stuff about me will surface again."

Lily grew suddenly defiant. "Well, I don't care if it does. I'd like another shot at embarrassing certain members of the press."

Poppy glanced toward the door as her friends Sigrid and Marianne came through. "What happened?" she called to them. Both had left work early to go to the courthouse; now they looked mutually dismayed.

"Halfway there we got Cassie on the phone," Sigrid said, taking the TV remote from Poppy's desk and aiming at the set. "She told us to stay home. She said no one would ever see us there, least of all Heather. The place is mobbed."

"With people from town?" Poppy asked as the television went on.

Marianne answered, "Loads. Dulcey Hewitt even showed up with a crowd from the Ridge—kids, cousins, you name it. The kids adore Heather. She's the one who reads to them at the library. But Cassie says there's a slew of media. Look at that picture. Oh, yuck."

"What's happening?" Lily asked at Poppy's ear.

"Looks to me," Poppy said, turning her chair sideways so that she could see the TV, "like they're all just standing around in front of the courthouse."

"The hearing's going on," Sigrid called back. "They're waiting for a ruling."

"Waiting for a ruling," Poppy told Lily.

"Poor Heather," Lily said. "Can't Cassie put someone on the stand to say Heather was nowhere near California when the murder occurred?"

"Who? When has Cassie had time to go looking for someone like that? If we figure the FBI was at Micah's at six, this thing's been going on for less than eight hours. What is he saying?" she asked Marianne.

"That if there's bail, it'll be high," Marianne called from her post by the TV.

"If there's bail, it'll be high," Poppy told Lily.

"Bail!" Lily cried. "But she hasn't *done* anything."

"Risk of flight," Marianne called back.

"Risk of flight," Poppy related to Lily.

"Where was Heather before she came to Lake Henry?" Lily asked.

Poppy recalled something about the Northwest. Or the West. "Idaho, I think." Or was it Illinois?

"You *think?*"

"It never mattered. Heather is Heather."

"Does she have family who should be called?"

Poppy hadn't thought about family, the same way she hadn't thought about Heather's ever having lived elsewhere. She had always accepted Heather for who she was, not who she'd been, which was how Poppy lived herself. She didn't dwell on the past. She couldn't do that and still wake up smiling each day.

And Heather? Heather had fit into the fabric of Lake Henry so easily that it was hard to remember she wasn't a native. "If she has family elsewhere," Poppy told Lily now, "she's never mentioned it. No one's ever come to visit."

"That doesn't mean no one exists," Lily's voice warbled as the connection worsened.

"Micah will know. If there were calls to make, he's probably done it from the courthouse."

"Is . . . anything . . . to help?"

Poppy filled in the blanks. "No, nothing any of us can do yet. Cassie says this is just a procedural thing. But you're starting to break up, Lily, and my phone bank's going nuts. I'd better go." She listened, heard no response. "Lily?" But Lily was gone. "Anything yet?" she asked the pair standing vigil by the TV.

"Waiting," Sigrid said.

Not knowing what else to do, Poppy punched in her next call.

Chapter Four

Griffin drove a gray Porsche. His prized possession, though, was the GPS unit he had installed in it the year before. Since he loved to drive and was forever behind the wheel tooling over back roads chasing down stories, over time he had done his share of getting lost. No more. All he had to do now was to punch in a destination, and a sexy female voice articulated the directions as they appeared in living color on a screen.

He had chosen that particular voice from a menu of several, because she made him feel less alone. He called her Sage and imagined her to be a siren of the barefoot-and-pregnant type, very down-home and country—this before he had met Poppy. When he talked to Sage now, he pictured Poppy.

Actually, had he been going straight to Lake Henry, he wouldn't have had to consult Sage at all. He knew the route by heart. For each time he had driven it in the flesh, he had made the trip ten times in his mind.

Now, though, he was headed for another New Hampshire town, West Eames. He had been monitoring the progress of the case on the radio during the drive north from New Jersey, and figured that he might just be able to arrive in time to catch the hearing.

His cell phone rang. The return number was one he had dialed an hour before. "Hey, Duncan. Whatcha got?"

Duncan Clayes was an old college buddy, currently a reporter for a San Francisco daily. "Lisa Matlock was born and raised in Sacramento," he said in a tone that said he was reading his notes. "The mother left when she was five. She was raised by her father. Years before, he'd done time for breaking and entering. He had a job making deliveries for a take-out restaurant at the time Rob DiCenza was killed. They lived pretty much hand-to-mouth."

Griffin already knew the financial situation. He had learned it through a call received shortly after he'd crossed the Tappan Zee Bridge. With Duncan, he was homing in on elements of the story that might prove or disprove a connection to Heather Malone. "Is the father still alive?"

"No. He died of a heart attack two years after Lisa disappeared. The FBI staked out his grave for months, but she never showed."

"Did the mother?"

"No. Not when he died, not when Lisa vanished. The FBI didn't have a clue about her at the time, still doesn't."

"Are there siblings?"

"Nope."

"Other relatives?"

"An aunt on the father's side. The Feds watched her for weeks after DiCenza died—twenty-four-hour surveillance, a tap on the phone. They did it again when the father died. If there was any contact between Lisa and her, they never knew it."

"Did Lisa have friends?"

"At the time of her disappearance, her father said yes, but none came forward, certainly not to help her. The father claimed that someone reached them first."

"Someone from the DiCenza family?"

"Thereabouts. Rob was a fast one, moving from one girl to the next. He apparently liked his women young and innocent."

"So what was the relationship between Lisa and Rob?" Griffin asked.

"Initially, the DiCenza family said there wasn't one. After the murder, though, DiCenza friends came forward saying Lisa and Rob were arguing that night, which suggested that they knew each other. When word leaked that they were sexually involved, the family changed its story and started talking of extortion. They said Rob had dated the girl a time or two and was trying to end it, but that Lisa was shaking him down for money to keep quiet."

"Keep quiet?" Griffin asked. "After a date or two? What would she have had to keep quiet about?"

"She was the daughter of an ex-con and she was poor—not the kind of girl his parents wanted, and since the family was headed for big visibility with the vice presidential nomination, she could have held Rob up for money. The family was uptight about its image. *Way* uptight."

Griffen knew that, too. It was public knowledge and something that he had been reminded about by another source no less than twenty minutes before. "So public opinion said she was a gold digger?"

"Public opinion, egged on by family spin. She disappeared, which smacked of guilt, and the longer it went on, the worse it became. Then Charles DiCenza got the VP nod three weeks after his son was buried, and party operatives milked the sympathy factor for all it was worth. By then, Lisa Matlock would have been stoned if she'd suddenly appeared."

"Your exit will be coming up in a mile," Sage warned. "Please make a left at the end of the ramp."

Griffin moved into the right lane. "Where'd you get this stuff?" he asked Duncan.

"The paper's archives."

"Is there more?"

"I could find it. You didn't give me much notice."

"Find it."

"Anything in particular, or everything in general?"

Griffin didn't know. When he had started the drive, he had made one call, thinking he would get a little background information. One call had led to a second. Duncan had been the third. Griffin supposed it was the journalist in him, always curious. Then again, perhaps, the more he knew, the more he would have to offer when he reached Lake Henry.

So he told Duncan, "Everything in general, plus as many photographs of Lisa Matlock as you can get. Overnight them to me care of General Delivery at the Lake Henry Post Office. Do this, and we'll be even." Several years before, in the course of writing one of the in-depth freelance pieces for which he was known, Griffin had come across a valuable tip to an adjacent story. He had given it to Duncan, who had needed the break.

When Duncan's career had taken an upward turn as a result, he had sworn that if he could ever do anything for Griffin, he only had to ask.

So Griffin asked now. Reaching his exit, he ended the call. He coasted down the ramp and turned left.

"Continue straight for five miles," Sage prompted.

He glanced at the monitor as he completed the turn, trying to calculate any slowdowns he might encounter. He wanted to get to the courthouse before the whole thing ended, but this road was no highway. Granted, the lanes were generously wide, but there was only one in either direction. Five miles could easily take fifteen minutes.

He reached for the phone to call Poppy, thought twice and, instead, focusing on something with better odds for success, punched in a different number. This one belonged to Ralph Haskins, an old family friend whose skill as a private investigator had proven invaluable to Griffin's father over the years. Ralph was always pleased to hear from a Hughes. He was also totally aware of the breaking news from New Hampshire, which meant that Griffin didn't have to fill him in or give explanations when he asked for as much paperwork on Lisa Matlock as Ralph could find. Randy would have paperwork, but Randy's channels were public—and besides, out of pride alone, not to mention resentment, Griffin would love to best his brother in this. Ralph was his strongest hope. He worked behind the scenes, between the lines, and underground. He had a network that was unsurpassed, and had a way of getting information other people couldn't. Griffin knew that the smallest bit of intelligence gleaned from a medical record, school record, telephone or credit card bill might offer a clue.

Ralph hadn't been able to find Griffin's sister, Cindy, but then, she knew Ralph and knew how he worked, which made it easier for her to stay one step ahead. Perhaps because of his frustration with that, he was eager to help Griffin now.

Leaving him to it, Griffin ended the call and pressed the radio's scan button. Moments later, he was listening to the strongest of the local stations, going from one to another. They told him that the hearing was still in progress.

* * *

When he arrived in West Eames a short time later, he had no trouble
finding the courthouse. It was a sweet frame building that looked like a
church, but there was no mistaking the crowd milling on its front steps.
He spotted several crews of local reporters; as he drove past looking for a
place to park, other crews were scrambling to set up across the street.

He parked the Porsche on a side street and was quickly hit by the cold
when he climbed from the car. Pulling on a parka, he jogged past charming little homes whose eaves dripped with ice, over two blocks of packed
snow to the center of town. He reached the courthouse just as the first of
those who'd been inside pushed open the large granite-gray double doors
and spilled out.

He didn't see Heather. Nor did he see Micah or Cassie. Those coming
out looked angry, not a good sign to someone praying the whole thing
would be dismissed there and then.

Feeling a sense of dread, he headed for the television camera closest to
the door and positioned himself near the soundman. Within minutes,
the correspondent emerged from the crowd, inserted the earpiece that
she was handed, caught up the microphone, and, awaiting her cue,
looked at the camera.

"You look good, Amber," Griffin called.

Amber Abbott glanced at him in a moment's surprise, then grinned.
"You, too, Griff. Doin' a story?"

"I don't know. Maybe. What happened?"

Eyes back on the camera, Amber adjusted the collar of her chic wool
topcoat so that it didn't obscure her jaw. "She's being held without bail
for thirty days."

Griffin's heart fell. "Held?"

"Pending receipt of the governor's warrant from California." Receiving
her cue, Amber spoke to the camera. "Yes, Philip, the hearing here in
West Eames has just concluded . . ."

Griffin moved away, having to snake through crowds that had closed
in around the building. A part of him wanted to hide, thinking that

everyone would know him for the traitor he was, but the stronger part of him needed to know more.

He looked around for a familiar face, relieved to spot John Kipling, with his brown hair, close-cropped beard, and Sherpa jacket, coming out of the courthouse into the harsh winter sun. Griffin's relief faded, though, when he saw the furious look on John's face.

Seconds later, John's eyes met his. He had been seen. There was no turning back.

Fighting his way up the stairs against the crowd, Griffin extended a hand. He was relieved when it was met with goodwill, and quickly pushed aside his guilt. "How can they hold her? She's been a model citizen."

John urged him back down the steps with the hitch of his chin. "Cassie argued that, but she didn't have a prayer of winning. Lisa Matlock went underground fifteen years ago. Odds say she'd do it again in a heartbeat."

"You're assuming the woman in there is Lisa."

"Not me," John cautioned. "The judge, the prosecutor, and the FBI. *And* the DiCenzas," he tacked on dryly. "Charlie DiCenza may have struck out as a vice presidential candidate, but he still has clout. Word has it he was brought into the loop long before anyone up here was, and he's been making calls. He wants his son's murderer caught and punished. Short of someone producing DNA evidence that proves Heather isn't Lisa, this outcome was a *fait accompli*. The hearing was over before it started. There was no way she was being released."

"So is there DNA evidence?"

"No. There was never any reason to collect it. Lisa had no record."

"Which raises the question of why she allegedly ran the guy down. She was eighteen years old. She was pretty and smart. She'd been accepted to Berkeley on scholarship. Is that someone who needed to resort to extortion?"

"I wouldn't think so," John replied as they reached the bottom of the steps. Starting down the sidewalk, he shot Griffin a glance. "On scholarship? Was that in the papers?"

"No. I got it from a contact."

John didn't respond to that. As soon as the crowd thinned, he began walking faster, seemingly lost in his thoughts. Suddenly he stopped and, eyes haunted, looked at Griffin. "You should have been in there, man. The judge barely listens, then says he's holding her for thirty days without bail. There's total silence—disbelief—then pandemonium, but I'm not even sure Heather realized people were on her side. The court officer starts to lead her away and she turns back to look at Micah with tears streaming down her face." He paused, swallowed. "I've never seen such pain."

Griffin heard much of it in John's voice and felt a resurgence of guilt. The only thing easing it was the belief that this situation was temporary. "Cassie'll get her out."

John pulled up his collar and resumed walking. "Yeah, but do you know what it'll take to do that? Only part of it's the thirty days of Heather's life, and of Micah's and Missy's and Star's. She's part of a family, y'know? The other part's the money. Know how much this'll cost? Okay, so Cassie won't charge for her time. But her out-of-pocket expenses to do a case like this might be high."

"She's innocent," Griffin insisted.

"Well, it'll cost her to prove it. I don't know how they're going to do it. Micah doesn't have that kind of money."

Griffin did. He would foot the bill in an instant. Not that Poppy would let him do that if she knew the truth. Nor would Micah accept it. They wouldn't want money from the guy who'd caused the mess in the first place.

John went on. "Micah *particularly* won't have that kind of money if he blows the sap run. He took out loans for the new equipment and had it all figured out, exactly what he needed to gross each year to pay down the loans. If Heather's in jail and he's preoccupied, or if something doesn't work—one piece of the puzzle doesn't fit right—he's in trouble. Sap'll be running within the month, and Heather's sitting in jail. The timing of this sucks." He stopped again and eyed Griffin strangely. "What are you doing here?"

Stopping alongside him, Griffin rubbed his hands together for warmth. "Here? I was heading for Lake Henry and got sidetracked."

"Where've you been? Last time we talked, you were interested in Poppy. Disappearing for weeks doesn't say much for that." He set off again.

Griffin kept pace. "She hasn't exactly been encouraging."

"You knew she wouldn't be. You knew she had issues. Does she know you're coming now?"

"No. I thought I'd surprise her."

"Poppy doesn't like surprises."

"Right," Griffin said. "But it's my only shot of getting a foot in the door."

John stopped at a Tahoe with *"Lake News"* written on the door. "Why now?" He pulled keys from his pocket. "If you're thinking of writing about Heather, think again. Know how Poppy feels about people who make money off the bad luck of others?"

"I sure do," Griffin said. "She told me that back in September. But I'm not writing about Heather. I can't. I'm in the middle of something else."

"So why did you talk to your contacts about Heather?"

"Hell, if I can come up with something that'll help . . ."

"Why would you do that?"

"Because I think Heather's being railroaded."

"You think she's innocent? Because she's Poppy's friend?"

"In part."

John stared at him. "Keep going. Poppy's gonna want to know the rest."

Griffin was silent. When John didn't budge, he felt a sinking inside. John knew, then. He had seen the interview with Randy and had put two and two together.

Denying it would make things worse. So Griffin admitted, "Yeah, she's gonna want to know the rest, but that'll be harder for me to explain. It wasn't deliberate. When I remarked about that picture on my brother's wall, the last thing I expected was that Randy'd come snooping up here."

John's stare grew vaguely blank before turning into a puzzled frown. "Randall Hughes. Oh God, I'm slow."

It was a minute before Griffin realized what he'd done. With a frustrated sound, he hung his head. Then he raised it and sighed in chagrin.

He didn't know what John thought he was keeping from Poppy, but he'd surely stepped into the trap. "Guess I'm slower than you."

John looked as angry as he had when he had come through the courthouse doors. "You led them here."

"No," Griffin replied. "I remarked on a similarity. Randy took it from there."

"Same difference. Poppy figured it was someone who was here in the fall. She won't be happy it was you."

Griffin actually took that as a positive sign. It suggested at least that she felt *something* for him.

"Are you going to tell her?" John asked.

"Probably. I'm not good at keeping things in." *As you just saw,* he wanted to add. "On the other hand, if one of my people comes up with something that proves Heather wasn't Lisa, I'll be in the clear." When John said nothing, he tacked on a less sure, "Don't you think?"

John looked at him a minute longer, then shook his head and unlocked the car. "What a mess," he mumbled as he slid inside.

Griffin caught the door before it could close. "I need a place to stay. Will anyone in town rent me a room?" The nearest inn was a fifty-minute drive from Lake Henry. He didn't want to be that far away, especially not in winter with snow a common thing in these parts. If he was to be of help, he needed to hang out in the general store and pick up gossip at the post office. He needed to be seen around town enough so that people got used to him. That was the only way he would get the inside scoop on Heather, and he needed that. An in-depth study of the vanished Lisa was only half the story; an in-depth study of Heather was the other.

Not that he was doing a story. He had a book to finish and didn't have time. But, boy, this subject sure fired him up more than a watered-down tribute to Prentiss Hayden did.

John looked out the windshield. "The town's going to shut out the press."

"I'm not the press. I'm Poppy's friend."

He glared at Griffin. "That's worse. Know how protective Lake Henry is of Poppy? She's special. Very special. She might be rosy and upbeat, but her life is no cakewalk."

"I know that," Griffin said, and he did. He knew things about Poppy that he doubted even John knew, and he hadn't relied on Ralph Haskins or any other contact to do the research. He'd done it himself.

John started up the Tahoe. He revved the motor once, let it idle, revved it a second time. Then his eyes found Griffin's. "Charlie Owens, owns the general store? His brother moved away a dozen years ago, but he left a place here that needs checking all winter. If you want to earn brownie points with Charlie—and brownie points with Charlie can take you a long way in this town—you could stay right there and do the checking for him." He gave Griffin a guarded once-over. "Nah. Maybe you couldn't."

"Why not?"

"It'd be roughing it. The place is bare bones. Middle a winter? It's tough."

"I can handle tough," Griffin said. He had hiked a good part of the Appalachian Trail and was no stranger to rustic accommodations. Wasn't he already wearing insulated hiking boots? Besides, house-sitting was far better than renting a single room. It would give him space to set up shop. He had a biography to write. "Does it have a roof?"

"Yeah."

"Heat?"

"There's a woodstove."

"So what's the problem?"

"Wind. Snow. Access. Little Bear's an island. It's a quarter mile out."

Griffin had never lived on an island. "How do you get there in winter?"

"Walk or drive. It'd be easy if you had a truck. The Porsche?" John had drooled over it the last time Griffin had been in town. Now he said a pedantic, "I don't think so." He moved to close the door, but Griffin held it firm.

"I'll rent a truck. I was planning to once I got here anyway."

John brightened. "Well, there's an idea. My cousin Buck's looking to sell his. His girl just had a baby. You could pay him twice what he's asking and win over a whole other side of town."

"Done," Griffin decided. "Where do I go?"

*　*　*

John's cousin Buck lived on the Ridge, which was Lake Henry's version of the wrong side of the tracks. Given that the Porsche wouldn't go over well there—or, more aptly, would go over so well that people would pour from their homes wanting a piece of it—John suggested that Griffin stash it in a boat shed at the local marina for the duration of his stay. That put Griffin in John's car for the ride to the Ridge.

When Poppy passed John's Tahoe in the center of town, though, she was too preoccupied to look twice. She waved in reply to John's honk, but she neither thought about another person in the car, nor had time to stop. Micah had called and asked if she would pick up the girls at school. She had left home to do it the instant Annie Johnson arrived to cover the phones.

Now, with a weak sun falling fast behind the evergreens, she pushed the Blazer as fast as she could on roads that were starting to ice up again. The attention required was a welcome break from her thoughts, which vacillated between outrage that Heather was being held in jail and near panic. She didn't *know* where Heather had come from, only that she was a good person. Poppy liked to think that she was one, too, but she had a past. So maybe Heather did, too.

Not liking this train of thought, she was happy to reach the school. Pulling on her gloves, which were padded and full-fingered for winter wheelchair use, she got herself out of the Blazer, and, with a bit of pushing, pulling, and wheeling, found a spot on the sidewalk where the girls would see her. She wasn't the only one there, but she was the only one foolish enough to be out in the cold. Other parents waited in the warmth of their trucks, while school buses lined the drive.

Poppy knew the parents in each of those other vehicles, but she didn't look their way. To do so would be to invite talk about Heather, yelled from one rolled-down window to the next. Instead, she burrowed into her parka, which was turquoise to match her chair, pulled a scarf tight around the collar, tucked her gloved hands in her pockets, and tried not to shiver. Moments later, the school bell rang. Moments after that, children in a rainbow of parkas poured from the doors, running off in whatever direction would take them home.

Normally, Heather would have been in the line of parents. Though the bus could easily transport the girls, she had always wanted to take them home herself. Now Poppy was there in her place. It struck her that with Heather being held in jail for thirty days, this wouldn't be a one-time shot. It also struck her that as long as the nightmare went on, she needed to do this. Heather was her friend, but she felt a responsibility that went beyond that.

She was saved from dwelling on such thoughts when Missy and Star emerged from the school. Side by side and eager, they set off at a run toward the parents' vehicles. Almost simultaneously, they caught sight of Poppy and stopped cold. Their excitement died. Poppy wasn't Heather.

Missy was the first to start forward again; Star was slower. In the time that it took for both of them to reach her, Poppy realized that not only wasn't she Heather, but she wasn't a parent, wasn't a therapist, wasn't a lawyer. She didn't know how to explain what had happened. Micah might know, but Micah wasn't here. That left Poppy, who had absolutely no idea what to say.

Unfortunately, that wasn't good enough. The questions started the instant Missy reached her side. "Where's Heather?"

Poppy held Missy's unzipped parka closed with one hand while she opened the other arm to Star. "She's in West Eames."

"Why's she there?" Missy asked.

How much to say? "There are things she has to do there." Poppy smiled to make light of it and gestured more broadly for Star to come. "So I'm here picking you up."

Missy wasn't that easily satisfied. "She said she'd be back."

"When did she say that?"

"When she left this morning. But she didn't look good. She didn't look like she wanted to go anywhere."

"Sometimes we have to do things we don't want to do." *Like be evasive with children,* Poppy thought, and in the next instant wailed a silent, *I am not good at this.* She tried another smile. It brought Star a bit closer. "I was thinking we could go home and make maple cookies."

"Whose home?" Missy asked wisely.

"Yours," Poppy said. Her own home might be better suited for working in a kitchen from a wheelchair, but she didn't dare take them there, not with the phone lines blinking and Annie alternately discussing the day's events with the locals and diverting the press.

"Is Daddy there?" Missy asked.

Poppy made a show of nonchalantly considering that. "I . . . don't think he is yet."

"He should be. He was supposed to be checking trees."

Star had finally come within reach. Poppy drew her close to the chair as she asked Missy, "Checking trees for what?"

Missy sighed. "Fallen-down ones to chop. In the sugarbush. Is Heather gonna be back for dinner?"

More nonchalance. "I . . . actually, I don't think so."

"When *is* she gonna be back?"

Ten days? Twenty days? Thirty days? How in the world do you explain this to a child?

I'm no good at this, no good at all, Poppy thought again. She was starting to tremble. "Soon, I hope, but I'm real cold, Missy. Another minute and, forget the ten toes that I cannot feel, my wheels are gonna freeze. Let's get in the car. Want a ride, Star?"

Star's lower lip looked none too steady. Eyes sorrowful, she shook her head.

"Give Missy a hand back there, then," she said and pushed at the wheels to start them turning. As soon as she and the girls were in the Blazer, she turned the heat on full force, and even then, it wasn't overly warm, which said something about the cold outside.

But the cold was the least of Poppy's worries as they headed out. Missy's questions didn't stop.

"What if Heather isn't home by morning?"

"Then your dad will help you get ready like he did this morning."

"What if he can't? He leaves before Heather sometimes. What if we don't get breakfast, like we didn't today?"

"You did." Poppy stopped, put her left blinker on, and waited for the trucks ahead of her to turn off the schoolhouse road onto the one that led through the center of town. "You got breakfast at *my* house."

"Will you get it for us tomorrow?"

Pretending it was a game, Poppy sang gently, "I'll get it for you *any* day." She reached the head of the line, but had to wait for Buck Kipling's rattletrap of a truck to pass. She had barely made the turn when she felt a small hand on her shoulder.

Star was there, saying in an even smaller voice, "Did Momma go away?"

"No, honey, she's just over in West Eames."

"Is she gone for good?"

Put your seat belt on, Poppy wanted to say, but Star seemed so frightened that Poppy couldn't make herself say it. Instead, driving with greater care, she tipped her head and touched her cheek to the child's hand. "She is not gone for good."

"What if she never comes back?"

"She'll be back. She loves you."

It was a minute before Star spoke again, and then it was more an aching sigh than anything else. "I want Momma."

Poppy had never felt so helpless in her life. "I know you do, baby. I know you do."

*   *   *

Griffin passed the red Blazer before he realized who was driving it, but that was fine. He wasn't ready to face her yet. He had to stop at Charlie's for instructions and supplies, then drive around to the far end of the lake. He figured he had less than two hours to get to Little Bear, open the place up, and get the woodstove going and the electricity on before darkness set in. He didn't have time to spare.

The general store was packed with people coming in from West Eames and those wanting to hear what they'd seen. Some stood talking in the aisles of the store, while others headed for the café. The greatest number of them congregated around the woodstove.

Grateful that no one paid him much heed, Griffin found Charlie at the cash register. Quickly he explained what he wanted to do. Charlie agreed, albeit with more caution than warmth.

"Is there a key?" Griffin asked.

Charlie shook his head. "Nope. Door's never locked."

"What do I need to know?"

Hand on the till, Charlie considered that for a minute. "Wood's in a pile on the porch. If you need to chip a little at the pipes for water, use the ice chisel inside the door. Electricity, just throw the switch."

It all sounded easy enough to Griffin, who, wary of pushing his luck by mixing with the townsfolk, stayed only long enough to buy coffee, bread, eggs, cheese, deli meat, and canned soup. At the last minute, he added a six pack of beer and several gallon jugs of water. Figuring that he would need something to help start the fire, he topped off the three large shopping bags with several of the newspapers that were for sale. Then he went back out to Buck's truck and, not trusting that the food wouldn't freeze in the steadily dropping temperature if he put it in the bed of the truck, stowed it in the cab. It took several tries before the engine came to life, but then he was on his way.

Heading out of town on the road that circled the lake, Griffin followed John's directions, going past quaintly named roads leading to coves that lined the shore. The bad news was that the closest access to Little Bear Island was at the far end of the lake from town, around myriad turns in the road, heading away from the lake and then back, making what would have been a five-minute drive had he been able to go directly more like a thirty-minute one. The good news was that Buck's truck held the road well—and that Griffin would have his own place for as long as he stayed, not to mention those brownie points he would score with Charlie once the guy had a chance to think about it.

Little Bear Road was perfectly marked with the same kind of well-kept sign that marked the rest of the roads in town. *Drive all the way down,* John had instructed, *then right out onto the lake.*

Onto the lake? Griffin had asked skeptically. *Can I do that?*

Sure, John replied. *We had some melt yesterday, but it's frozen back up today. There's trucks out to bobhouses all the time. No one's fallen in yet this year.*

Needing to convince himself that he was up for the challenge, Griffin set his qualms aside, particularly when he saw that Little Bear Road was plowed. He turned in, putting on his headlights when the road plunged him into the darkness of a thick forest of trees that blocked out what was left of the day.

No sweat, he told himself with a glance at his watch. He still had more
more than an hour to get out there and get settled. *Piece a cake.*

When the road ahead brightened and the lake came into view, he
smiled. Seconds later, his smile faded when the plowed portion of the
road abruptly ended and the truck got stuck. Praying that it was a momentary aberration, he shifted, backed up, shifted again, and went forward with greater force. He moved ahead just a bit before stopping again.
This time, when he tried to back up, he couldn't do that either. No matter how he shifted, how he steered, what brilliant little tactic he thought
he'd used, he couldn't budge the thing. All four tires of the truck were in
snow nearly to their upper rims, which Griffin discovered when he
climbed out of the cab and sank in well above the top of the hiking boots
of which he was so proud. He looked ahead at another ten feet of un-
plowed snow, then at the lake. Its surface sat two feet lower than the land
and was covered with just as much snow.

Not wanting to waste time, with the shadows on the lake growing
longer as he watched, Griffin studied Little Bear Island. A quarter mile
out, John had said. It didn't look far. He figured he could cover the distance easily enough on foot. He didn't have gloves—they were back
in Princeton—but he'd had cold hands before. Cold hands wouldn't
kill him.

So he pulled on his time-worn, good-luck Yankees cap and climbed
out of the truck. Putting his overnight bag on one shoulder and his laptop bag and briefcase on the other, he took a shopping bag in each arm
and set off.

The good news was that the ice held him easily. It didn't moan or crack
or move, but showed every sign of being as thick as John had said it was.
The bad news was that not only were his ears freezing, but his jeans
didn't keep out the snow any better than his hiking boots did.

Mindful of the lowering sun, he slogged on. He knew there was ice
under the snow, because he slipped on it from time to time. Fortunately,
he was athletic enough to keep his balance.

If the temperature was falling, he didn't feel it. Lifting his feet high to
cross through the snow, he built up a sweat in no time. This countered
the wetness where the snow seeped through his clothes. Being warm,

though, didn't keep his thighs from screaming in protest. He wasn't used to goose-stepping. It couldn't be done with any kind of speed, particularly loaded down as he was. Worse, what had looked like a short distance from shore seemed to take forever to reach, and then there was the matter of his hands. Yes, he'd had cold hands before. But this was *cold.*

Determinedly, he kept his eyes on the pine trees ahead, and he forced his legs to keep moving. He couldn't even see the cabin until he got close and rounded the island, but when he reached it, he felt a surge of pleasure. The cabin was made of logs, charming in its rusticity. It occupied the only clearing on the island, which, itself, was less than an acre.

He waded up to the front door. Firewood was piled immediately to its left, under a porch overhang that hadn't kept snow from blowing over it.

Eager for shelter—not to mention for a place to unburden his arms, which were aching mightily, and a fire to warm his hands, which stung painfully—he tried to open the front door. When it resisted, he set one of the brown bags on the woodpile and tried again. It wasn't until he had set the other bag down as well and put all of his strength into the push that the ice crusting the doorframe gave way. Snatching up the bags, he whisked them inside and closed the door.

Darkness. Cold. Mustiness.

Electricity, Charlie had said cryptically, *just throw the switch.* The problem was finding the switch in the dark.

Depositing his belongings, he quickly pushed back the little café curtains that hung on the windows. That helped some with the darkness, though the light outside was pathetically weak. He spotted a switch on the wall, threw it, got nothing. He tried another switch and another, finally realizing that there had to be a master switch. Intent on calling Charlie, he pulled his cell phone from his pocket, only to find that he was in a no-service zone.

This did not please him. If he had no phone reception, he wouldn't be able to talk to friends, access e-mail, or log on to the Web. Without phone reception, he couldn't work. Unless he had an antenna installed. He could do that himself. But not now, not tonight, not with darkness falling fast.

Afraid of dallying, he looked around. The room in which he stood housed the living room and kitchen. Heading for cabinets in the kitchen, he opened one after the other until he found candles, a lantern, and matches. In no time, he had the lantern lit, but the relief was small. The woodstove sat inside the fireplace, looking as dark as the cabin and twice as cold.

Blowing on his hands for warmth, he rubbed them together to combat numbness as he went back outside. He brushed snow off the top of the pile of wood, but it was another minute before he was able to dislodge pieces that had been frozen together. Needing them to be as dry as possible, he whacked several together to free them of errant snow and ice, and, in the process, whacked his thumb.

The good news was that it hurt, which ruled out frostbite. The bad news was that it *really* hurt.

Ignoring the pain, he carried as much wood as he could inside. Making tight rolls from some of the newspapers he had bought, he placed them inside the stove, placed wood over them, opened the damper, and struck a match. The paper burned, then went out; the logs didn't catch.

No longer working up a sweat, Griffin was growing colder by the minute. Swearing softly, he began chipping at one of the pieces of wood with the ax he found just inside the door. When he had enough kindling, he removed the logs, added more paper, then kindling, then logs.

He held his breath—a challenge, given that he was shivering—and watched the paper burn and the kindling catch. He didn't breathe freely until the first of the logs hissed softly and burst into flame.

Buoyed by the thought that the heat of the fire would grow and begin to spread soon, he went to his overnight bag, dug out a sweater and knotted it around his head to protect his ears, pulled out a pair of socks and pushed his hands inside, then set off in the near-darkness to get the rest of his gear from the truck.

Chapter Five

Poppy was worried. The oven had long since cooled, the smell of maple sugar cookies had begun to fade, the milk glasses had been washed, and the girls would be wanting supper, which, taken alone, was no problem. She would happily make them supper. But they wanted Micah.

So did she, if for no other reason than to find out what was happening. Poppy's friends had begun calling her here, but she didn't have any more answers than they did. With each call, the girls grew more uneasy. After an initial spate of questions, they had taken to sitting quietly by her wheelchair. She tried reading to them, but they were distracted, uninterested. She tried getting their imaginations going with the dollhouse village in the spare room, but they were quickly bored with that, too. Now, silent and serious, they were watching television. Not even Barney could make them smile.

Poppy had barely heard the sound of Micah's truck when the girls were up and out the door. She hung back, waiting until Micah shooed them inside again. His face was ashen and his eyes so dark that Poppy felt a jolt. She hadn't seen those eyes so dark in years. The light Heather had put there was gone.

The girls stood inside the door, watching their father and waiting.

Poppy raised her eyebrows, inviting him to speak.

Micah simply shook his head and set off for the kitchen.

* * *

By the time Griffin returned to the truck, loaded himself up with the rest of his things, and trekked back to the cabin, he was colder than ever. He wanted heat—*high* heat and *lots* of it—but everything in the cabin had been so cold for so long that the warmth of the woodstove was slow in spreading.

He fought with frozen, snow-crusted laces and stiff fingers to get his hiking boots off, then pulled on two layers of dry socks and a dry pair of jeans. The sweater he'd used on his head went over the sweater he already wore, and the Yankees cap went back on his head. Using the candle in its lantern for light, he searched the cabin and pushed every switch he could find, but couldn't get the electricity to kick on.

Without electricity, he had roughly two hours of laptop use. Long term, that would be a problem. Short term, he was more concerned with warmth.

So he searched the cabin again. This time he found an oil lamp and a tin of kerosene. With that lit, he went into the bathroom. It was a tiny room, with a tiny toilet, a tiny sink, and a shower stall that would have been tiny, too, had there been anything closing it in—not that Griffin cared. Taking a shower was the last thing on his mind. He'd had enough trouble taking off his jeans to put on a dry pair. The idea of stripping down in a room with the look and feel of a refrigerator did not appeal to him.

The toilet did. But there was no water in it. He pulled the flush knob that sat on top. Nothing happened. Same thing when he tried to run water in the sink. Nothing.

If you need to chip a little at the pipes for water, use the ice chisel inside the door. Charlie had said, so Griffin went looking for the chisel. Oh, it was there as advised, right inside the door near the ax and a shovel. Griffin picked it up and looked around. Chip a little at the pipes? *What* pipes?

It occurred to him then that he'd been set up. If John hadn't known the pitfalls of the cabin on Little Bear Island, Charlie surely did. They wanted him to fail, wanted him to come running for cover on the mainland.

Well, he wasn't about to do that. Dropping the chisel by the door, he pushed his feet back into his wet hiking books, and, with the laces hanging loose, went outside and relieved himself in the woods. He was retracing his steps when he spotted the generator crouched low by the cabin's rear wall. Feeling a small sense of victory, he waded through the snow and brushed it off. He checked the propane and the oil—he was no dummy. Then he found the pull-start and pulled. When nothing happened, he pulled a second time, then a third. Fearing that he'd flooded the thing, he gave it a moment's rest, but he was no more successful when he tried it again.

So he kicked it for the satisfaction that brought and went back inside, where the woodstove had started to warm the area closest to it. Thinking that this was a good sign and needing to feel in control, he pulled an iron saucepan from the kitchen cabinet and set about heating soup on the woodstove.

The soup was barely hot when he realized that the small scratching sounds he heard weren't coming from the pot.

* * *

Poppy stopped at Cassie's on the way home and gave a short beep of her horn. A coatless Cassie ran out, slid quickly inside, and shut the door against the cold.

"What is happening?" Poppy asked quietly. Micah's silence had shaken her. It suggested serious problems, rather than what should be a simple case of mistaken identity.

Cassie's face reflected only the red glow of the dashboard. "What did Micah say?"

"Not much. He was nearly catatonic, and I didn't want to push things with the girls right there. But it should be easy to prove who Heather is. You produce something from her childhood—a relative, a report card, a high school yearbook, a doctor, a friend. Did she give you names?"

Slowly, Cassie shook her head.

"Why not?" Poppy asked, nearly as unsettled by that headshake as by Micah's silence.

"She wouldn't talk."

"Why *not*?"

"I don't know. She was very upset. It's like she was traumatized by the arrest itself."

"Well, I would be, too," Poppy argued, because she could feel the panic that Heather must have felt, "but she's always been practical. She's always been one to accept and move on."

"Something emotional is happening."

"What? Why?"

"I don't know."

"But this is how you solve the problem," Poppy insisted. When Cassie sent her a wry look, she voiced that niggling fear. "I've been thinking hard, trying to come up with what I know about where Heather was before she came here, and I'm not finding much. Are you?"

Cassie didn't answer.

"Okay," Poppy went on, hanging on to hope, "but Micah must know some of it. Did you ask?"

"About a dozen times," Cassie grumbled. "I asked *both* of them. It's called an alibi, and it would be simple to establish under normal circumstances, but these circumstances aren't normal." Her voice died abruptly.

"What," Poppy coaxed.

Cassie started to say something, stopped, then seemed to shift gears. "Maybe someone in town knows. Like Charlie. He hired her when she first got to town. I'm talking with him first thing tomorrow."

Poppy was frightened. "She's hiding something, isn't she?"

"I don't know."

"Something happened to her before she came here."

"Do you think so?"

"Yes, I think so, because I don't know what *else* to think. How else do you explain her not being able to talk? How else do you explain her telling us nothing about her life?"

"So what might've happened?"

Poppy had given it some thought. "Rape. Domestic abuse. If so, she may have post-traumatic stress disorder. Or maybe she lost her family in a totally tragic way like . . . like . . ."—she seached for an appropriate image—"like a house fire, and it was so awful that she's just blotted everything out. Or maybe she had an accident like mine, only without the paralysis. She did say the scar was from an auto accident."

When a sudden knock came against Cassie's fogged-up window, they

both jumped. Swearing softly, Cassie rolled it down to reveal in incre-
ments the face of her husband, Mark.

"Hi, sweetie," she said.

"The buzzer went off."

"Take the casserole out and put it on the counter."

"The kids want you inside. They haven't seen you all day."

"I know. I'll be in in a sec."

Mark gave her a skeptical look. Then he turned and left.

"He's a saint," Poppy said.

Cassie rolled up her window. "Yeah, well, his patience is starting to
fray. He thought my hours were too long before. This won't help. Hell,
Poppy, it's not like I *ask* for cases like these, but when they come, I can't
turn my back. I know that I have three kids. And, yes, I know the oldest
is only six and that these are the critical years in their lives. So am I taking advantage of the fact that my husband teaches high school history
and is therefore around more than me for the kids? Of *course* I am. But I
do what I can." She let out a breath. Then she leaned over and gave
Poppy a quick hug. "Call me if you hear anything useful, okay?"

*   *   *

Poppy didn't hear anything new or useful, at least, not on the matter of
Heather. People were back in their own homes, answering their own
phones, and the few who called her were asking the same kinds of questions she had asked Cassie. Disbelief had become frustration. People
wanted a surefire *something* to exonerate Heather. Like Poppy, they were
looking for an alibi.

These calls only made Poppy feel worse. No one seemed to know any
more about Heather's past than she did. All fingers pointed to Micah as
the one who should know something, and Poppy did try to call him. But
when he finally picked up after four rings, he was monosyllabically terse.
Yes, he had fed the girls. No, they weren't happy. Yes, the press had called.
No, he hadn't talked with them. Yes, he was trying to remember what
Heather might have said about where, when, and with whom she had
been before coming to town. No, he hadn't come up with anything.

Poppy wanted to know why. She wanted to know how a man who had lived with a woman for four years could not know about her past. She wanted to know what they *did* talk about when they were alone.

But Micah didn't volunteer that information, and she couldn't get herself to ask. And then she was distracted.

Mary Joan Sweet, president of the local Garden Club, called her, claiming to have seen Griffin Hughes driving Buck Kipling's old truck through town. But Mary Joan, with her delicate pansy face framed by wispy gray hair, was known to be nearsighted, so Poppy could comfortably discount her claim. Leila Higgins, on the other hand, was a credible source. She called Poppy to report seeing Griffin in the general store, which was easy enough to prove. Poppy called Charlie.

"Yup," Charlie confirmed, "he's here in town. Gave me the brightest spot in a pretty lousy day. He's staying out at my brother's place on Little Bear."

Poppy didn't hear the last for grappling with the first. "Why's he here?"

"He's chasing after you," Charlie teased, but she didn't hear the teasing, either. She had told Griffin she wasn't interested. She had told him that more than once.

"He must be chasing after Heather," she decided and vented her annoyance on Charlie. "I can't believe you gave him a place to stay."

"He wanted to stay in town."

"He's a journalist. He'll use us."

"He says he's working on something else entirely, but the thing is, if he's determined to snoop, I'd rather he be under my thumb so I can keep an eye on him. Besides, we need answers about Heather. Maybe he can get them for us. So he uses us, and we use him back. Hell, we can play the game, too."

"Okay," Poppy tried. "Forget Griffin. Tell me what *you* know. You hired Heather when she first came to town. Where was she before here?"

"Atlanta."

Atlanta. Poppy had never heard Heather talk about Atlanta.

"She worked at a restaurant there," Charlie said, "but only for a few weeks. She needed money."

"For what?"

"To live. To come here."

"Why here?"

"I don't know."

Poppy needed a reason. It would give Heather credibility. "Small town? Lake? Loons? What?"

"I don't know."

"Didn't you ask?"

"Poppy," Charlie chided, "this was fourteen years ago. I probably did ask at one point or another, but the fact is I was more interested in whether she could waitress."

"Did you check out a reference before you hired her?"

"I sure did. The guy who owned the restaurant gave her a glowing one, just like the one I'd give her if I was asked."

That brought Poppy back to Griffin. "He'll ask. He'll prod. He may be working on something else, but guys like that keep their fingers in lots of pies at once. Trust me. He'll get things from you that you didn't think you knew."

"Maybe that'd be good—you know, if I can remember something that'll help Heather. It sure is a help to me, Griffin's being on Little Bear. It's at the far end of nowhere. I wasn't looking forward to traipsing out there to check on the place."

At last the words registered in Poppy's mind. "Griffin's on Little Bear? But Little Bear's all closed up."

"Yes, it is."

"The place must be frozen solid."

"Yup."

"He won't get water."

"Not this time of year."

She heard his smile, and suddenly it seemed fair game that a guy who had enough money in the bank to stick his nose into other people's business at will should be stuck out in the cold with a minimum of amenities in the depth of winter. Unable to resist a momentary satisfaction, she said, "You're bad, Charlie," and let slip a small smile of her own.

* * *

Red squirrels. Griffin wouldn't have known that if he hadn't followed the scratching sounds to a spot overhead, not far from the woodstove. He pulled out a ceiling tile and caught a pair of them tearing the insulation apart. Bits of stuff fell down on him, not all of it insulation. Not wanting to know what that other stuff was, he replaced the tile as quickly as possible and returned to the spot he'd staked out for himself in front of the woodstove.

He felt hamstrung. Forget his thumb, which throbbed, and knuckles that were raw from the cold. Legs, arms, back—he ached all over. He would have killed for a hot shower. Hell, he'd have killed for a *warm* shower. Barring both, he yearned, positively *yearned,* for the sleeping bag that was stashed in the closet of his bedroom in Princeton. It was top of the line and good to twenty below. Even with the woodstove generating steady heat, the cold had so penetrated everything in the cabin that it made the stove's job twice as hard.

Normally, he'd have passed an evening at home watching television, surfing the Web, even writing Hayden's bio, but he couldn't do any of that here. Nor could he run down the street to the pub to catch a Knicks game or have a beer with friends. Charlie's Café was the closest anything came to a pub; it was closed for the night, and even if it hadn't been, he wasn't running anywhere. Not tonight, not in the pitch-black, with the wind kicking up and the air outside the cabin colder than anything he'd ever known in his life. The air inside the cabin wasn't much better.

And all that was before he thought of the truck. Oh, it had heat. He had felt that on the drive out to this godforsaken end of the lake. But it was stuck in the snow, likely to be frozen solid by morning, which would make things interesting, particularly with his cell phone useless.

Of course, he'd been set up. No *doubt* about that. He figured there might be folks in town at that very minute, sitting around Charlie's after hours, chuckling at the idea that the city boy was freezing his butt off in the dark, with no running water, no electricity, no phone. He wondered if Poppy was there, but rejected the idea. Truth be told, he didn't want to think she took pleasure from his discomfort.

Besides, having driven for seven hours, then trekked through snow and cold, he was beat. So he took cushions off the sofa, laid them out near the woodstove, then took blankets from the bedroom, which was the only other room in the cabin. Stretching out on the cushions in front of the woodstove, he covered himself, but he pushed the blankets back off seconds later. They were nearly frozen themselves. Relying on the direct heat from the stove, he curled into a ball and let determination ease him to sleep.

*   *   *

Micah couldn't sleep. He tried, but well past midnight he was still wide awake. The bed was too empty and his fear too intense. Needing to do something useful, he pulled on his jeans, pushed his feet into boots and his arms into a parka, went out back to the sugarhouse, and flipped on the lights. He avoided the woodpile where Heather's knapsack was hidden, and, instead, heaved up a coil of piping from the to-do pile and began combing it foot by foot for spots that looked weak. Weak spots could break into tiny holes and let sap drain out onto the snow and be lost. He couldn't have that. Give or take, depending on first run or last, it took forty gallons of sap to yield one gallon of syrup. Lost sap was lost syrup, lost syrup was lost business, and business was what Heather did best.

Dropping the piping, he went into the new addition. With his back to the kitchen side, he faced the office side, studied the pile of papers on her desk, and felt the start of panic. The papers were in folders, neat and orderly as Heather's mind worked, but Micah's mind didn't work that way. He knew that the folder labeled "ART" held sketches of the new logo as it would appear on the labels they planned to use on syrup tins, and that the folder labeled "VAC" held information on the vacuum system they had just installed to draw more sap from the trees. There was paperwork to be done for that, and then there was the folder labeled "EVAP," which held details on loan payments for the new, larger evaporator that they had bought and used the season before—the efficiency of which had told them they could handle more syrup, which was why they had bought the vacuum system, ordered new labels, and put on the addition.

Information on all of it was in the computer, which sat there like an ugly troll on the desk, and then there was e-mail. E-mail was Heather's major link to suppliers and customers.

Micah was an expert with a chainsaw, a drill, and a bit, but he was in over his head when it came to a computer. Heather wasn't. Hardware . . . software . . . she got it all. She knew about everything on this desk. It all had to do with his business. If she didn't get back soon, he'd be in big trouble.

Breaking into a nervous sweat under his parka, he returned to the house, but Heather's touch was everywhere there, too. Copper pots hung in the kitchen from the frame she'd had him mount on the ceiling; plants thrived in the greenhouse window she'd had him install behind the sink. The sofas were draped with afghans she had knitted. Half-made dresses for the girls in pretty patterns were folded on the sewing machine.

Unwilling to see more, he shut off the lights and returned to the bedroom. Sitting there in the dark, he felt numb, though certainly not from the cold. The house was plenty warm, thanks to a furnace that spread heat through the rooms.

He hadn't had the furnace when he first met Heather. He had a blower system then that worked off the heat generated by the woodstove, and the system had been fine, assuming the woodstove stayed lit. Letting it die out had been a source of constant contention between Marcy and him. She didn't think it was her job to hang around the house just to keep it going, not when she had a husband who was in and out of the place all day long—and she was right in a sense. He certainly was nearby. Even when he was doing renovations or additions for other people, his jobs were local, so he was home for lunch. During sugaring season, he was around even more.

His side of the argument said that she was the one *in* the house. She was strong and healthy, and it wasn't like he was asking her to chop down the tree, cut and split the logs, and carry armloads at a time to the hearth. He did those things. All he was asking was that she add one or two logs to the stove when the flame got low.

What he really meant, he had realized after she died, was that he didn't see why she had to be out all the time. Having babies hadn't slowed her down. She simply strapped the girls into the car and took off to see friends, shop, do whatever struck her on a given day. She had a kind of frenetic energy, and he'd found it exciting at first. Born and raised on the

Ridge, she was like a bright light that was never still. He had tried to follow it, but in the end, he had failed. He was too much a creature of habit.

Habit? Necessity. He had inherited the sugarbush from his father, and the sap season was short. He had to make the most of every minute, couldn't slack off. And when it was done, when the sap was boiled down and bottled and sent to the many dozens of stores in northern New England that sold it through the year, he had to earn money another way. Frenetic energy was a luxury he couldn't afford.

That frenetic energy had killed Marcy. No one had said it in as many words, but it was clear as day. She'd been driving too fast on icy roads. Always too fast, too eager, too ready to get somewhere.

Heather was the opposite, with her soft, steady voice, her clear silver eyes, and her common sense. She loved being at home. She loved sugaring. She loved the girls. Though he was guilt-ridden each time he thought it, she set a far better example for them than their mother had. He had always trusted Heather with them, had never worried when she was with them, not once, not even at the start.

A small whisper of sound came from the door. He looked around just as Star slipped into the room. She didn't say anything, simply ran softly around the bed and came to lean against his thigh.

As he stroked her hair, he felt a catch in his throat. She was a beautiful child inside and out, and so knowing. He didn't have to ask why she was awake. Her worries might be fewer than his, but many of them were the same.

Where's Momma? Why isn't she here? When will she be back? Why did she leave?

She hadn't left, he wanted to say. She would be back in the morning, he wanted to say. But he didn't know whether either was true. Feeling as lost as Star, he scooped up the child and held on until the frightening moment passed. Then, needing to be alone with his confusion, he carried her back to bed.

*   *   *

Griffin slept poorly. He was cold, and he was sore. Cushions on the floor—*thin* cushions on the floor—couldn't compare to his own bed, and even if the rest of the cabin were ever to thaw enough to allow him to use the bedroom, the bed there didn't promise much more comfort. He was five ten and of average build. Charlie's brother had to be smaller than that, and he sure as hell didn't share this place with a woman. There was barely enough room in the bed for one person, let alone two. In fact, not much at all in the cabin suggested that a woman spent time here. Everything was basic, wood-brown, life at its most spartan—which was probably exactly what a cabin in the middle of a lake was supposed to be.

He told himself that. He told himself he was paying his dues. He told himself he was getting on Charlie's good side.

Using this thought as a mantra, he dozed off, but he was awake again two hours later. The wind had picked up and it wasn't the howling that bothered him, though it was an eerie sound, so much as the way the cabin shook with each swirling gust. He thought about the trees that were surely swaying, wondered if any might fall and how he would summon help if he were trapped inside here.

He needed to use the bathroom, but there was no way he was going outside. So he stifled the urge and went back to sleep.

He woke again and fed the woodstove. Once the blankets had warmed, they were a help in cushioning and layering, and he drifted into a deeper sleep. This time he awoke to a hint of daylight coming through the center of the café curtains.

The good news was that the wind had died down. The bad news was that in the silence it left he could hear the scurry of feet overhead, which said that the squirrels had gravitated to the warmth. Giving them wide berth, he got up and out of the way, gingerly manipulating stiff muscles and joints until they were marginally warmed.

He opened the curtains on a world dense with fog. He couldn't see more than a dozen feet beyond the cabin. The lake might have been an ocean, with him thousands of miles from shore.

Unsettled, he returned to the woodstove. His hiking boots were still damp. He opened them wider and repositioned them, then set a pot of coffee on to perk. When it was barely done, he poured a cup and drank it while he scrambled eggs in a heavy iron skillet. He ate them straight from the pan, standing up, shifting from one foot to the other. Finally, when he had nothing else to distract him and couldn't possibly wait any longer, he put on his boots, went outside, and ran straight for the trees.

The relief was well worth the biting cold. He took a deep breath, dropped back his head to look high into the hemlocks, smiled at the crispness of the air and the pleasure of the physical release. When he was done, he turned back toward the cabin and caught sight of the lake. The fog had begun to lift, leaving startlingly beautiful tiers of light. Highest up were the clouds in shades of gray, beneath them the shore in gradient levels of gray-green to moss, then the lake itself with snow riffles shaped by the night's wind.

The clouds lifted even as he watched. When they thinned enough to allow bits of sun to break through, the snow came alive with glitter, but it was what he heard then that made him catch his breath. From some-where—nowhere—came the haunting call of a loon. At least, he thought it was a loon. He had heard a few when he'd visited Lake Henry in Octo-ber and had seen them on the lake. He didn't see any birds now on the frozen expanse and guessed that they were in a hidden little patch of wa-ter, but that didn't lessen the effect. If anything, it added a surrealism to the scene.

In that instant, he wasn't thinking of paying his dues or proving him-self or getting on anyone's good side. He had always loved the outdoors, and this was the outdoors at its best. As he stood there and the loon call came again, the shore grew more distinct. He made out his truck. Farther along the shore he picked out one small cottage, then farther on, another. He heard the sound of an engine or a chainsaw—he didn't know which, didn't care. It worked well with the smell of the woodsmoke coming from his stove.

The loon moved on and ceased to call. He began to shiver, but he stayed there, standing now on the edge of the island, until his ears stung from the cold. Back inside, by comparison comfortably warm, he was in-vigorated.

He could do this, he decided. He could find the switch to turn on the lights; he could get the water running. He could make this cabin work.

All he had to do was get the truck out of the snow, and he'd be on his way.

* * *

Poppy worked out until her arms and shoulders ached. Lulled by the fog as she faced the lake, she focused on her upper body, moving from one part of the weight machine to the other. She pedaled the recumbent bike with her arms, which in turn moved her legs through a range of motion. She used the standing table to keep her lower extremities as attuned to weight bearing as they could be. But she ignored the parallel bars on the far side of the room. That piece of equipment had been her physical therapist's idea, not hers. She hadn't wanted it there, didn't see the point. She wasn't walking again. She could accept that.

Finishing up, she showered, had breakfast, and answered the phones long enough to know that Micah had taken the girls to school, that Cassie had learned nothing more from Charlie than Poppy had learned herself the night before, and that Griffin had survived his night on Little Bear. He had shown up at the general store with a bruise on his thumb from whapping frozen logs together, a purpling slash on his cheek from slipping against the truck when he was shoving pieces of birch bark under his tires for traction, and stories about hearing a loon. The reports said that he was undaunted, and had come looking for gloves, high winter boots, thermal underwear, and the secret to turning on the lights at the island.

Everyone in town knew that the fuse box was behind a small panel in back of the peanut butter in the kitchen cabinet, that the loons were gone for the winter, and that Buck Kipling kept a set of tire chains under the seat of his truck.

Poppy wondered if anyone had told Griffin about the chains.

She wondered if anyone had told him that he wouldn't get water running until the pipes were fixed, and that they couldn't be fixed until spring.

She wondered when he would show up at her place.

Not wanting to be there when he did, she set off in the Blazer the instant Selia McKenzie showed up to man the phones. By ten, she was at Cassie's office in town, and within minutes of that, they were off to visit Heather at the county jail in West Eames.

Chapter Six

The county jail was a squat brick building behind the courthouse. Poppy's heart pounded in trepidation as she propelled her wheelchair up the well-shoveled ramp. She stayed close to her friend while Cassie talked them inside. There was a standard search, modified to accommodate dangers that a wheelchair might hide, during which Poppy was desperate to say something like, *You're suspecting the wrong people! Always the wrong people!* A dozen years ago, she would have spoken right up. Wisely, now, she held her tongue.

They were ushered into a small room reserved for meeting with lawyers. The walls were bare concrete with a smattering of graffiti. A card table stood off to one side. Cassie dragged it to a more comfortable spot away from the wall and pulled up two folding chairs.

A short time later, Heather was led in. She wore an orange jumpsuit and looked as if she'd barely slept. Her eyes widened when she saw Poppy, and for a minute she hesitated. It took Poppy offering her arms before she ran over for a hug.

After a minute, Poppy eased her back. "How are you doing?"

"Awful awful awful," Heather whispered and started to cry. When she tried to hide her face, Poppy hugged her again. After a minute, Heather pulled back on her own.

Gently Cassie asked, "Are you all right here?"

Heather nodded as she blotted her eyes with the heel of her hands. Rather than taking a seat at the table, she backed up to the wall. "Where's Micah?" she asked in a thin voice.

"He'll be here this afternoon," Cassie replied. "He wanted to come with us now, but I asked him not to."

"Why?"

"Because we need to talk—you, me, and Poppy. We need to talk about where you were before you came to Lake Henry. I thought you might feel freer without Micah here. Charlie told us about the restaurant in Atlanta. That's the kind of information we need. My paralegal is at the office right now trying to contact the guy."

"Why?"

"Because if we're going to prove that you're Heather Malone, we need affidavits from people who knew you before the date of the murder in Sacramento. I need leads, Heather. Help me, please."

Heather took in a slow breath. Exhaling, she put a hand over her mouth. For a minute, she looked like she was going to be sick. She swallowed once, then again, and seemed to regain control.

Poppy wheeled over to her. "What is it? What happened?"

Heather's eyes welled again, but she said nothing.

"It doesn't matter what it is," Poppy tried. "We don't care. It won't change how we feel about you. We're with you through this all the way. That's what being friends is about."

"Did John write a piece?"

Lake News, John's newspaper, appeared each Thursday. "He's a friend, too. The article covered only the facts of your arrest. It didn't get into speculation."

Heather nodded. Eyes moist and filled with pain, she asked softly, "How are Missy and Star?"

Feeling rebuffed, Poppy sat back in her chair and said a less gentle, "They're terrible. They want you home. They're sure that you're gone for good, just like Marcy."

Heather drew in a shaky breath but made no reply.

In the ensuing silence, Cassie rose abruptly. "This is not fair to them, Heather. They love you. So does Micah, and here he is, hit with all this just as sugaring season is about to start. You're his partner in all that, so it's not fair to him, either. And it's not fair to us. We're your friends, and we love you, but those facts don't take us far in a court of law. Here's the scoop, sweetie. We need facts. We need hard facts documenting who you are, like where you were born, where you grew up, where you went to school."

Heather frowned, swallowed, murmured, "We had no money."

"Public schools are free," Cassie replied. "Where did you go to school?"

When she didn't answer, Poppy asked, "Did you get a driver's license somewhere?"

"I used to baby-sit," Heather said.

"For whom?" Cassie asked.

"They're all long gone. My dad had trouble holding a job. It was worse after my mother left."

Left. Poppy had assumed that the woman was dead, since Heather had never mentioned her mother. *Left* was something else, something that could raise all kinds of issues, which made Heather's silence on the matter all the more puzzling. They had talked about mothers. Poppy knew they had, and many times—Poppy and Heather alone, Poppy and Heather with Marianne, Sigrid, and Cassie. Most women had issues with their mothers. Heather must have taken part in these discussions, or the others would have questioned her on it. Of course, there were ways to take part in a discussion without talking from firsthand experience.

"Left?" Cassie asked.

"Where did she go?" Poppy asked.

"I don't know."

"How old were you when she left?" Cassie asked. When there was no answer, she asked, "So your father raised you? Where?" Still there was no answer. "Talk to us, Heather," she warned. "I need to know these things. Give them to me, and I can get you out of here. Without them, my hands are tied."

Heather huddled into the wall. "I can't."

"It's *that* bad?" Poppy asked.

Heather nodded.

"Worse than being sent back to California and tried for murder?" Cassie asked, then warned, "Because that's what'll happen, sweetie, if you don't help me out here."

Heather put her forehead against the concrete wall.

"Don't," Poppy begged.

"Talk to us," Cassie pleaded.

Heather took her head only far enough from the wall so that she could press her palms to her temples.

Cassie took a step back. "The problem is that if you won't talk, people will assume guilt."

Heather pressed harder.

Poppy tugged at her arm. "Help us, Heather. Give us a date, any date. You don't have to relive the whole nightmare, if that's what it was, just give us one person who can vouch for your being you, just one person, just one name, one place, one date . . ." She could have gone on, but it wouldn't have helped. Heather had put her hands over her ears.

"I think we're done," Cassie said in a no-nonsense voice.

"No," Poppy cried, turning to her, but Cassie's face was set.

"We've asked, we've coaxed, we've begged," she said loudly enough for Heather to hear, hands and all. "I don't know what more we can do. Heather has thirty days to decide if she wants to visit California. At the end of those thirty days, she may not have a choice. If that governor's warrant presents evidence that we can't counter, she'll be on the first flight out, and once she's there, it'll be prison, not jail. It'll be hardened convicts on the next cot and in cells on either side, not someone spending the night for driving under the influence. Californians have no sympathy for Lisa Matlock. Charlie DiCenza is out for blood. So if Heather's prepared for hard time, fine. If not, she needs to listen to reason and talk." She went to the door and rapped hard. Within seconds it opened, and Heather was retrieved by a guard.

Watching her leave, Poppy felt utterly helpless. The instant the door closed, she turned on Cassie. "We should have kept at her. We should have worked at it from the personal side—the five of us being close friends—friends wanting to help. If she doesn't have family, we're her only hope. We should have told her that."

"We did. She's not hearing."

"But what you said was *cruel.*"

Cassie sighed. "What it was was blunt. Gentle coaxing hasn't helped. I tried that yesterday. Maybe this will."

*   *   *

Within minutes of dropping Cassie at her office, Poppy put in a call to Maida. "Hi, Mom."

There was a pause on the Palm Beach end, then a cautious, "Poppy? Are you all right?"

"I'm fine," Poppy said lightly.

That brought another pause. "You don't usually call. Is this about Heather?"

It certainly was, though for the life of her, Poppy didn't know why she thought her mother might help.

"I've gotten calls," Maida went on. "I know she's in jail."

"She'll be out soon. We're working on gathering evidence to prove that she is who she is."

"And is she?"

Poppy felt a twinge of annoyance. "Of course, Mom. Why do you ask that? She's my friend. Wouldn't I know if she'd committed murder? Wouldn't I *know* if she'd done something as bad as that?"

After yet another pause, Maida said quietly, "Maybe . . . maybe not."

"Why do you say that?"

"Well, I don't know." Maida sighed. "It's just that sometimes you know people, and sometimes you don't."

"Heather isn't people. She's a friend. You know a friend."

"Not always."

The conversation wasn't helping Poppy, though she didn't know what she wanted. She had always detested the kind of perfection that Maida pushed. Conversely, she might have liked the assurance that Heather's secrets were innocent and pure.

Poppy sighed. "You're not making me feel better."

"Is that why you called?"

It had to be, though she had never done it before. Maida was her mother; she was of a different generation from Poppy and had a different approach to life. Maida wasn't Poppy's friend by any measure of that word. "Well," she said after a pause, "maybe not. I just . . . wanted to call."

"I'm sorry if I've disappointed you."

It wasn't disappointment, exactly. Or maybe it was. "You haven't."

"I have a way of doing that with you and Lily."

"No, really. It's okay. But hey, Mom, I'm almost home. We'll talk another time, okay?"

* * *

Shortly before noon, the FBI returned to Micah's. He was up the hill in the sugarbush, taking his anger out on the winter debris. His chainsaw had cut up a storm of downed limbs and dead branches when he finally killed the engine and came up for air. That was when the sound of a car breached the silence of the clear winter air. Returning to the house as fast as his snowshoes allowed, he came down the last hill just as two agents were looking around. They were different ones this time, but he knew what they wanted.

"We have a warrant to search the house," one said, unfolding a paper that Micah had no doubt was official.

He considered his options. "What if I say no?"

"We break down the door."

"Do I have a right to a lawyer?"

"Do you need one?"

"Not me. Heather. You're looking through her stuff."

"Her 'stuff' has no rights. This warrant says that."

No Cassie. No rights. No choice. Micah trudged over to the porch and took off the snowshoes. He might not be able to keep them out, but he sure as hell could watch what they did inside. He didn't trust that they wouldn't try to plant something there.

* * *

"Micah, what do you know?" Poppy asked. She had returned to a barrage of media calls directed at his very available phone number, but she didn't see any point in telling him that. "You lived with Heather for four years. You have to know something."

"They're here searching the place," Micah replied angrily. "For all I know, the phone is bugged." He hung up.

Poppy called Cassie, who promised to head to Micah's. She took several calls from townsfolk asking questions she couldn't answer. Then, putting the phone bank on audio, she wheeled to the window and looked out over the lake. Visually, it was as clean, crisp, and pure as it had been the day before. Emotionally, however, it felt old today—and not unexpectedly so. Poppy experienced this same shift every year in the middle of February, when she suddenly ached for spring—and she wasn't the only one. Ice Days were held in February to give the townsfolk something to look forward to at the end of a long winter, and after Ice Days came the sap. Sugaring season was about celebrating the first crop of the year. It was about a strengthening sun, about townsfolk loosening their scarves and trekking through melting snow, about the promise of spring.

Poppy was ready. She craved a warmer sun. She craved grass on the ground and buds on the trees. She craved ice-out. She craved loons.

After a bit, she returned to the phones. The occasional call came in, but her heart was elsewhere. Frightened for Heather, unsettled by her conversation with Maida, and tired of asking questions she couldn't answer, she had nothing better to do as she ate lunch at the console than to wonder when Griffin would show up. She was surprised that he hadn't been there already. Each time she heard the slightest sound that might be a car on the drive, she held her breath.

Car on the drive? Make that *truck* on the drive. *Noisy* truck, unless Griffin had a way with tinkering under the hood of a car, which she seriously doubted since he was a city boy through and through. Car? *Truck,* Poppy. *Truck.*

* * *

Though she made a point of looking at everything else as she drove around the lake and through town that afternoon, she didn't see the truck, and once she arrived at the school and got the girls into the Blazer, her concern for them pushed thoughts of Griffin away. Missy had heard that Heather was in jail and wanted to know if it was true.

Poppy could curse Micah as much as she wanted for not telling the girls himself, but with Missy asking straight out, she couldn't lie. "Yes, she's in jail."

"Why?" Missy asked, her dark eyes looking positively huge with her bulky wool hat nearly touching her lashes.

"Because somebody thinks she's someone else."

"Can't she tell them who she is?" Missy asked with perfect logic.

"She can, but we need proof. Cassie's trying to get that now."

"What's proof?"

"Evidence. Like a spelling test with your name on it," Poppy said. "If you had one in your knapsack right now, it'd tell me that Melissa Smith was in school on this day in February."

Melissa pushed out her lower lip. "There is one in here. We had a test today. I got five words wrong."

"Five out of how many?" Poppy asked. Five out of, say, thirty wasn't bad.

"Five out of ten. That's *half*," the child informed her.

"Oh." That was bad. "Well. They must have been hard."

"That's *not* why I got them wrong," Missy stated. "I got them wrong because Heather didn't study with me."

Poppy looked for Star in the rearview mirror. The child's face was half-hidden by the hood of her parka. The part that might have been visible was turned to the window.

Wondering what the little one was feeling and thinking, Poppy told Missy, "I could've helped you. You should've asked. I'd have loved to help you study. I'm a good speller."

"Did you get all A's when you were in school?"

"No."

"Why not?"

"Because I fooled around and didn't pay attention, which was not a good thing to do at all. I didn't learn as much as I could have or should have, and I disturbed kids who *were* paying attention, and I got a reputation for being a problem in class, *and* I disappointed my parents. Fooling around in school is not a good idea, Missy."

Missy must not have liked the answer, because when Poppy glanced back, the child was flopped against the seat, staring at the handle of the door.

"Yes?" Poppy prompted. She shot another look back in time to catch the one-shouldered shrug Missy gave, and decided to let it be. "How was your day, Star?" she asked as she drove on through town. When Star didn't answer, she glanced in the rearview mirror. "Star?" Still, there was no answer.

And so it went for the next two hours. Poppy asked questions or suggested activities, and the girls either shrugged or were silent. She made maple apples, baking Cortlands in the dark amber, late-season syrup that was less subtle than the earlier, lighter, premium syrup but best for this purpose. The girls handed her whatever she couldn't reach in Heather's kitchen, but other than asking when Micah would be back from West Eames, they didn't initiate conversation.

Then Star went outside—just picked herself up from coloring at the kitchen table, walked right through the back hall and out the door.

Poppy watched her in surprise. "Star?" When the child didn't stop, she wheeled around to follow. "Star, where are you going?" The door clattered shut.

Dusk had fallen. It was dark and cold. Star wore no boots, no jacket, just sneakers, corduroy overalls, and a skimpy sweater.

Holding the back door open, Poppy watched the child climb the snow on the hill and fade out of view. "Come back here, Star!" she called.

Star didn't reappear.

"My God," Poppy murmured, "she can't go out like that." It was a Maida comment, straight out of Poppy's childhood, and ignored then by her as surely as it was ignored now. Poppy had visions of Star getting lost, being attacked by a fox, freezing to death in the frigid night air before Micah could find her. And Poppy couldn't do anything to stop it. She couldn't go after Star, couldn't trek up that hill when it was bare, much less in the snow.

"Star, get back here this minute!" she yelled at the top of her lungs, then said over her shoulder, "Missy, put on your jacket and see where she is!"

"She's okay."

"She's not!" Poppy cried. "She doesn't have a coat!"

"She's only going to Heather's tree."

"What's Heather's tree? *Where's* Heather's tree? Go after her, Missy. I *can't.*" She grabbed Missy's coat from a low hook and handed it to her. "Boots, too," she said, "and take Star's." The girl filled her arms with the things Poppy handed her and set off.

Poppy found the switch for the back light. She sat at the door and watched Missy trudge up the hill through its beam and fade into the dark, then she waited. She imagined the both of them vanishing, wandering off into God-knew-what. She imagined rescue teams combing the woods in the cold and damp. She imagined all sorts of horrors. Sitting there helplessly, waiting for them to return, she had never resented her handicap more.

It might have been one minute or five. Poppy didn't know. Then Missy reappeared in the outer reaches of light cast from the back porch. For a minute Poppy thought she was alone. When she saw Star behind, she fought back tears of relief. She lost the battle when Star reached her. Snatching the child up, she cried softly against her silky hair.

"Don't you ever do that to me again, Star Smith," she scolded brokenly.

"Heather's tree was lonely. I wanted it to know I was here."

"Well, I need to know you're *here*." She held the child back. "I need to know you're *right* here, because I can't go after you, Star. If something happened to you up there, I wouldn't be able to help. I wouldn't be able to help, Star."

* * *

I wouldn't be able to help. Poppy was haunted by that thought as she drove home. It occurred to her that she had no business filling in for Heather if she couldn't begin to do what Heather did. But she felt a responsibility—and it wasn't to Micah, or to Missy or Star. The responsibility she felt was to Heather alone.

Given her limitations, that responsibility was awesome.

Under the weight of it, she was teary still, feeling utterly incompetent as she turned in at the road to her house. She barreled on toward the lake until her headlights picked out Buck Kipling's old heap—now Griffin Hughes's old heap. At the sight of it, she felt a surge of anger.

She slammed on the brakes. The Blazer skidded. She steered into the skid, caught it, and continued on. Passing the truck, she pulled up as close to the house as she could. She thrust the gear shift into park and, furious now, maneuvered her chair onto the lift and down.

There was some solace in the fact that she was on the ramp before

Griffin got out of the truck and reached her side. But the solace ended there. Vulnerable as she felt, he was the last person she wanted to see.

She barely gave him a glance as she continued on to the house. When he reached to open the door for her, she angrily waved him aside, opened it herself, and wheeled in. She went straight to the bank of phones, and yanked off gloves, jacket, and hat, while Selia McKenzie ended her call.

Selia was one of two regulars Poppy used. Annie was a high schooler and great for filling in after hours, but Selia was the one most often there during the day. From the Ridge, she was forty-two and a grandmother seven times over. She was quick, patient, and as desperate for the money as she was for escaping the bedlam of her life at home, which made her an ideal employee.

Wheeling up to her now, Poppy held out a hand for the headset. "Anything new?"

"Lots of media," Selia said and moved her chair aside to make room for Poppy's.

"You told them no."

"Correct. There were also calls from around here wanting to know what you know."

"Which is nothing," Poppy snapped. Putting on the headset, she turned to the bank of buttons. Just when she needed something to happen, not a one was lit.

Selia took her car keys from the end of the table and left.

Griffin came up and planted himself directly in front of her desk.

Poppy focused on the phone panel. She knew her eyes were red, and guessed that her skin was flushed. Her heart was beating crazily in sheer annoyance.

He pushed his hands into the pockets of his jeans. She could see that without looking at him, thanks to peripheral vision. It also told her that he was of average height and build, with wide-set blue eyes, wavy auburn hair, and a straight nose.

The phone bank didn't blink.

Slowly, defiantly, Poppy raised her eyes. By the time they met Griffin's, she was boiling. *Why are you here? Didn't I make myself clear enough? Why can't you leave me alone?*

She didn't say a word, just glowered. And then he had the gall to say, "You look like you could use a knight in shining armor."

She exploded. "And you're it? I. Don't. Think. So. Besides, I couldn't get on a horse and stay there if my life depended on it." Her eyes filled with tears. "I answer phones. This is what I do best. I can't climb hills, I can't snowshoe or ski, I can't dance or run or even *walk* down Main Street, and I certainly can't take care of kids, which is good reason why I'll never have them."

"Is that what you were crying about?"

"That, and a million other little things. I have a right, y'know." She produced a singsong mimic. " 'Poppy's a saint. Poppy's always smiling. Poppy never curses her fate in life.' " Her pitch returned to normal. "Well, I do. My best friend is in jail, her kids are lost without her, her significant other is on the verge of *the* busiest weeks of the year for his business, and I'm stuck in a wheelchair—and with *dirty hands.*" She glared at them. "I *hate* these hands. No matter what I do, they're callused, and they get dirty whether I wear gloves or not." Sticking them under her thighs and out of sight, she glared at Griffin. "If things were different, I'd be helping Micah in the woods, *with* the girls, but the reality is that I can't help *any* of them. Right now, I *hate* this chair."

She stared him in the eye, daring him to say something patronizing.

What he said, after a moment's thought, was, "Want a kiss?"

"I do *not* want a kiss!"

He pulled a small foil-wrapped candy from his pocket and held it out.

She tried to make like she'd known all along what he meant. "I said no. I get them from Charlie's too, y'know. Kisses are a dime a dozen."

"Actually, a dime for ten," he said. Returning the candy to his pocket, he went around the desk to the back of the room. A long sectional sofa was there, dividing its focus between the television and the fireplace, which sat waist-high in a floor-to-ceiling wall of fieldstone. A low fire burned there.

The fieldstone wall also held a woodbin. Removing a log, he added it to the fire and brushed his hands together. "Reverse psychology won't work," he said as he returned.

"Excuse me?"

"Turning me off with a show of self-pity." He sat against the edge of the desk. "All of us have moments of self-pity."

"When do yours come?" she asked.

"When I think about my sister and wonder why I can't find her," he said. He began to gnaw on his lower lip, suddenly apprehensive. "Actually, no. Right now, I'm feeling sorry for myself because I inadvertently mentioned something to my brother that probably resulted in bringing the FBI here. If I could turn back the clock, I would, because I know you're going to hate me for what happened to Heather, which means I've lost something I wanted. But you might as well know. It was me. My brother is FBI. He's on the cold case squad. When I left here in October, I went to his office and kept staring at the picture of Lisa that was hanging on his wall. She looked so much like your friend. I'm sorry."

The confession stopped Poppy cold. She hadn't expected it, hadn't suspected Griffin of this. Taken so by surprise, she was without words. After a minute, feeling utterly deflated, she lowered her head to her folded arms. She was suddenly dreadfully tired. And sad. Profoundly sad. She didn't know why, but there it was.

With her head on her arms, she began to cry again. It was quiet and deep now, a soulful weeping, the venting of so many confused emotions that tears were the only possible form of expression.

She didn't look up. Her head stayed on her arms, not out of embarrassment but from an aching fatigue. "Oh God," she whispered finally, pressing her eyes to her forearm. "It's been a wretched two days."

When Griffin said nothing, she mopped her eyes with her hands, raised her head, and dared to meet his gaze. "What?" she invited in a nasal voice and dropped her hands. "No slick words?"

Not only didn't he come up with any, but those blue eyes of his actually seemed unsure. "I don't know what to do. I want to go over there and give you a hug, only I don't know if you want that."

"I don't need hugs," she informed him as archly as one who was all blotchy could do.

"Not need. Want, maybe."

There was no "maybe" about it. It had been a long time since Poppy had been held by a man. It had been a long time since she had been held by *anyone,* certainly not in the full way that would have given her the comfort she craved. Her chair was the proverbial third person, always there to remind her of her handicap.

She drew in a long, ragged breath. "I'm fine." But she couldn't talk about this. "So. You were the one who told them about Heather." It was safer to focus on that than on her own private needs.

"No. I just told my brother that someone here reminded me of Lisa. He's a good snoop."

"But not good enough to find your sister."

Griffin compressed his mouth and shook his head.

His admission gave Poppy a vague sense of power. "So what good is he? What good are you? And why are you here? Major question. If you're looking for me, the me you might have scored with left here twelve years ago, and if you're here looking for a story, you're still in the wrong place. I'm not helping you out."

"Turn that around. I was thinking I could help you out."

"Were you." It wasn't a question. She didn't want his help. "That's some bruise on your face, by the way."

A mite gingerly, he fingered the purple slash. "There was a struggle before I could convince the truck which of us was in charge." His hand rasped coming down over the stubble on his jaw. It was even darker than the auburn his hair had become since the autumn before.

"Your thumb looks awful, too. Who *is* winning the war?"

"Me. Definitely me. I got the cabin warmed up and the electricity on. I can't get the water going, but I'm working on it."

"Don't bother," she took pleasure in informing him. "The piping is bad. It can't be fixed until spring."

Griffin looked dismayed. "Are you serious?"

"Totally. We all know it. And another thing. There aren't any loons here this time of year. What you heard was Billy Farraway playing his loon pipe. He's seventy-five years old and spends the winter moving his bobhouse around." She wondered if Griffin had ever been ice fishing. "Do you know what a bobhouse is?"

"Yes. But I didn't see one near the island."

"You wouldn't if it was tucked behind one of the other islands on the lake. Do you know how many of those there are?"

Griffin smiled. "No. How many?"

"Thirty-eight. Thirty-eight islands on Lake Henry, and as lakes go, we're not overly big. If you haven't met Billy yet, just wait. He'll find you."

"A loon pipe? Are you sure? It sounded very real. I was talking at Charlie's about hearing a loon. No one there mentioned Billy."

"They wouldn't," Poppy replied and held his gaze until he got the message.

"Ahhh. They were letting me put my foot in it deeper."

She nodded. It struck her that between the bruise on his cheek, the one on his thumb, the stubble on his jaw, and the rumple of his hair, he looked a little worse for the wear, but it was a good worse. More rugged. She motioned him to move back from the desk so that she could see him head to toe. When he had done it, she said, "Nice boots. Nice vest. Nice thermals up there under that nice flannel shirt. Warm now, Griffin?"

He smiled again. "Yes, thank you. Quite warm. Your house is very comfortable." He meandered around the desk and sank into the sofa.

Poppy turned to watch. She liked the way he moved. She liked the way his shoulders looked when he put both arms along the back of the sofa. She also liked the way he smiled.

Then his smile faded. He shot a glance at her over his shoulder. "Have you seen Heather?"

Reality returned. "Yes. She's in bad shape. If you were the one who tipped off the cops, that makes me feel responsible, too. You came in October to see me."

He stretched out his legs and crossed his ankles. "So we can sit here and fixate on that, or we can talk about how to solve the problem. I take it it's a matter of proving that Heather is Heather. What does she say on that score?"

"Not much," Poppy remarked. "She seems unable to talk about this. And don't ask me why, because I don't know."

"Is that what upset you just now?"

Poppy thought about the crying jag he'd witnessed. "I don't usually do that," she said.

"I'm sure."

"I was taking care of the girls. The little one, Star, wandered out into the woods and I couldn't go after her. I was totally panicked. It's been a while since I felt as helpless as that." And then there was Micah, returning all stony from visiting Heather. And then Poppy's talk with Maida. She still didn't know what she had wanted her mother to do.

"You're good to be staying with them," Griffin said. "I can't believe half the town hasn't volunteered to do it."

"They have. But the girls are mine." She rushed to explain. "I mean, only in a way. Of course, the girls are Heather's." But she had to qualify that, too. "Not legally, but in every other sense."

"Why not legally?" he asked. "She could adopt them."

"She and Micah aren't married."

"Why not? They've been together . . . how many years?"

"Four," Poppy said. "Heather never pushed Micah. She didn't need to be married. She never wanted the girls to think that she was trying to make them forget their mother."

"Did you know the mother?"

"Yes."

"What was she like?"

Poppy struggled to say something positive. "She was very pretty. She died in an auto accident when Star was two months old."

Griffin blew out a surprised breath. "Were she and Micah in love?"

"Yes. For a little while, at least."

"Until Heather came along?"

"Oh, no. No. That wasn't it. Micah didn't cheat on Marcy. He's a loyal guy."

"So what was the problem with his marriage? And don't give me that look. There's a whole lot you're not saying. I can sense it."

Poppy said, "There's not a 'whole lot.' It's just that Marcy grew up here in town, but I think she always wanted something more."

"If she wanted more, why did she marry a local?"

"Probably because Micah's tall, dark, and handsome. Yes, it's a cliché. But that's what he is. He's also silent, which means he's a mystery, and that adds to the turn-on."

"Does he turn you on?"

"No," she said pedantically. "I don't personally *like* the silent type, and besides, I never knew him well before Heather. It takes a lot of work to get to know Micah, a lot of work to find out how softhearted he is, which means that *you* may be able to worm the occasional bit of information from me—like you're doing right now, Griffin Hughes—but you won't get anything from him."

"It's an issue of trust between you and me. You trust me."

"Excuse me?" she asked. "I trust you? Didn't you just say you pointed the FBI our way?"

"No. I said that my brother picked up on things I said that *inadvertently* resulted in his finding Heather. I told you the truth. You trust that I'll do that."

"I do not."

"Yes, on some deeper level you do. So is Micah approachable? If I went to talk with him, would I be welcome?"

"Not if he knows you caused all this."

"What if he didn't. Could I get him to talk?"

"About the weather, the woods, or the sap? Maybe. Suggest writing about Heather, and he'll cut you down cold."

Griffin sighed and sat forward. "I can't write about Heather. I'm doing something else."

"What's to keep you from doing two stories at once?"

Coming up from the sofa, he returned to her desk. Taking paper and pen, he wrote down a name and a number, and pushed the pad her way. "Prentiss Hayden. Give him a call. He'll tell you about the deadline that's closing in fast."

"Prentiss Hayden?" Poppy didn't have to be told who he was. The man was a political legend. "I'm impressed."

"Don't be. I wasn't his first choice. Two others came before me. Both quit before they'd written a word."

"He's demanding?"

"Very."

"If that's so, what're you doing here?"

"Obviously not winning *you* over," Griffin said with a snort and pushed a hand through already-mussed auburn hair. "Okay. I'm here to ease my guilt. If it hadn't been for me, this wouldn't have happened. But I can help reverse it. I have contacts all over the country."

"From your work?"

"Some from that. Some from my father. He's a corporate lawyer turned CEO. He turns companies around. He's built something of a name for himself."

Poppy knew that Griffin was independently wealthy. He had told her that back in the fall. Now something rang a bell. "Not Piper Hughes."

"Yes. Piper Hughes."

"But you told me your father was a Griffin, too."

"He is. Griffin P. Hughes. The 'P' is for Peter, but he was always a charismatic kid leading the crowd, so he became Piper, as in Pied Piper, to distinguish him from his father, who was the first Griffin."

"What did they call *that* Griffin?"

"Griffin. My dad's done well, but Granddad was actually the source of the big money."

"What'd he do?"

"Made cookies. Hummers."

"You're kidding," Poppy said with a grin, conjuring up images of chocolate, peanut butter, and graham cracker crunch. Hummers had come second only to s'mores at the Blake house, and s'mores, like hot dogs, were best only at summer cookouts on the lake. Hummers were a winter staple.

Griffin grinned back. "I wouldn't kid about that." He picked up the remote and flipped on the TV. "Hummers were serious stuff back home."

"I haven't had one in a while."

"No loss. The business was sold a dozen years ago. Then my grandfather died and left us each a bundle from the sale." He switched channels. "No more breaking news."

Poppy's grin faded. "Not about Heather. Not for twenty-nine days."

"Less than that, if we come up with something good. Charges can be dropped."

"Which brings us back to your contacts. Okay, Griffin. What's the price?"

"A shower."

She rolled her eyes.

"I'm serious," he insisted. "We rich boys are used to hot water. I have none, and now you tell me that I won't be able to get it. Know how grubby I feel? So let's make a deal. One piece of new information—on either Heather or Lisa—in exchange for one hot shower."

Appalled, Poppy put a hand on her chest. "I am not letting a strange man use my shower. That'd be like getting a roommate from the want ads."

"It's done all the time. I'm told it works well. Besides, I'm not a strange man. You know me." He pointed at the pad of paper near her hand. "If you want a reference, call Prentiss. Better still, ask for his wife. I stayed with them for a month."

"Ahh. The postcard from Charlottesville."

"She'll tell you I'm a decent guy."

"But why me?" Poppy cried. Showering was such an intimate thing. "Why here? Go ask someone *else* for a hot shower."

"Yeah, and have them laugh at me? They're already laughing about the loons. And the water. No water means no plumbing, and no plumbing means a hole in the ground. I'd put money on the fact that right now, right this minute, someone is over at Charlie's taking bets about when I'll cave in and go north to the inn."

"If they're not doing it now, they'll do it later. Thursday nights there's music in the Back Room. Music and talk. I'd advise you not to go."

"Why not?"

"Because thanks to what's happened to Heather, this is not a night for a new face."

"And you think they're going to let me in their *showers?* So what do I do? Come on, Poppy. Take pity. Be a sport."

Poppy didn't want Griffin showering at her house. She really didn't. But he did have a point. Besides, being a sport was second to being a pal, which had nothing to do with romance. Being a sport was safe. Lord knew, she had experience at it. She was a best friend to most of the men in town. She could certainly be a sport when it came to Griffin, especially if it meant getting information that would help Heather.

"If you think I'm providing towels," she warned, "think again. This isn't a bathhouse. And I am not doing your laundry."

"I'm not asking you to. I'll use the laundromat. Laundromats are great for picking up information. Even rich boys know that."

"The town won't tell you a thing," she warned.

"We'll see."

*   *   *

"The town won't tell him a thing," Charlie Owens was saying. He and his wife were in the back office of the general store with John and Lily Kipling. The four had had dinner in the café and now, with chocolate chip cookies baking under the watchful eyes of the next generation of Owens, and the woodstove fired up, they were nursing cappuccinos in the last few minutes before going out to meet and greet in the Back Room. "He seems like a nice enough guy, and his being on Little Bear saves me having to bribe one of the kids to go out there. But we've been through this before."

Lily said, "Poppy likes him."

"If you were to ask her, she'd say no," John teased.

"She's defensive. It's understandable."

"Is she afraid of being hurt?" Annette asked. "Strung along, then dropped?"

"Speaking of being strung along," Charlie said, "what's with Micah? I feel silly knowing so little about Heather and thinking myself so close to her. Micah's a hundred times closer. What does *he* know?"

Camille Savidge wasn't sure. She sensed that Heather kept secrets. Now, eavesdropping on the conversation from an adjacent office as she did the store's books for the week, she wanted to say that Micah didn't know a whole lot—and that Griffin Hughes wouldn't get much even if he went to the source.

The problem was that Heather needed help. Camille wasn't sure that Cassie had the resources to get the job done. If Griffin did, that was something to consider.

Chapter Seven

On Friday morning, Micah talked with the FBI. The agents had requested a meeting, and, though it was the last thing he wanted to do, Cassie urged him to cooperate. She argued that a refusal would only whet their appetites. She also said that since he was honest and straightforward, he would be a solid witness on Heather's behalf.

The meeting took place at Willie Jake's office, and Cassie was with him the whole time, but neither fact gave Micah much solace. He was a pretty straightforward guy. Ask him a question, and he could answer. Ask him the same question again, then again, and again, and he got pretty steamed. He didn't like people implying that he wasn't telling the truth.

So he was feeling raw when, after two hours of questions, he and Cassie were finally able to head to the jail. Cassie made it clear to him that the only reason she was along for this part of it was to get him the privacy of a lawyer-client meeting room. Five minutes into the visit, she found a reason to leave Heather and him alone.

As soon as the door was closed, Micah pulled Heather close. He missed the rosemary scent of the soap she used at home, but the softness of her was the same. Closing his eyes, he focused on the familiarity of her body against his. So much else had changed. He needed this.

"Cassie's angry with me," Heather said in a voice muffled by his shirt.

"So am I. Talk to me, baby."

He had never said those words before, never had to. Heather had always known without asking that he liked his eggs over easy, his shirts folded rather than hung, and the junk mail tossed out before he got home, just as he had always known that she loved blue lupines, red shoe-string licorice, and hot coffee waiting when she reached the kitchen in the morning.

He made great coffee. But he had often suspected that he could have burned the grounds in the making and she still would have smiled. She was always simply touched that someone thought to do this for her.

At least, he assumed that was the thought behind her pleasure. He knew it was behind his own. Heather was the first person in his life who seemed to want to make him happy.

Now, though, she didn't answer, just held him as if there was no to-morrow. In Micah's mind, no tomorrow didn't seem too far off the mark. He had always known Heather had a past. But he hadn't imagined it was something so bad that she wouldn't speak up, especially to defend herself against a charge of murder.

"Say something, baby," he pleaded. "Say something so all this makes sense."

She didn't speak.

"I know there are things," he said into her hair—dark hair, with silver strands that might well have come from trauma. "I never asked. I didn't want to upset you."

She remained silent.

"It never mattered to me," he went on. "I just wanted you."

He hadn't planned to want her. Four and a half years ago, when Heather had entered his life, he was in mourning for his wife. He had two babies, two businesses, and no free time. He wasn't supposed to want a woman. And he hadn't wanted Heather when she first offered to baby-sit during the day while he worked. He liked her. He trusted her. It seemed like a good deal.

At the beginning, he came home during the day to check up on the girls. But he kept at it long after he knew they were fine. During summer and fall, when he was doing carpentry, he came home for lunch; during sugaring season, he came in for coffee, lunch, and snacks. Heather was a quiet, smiling presence in his home. He began to look forward to see-ing her.

And the change from baby-sitter to lover? It happened after they'd kissed.

Well, they hadn't just kissed. How to stop at a kiss with Heather? It had been building for weeks, like sap rising in the growing heat of the sun. Try as he might to tell himself that it was inappropriate, Micah hadn't been able to keep from lying in bed at night in an agony of wanting that got worse and worse and worse.

Heather didn't encourage him. She never touched him. She didn't look at his chest or his legs or his fly—always only at his face. But the effect those silver eyes had was amazing.

Then one day, when the sap was boiling hard and he and a crew were late in the sugarhouse, she stayed to put the girls to bed. Later, when everyone else had left, she went over to help him finish and clean up. There, with the air sweet and warm, and his body hot and heavy, he thanked her for her help with a kiss.

It was the most natural thing in the world. But it wouldn't stop. They kissed, they touched, they undressed. He used no protection. He couldn't. He needed to feel every bit of her. He didn't care if he made her pregnant. Part of him *wanted* to do it. He was so in love he couldn't think of anything else.

He still was that much in love. Now, though, the place that had brimmed with Heather was a gaping hole. He'd been alone for two nights, and he felt a pain he had never felt when Marcy died.

"They keep asking me what I know," he said.

"Who?"

"FBI. They think I'm an accomplice."

"To what?"

He felt a flash of annoyance. He didn't like being taken for a fool by anyone, least of all by Heather. She knew *to what.*

"They searched the house," he told her more harshly than he might have, but the mere thought of it brought back the fury he had felt at the time. "Turned the place upside down. Went through drawers and cabinets. Pulled up the rug and the mattress. They went through the sugarhouse, too." They had even pulled a few logs off the woodpile, which had given him a fright. But they'd soon stopped and moved on. "They didn't get much of anything except the computer. They picked it up and carted it off."

Heather drew back. "But that has all our files."

"They think there's more in there."

"No, no, no, no." Her silver eyes sparked. "It's all to do with the business."

"They think there's coded messages."

"Micah, it's all *business*," she cried in outrage. "They can't take that. You *need* those files."

He snorted. "For what? I can't work that machine."

"Camille can. Call her."

"What good'll that do, if they have the machine?"

Heather drew herself straighter. She gave a quick toss of her hair and a small, smug smile. Then she whispered, "Backup disks. She makes them each time she comes to do the books. We thought it was a good thing in case there was ever a fire."

Well, that was something, Micah decided. But it still didn't mean that the business wouldn't fail if Heather wasn't back soon.

"I'm alone, baby," he told her, unable to keep it in any longer. "I lie in bed alone in the dark and I'm wondering. All the time wondering. I don't know much more'n anyone else. All I know is I wanted to marry you, but you wouldn't. I wanted us to have kids, but you wouldn't. Tell me why."

She wilted with frightening speed, became this other person he didn't know at all. "I have."

Very slowly he shook his head.

She tried, "I couldn't . . . I'm not . . . there's Marcy."

"Marcy's dead."

She said nothing. He tried to read something in her eyes, but the sadness there simply set his head to spinning. That sadness didn't belong to his Heather. It belonged to someone else.

Feeling dislocated, he stepped back. Moments later, Cassie returned and they left.

* * *

Micah stewed the whole way home. With each passing mile, he became more convinced that Heather was hiding something important. It galled him to think that she didn't trust him—trust *him*—enough to say what it was.

Pulling up at the house, he slammed out of the truck and strode around back. Crossing the clearing to the sugarhouse, he went straight to the woodpile inside. There he stopped. He stared at the area where the knapsack was hidden, as if he could see it right through the wood. He ran a hand around the back of his neck, dropped his arm, flexed his fingers.

Heather had brought the knapsack with her when she had moved in. He had seen it with her things, then it had vanished. He had found it by accident a while after that, when he'd been taking Christmas ornaments from the closet, and it had fallen off the shelf. He had quickly put it back and hadn't touched it again. He hadn't wanted to see what was inside.

He still didn't. He could call himself a million kinds of fool, but he was too frightened to open the damn pack.

Turning on the heel of his scuffed boots, he went back to the house. In no time, he had pulled on a wool hat and gloves and, snatching up snowshoes on his way through the back hall, headed out again. He stopped at the outer woodshed for a chainsaw, a long-handled ax, and a sled. Then he headed up the hill.

*   *   *

Griffin pulled up behind Micah's truck. As soon as he turned off his engine, he heard the chainsaw, all the more so when he opened his door. The growl of the saw was distant, but distinct.

On the chance that someone other than Micah was using it, he went up the front steps and across the porch to knock on the door. There was no answer.

Going around back, he knocked there. Then he went to the sugarhouse, opened the door, peered inside. The room held numerous large pieces of equipment, but its centerpiece was a stainless steel pan easily six feet wide by sixteen long. The rear part sat higher than the front, but the whole of it rested on a brick arch with a wrought-iron door underneath. Above was a hood, from which a steel chimney rose to the cupola. The cupola was directly above the evaporator, and nearly as large.

"Hello?" he called.

When no one answered, he ducked back out and went around the sugarhouse. A woodshed, piled high with logs, stood against the east end of the fieldstone structure, close beside a huge set of double doors. Behind the sugarhouse, on the north, were two large steel tanks. Another tank, even larger, sat on a platform a few yards up the hill, and yet other machine stood off to the right. A bit farther off, nearly hidden in a stand of billowy firs, was a doorless garage, in which he could see a large tractor with a yellow plow on the front.

He headed up the hill toward the sound of the saw. Once past the tamped-down stretch, his boots sank deeper in the snow, but they were the right boots now, and besides, he figured that the saw couldn't be far. He crested one small rise and saw an evenly spaced stand of bare maples with snow on their limbs. He had to steer right and crest another rise before he finally spotted Micah in the distance. He was out of breath and sweating under his thermals before he was halfway there. By then, Micah had spotted him and killed the saw.

Had Griffin been a timid man, he might have turned and run. Micah Smith was a head taller than he was, the chainsaw might have been a toy for the ease with which he held it, and, below an orange wool hat, his face was threatening and dark.

Truth be told, Griffin couldn't turn and run, even if he *had* been timid. He could barely *wade* through the snow those last few yards, but wade he did, trying to look as pleasant and nonchalant and non-threatening as possible. When he was within striking distance, he stuck out a hand.

"I'm Griffin Hughes."

"I know who you are," Micah said and turned back to the tree he had downed. The stump was a dozen feet off, surrounded by sawdust in the snow. The branches had been removed and stacked in long pieces. With a quick pull, he set the chainsaw to snarling and went to work on the trunk.

Griffin watched. Micah made a clear cut, then moved down two feet. The tree trunk was easily twelve inches in diameter and, to Griffin's eye, looked healthy enough. When curiosity got the best of him, he plodded around so that Micah could see him. Then he yelled over the sound of the saw, "Was it sick?"

"No," Micah yelled back. He finished another cut and moved on to the next.

"So why'd you chop it down?" Griffin called.

Micah finished another. "Snow," he said and moved on.

"Snow what?"

Micah sawed off that piece, moved down the trunk, severed another. Silencing the chainsaw then, he straightened and, with resignation, said, "It was a good tree. I put it in as a sapling a long time ago, and I've tapped it for two years now. South exposure, it got good sun and had a broad crown." He looked around the sugarbush. Some of the trees had a handful of withered brown leaves that hadn't had a chance to fall off before being frozen in place. "It was too broad for it's own good. The first snow came in October, wet and heavy on a full head of hair. The weight was too much." He hitched his chin toward the longer branches piled on the snow near the stump. "The biggest of those broke right off under the weight, took nearly half the crown. A tree won't produce sap without the starch brought in by the leaves. No leaves, no starch, no sap. If I left this one standing, it'd only take sun away from more promising trees in the grid."

He started up the chainsaw and went at the next section of trunk.

Griffin continued to look around the sugarbush. The maples were utterly still, seeming too cold to even shiver. They were carefully spaced, and while his island was mostly evergreen, the only evergreens here stood off in a group on the side. Had Griffin been poetic, he'd have said they were watching everything that happened there.

"Windbreak," Micah called over the sound of the saw. "Protects the maples from a northwesterly blow."

Griffin could understand the why of that, but he had dozens of other questions. That said, he wasn't pushing his luck. Instinct told him that he was privileged to have gotten as many words from Micah as he had. So he settled for calling over the growl of the saw, "Do you sell the wood?"

Micah finished the cut. "No."

"What do you do with it?"

"Burn it. Evaporator can use up to a cord of wood a day. If the season's long, I'll need all I can get." He went back to work.

Griffin spotted the ax, and was sorely tempted. He'd been barely a teenager when his grandfather had taught him how to split wood at the cabin in Wyoming. He had spent the best summers of his life at that cabin, and had indeed split many a cord.

Warmed by the memory, he picked up the ax. Testing its weight, he shifted it in his gloved hand until there was a sense of familiarity. Then he took the first of the large logs in the line of severed sections and stood it in the snow. Legs spraddled, he raised the ax high, eyed the soft spot he wanted, and struck. Like a shot, the log split down the middle.

"All *right,*" he crowed and looked up half expecting to see his white-haired grandfather grinning from ear to ear.

The sight of Micah, glowering, was a shock. "Don't sue *me* if you cut off your toe."

"I won't cut off my toe. I was taught better."

With a disparaging snort, Micah revved up the chainsaw and turned away.

Feeling invigorated, Griffin split each half of the log again, then started over with the next log, and then the next. Finding a rhythm, he worked his way down the tree.

When Micah was done with the saw, he began loading the split logs onto the sled.

Griffin finished his part and, game for more, eyed the pile of branches. "Is that kindling?"

"Another day. Grab the reins," Micah instructed, tossing his chin toward the back of the sled, where leather straps trailed from the corners over the trampled snow. Griffin caught up the two just as Micah began to pull.

It should have been easy at the back end. Micah was the engine. All Griffin had to do was hold on tight enough to prevent a runaway sled. By the time they had gone all the way back down the hill and reached the sugarhouse, though, his arms were as tired as his thighs. "What the hell's the tractor for?" he called as Micah kicked and pulled the sled around to the exact spot he wanted.

"To make things easier."

"So why didn't you take it up there?"

Micah shot him a cold look. "Because I felt like working at things. You have a problem with that?"

"Nope," Griffin said, because he wasn't having Micah think he couldn't hack it. "Not me."

And the work wasn't done. When Micah started tossing wood from the sled to the top of the pile by the sugarhouse wall, Griffin chipped right in. He figured that sore muscles were a small price to pay for a bit of respect.

Still, he was flagging badly when Micah straightened and, alert now, turned toward the road. "Poppy," he said.

Just when Griffin needed a rush of adrenaline, the sight of the red Blazer brought it. It came down the road with the crunch of tires on packed snow and disappeared in front of the house. He was setting the last of the logs up on the pile when two little girls rounded the corner at a run and made for Micah. They were beautiful children, one slightly taller than the other, both with bright jackets and hats, long dark hair, and big dark eyes. Griffin imagined he saw hope in those eyes as they looked up at their father.

Not wanting to see that hope die when they asked about Heather, Griffin took off his gloves, raised a hand in a wave, and said on an up note, "Good workout. Thanks."

He strode off, around the house to the front. Poppy was already out of the Blazer and up the ramp at the end of the porch. He took the porch steps by twos, nearly collapsing on the top one, his legs were that weak, but he reached the door in time to open it for her.

Sending him a wary look, she rolled past. Once she was inside and clear of the door, she pulled off her chair gloves, took a cloth from a side pannier, and began to wipe loose bits of snow from her wheels. "Are you bothering Micah?" she asked.

"Nope. Just working up a little sweat." He pulled a candy from his pocket. "Want a kiss?"

She glanced at the candy and seemed about to say something tart when the back door slammed. Her eyes flew that way, reflecting concern.

Taking the cloth from her hand, he hunkered down and finished up. From the back hall came shuffling sounds as the girls took off their things, then a soft running. The smaller of the two appeared first, then the older. Both stopped just inside the front room.

"Who're you?" the older one asked.

"He's . . . uh, he's . . ." Poppy tried, and as endearing as Griffin found her unsureness, he couldn't let her suffer.

"Griffin," he said. Dropping the cloth on his thigh, he held out his hand. He stayed on his haunches, hoping to be less intimidating that way.

"That's Missy," Poppy told him, "and Star just behind."

"Missy." Griffin mimed shaking her hand, then did the same with the younger child. "Star." So. Smiths didn't shake hands. In Micah's case, he assumed it was animosity. In the case of the girls, he figured it was caution. They had never seen him before. He was a stranger.

Instinct told him that getting the girls to like him would help him with Poppy. So he said, "I'm pleased to meet you both. I'm a friend of Poppy's. And I just helped your dad chop wood."

"Are you sugarhelp?" Missy asked warily.

"She means hired to help with sugaring," Poppy explained.

"Oh, no," Griffin told the girls. "Just a friend." He smiled. When neither of the girls smiled back, he reached into his pocket, pulled out several candies, and tried a hopeful, "Want a kiss?" The girls looked at his hand. He figured that if he could get the older one to accept him, the younger one would follow. "Missy?"

"It's Melissa," she said, standing her ground, "and we don't eat *chocolate* candy here. We eat maple sugar candy."

"Ah. I didn't know that. I mean, I should've. It makes sense. Do you make the candy yourself?"

"With Heather," the little girl said, daring him to ask more.

But before he could, Star slipped out from behind and came forward. Her eyes were on Griffin's hand. "I like chocolate," she said in the smallest little voice. "Is that from Charlie's?"

"It sure is," Griffin replied. "I used to get these at the country store near my granddad's cabin in Wyoming."

Poppy cleared her throat.

He shot her a glance. "It's true. You don't think that a guy who could invent Hummers would live in Trump Tower, do you?" Something touched his hand.

"Do these have nuts?" Star asked as she turned one of the kisses in his palm.

Griffin scrutinized the wrappers. "Not these." Shifting the kisses to his other hand, he dug back into his pocket. He came up with a single one, checked the color of its wrapper, and grinned. "This one does. I knew I had an assortment. Want it? Poppy doesn't. She's on a diet."

"She doesn't need to diet," the child said, savvy enough on that score. She took the candy from his hand, unwrapped it with careful skill, and took a bite. The chocolate was still melting on her front teeth when she looked at Griffin. "I like the ones with nuts. If you come again, bring those." She turned and went back into the kitchen. Missy must have gone there, too, because she was nowhere in sight.

"You're playing with fire," Poppy warned. "That child is vulnerable."

Griffin held up the cloth, arched his brows, and pointed to the pannier. As he tucked it in there, he said, "I won't hurt her. She sensed that. Children are like animals that way. They feel vibes."

"How do you know?"

"I have twelve nieces and nephews. I watch them. They know right away whether someone coming into the room likes kids or not. Hey." He grinned. "I have something for you."

"I told you. No kisses."

"Nope," he said and stood. Even with one hand on the arm of Poppy's chair, he felt the strain in his thighs. A groan escaped before he could bite it back.

Poppy smiled. "Oh my. You have a little problem."

"Nothing a hot shower won't fix," Griffin said and put his mouth to her ear. "I got a pack from California. When do you want it?"

*   *   *

With the phone bank set to beep when a call came in, Poppy sat by the hearth in her home blotting out thoughts of everything but the pack on

her lap. She had glanced through it all, but was most drawn to the photos. They showed Lisa Matlock in a formal high school graduation shot,
a less formal hiking-club shot with her head circled, a distant view of her
as she worked serving food in the background of what looked to be a
wedding, and a blow-up of her driver's license.

"What do you think?" Griffin asked, coming up from behind.

Poppy put the formal graduation shot on top and studied it for the
longest time. With each passing minute, her heart felt heavier.

No resemblance, she wanted to say. *These are two distinctly different
women.* At the very least she wanted to say that they might have been
identical twins and still she could tell the difference between them. But
she couldn't even say that. All she could manage was a discouraged,
"Amazing."

"They look alike."

"Yes." She glanced up at Griffin. He was still fresh from the shower
and looked handsome indeed. She might have dwelt on how much so, if
the other matter hadn't been so weighty. "If this was the one your brother
had on the wall, I can understand why you stared. The resemblance
is . . ."

"Uncanny."

It was, indeed. "Which doesn't mean it's her," Poppy hastened to say,
and not out of sheer obstinacy. She was grateful to Griffin for having gotten these, because it did explain why there may have been a mix-up. Still,
she was Heather's friend. Out of loyalty alone, she wasn't ready to say that
Heather was Lisa. "People do look alike. There are only so many different
eyes, noses, and mouths. Same with hair." She guessed that fifteen years
later, Lisa Matlock might have silver strands there, too.

"And smiles? That was what got me when I was here in October. Even
aside from the scar, the smile is the same."

Poppy actually found the eyes more gripping. The graduation shot
was in color, and those eyes had the same irridescence as Heather's. "Ac-
cording to these records, her school grades were good. Same with recom-
mendations. It's no wonder she was offered a scholarship." She singled
one page out from the rest. It was a medical report from the emergency
room of a Sacramento hospital, made eight months before Rob DiCenza's

death. The cut at the corner of Lisa's mouth wasn't the only thing mentioned. There had been other facial bruises. The doctor noted that though the patient denied it, he suspected domestic abuse.

"Why didn't he pursue it?" Poppy asked, knowing that Griffin was reading over her shoulder.

"He had no legal obligation to do that. Lisa said she was eighteen. It was a lie, but he didn't know it. He might have pursued something if she'd come in battered time and again, but she didn't. If there were other incidents, she went to a different hospital."

"Your person didn't find other records?"

"Not yet. He's still looking."

Poppy returned to the graduation photo. She compared it to the other photos. The scar was there in all but the driver's license. "When did she get her license?"

"Right after she turned seventeen."

"The date of birth here says April. Heather's birthday is in November."

Griffin said nothing.

"You're thinking Heather may have lied." Poppy wondered it, too. "We know that Lisa is capable of lying, if she told the doctor she was eighteen when she wasn't. But no one who knows Heather here can think of any time when she lied."

The phone bank beeped. Poppy wheeled around and returned there, setting the papers on the sofa as she passed. Not surprisingly, the call coming in was on Micah's line. One of every four she received lately was for him.

She was on edge even before she answered. "Hello?"

"Micah Smith, please," said a deep-voiced man.

"Who's calling?"

"Samuel Atkins, *Sacramento Bee.*" His tone was nonchalant, like Micah was someone he talked with regularly.

"Samuel Atkins, *Sacramento Bee,*" Poppy repeated less nonchalantly. "And you think I'll just put the call through to Mr. Smith?"

"Who is this?"

"His press secretary. He isn't taking calls. He isn't doing interviews."

"I'm prepared to pay."

"Well, that's a new twist," Poppy said, "but it would mean prostitution on the part of Mr. Smith. He isn't that desperate, Samuel Atkins, *Sacramento Bee*." She punched off the call with a flourish and a snort. "That man has called before," she told Griffin. "He used another name, but I know the voice." She let out a breath, then drew in another and told herself to relax. Tossing the headset on the desk, she went back to the sofa for the packet Griffin had brought.

She returned the graduation photo to the top and searched it for something, anything that didn't match. Lisa's ears were pierced; so were Heather's. Lisa's hair was long, dark, and wavy; so was Heather's. Lisa even had the same uneven edge on her two top front teeth.

"So," Poppy reasoned, "if I were Lisa, and I was as smart as she was, wouldn't I have done something to change my appearance?" She looked up at Griffin. "I mean, right there you have the best argument for why these women can't be the same person. It would be just dumb to disappear and then resurface somewhere else looking exactly the same."

"Unless the somewhere else was the last place on earth where you think a lawman would look," he reasoned. "And if she left no paper trail—if she used a new name, new driver's license, new Social Security number—it wouldn't have been so dumb. Changing the paperwork is a hell of a lot easier, and cheaper, than plastic surgery. A few questions on a street corner will tell you who to see where, and a little money closes the deal."

Poppy tried to imagine Heather doing that. It still didn't fit. "So do you have anything on Heather yet?"

"No. But I'm working on it." He gave a short smile. "Not that I'd give you everything I have at once, not if I want a shower a couple a times a week. You have a great shower, by the way."

Pointedly, Poppy said, "Once you get my shower chair out of the way."

"Light as anything, and worth it. We rich boys are suckers for oversized stalls."

"We paraplegics need them, along with meds every day. If you snooped in the medicine chest, you'll have seen those, too." He kept acting like everything was normal. Only her life wasn't normal—at least, not by most people's standards.

"I didn't snoop," he told her. "I didn't have to. Last time I left here, I boned up on paraplegia. I know about daily meds. They control muscle spasms."

" 'Boned up on paraplegia,' " Poppy repeated. "That makes me very uncomfortable." It struck her that he might have gotten hold of her medical records, just like he had Lisa's. That was illegal. Not that she minded when it came to Lisa. Which, of course, made her a total hypocrite.

So she didn't argue the matter of violation of privacy and said instead, "Know what happens if I don't take the pills? These muscles can very well knot up. It's totally gross. So I'm thirty-two, and I pop pills every day. I'll have to be on them every day for the rest of my life."

Griffin didn't look fazed. "Is it any different from a diabetic taking insulin? Sorry, angel, but that won't scare me off."

She held his gaze. "I am not an angel. I thought I made that clear yesterday."

"All you did yesterday was to tell me that you have moments of self-pity, and I told you that the rest of us have those, too. So I'm still not turned off."

"Okay," Poppy goaded. "What if I told you I have a dark past."

"You mean, the accident?"

For a split second, she wondered just what he did know. Unable to think about it herself, though, she said, "Before the accident. I was an impossible child to raise. I was bratty and rebellious. My mother'll vouch for that."

"Poppy, why do I care how you were as a child?"

"Because . . . because that's my true nature."

He considered that for a bit. Then, still pensive, he said, "I don't think so. I think people's natures change. They may be one way as a child and another as an adult. Life does that. Things happen, traumas take place, people learn and wise up and adapt. That may be the case with you. It may have been the case with Heather."

"Then you do think she is Lisa?" Poppy asked, pleased to get away from talking about herself. "If so, you're no friend of mine." She pointed toward the door. "Leave. Now."

He grabbed her finger and shook it gently. "I do *not* think she's Lisa. I think she's Heather."

He didn't finish the sentence. Well, he did. But Poppy heard a final word. *Now.* He thought that Heather was Heather . . . *now.*

She retrieved her finger and prepared to argue. Mustering loyalty, frustration, and fear, she opened her mouth. Then she closed it again. Her eyes fell to Lisa Matlock's graduation photo. If she hadn't known differently, she would have sworn it was Heather's.

*   *   *

Micah wasn't good at doing hair. Missy told him so in no uncertain words when she climbed out of the bathtub, put on her nightgown, and asked him to help with the brush. He hadn't finished three strokes when the bristles caught on a snarl and she cried out in pain.

Pain was the last thing he had wanted for his girls. He had tried to shield them when Marcy died, and now he was doing it again. He could cook. That was easy enough. He could read stories. That was easy enough, too. Hair was something else. And even if he'd been able to help, they wanted Heather.

So did he. Only she wasn't here. She was sitting in a jail, shutting him out of her life in a way that made it impossible for him to help get her home. He wondered what she was hiding. The possibilities tormented him. He felt alternately furious at her, then guilty for feeling that way. He told himself that she might have lived through awful things. He tried to understand. But he hated being shut out, hated being in the dark, *hated* feeling impotent.

Needing to do what he was best at, he put the girls to bed and then went to the corkboard that hung on the kitchen wall. A shopping list was tacked there, a school calendar, and samplings of the girls' art, along with miscellaneous phone numbers and notes written in Heather's hand. He had no idea what half of them meant.

He did know what the list in the middle was about. It was everything he needed to get done so that when the sap started to run, he was ready to boil. He had cleared enough of the sugarbush. Now he had to lay tubing through fifty acres' worth of trees. The last few years, Heather had helped him with that. Not this year.

Gritting his teeth, he stomped out the back door. The snow underfoot was packed, but he knew it wouldn't be for long. A midday melt wasn't far off. He didn't have to check his journal, his barometer, or the Weather Channel. Nor did he rely on other signs, like hearing the caw of the crow or seeing raccoon tracks in the snow. He could feel it in his bones. He hadn't grown up a sugarmaker's son for nothing.

Nights like this were for washing pans, tools, and spiles. It had all been done the April before, when the sap had grown buddy and turned dark and stopped flowing. Now it had to be done again—everything washed in a bleach solution and triple rinsed to prevent even the slightest off taste. Cleanliness was crucial to a sugarmaker's operation, if the final product was to be top quality, and if the goal wasn't top quality, then he figured it wasn't much worth doing.

He had barely gotten the propane going to heat the water when he had an awful thought. If one of the girls had a nightmare, he wouldn't be able to hear. If one of them was sick or frightened, and he had the faucets going here, he wouldn't know a thing. He had counted on Heather keeping tabs on them while he did this.

Thinking that he couldn't afford not to use this time to wash, he went ahead with the job, filling the large stainless steel sink, adding the right amount of bleach.

Then, thinking twice, he let the whole thing out, turned the propane off, and stomped back to the house.

Chapter Eight

Griffin bolted up from a dead sleep Saturday to the fierce growl of a motor. Convinced that something was about to crash through the cabin wall, he pushed off the blankets and jumped up. A beam cut through the dark, penetrating the curtains, lighting the room. Pulling the door open, he peered into a headlight. It was blinding in the predawn dark.

"Who's there?" he called, shielding his eyes. When he realized that whoever it was couldn't hear him over the engine's noise, he waved an arm.

The headlight veered to the side, taking the noise with it. In the light reflected off the snow on the lake, Griffin made out a snowmobile. He caught sight of something large behind it, before the whole thing disappeared around the back of his island. Seconds later, the engine went still.

Closing the door, he checked his watch. It was barely six in the morning. The woodstove had burned down during the night and the cabin was cold, though nowhere near as cold as it had been when he had first arrived. He also had extra logs inside now, which meant that they were dry and ready to burn.

He added several to the woodstove. They quickly caught flame.

In the light from the blaze, Griffin pulled on his clothes and boots, grabbed his parka and the battery-powered lantern that he'd purchased at Charlie's, and went outside. The path to the lake was packed down now and easily crossed, and once he hit the lake itself, he walked in the ruts made by the snowmobile and its trailer. They led him a short distance off the tail end of Little Bear. He raised the lantern.

"How ya doin'?" came the voice of an old man.

Griffin approached. "Billy Farraway, I take it?"

"The same."

"They said you'd get here sooner or later."

"Sooner's only because of Ice Days. I was up on the far side of Elbow Island, and the fishin' was good. But others'll be setting up shop there this weekend. Don't see the point in sharing my space with whoever chooses to fish. There should be trout here. Got any coffee?"

"Not yet. I can make some," Griffin offered.

"You do that while I set up house. No need to fuss. I take it black."

Griffin returned to the cabin, perked a pot of coffee, and carried two large, steaming mugs back outside. By then, dawn had spread over the lake. In its pale purple light, he saw that Billy Farraway's house was . . . indeed, a house. It was small, no more than eight feet by ten feet, and made of wood, with a tin roof and a pipe for exhaust. It sat on a platform, which rested on runners, now immobilized by bricks front and rear.

As Griffin approached, a dim light began to shine through the house's single small window. He opened the door. Inside was a cot piled with down covers, a cushioned chair, and a stove. Shelves on the walls supported canned goods and books. One basket held bananas, another eggs. A blackened fry pan sat on top of the stove.

The old man himself was a vision of bushy gray hair and eyebrows, ruddy hands and cheeks. His clothing was a mix of Sherpa and wool, all well-worn but not tattered. He was on his knees, feeding the stove from a pile of wood on the side.

Closing the stove door, he said, "This is the big danger, y'know. Fire. Gotta watch it close."

Griffin handed him one of the mugs. "Are you out here all winter?"

"Just about."

"With your loon pipe."

"With my loon pipe." The old man drank from the mug.

"What about when it storms?"

"What about it? I got a roof here. I got food." He turned on his knees, reached into a corner, and pulled up on a hook. A trap door opened. "I take my auger and make a hole right here. Drop the line, set the trap, close the hatch, then wait for the flag to flip and tell me I have a bite. Meantime, I'm warm enough."

Griffin eyed the woodbin. "That little bit of wood won't last you long."

"The woodman delivers."

"Who's the woodman?" When Billy pushed the question aside with a negligent wave, Griffin asked, "Where do you live when it isn't winter?"

"Downtown. I got a camp on the shore. There's a bunch of us old guys."

"Where are they now?"

"Florida." He snorted. "Won't get *me* there." He put the mug to his mouth, took another swallow, set it down. "Nah. Lake winter's in my blood."

"You've lived here all your life?"

He nodded. "All my life." He kept nodding. "This is my season coming up."

"Spring's your favorite?"

The old man looked lost in thought. "Don't know what happened with her, though. I liked her."

"Spring?"

"Heather." He shot Griffin an annoyed glance. "Heather. Who'd you think I was talking about? Who's *anyone* around here talking about? Doesn't matter if you live on the lake like I do. You hear. You hear lots. Course, they don't ask me what *I* know."

"What do you know?" Griffin asked nonchalantly.

Billy looked at him long and hard. "I know that I don't know *you*."

Griffin held up a hand. "I'm safe."

Billy snorted. "I know about sugaring, I'll tell you that. Know how to drill to hit sapwood. Know how to keep the pan from burning. Know ju-ust that instant when the boil changes texture and you got syrup."

"How do you know that?"

He frowned, then scowled. "Achh. Doesn't matter." His brows rose and his expression brightened. "Want to watch me wet a line?"

* * *

During Ice Days, Poppy drove an Arctic Cat. She didn't own it. The local dealership was run by a friend, who happily hoisted her up, strapped her in, and provided helmets for her and her crew. Poppy felt safe in the Cat. It was an all-terrain vehicle with four large, deep-treaded tires, an automatic gear shift, and a rear box that could hold up to three hundred pounds of food, drink, or kids. It didn't go fast, but that was fine. Poppy didn't need speed. Slow and steady suited her.

Today the rear box contained two dozen large pizzas in insulated bags. They were held in place by bungee cords and Missy and Star, the two girls half-hidden under their helmets.

Poppy raised her faceplate and looked back. "You girls okay?" Both helmeted heads bobbed. "Ready to go?" There were two yips of assent.

She gave them a thumbs-up, or as much of one as she could with heavy ski gloves on her hands, and waited. They each raised a mittened thumb and grinned.

The grins were what Poppy wanted most. There had been none at all that morning when Micah had dropped them off. They'd been half-asleep, wearing nightgowns with their parkas, hats, and boots, none too happy to have been uprooted at first light for a reason other than seeing Heather.

"Gotta work," was all Micah said when Poppy opened the door, and she didn't argue. Yes, the girls needed him. With Heather gone for however long—and Marcy gone for good—he was the only parent they had left. But Poppy knew enough about sugaring to understand the pressure he felt.

She had grown up with seasonal pressure, albeit with apples rather than sap. She knew what it meant to harvest those apples and get them to market while they were crisp, then press the rest into cider before they spoiled. Sugarmaking wasn't much different. A small window opened, during which time the work had to be done. A family's income depended on it.

Cidermaking was the last crop of the year, sugarmaking the first. With it, the cycle started again. Poppy had always loved the poetry of that.

She wasn't thinking of poetry, though, when Micah arrived with the girls. Barely awake herself, she had taken the two right back to bed with her. They piled the pillows high, pulled up the quilt, and turned on the television—and for Poppy, it was sinfully sweet. In her own home, with the girls right there, she felt safe. She felt useful. She felt able. Pushing aside her nagging thoughts of Heather, she took pleasure in the warmth of the two little bodies snuggling close, and relief that at this moment the two were content.

Likewise, as they sat on the Arctic Cat now, their grins were a balm.

Facing forward, she lowered her faceplate and shifted her wrist. Taking care where the rocky shoreline made bumps in the snow, she drove the Cat out onto the lake to the pizza hut that Charlie had set up. When Charlie's two oldest boys had unloaded the boxes, she returned to shore for another load. After the pizzas came drinks, and after that, hot dogs, hamburgers, buns, and relish.

Work done, they explored. They drove around in a slow arc, passing incoming snowmobiles, cross-country skiers, and snowshoers. Farther out, there were car races to watch, and farther still, open patches where ice sailers caught the wind in a stream of vivid colors against the snow.

When they had seen it all, she retraced the route. By the time they were back at the town beach, the girls were hungry enough to share a hot dog and a slice of pizza, and the crowds had arrived. Pickups lined the road; snowmobiles formed impressive side-by-side displays. Snowsuited crowds milled on the lake, their breath white as they talked, their cheeks red. They wore every color of the rainbow, bringing gaiety to stands that sold not only food, but T-shirts, fur hats, and wood plaques. Aware that there was prize money at stake, spectators and fishermen mingled around the big board at the fishing derby headquarters, applauding the arrival of new catches as each was weighed, tagged, and hung on display.

Poppy knew that if past years were any indication, there were out-of-staters in the crowd. She was sure there were media people among them, and tried to pick them out, but the only one she spotted for sure was Griffin. The bright sun brought out the red in his hair, and with only a blue wool headband to keep his ears warm, that hair was a beacon. She seemed to see it everywhere. She refused to look for it, but there it was.

He caught her eye once and waved. She waved back and returned to the conversation at hand, because there always was that. Ice Days was a social event. People who had been inside for the worst of the winter months were aching to be outside, aching to see friends, aching to talk. There was incidental gossip—a birth, a death, a divorce. There was talk of the weather—of snow that was forecast, of how long it would last, how cold it would be, what impact it would have on Micah, when the sap might start to run. Of course, there was talk of Heather, and since Poppy was Heather's closest friend, she was a target for questions.

The first few questions were the least harmful, running along the line of the ones Poppy so often asked herself. *Why Heather? Why so suddenly? Why Lake Henry? Why now?*

Then came observations that should have been innocent, but carried a probing edge. *Did you see the picture they showed on TV? That one sure looks like our Heather. What do you think?*

By midday, the questions went deeper. *Where is she from? Why don't we know that? Where was she born? Where did she grow up? She must have people somewhere. You're her friend, Poppy. What do you know?* And then, *What does Micah know? He has to know more than we do. He's lived with her these last few years.*

Consternation seemed to be the bottom line. *We don't know a thing. She's been one of us for fourteen years, and we're in the dark. How can a person keep so much of herself hidden?*

*   *   *

Griffin mingled with the crowd on the lake, trying to be as easygoing and friendly as possible, and it wasn't a struggle. He'd done Aspen, Vail, and Snowmass. He'd done Jackson Hole. He was familiar with lively winter scenes, and this one charmed him. What it lacked in sophistication, it more than made up for in sincerity. People were pleased to see one another. There was genuine affection, genuine enthusiasm.

Having been born with a natural curiosity, asking questions was his thing, but he kept them innocent now. He asked about the bobhouses that had appeared overnight, asked about bait the fishermen used, asked who had designed the T-shirts commemorating the event, asked about the ski races to be held the next day. He asked whether the townsfolk weren't nervous that having so many people on the lake would crack the ice. He asked whether they weren't nervous that having *cars* on the lake would crack the ice.

He wanted to ask about Heather. He was as curious as anyone else. But being an outsider—media in their eyes—he didn't dare raise it himself. He did lean close when he heard the locals talking.

Inevitably, when they caught him at it, they quieted right down.

He gleaned a little bit from Charlie's sons, who were running the pizza stand. At sixteen and eighteen, they were less suspicious than their elders, or so he thought. They confirmed that Heather had worked at the café right up until the time she moved in with Micah, that she used to baby-sit for them when they were kids, and that she had been the one left in charge of the store when their parents went on vacation. When Griffin asked if she'd ever talked about herself, the boys looked at each other and shrugged. They repeated the gesture when he teased them about knowing her secrets. And when he suggested that they wouldn't tell if they did, they simply smiled.

He wandered off and, for a short time, just stood there on the packed snow that covered the ice that the townsfolk swore was thick enough to hold an army. Snowmobiles skirted him. People walked around him. Some approached, caught his eye, passed right by.

Poppy was everywhere, tooling around in her hefty four-wheeler with the two little girls in the box on the back. He caught her eye once and waved—and she waved back, but she didn't come over to him. Here in town, she was in her element.

He, on the other hand, was persona non grata.

In time, he grew lonely. By early afternoon, he traipsed back to the truck, fully intending to return to Little Bear. He had work to do. The island might not have cell reception, but the downtown did, and he had already received three messages from Prentiss Hayden.

He definitely had work to do. Yet Buck's truck didn't head for the Little Bear end of the lake. It headed for Micah's.

*   *   *

How can a person keep so much of herself hidden?

Poppy didn't remember who asked it. She began to think more than one had, because she kept hearing the words. It didn't seem to matter where she was—in the Arctic Cat on the lake, taking a hot chocolate break by the woodstove at the general store, or back on the lake—they followed her wherever she went.

Desperate for an escape, fearing that the day would be gone all too soon, she took the girls for a pleasure ride. The sun wasn't as high as it had been an hour before, but a warmth lingered in the fingers of yellow that covered the lake.

"Hold on," she called back. Lowering her faceplate, she accelerated with the turn of her wrist. The Arctic Cat bucked over a ridge, then hit the lake with a growl and took off.

Startled by the sudden speed, she immediately slowed and looked back. The girls were strapped in and secure. She gave them a thumbs-up, which they returned.

She drove straight out, past the concession stands. Turning the large handlebars then, she wove in and out of the bobhouses, exchanging waves with the fishermen grouped there. When Missy gave a tug at the back of her coat and shouted, *"More!"* she circled around and repeated the zigzags. The delighted squeals she heard from the rear box warmed her heart.

Settling into the trail left by the snowmobiles, she drove on for a bit until they reached an untouched part of the lake. Unable to resist, she turned the Arctic Cat onto the virgin snow and upped the speed. It was exhilarating. The path was open; the air was clear; the world was pure. For a few minutes, her handicap ceased to exist. Invigorated by that, she drove on through lengthening afternoon shadows, and if the speed crept up and up and up, it was worth the escape. For those few minutes, feeling an incredible freedom, she not only forgot that she couldn't walk, she also forgot about Heather.

Then she felt a sudden catch inside—a flash of memory—a stab of fear. Slowing quickly, she looked back. The girls were fine. She gave them a thumbs-up. They gave her one in return. At a saner pace, she made a large circle and headed back to town. The closer they got, the slower she went, so that she was all but creeping when a helmet tapped hers. Seconds later, Star's cheek settled on her shoulder. The little girl raised Poppy's faceplate.

"There's face painting over there," the child said.

Letting the Artic Cat idle, Poppy focused in on a sheltered spot near the shore. "Oh my," she exclaimed. "We nearly forgot." Shifting, she headed that way. Pulling up close, she turned off the Cat. In no time, both girls had dropped their helmets in the rear box and scrambled out.

"Hi, Aunt Poppy!" came a shout from the short line of little girls. It was six-year-old Ruth, her sister Rose's youngest, waiting her turn. The middle daughter, seven-year-old Emma, was right beside her. In the space of a breath, so were Missy and Star. Missy and Emma were classmates and friends.

Rose separated herself from a group of mothers standing nearby. She was as well put-together as always in a plum-colored parka and pants, with navy hat, gloves, and boots. As she reached Poppy, she put a hand to her throat.

"I was watching you," she half whispered. "I can't believe how *fast* you were going."

It was a Maida moment. Poppy steeled herself against a wave of guilt. "Oh, I wasn't going that fast."

"You were," Rose went on, sounding frightened. "You started speeding up as soon as you cleared the bobhouses. I was amazed. We all were—it wasn't just me. You kept going faster and faster. All I could think was that this thing would flip right over and the three of you would fall out and be crushed."

Poppy tried to make light of her fear. "Rose, these things don't flip. We're talkin' a megawide wheelbase. They stick to the ground like glue."

"You were going over snow and ice, not ground. It'd be one thing if you were alone. But with the girls?"

"The girls had helmets. And they were belted in."

Rose looked at the girls, then at the lake. "I don't know if you should be doing this."

Poppy had an uncomfortable feeling. "Why not?"

Her sister made a dismissive gesture.

"No, Rose. Tell me. Why not?"

"You know," Rose said with a glance at Poppy's legs. "And it isn't just this," she added, rapping a gloved hand against the Arctic Cat. "I know you're Heather's friend, and helping with the girls is a wonderful gesture, what with everything else Micah has on his plate. But isn't it taking an awful lot on yourself? I mean, what if there was a problem? What if one of them fell? Could you pick her up?"

Poppy bristled. It wasn't that she hadn't asked herself the same questions, and not so long ago. Having Rose ask them, though, was humiliating. So she said a defiant, "Yes. I could pick her up."

"How?"

"The same way anyone else would—in my arms. My arms are strong, Rose. I'll bet they're stronger than yours."

Rose sighed. "They may be. But spills are only the start. You've never been a mother. You don't know what the challenges are."

"Blind women have kids," Poppy argued, because Rose was *offensive*. "Deaf women have kids. Women with *rock-bottom IQs* have kids. Are you saying I'd be any worse off? But hey, I'm not planning to have kids. I know the risks. I know the problems. All I'm doing here is helping my friends. If you're so worried about Missy and Star, why don't you pitch in, too?" She regretted it the minute she said it, because she knew what was coming. Rose was nothing if not the consummate mom.

Sure enough, she said with genuine enthusiasm, "That's actually a terrific idea. Hannah's staying over with a friend." She lowered her voice to murmur a wry, "Would you believe that?" Then she went on. "We figured these two would be exhaused after today, so Art is renting a couple of movies, and we're bringing in pizza. I'd love having Missy and Star, too. Do you think Micah would let them come?"

Poppy figured that Micah would be working well into the night and would be glad that they had somewhere to go. She had been planning to suggest that they stay with her, but given the choice, they were better off with their friends. Emma and Ruth were sweet children, and Poppy trusted Rose. She didn't always like her, but she trusted her.

Of course, that meant Poppy would spend the evening simmering about what Rose had said, but it couldn't be helped.

* * *

Griffin felt a keen sense of satisfaction. Micah hadn't said more than a handful of words all afternoon, but as daylight waned, the main room of the sugarhouse, which was warm and moist and smelled faintly of bleach, was filled with the fruits of their labor. They had washed and triple rinsed innumerable coils of plastic tubing, many buckets of spiles, and a dozen implements of the stainless steel variety. Thermometers, hydrometers, refractometers, skimmers, and scoops—Griffin had no idea what they were for, and he wasn't about to ask. It felt like small talk, for which Micah didn't seem to have the patience. Indeed, what few words Micah had said seemed more to himself than to Griffin.

"No matter that this was all washed at the end of last season. Can't take the risk," he murmured at one point, and at another, "Microorganisms grow behind your back. They can ruin the quality of the syrup," and at another, "Gotta keep washing. Keep washing the whole time."

Now, though, curiosity nagged. Griffin figured that a few questions while they cleaned up wouldn't hurt. Pausing while wiping down the long steel sink, he pointed to a large machine not far from the smokestack. "What's that?"

Micah shot the item a glance. "R.O." He bent over to wipe down the legs of the sink. "Reverse osmosis machine. It removes water from the sap before the sap even hits the evaporator. Saves time. Saves fuel."

"And that?" Griffin asked, indicating another machine.

"A filter press. As soon as you have syrup, you pour it hot through there. You can't have sugar sand in your syrup, not in top-quality syrup. Lower-quality syrup, lower price."

"So how much do you make?" Griffin asked, wondering about the profit margin.

"In a good season? Twelve hundred gallons, give or take."

It wasn't the meaning of "make" that Griffin had intended, but he rode it out. "What makes a good season?"

"First off," Micah said, squatting now to wipe the floor under the sink, "a good summer before. If a tree gets sun and water, it thrives. A thriving tree produces sweeter sap. Then you need a good late winter and early spring. Sap can run for six weeks. Or it can stop after two. Obviously, the longer it runs, the more you make."

"What determines the length of the run?"

"The weather. Sap runs when the nights are below freezing and days are above. A fifteen-degree swing is ideal. All cold or all warm, and the sap won't flow right. If you get a snowstorm and there's damage in the sugarbush, you've got trouble unless you can fix it quick. You get *no* sap to boil if the mainline's broke. In any event, you have to do what you can before the buds start to swell, because after that, the taste of the sap is off."

"You learned all this from your father?"

"And his father. And my uncle." Sitting back on his haunches, he looked at Griffin and came close to smiling. The expression gentled his face, made it less dark and forbidding. "Sugaring's always been a family thing. Back before the Civil War, it was billed as the only crop that didn't use slaves. Immediate family, extended family, adults, kids—everyone helped. My mother used to bottle and can. My grandmother kept everyone fed. The men, they were doin' the rest of it themselves at a time when you didn't have reverse osmosis machines or filter presses. Hell, they weren't using tubing when I was a boy. I remember *buckets*." He paused, seeming lost in the thought, and it was a pleasant one, to judge from his expression.

Then the pleasure faded and there was fatigue. "Of course, they didn't have the acreage I have now. There's no way I could haul buckets in from fifty acres every day, and you just can't get help. Four weeks a year? Six weeks at best?" He grunted and went back to wiping the floor. "Young guys want the big money that comes from the trades. So we use tubing now, and it cuts the work way down. That keeps it a family operation. At least, it's supposed to be. I was counting on Heather."

He stopped short.

Griffin remembered the warmth a minute ago. He wanted to think that Micah had let a wall down. If any part of it remained down, there was hope. "I wanted to talk to you about that."

Micah shot him a disparaging look. "I was wondering when that'd come." He gave the floor a last few swipes.

"I can help. I have contacts. I can get information other people can't. You need to know about Lisa? I can get information on Lisa. Give me clues about Heather? I can get info on her, too."

"What's in it for you?"

Griffin couldn't get himself to talk about guilt. The softer side of Micah was gone now. Mentioning Randy would be disastrous. So he said, "Poppy. I like her. I want to help her friends."

Micah went from his haunches to his feet. "Did she send you here?"

"No. She wouldn't. She's protective of you. She's not sure I'm a friend."

"If she isn't sure, why should I be?"

"Because you have my word. And my reason goes beyond Poppy," he added, feeling that he was telling the truth, albeit not the whole truth. "I come from a different place. I've been lucky that way—spoiled that way—but I do have these contacts. I use them for all sorts of stuff that I don't really care about. This I care about. I like Lake Henry. I like the people here. Lily Blake got a raw deal last fall, and Heather's getting one now."

Micah started snatching up wet cloths from around the room. "I have Cassie."

"You do. But Cassie's resources are finite. Mine are greater."

Arms half filled, he turned to Griffin. His eyes were dark. "What'll it cost me?"

"Nothing. That's what I'm saying. I'm a friend. I have a network of friends. This won't cost me anything, so it won't cost you anything. The thing is, you're the linchpin here. You're the one who has the most information right now. You're the one who can point me in the right direction."

With a snort, Micah went back to collecting wet cloths.

"I don't need much," Griffin coaxed. "A birthplace would be great, but if you don't know that, a town, a school, a church?"

"I can't tell you."

"Can't or won't?"

"Can't." Arms laden with cloths, he went out the door.

Griffin grabbed up their jackets and shirts and followed him. "Because you don't know? When you first met her, she must've talked about where she'd been." The cold air was sharp in his heated lungs.

"Why? She'd been in Lake Henry a while by then. Why would I ask about the other?"

"Curiosity?" Griffin offered. "Okay. So you didn't ask. But you've been together four years. She must have mentioned something, must have dropped hints."

"If she did, I didn't get them," Micah muttered as he strode toward the house along the path of packed snow. His boots crunched with each step.

"Mail," Griffin tried. "Does she ever get mail?"

"All the time. We run a business here."

"Personal mail. A birthday card, a postmark from somewhere strange."

"No. But I'm not the one who picks up the mail. What do I know?"

"You're thinking she might have hidden something?"

"*No.*" He pulled the back door open and went inside.

Griffin caught the door before it slammed and followed him in, through the kitchen, to the adjacent laundry room. "It's not like we need a biography. All we need is one thing. One thing to put her in a place other than the one where Lisa Matlock can be proven to be at a given point in time."

Micah stuffed the washer with towels and dropped the rest on the floor. In a tight voice, he said, "I don't have one thing."

"A trip she took," Griffin tried. "A birthday party. A birthday *present*."

Soap went in. The lid slammed down. The washer went on.

"A relative, any relative," Griffin went on, following him back into the kitchen. "A hobby. A *dream*. Dreams tell a lot."

Micah turned on him fast. His voice was controlled, but just barely. "She didn't dream. She worked hard and long, and she slept deep."

"Christ, man, you must know something," Griffin charged, pushing, hoping that the heat of anger might produce a crumb. "She had to be somewhere before she came here."

Micah lost it then. Eyes blazing, he shouted, "If she was, I don't know where! I don't *fuckin'* know where! Do you think that makes me feel good?"

A dead silence followed the outburst. In its midst, Griffin caught the smallest movement in the corner of his eye. Glancing back at the door, he saw Poppy. Her eyes were on Micah. She looked devastated.

Griffin let out a breath. "No, I don't suppose it does," he said quietly.

He glanced at Poppy again, but she continued to look at Micah. Discouraged, he said, "I've done enough for today, I guess," and let himself out the back door.

* * *

Poppy didn't think she had ever heard Micah shout before. Beyond being silent, he was controlled, private, and proud. The admission he'd just made must have hurt.

"I'm sorry," she said softly. "I didn't know he'd come here."

Hanging his head, Micah wrapped a large hand around his neck. "What does it matter? Maybe he'll let it go now."

Poppy wasn't sure. She wasn't sure Griffin should let it go. He did have contacts, and everyone else was stymied.

Quietly, she asked, "Is it true? Do you really know nothing?"

He raised weary eyes. Hurt eyes. "I know nothing." Suddenly alert, he glanced past her. "Oh Christ. Did the girls hear?"

"No. I left them in town with the Winslows. They were having their faces painted with Emma and Ruth, and even Star was having fun. Rose invited them over for dinner and movies. She'd like to turn it into a sleepover, but I told her I'd have to check with you."

Turning away, he went to the sink. "Fine. They'll be better off there. I'm not good for much."

"I wouldn't say that. Neither would Heather."

He turned, hands braced behind. "I can't do a damn thing, Poppy. I don't *know* a damn thing. I've been going over everything, thinking back." Raising his arms, he pushed his fingers into his hair. "I've been digging, digging, digging, and I'm hitting rock." He dropped his hands in defeat. "How can I know so little? We were close. She knew me inside out. She knew what I was thinking. I thought I knew what she was thinking, too." He paused, eyes tormented. "I was a fool. A person doesn't just . . . just appear out of nowhere at the age of nineteen with no history at all. Why didn't I ask?"

"Because it didn't matter."

"Clearly it does. How could I not know any of it?"

"Because she didn't say."

"But why *not?* I'm her man. Why didn't she say?"

"If it was bad . . . if she was afraid . . ."

"Of me? But I love her. She knew that. And besides, how can someone like Heather have done something so bad? She's so *good*. She's patient and kind and understanding. She's generous. In all the time I've known her, there's been nothing—*nothing*—she's done that was bad. She doesn't yell at the kids. Doesn't yell at me. She doesn't have a mean bone in her body. So what could she have done that was so bad?"

"I don't know," Poppy said. "I wish I did."

"She never said anything to you, either?"

"No."

Studying the floor now, he considered that news. His jaw flexed spasmodically. Finally, like a man condemned, he looked up. "Do you think she's Lisa?"

"No," Poppy said. "No. I think it's something else."

"If it's something else, why can't she say?"

"Sometimes you just can't."

"I'm sorry. That doesn't work for me."

Poppy laced her fingers. They lay in her lap, on thighs that looked perfectly normal under flannel-lined jeans but weren't good for much at all. Just then, she felt as useless as they were.

But there was no one else to help Micah. She had to try. So she said, "Suppose something terrible happened to her—something so horrible that if she kept thinking about it, it would have driven her mad—something so upsetting that she couldn't eat or sleep or think about anything else."

"She should have told me."

"But how do you survive something like that? How *do* you survive?"

Micah remained silent and tense.

"You push it out of your mind," Poppy went on with the conviction of one who had been there. "You deny that it happened. I don't know what Heather lived through. I do know what she's like now, and it's everything good that you say. So how to explain why she can't talk about the other?"

Micah didn't answer.

But Poppy was desperate that he understand. "She loves you, Micah.

She loves the girls. If she can't talk about the past, maybe it's because she can't *let* herself do it." Oh boy, did she know about that, too. "Okay. So maybe you don't work this way. But don't you think it's possible—just possible—that a person who has gone through something bad may need to let go of the past and become someone else in order to survive?"

*   *   *

Micah came close to opening the knapsack that night. He actually removed it from the woodpile and fingered the discolored buckle. He told himself that there was probably nothing inside—that it might well have been a gift from one of Heather's parents, and therefore had sentimental value.

But that didn't explain why she'd kept it hidden in the closet these four years, rather than in a dresser drawer. He never went through her things. A dresser drawer would have been safe.

But if she kept the pack for sentimental reasons, she would have showed it to him. He could appreciate sentimental value. Wasn't that why he'd kept up the sugarhouse? Sugaring had been in his family for two generations before him. There was sentimental value in keeping it going.

Actually, now, there was more. Thanks to Heather's ability to see a larger picture, he was seeing a larger profit. That stood to be even truer this year.

So. Heather had done good and, in that sense, opening the knapsack behind her back seemed like a betrayal.

But that made no sense, not with her in jail, not with the kind of charges they were talking about.

So why didn't he open the knapsack? Was he afraid of finding nothing? Was he afraid of finding *something*?

He even went so far as to ask himself what the worst something could be. The worst was identification papers saying that Heather was Lisa. Coming in a close second, though, was documentation that Heather was married to another man. This would explain why she hadn't been willing to marry Micah.

So why hadn't she gotten divorced?

Maybe the guy had threatened to kill her. Maybe disappearing was the only thing she could do. Maybe that was what Poppy meant by becoming somebody else in order to survive.

Or maybe she was Lisa. If so, she had committed murder and would go to jail.

If she was Lisa, he wasn't ready to know. So he put the knapsack back in its groove, piled the wood back to cover it up, and walked away.

Chapter Nine

It began to snow in the wee hours of Sunday morning. By the time day broke, a three-inch blanket lay on the ground. Feathery and light in the cold air, it turned the view from Poppy's bed into frosted candy, but that didn't help her mood. After spending most of the night drifting in and out of a troubled sleep, she awoke feeling weighted down.

She stayed in bed later then usual. When she finally pulled herself up, she showered and, needing a lift, put on a lime green sweatsuit. Finger combing her hair, she went to the bank of phones to switch it on, then thought twice. Turning away again, she pulled the Sunday paper in from the front door and went to make a pot of coffee.

She skimmed the front page and was relieved to see nothing about Heather. She skimmed the front pages of each section and tried to decide what she wanted to read. But when the coffee was ready, she set the paper aside and wheeled herself to the living room window.

Sitting there, just . . . sitting, she watched another half inch of snow accumulate on the limbs of the hemlocks near her house. Bits of it fell to the ground under the tiny feet of a pair of cardinals as they flitted from one tree to the next. The male was a vivid red; against the snow, even the duller female stood out. They flew to her deck, where they left a trail of chicken-scratch prints on the fresh snow before flying off again.

Pulling lotion from her side pack, she lathered her hands and absently scrubbed at the calluses on her palms while she followed the play of a pair of chickadees. She wondered about the freedom of flying, of taking off, soaring high, and disappearing—wondered what it would be like to start fresh and unblemished—what it would be like to have hands that were soft and clean.

It would be nice, she decided. It would be nice.

The problem with dreams, of course, was the waking up to a reality that was, by contrast, far more onerous. She grappled with that a bit and finally turned on the phones, but they offered no escape. Not a button was blinking. The world of Lake Henry was either sitting in front of a fire and taking its own calls, or was in church, or over at the mountain, where Ice Days had shifted for ski races, snowboard contests, and toboggan runs.

Putting the phones on audio, she returned to the window, which was where she was later when a truck came down the drive. It wasn't the plow crew with its scrapes, stops, and backup beeps. This truck was Griffin's. It moved slowly through what now looked on the back porch rail to be four inches of snow, and it stopped beside the Blazer.

Poppy didn't move. She didn't know how she felt about his coming— couldn't muster anger, or even a milder annoyance, unless it was aimed at the random little bits of anticipation that slipped past her guard. So she sat and listened.

A door opened; there was a pause; the pause lingered; the door closed. She heard him clomping up the ramp through the snow—and suddenly wondered if he'd brought lunch. A hot treat from Charlie's would be nice. Charlie did a great chili. She could go for some of that. His pulling a sack from the front seat would explain the pause.

He stomped his feet at the front door. The mat there was just textured enough to take muck from Poppy's wheels without hindering her movement. Apparently, it didn't do the job he wanted. Watching him in her mind's eye, she saw him backtrack to the post at the top of the ramp, whap his boots against it, then return to the door.

He knocked. She said nothing. He knocked again, then turned the knob, opened the door, and called, "Anyone home?" Spotting her, he smiled. "Oh. Hi." He slipped inside and closed the door. "How're you doing?"

"I'm okay," she said. She was pleased to see him, but sorry that there was no paper bag. Charlie's chili would have been nice. "You're all bundled up."

He toed off his boots, pushing them aside, his jeans breaking over his wool socks. He pulled off his headband and shook it free of snow, then brushed off his hair. "It's really coming down."

"They must love it at the mountain. I'm surprised you aren't there."

"I was," he said, though he didn't move from the door. "I thought you'd be there, too. You seemed to be having a good time yesterday."

"Yesterday was on the lake," she said. "Anyone could have a good time then. Today's for skiing and all." She wrinkled her nose in dismissal.

"Have you ever skied?"

"You don't grow up here without skiing. I used to do it all the time."

"I mean, since the accident."

She was surprised that he asked. Most people didn't. But then, Griffin, being Griffin, would ask questions. "No," she said. "I have this slight . . . problem."

"Never tried a sit-ski?"

She felt the same twinge of discomfort that she had felt once before. "What do you know about those?"

"Only that they're supposed to be fun."

"Ah. You've talked with people who've used them."

"Actually, yes," he said and opened his parka several inches. She saw a red waffle-weave shirt in the vee and, from the bunching at his middle, guessed he had a fleece in there, too.

So. He knew about sit-skis. She didn't know how she felt about this, either. She tried to feel anger—some sense that her privacy had been violated—but it wouldn't come. All she could do was ask a neutral, "Did you talk with people about sit-skis while you were boning up on my disability?"

He didn't flinch. Those blue eyes held hers without remorse. "I wouldn't call it boning up. I was curious."

So was she. "What do you know about my injury?"

"Only that it's to the lower spine. It's an 'incomplete injury.' "

"Which means," she picked up, wanting it all out, "that I'm not as bad off as some, that my abdominal muscles function, so I have control of things that some paraplegics don't, that I could probably get myself to walk, though it wouldn't be smooth or practical, and it certainly wouldn't be pretty. Someone here in town blabbed. Who was it?"

"If I said, you'd never talk to him again."

"Him. Was it John? Charlie? My physical therapist? My masseuse?"

"Whoa. A masseuse here in town? Any good?"

"Griffin."

He held up his hands. "Let's not argue. It's just that you looked so pleased yesterday on the Arctic Cat that I was sure you'd be doing something like that on the mountain. Would you toboggan with me?"

"No."

"Go on a snowmobile?"

"No."

"Because of the accident?"

"*No,*" she said, though of course it was a lie. Like skiing, snowmobiles had been a way of winter life when she was growing up, but she hadn't been on one since the crash twelve years before.

"Out of fear?" Griffin asked.

She sighed. "Why are you harping on this?"

"Because I know that you can do these things, and I want to do them with you."

"I told you I couldn't," Poppy reminded him, though, here too, she couldn't feel anger—because she didn't sense malice on his part. He was a nice guy. "I told you that last fall. If you got your hopes up, that's your problem. I look at the positives—all that I *am* comfortable doing. I'm much more fortunate than some, and I'm grateful for that. I'm perfectly comfortable with my life."

"Okay," he conceded with a self-deprecating smile. "You're right. You did tell me last fall. So maybe it's just that I'm desperate to be with a friend, because I'm feeling like a pariah around here. No one would talk to me at the lake yesterday. No one would talk to me at the mountain today. So I drove over to Charlie's. The place was next to dead."

Poppy wasn't surprised. "They're all at the mountain." She actually felt bad for him, and that made her feel better, like she was doing a good deed by talking with him when no one else would. It justified his being there, in a way.

"Except for this one lady," Griffin went on and launched into a story as he stood there at the door. "She says she's not from Lake Henry, but there she was at Charlie's, and we got to talking, and before I knew it, she was opening her shoulder bag and out came a cat."

"Ahh." Poppy pictured the scene. It wasn't new, wasn't new at all. "Charlotte Badeau," she said.

He had taken a breath to go on, but held it a second too long. "How do you know?"

"She's the cat lady. She shows up whenever she thinks there'll be a crowd, and there'll be one at Charlie's later, that's for sure. She takes in strays and is always trying to find them homes. There were probably half a dozen in her car." Poppy had a sudden thought. "You didn't." She studied the bulge of his parka. He was a lean man. Fleece or no fleece, that was quite a bulge. "You *didn't*." When he didn't deny it, she felt a wave of absurd affection. On its heels came a warning. "You're a city boy. Do you have any pets—cats, dogs, gerbils?"

"No, but this little one—she's so sweet."

"You took it? You really did?"

He cradled the bundle. "Tell me you're allergic."

"I am not."

"Then you hate cats?"

"I *love* cats. We had them around all the time when I was a kid. It's just that Charlotte is insidious. She assumes that anyone and everyone can and should have a cat, but that isn't true. I've seen her send cats home with kids from the Ridge who can barely afford to feed them, much less have them fixed, so suddenly there's one litter, then a second, and before you know it the fisher cats are coming out of the woods in droves. Ever seen a fisher cat?" Griffin shook his head. "They're big, wild, weasily things that are ferocious and strong. They feast on these poor kittens, leaving bits of bodies around. It isn't a happy thing, either for the kitties or for all those kids with broken hearts."

Sober now, Griffin promised, "That won't happen with this one. She's an indoor cat, and she's already fixed. Besides, I'm a responsible guy. I bought everything I needed at Charlie's. I don't see any problem."

"I see two," Poppy said, because he was *so* sweet and sincere that the perverse part of her needed to show he hadn't thought this through. "A, cats want warmth, and the cabin out on Little Bear isn't warm unless you're there to feed the fire, which means you'll have to take her along with you if you're planning to be gone for any length of time, certainly when you're driving back home to Princeton, New Jersey, which leads to problem B. Cats hate cars."

He peered down inside his coat. "She didn't seem to mind the ride here. She slept most of the way. She's still sound asleep— oh," he caught himself up with an excited whisper, "no, she's waking up." His voice jumped an octave. "Hi, baby."

Poppy was thinking that the man was adorable, when she saw a tuft of orange fur against that red waffle-weave. Excited in spite of herself, she asked, "Is it a baby?"

"Not really. The cat lady says she's two, which she says is adult for a cat. But this one's small."

"Let me see."

Crossing the room in his stockinged feet, he opened the jacket enough so that the cat's upper half was exposed. Holding her rump with an arm, he squatted by Poppy's chair.

There wasn't just a tuft of orange fur, Poppy saw. The cat was entirely orange. "She's a redhead, like you," Poppy said in delight as she stroked the cat's warm little head. Granted, Griffin was more auburn than orange. But he had said that his family nickname was "Red." "Look at those closed eyes. She's still sleepy." The head had turned at the sound of her voice, and at her touch, the nose began sniffing her hand. Looking closer, Poppy caught her breath. "Oh my."

"Yeah," Griffin confirmed, "so how could I say no? Apparently, she was born sighted, but then something happened. Whoever had her couldn't deal, so they abandoned her on the side of the road. She was picked up and treated, but it was too late to save her sight. The cat lady's had her for a couple of months and would have kept her if she didn't have so many others."

"Were the others abusive to this one?"

"No. She said they were totally respectful, protective even. But this one wants a lap, and the cat lady isn't still for long."

"Are you?" Poppy asked.

"Sure am, when I work."

Poppy let the cat sniff her hands, then, unable to resist, she lifted her out of his parka and drew her close. "Well, hello," she cooed. She continued to stroke the cat's head while the cat sniffed her sweatsuit. "You're such a pretty little lady, such a *warm* little lady." The cat braced a paw on Poppy's shoulder, while she sniffed her neck, her ear, her face. "What do you smell? Hmmm? The cologne is by Ralph Lauren. Do you like that?" The cat butted Poppy's cheek en route to nuzzling a spot under her ear.

"She has good taste," Griffin said so sweetly, so gently, that Poppy was left without words. He was close, very kind, and handsome, definitely handsome with his wavy auburn hair, his blue eyes, and a shadow on his jaw that said he hadn't shaved since he had been in her shower two days before.

Looking at him now, something caught in her throat. In the space of a breath, she was swept back to the first time they'd met, she in her wheelchair, he on foot at the back of the meeting room in the church at the center of town. Prior to that, she had felt a connection between them on the phone, but in person it was stronger—stronger than anything she had known—stronger than anything even before the accident. Was it chemistry? She hadn't taken the chance of finding out whether it was or not, and, if so, whether her body could sustain it. She had been too frightened of failure.

She still was. But something inside her had mellowed. Or maybe it was the cat. How to be anything but mellow when a beautiful, blind cat was at hand?

The cat leapt to the ground.

"Wait!" Poppy cried, and her eyes flew to Griffin. "Catch her."

"No, no. She's okay."

"She doesn't know her way around. She'll hurt herself."

The cat looked back at them, her body arching gracefully. Seeming to draw her head up with pride, she straightened and sat back on her haunches facing the curved desks that held the phone bank. Her nose twitched ever so slightly, her whiskers aimed forward. Smoothly coming up on all fours, she began to walk toward the desks. With startling precision, she stopped at the nearest leg, explored it with her nose, rubbed it with her cheek, then her neck and back, on down her body. With the same uncanny exactness, she moved to the next leg and the next. When the desk had been mapped, she moved with regal grace toward the wall.

Poppy held her breath, fearing she would hit it head-on. Instead, she stopped short and turned to walk its length as if she'd done it hundreds of times before. She rubbed against the open archway, then, carrying herself nobly, proceeded on down the hall.

Griffin said a quick, "She's looking for the bathroom," and before Poppy could tell him that cats were like camels, he had dashed back to the door, pushed his feet into his boots, and raced out.

Following the cat, Poppy started down the hall just as the elegantly held orange tail disappeared into the kitchen, and the scene was the same there. The cat explored. She walked, she sniffed, she rubbed. At one point, she rose on her hind legs with her front paws on the cabinets leading up to the counter. Wheeling close, Poppy picked her up and gently set her on the granite.

There was noise back at the front door—open and shut, boots kicked off—then a padding trot down the hall. "Litter," Griffin announced, snowflakes still in his hair. He carried a large plastic pan, with a huge bag of litter inside.

"We need food," Poppy said. She had turned on a trickle of water. The cat had her rear paws on the rim of the sink, her front paws inside, and her mouth perfectly positioned under the trickle.

"Food," Griffin repeated. Setting his armload on the floor, he went back out.

By the time he returned, the cat had jumped down from the counter and was exploring Poppy's wheels. Not wanting to disturb her by moving, Poppy pointed Griffin in the direction of the dish she had taken from a roll-out drawer. He quickly filled it with pellets of food.

"Mmm-mmm," he said as if he were coaxing a child, "chicken and liver." He held the bowl under the cat's nose for the split second it took to get her attention. Looking around, he set it down in a corner out of harm's way.

The cat was there in an instant.

"How does she do that?" Poppy asked in amazement.

"She smells. She hears. She feels. Those whiskers are antennas. They tell her when she's near something, and her reflexes are so sharp that she can navigate with precision." He turned around and filled the litter box, then arched his brows at Poppy. "Where?"

She hitched her chin toward the room off the kitchen that held her washer and dryer. It was more a deep alcove than a room, with an ultra-wide opening and the same pocket doors that were in the rest of the house, ones that could be tucked neatly away in the wall to allow for the easy maneuvering of a wheelchair. In this instance, there was plenty of room for a litter box inside the door, around the corner, and out of the line of traffic.

Crunching sounds came from the food bowl. While Griffin positioned the litter box, Poppy filled a second bowl with water and set it down near the food. The cat took a sip, returned to the food, munched a bit longer. Every few mouthfuls, she turned her head sideways to chew, and the occasional bit of food fell on the floor. She sniffed it, pawed it, abandoned it. Poppy didn't mind the mess one bit.

When the cat was done eating, she sat up and set to cleaning her face, first with her tongue, then by licking a paw and using that to scrub her muzzle. With each pass of the paw the area widened, until it included her eyes, then her ears. One ear folded backward. Just when Poppy was thinking what a silky thing it was, it popped right.

The cat turned her head. Griffin was still hunkered down near the laundry room. He made a clicking sound and tapped his fingertips on the tile floor. The cat approached. Familiar with his scent, she gave his leg a full body rub in passing, and went on to the litter box.

Griffin straightened and brushed his hands together. "There. Now I feel better."

"You do," Poppy said with a chuckle. "She probably does, too. So what's her name?"

He looked pensive. "I was thinking about that driving over here. 'Baby' seemed a good enough name then, but now I'm not sure."

"You cannot call this cat 'baby.' That's an insult, given how courageous she is."

"So what's a courageous name for a girl?"

Poppy thought. "Gillian. That's a strong name." But the orange cat didn't look like a Gillian to her. "Whitney." That didn't sound right, either.

There was a sandy scratching, a tapping, then the emergence of the cat from the box. She paused on the laundry room threshold for an instant's orientation. Then, raising her tail, she walked with surefooted grace straight to Poppy.

"Victoria," Poppy said. "For majesty." With exquisite aim, the cat jumped up onto her lap. "Victoria?" Poppy asked the creature.

The cat gave Poppy's chin a rub and began to purr. Then she turned in a slow circle on Poppy's lap and, like silk drifting down, settled in a ball.

"And you can't take her to Little Bear," Poppy decided. "She's oriented here now. It would be cruel to uproot her again."

"But she's my cat," Griffin said.

"She can stay here."

"Only if I stay with her for part of the time."

With a hand on Victoria's warm neck, Poppy looked up, suspicious. There was a devious side to Griffin. There had to be. He couldn't be *all* goodness and light. "What does 'part of the time' mean?"

Griffin bounced a look off the ceiling and said a patient, "It means absolutely nothing except that I have work to do, and you have a huge desk with more than enough space for me to spread out my stuff. You have heat and electricity. You have a *bathroom*. And a fax machine. And cell phone reception. You have extra phone lines, so that I can use one to access the Internet without having to pray that my wireless connection will hold up. You also have a level head, so you know that what I'm saying makes sense. And you have a kind heart. Don't try to deny it. I didn't ask you to take in this cat."

No. He hadn't. And it struck Poppy that Victoria's arrival would raise a few brows. For years, Maida had urged her to get a pet—most regularly mentioning a Doberman, a rottweiler, or a German shepherd—but Poppy had repeatedly rejected the idea of a watchdog. She refused to think she needed one. Rose often urged her to take one of the litter of golden Lab pups that their own dog mothered. But a golden Lab pup grew into a golden Lab dog, and that could be large. There was no way Poppy, her chair, and something that size could fit into the shower for a wash, and Poppy didn't see the point of having a pet if she couldn't take care of it herself.

And then there was Charlotte, showing up with a basket of cats to give away at crafts shows, plant sales, and bake sales, Memorial Day parades, Fourth of July fireworks, and Labor Day picnics—and not only in Lake Henry. Charlotte was a regional institution. Children flocked to her baskets; adults steered clear. For Poppy to have taken a cat from Charlotte would have meant she was suckered.

Funny, but she didn't feel suckered now. Granted, she hadn't been suckered by Charlotte. If she'd been suckered by anyone, it was Griffin. But Victoria was warm against those abdominal muscles that did sense warmth, and, curled up in Poppy's lap, she was a perfect fit.

So, fine. Poppy wasn't at the mountain, because she didn't want to dwell on what she couldn't do. But she could do a cat. Thinking that, she felt better. She felt stronger. And then there was Griffin.

"Where's your stuff?" she asked. "Your papers and all?"

"At Little Bear," he replied.

She glanced at her watch. It was nearly noon. "If you were to go back and get what you need, then stop at Charlie's for chili"—she still had a yen for that—"could you be back by one?"

"Sure. Why?"

"Because if you can, and if you're willing to cover the phones while you work, I could go visit Heather. Think the driving's okay?"

*   *   *

The driving was fine, but then, Poppy was still feeling strong. She had chili in her stomach and the comfort of knowing that Griffin was at her house. He was working. Nothing wrong with that. He was covering the phones. It was perfect.

Besides, she was a pro at driving in snow. Give her a broad wheelbase, steel body panels, four-wheel drive, and big tires, and she was fine. By the time she passed through the center of town, the first of the plows had been through. She reached West Eames without so much as the hint of a skid.

By then, the chili was digested, Griffin seemed far away, and she was alone with her thoughts. To her chagrin, they were the same ones that had disturbed her sleep, and they weren't going away. Nor did she try to make them. This was what she had to discuss with Heather.

She hadn't counted on a large room filled with other inmates and their guests, or on the alarm that hit her seeing those others, who were so unlike Heather. But there was nothing to be done about either. She managed to grab a free chair and an empty space by the wall.

Heather spotted her immediately. After a quick glance around, she came over and slipped into the chair. She put her elbows on her knees, leaning close. Poppy did the same, giving them an element of privacy.

"I know," Poppy began, because she had seen that quick search of the room and the flicker of disappointment. "I'm not Micah. I'm sorry."

Heather seemed resigned. "I figured he was working, but when they said someone was here, I was hoping . . ."

"He's been washing all weekend. I think he's planning to lay tubing this week. He wants to be ready when the sap starts to flow. First run's always the best."

"I should be there. Are Missy and Star helping?"

"No. I think he needs to be alone."

"But he can't do it alone. Well, I guess this part he can handle. Has he called Camille about the paperwork?"

"I don't know."

"She knows everything, Poppy. Make him do it. Tell me about Missy and Star."

"They were with me yesterday. They slept over last night with Emma and Ruth. Today they're at the mountain with Marianne."

"They must hate me."

"They love you. But they don't understand all this. None of us do. That's why I'm here. Talk to me, honey. Tell me what happened."

Heather's eyes glazed over.

"No no no," Poppy whispered, grabbing her hands. "Don't *do* that. It doesn't help. When you tune out, you hurt yourself and everyone else. Talk to me. *Talk* to me. You and me, we could always do that. Way back, when Micah first asked you to be a nanny for the girls, we discussed it, remember? We went back and forth, pros and cons. We agreed that if you'd wanted a career, you'd have been better staying at Charlie's, but you really, really wanted to take care of the girls. Remember? I could see that. And then when things heated up between Micah and you? I could see how you felt. And then when it happened, you told me, because you needed to know it was okay, and you knew you'd get a fair answer from me, and I gave you one. So why can't you trust me that way now?"

"There's no point," Heather whispered.

Poppy whispered back a desperate, "Why *not?*"

"Oh, Poppy. Did you ever wish you could live your life over—just go back and do things different from how you did them the first time around?"

"All the time. You know that. One ride on a snowmobile—thirty minutes—and everything changed. I'd give *anything* to do those thirty minutes over again."

"But you can't. All you can do is go on."

"That's what you always said. We both did. We said it over and over again, trying to convince ourselves that was the only way to go. Only maybe it isn't."

"It is."

"Heather. They're going to try you for murder. Whether you're Lisa or not—"

"I'm not Lisa."

"—they'll take you back to California and put you on trial. They're out for blood. You could be totally innocent, but unless you give Cassie something to work with, you'll be convicted. So then there won't *be* any going on. It'll all have been bravado on our part. Nothing more."

"I'm not Lisa," Heather repeated.

Poppy looked down. She gave Heather's hands a squeeze. "Is that because it would be too painful to be Lisa?" When Heather didn't answer, she looked up. "Then is it too painful being *Heather,* to talk about what she went through before Lake Henry?"

Heather shot back, "Is it too painful being Poppy?"

Poppy had known the question would come. This was one of the things that had haunted her through the night. She welcomed the chance to air it, actually *needed* that chance. Even with all that was happening, all she didn't understand, she trusted Heather more than anyone else to listen without passing judgment.

Is it too painful being Poppy?

"Being the Poppy I was? Yes. It is. She did some things wrong, and that brings pain. There's pain, too, in good stuff that's lost."

"Like?"

"Her spirit. Her daring. Her *energy*. She was on the go all day, every day. I don't know where she'd have been today—maybe in another part of the country or the world, or maybe in Lake Henry in spite of it all—but she was fun. She was also difficult. And defiant. And foolish, and a lot of that's really hard to think about. But my situation's different from yours. For me, the past is done. Everyone knows I was born and raised here. No one's coming after me with handcuffs. Besides, if something happened to me, no one would be the worse for it. I don't have a Micah, and I don't have a Missy or a Star. They *need* you."

With a tiny tremor, Heather sat straighter. Wrapping her arms around her middle, she sat back.

"So maybe it comes down to punishment," Poppy suggested. "Something happened in your life, something so bad you can't talk about it. You could have married Micah and had more kids, only you didn't. Were you punishing yourself for whatever it was that happened before?"

For a minute, there were only low murmurs from the rest of the room. Then Heather asked, "Don't you do that?"

"Punish myself? How?"

"By limiting what you do."

"I do what I want. I accept what I can't do."

"But do you ever want to chance it? To take that little risk?"

"Like how?"

Heather gave her a you-know-how look. "Like with a man. Aren't you curious?"

"About what?" Poppy asked, whispering again. "Sex? I had it. I had plenty of it before the accident."

"That was then."

"I have a full life. I'm not looking for more." To make her point, she said, "Take Griffin. He's back in town."

Heather's eyes went wide. "He is? When did he come?" As quickly as excitement had flared, it died. "Oh. He wants to write about me."

"No. He says he just wants to help. He has contacts that none of us have." Poppy nearly told her about the pictures of Lisa, but something held her back. "And there are other kinds of help. He's at my house right now answering the phones, so that I can be here. But do I want to go to dinner with him? No. I'm home with the phones tonight, and having dinner with Lily and John tomorrow, then Tuesday night you all are over." Of course, Heather wouldn't be over this week. She might not be over this month. In fact, her absence could drag on longer, much longer.

"I love our group," Heather wailed softly.

"Then help us. Help us help you."

She looked torn. Tentatively, she asked, "Where are Griffin's contacts?"

Poppy felt a glimmer of hope. "All over. He has a network. If there's someone you need to find, or documents, or relatives—he's good at this."

"There'd be a price. There's always a price."

"He's rich. He doesn't need money." She couldn't quite get herself to tell Heather that Griffin's brother was the one who had tracked her down, which would ensure his doing everything for nothing. But the time seemed right for the other. "He has pictures. Pictures of Lisa. Looking at them is the most amazing thing. You can understand why someone made this mistake."

Heather sat very still. Her eyes had gone wide; they held Poppy's without blinking. Then, without taking a breath, she opened her mouth and, soundlessly, formed three words. Before Poppy could react, before she could even wonder if she'd read those words right, Heather was up out of the chair, across the room, and out the door.

Chapter Ten

Griffin had fun playing the role of telephone operator. Having been on the other end of the line enough times when he had called for information on Lake Henry and Poppy had blown him off, he did it now to others with flair. Three media calls came, and he was cordial but firm; Lake Henry had nothing to say on the matter of Heather Malone.

He enjoyed the other calls, too. Now that he was playing backup for Poppy Blake, people didn't shun him—or, in this instance, hang up on him. They asked where Poppy was and when she would be back. They asked who *he* was and knew precisely, once he gave his name. They asked why he had come, how long he was staying, and whether he was dating Poppy, and he answered in good humor, because the questions weren't one-sided. From the postmaster, Nathaniel Roy, who called to say that Poppy hadn't picked up her mail since Tuesday, he learned that she regularly read *Newsweek, People,* and the Patagonia catalog, which was no surprise, and *Martha Stewart Living,* which was. From the masseuse, he learned that she had a full-body massage every week, usually on Monday afternoons, though she wanted to change it this week, and if Griffin was interested, the menu included not only Swedish massage, but reflexology, hydromassage, and conditioning body scrubs. He learned that the logs in Poppy's woodbin were replenished every week by the same man who plowed her road, that she had played the trumpet in junior high to the chagrin of her mother, who thought the trumpet was boyish and encouraged her to play the flute, and that every summer, she completed the cross-lake swim that was a Fourth of July tradition in town.

He also learned that she hadn't dated anyone special since Perry Walker. Two people told him that, and if they wouldn't talk about Perry, that was fine. Griffin had already learned a bit about him, though none of it from Poppy.

Between calls, he plugged in his computer and logged on to the Web. He checked his e-mail and found nothing urgent, so he went right on to his search for his sister. It was something he did often, a pastime of sorts, a puzzle that he simply kept at, over and over again. Though separated by seven years, Cindy and he were the two youngest of the siblings. A bond between them stemmed from that. Griffin hadn't been any more able to keep her from leaving home than the others had, but he felt her loss more keenly—and he was the only one to whom she sent notes. They came few and far between, forwarded to him by his publisher du jour, and there was never a return address. What there was—always— was a New York postmark with a zip code that fell within a digit of the family brownstone.

That was deliberate, Griffin knew. He didn't believe for a minute that she was in New York, but guessed that she had friends who visited there and mailed her notes. Since tracing her from these was impossible, he had to settle for the solace of what she said—that she was alive and well and drug-free.

He had a theory. She was a talented poet—a *disturbed* poet, some said, but Griffin had always felt too much loyalty to say that. If she was clean and thinking clearly, she would sell her work when she needed money.

The crime, of course, was that she did have a trust fund. She could have access to it—could have all the money she wanted—if she told the family of her whereabouts. The fact that she should have to scrounge for money ate at Griffin.

That said, she wasn't without means. She would write. Poems, short stories, whatever. He was convinced of it.

So while Ralph Haskins followed more conventionally clever PI channels, Griffin regularly searched the archives of three dozen magazines that printed the kinds of pieces he knew she could write. He searched the names of contributors and plugged in some of his own. He didn't try Cynthia Hughes; she wouldn't use that, because Ralph would pick it up.

Nor would she use any variation of James, the brother who had given her drugs. Rather, Griffin typed in other appropriate possibilities. Most had to do with their mother, Rebecca, with whom Cindy had always had a love-hate relationship.

So there was Rebecca Hughes, and Rebecca Russell, their mother's maiden name. Elizabeth Russell was their maternal grandmother, and Elizabeth Casey, her maiden name. Griffin always tried Hugh Piper, taken from their father's name, and combinations of their brother's names, like Randi Griffin and Alexa Peters. On a given day, if he had time, he would try a bunch of others that might evoke a childhood memory.

This day he didn't have that time, so he simply ran the usual names, got the usual "no matches," and logged off. Then he spread his working papers over the desk and put in a call to Prentiss Hayden. He had been prepared to talk as if he was heavily into the bio. Prentiss nixed that, though, by launching into a spirited, "My telephone says this call is from New Hampshire. I should have figured it out sooner. You're up there, aren't you?"

"Sure am," Griffin said nonchalantly. "Quiet places are great for writing."

"Hah. You're up there for the DiCenza case. Who's the article for this time?"

"There's no article. I just happen to know people here, and it is a good place to write."

"While you snoop around," the senator said, but he sounded more interested than annoyed. "Are you learning anything interesting? There's lots of talk down here. Give me something to share, so I'll sound like I still have an iron or two in the fire."

"I don't have much to share. We're waiting this out, just like the rest of the country."

"Everybody's speculating here, and not about nice things. It's all ridiculous, of course, idle minds that have nothing better to do. As long as you're not wasting your time on it. Did you get the information you needed from my army buddies?"

"I did." Griffin had told him that several weeks before. "I've incorporated it into the body of the chaper on the war. I'm still worried about the other issue, though."

"What's it like up there?" Prentiss asked deliberately. "Pretty town?"

"You bet." Another call lit up the board. "I'm going to have to run, Senator. I'll get back to you, okay?"

He took the next call. It was a local one and easily dispatched. When it was done, he returned the Hayden papers to his briefcase, not at all disappointed to put it off for another day.

What did disappoint him was Victoria. She wouldn't sit on his lap. He whistled softly. He promised her treats. He made kissing sounds. He patted his thighs. He lifted her once and actually set her there, but she bounded back down and sashayed to the sofa with her tail in the air. She walked carefully around it, still mapping her space, he guessed. Once she jumped onto the cushions, the top third of that tail was the only thing he could see from the desk. It moved down the sofa. In time, it stopped, twitched, lowered. When he dared peek over the sofa back, she was curled in a ball in the corner directly opposite the fire. It was Poppy's spot, to judge from the chenille blanket on which Victoria so contentedly lay.

Poppy's spot. Poppy's cat. Griffin had lost out on that one.

Satisfied in an odd kind of way, he gave the phone bank several minutes to blink. When the buttons remained dark, he adjusted the headset for comfort and used one of Poppy's lines to make a credit card call of his own. Ralph Haskins answered after a single ring.

"Bad time?" Griffin asked.

"Nah," Ralph said. "I'm doin' surveillance. But I don't have much to tell you, or I'd have called you myself. I'm running into stone walls."

"As in stonewalling?"

"You got it, Red. I don't know whether the senator's people made a recent round or whether the directive is still in effect from fifteen years ago, but I'm talking to people who knew Rob and knew Lisa, and they won't say a thing. They claim that they don't remember, or that it was too dark to see, or that they were way on the other side of the party on the night Rob died, which was pretty much what they told the police at the time."

"But I thought there were witnesses saying Lisa threatened Rob."

"There were. I've tracked down three of those, and they all have similar stories. They didn't hear words. They saw anger and pushing."

"By Lisa?"

"That's what they say."

Griffin was dismayed. "If no one heard words, how could they say she was trying to extort him?"

"It's the family who claims that. They say there were phone calls to Rob in the days before she ran him down."

"That's hearsay."

"Nope. The family claims Rob told them directly, or so the record reads. The family won't answer my calls. I did find another ER appearance. It was in a clinic near Stockton. She used an assumed name and paid in cash, but after the murder, the staff was sure Lisa and that girl were one and the same."

"What name did she use?" Griffin asked, figuring it would be too much to ask that Lisa had used the name Heather Malone.

"Mary Hendricks," said Ralph.

"M. H., rather than H. M. Is that a coincidence?"

"I don't know. Could be. Lisa and Mary have the exact same blood type, type A. The Feds say Heather does, too, but they're not making much of that. Forty percent of Americans have type A blood."

"So what made her go to the clinic near Stockton?"

"A pair of broken ribs."

Griffin swore softly. "Do we know Rob did it?"

"She wasn't seeing anyone else. So when I mentioned this second ER visit to one of the DiCenza people, I was told that Lisa was a troubled young woman who was a pathological liar with a history of self-inflicted wounds."

"That could be true," Griffin thought aloud. "Or it could be that Lisa had a legitimate reason to fear for her life. I wish I knew her side of the story."

"So do the Feds, which brings me to another piece of news. Someone on the local FBI team played college football with Rob. He didn't have much good to say about the guy. So, okay. Maybe he has an ax to grind. Maybe he resented the DiCenza privilege and power. But he flat-out said

Rob was rough on girls. He said he'd witnessed one ugly incident where the girl might have been hurt if a group of them from the team hadn't pulled Rob off."

"Do his higher-ups in the FBI know about this?"

"Yes. They told him to keep his mouth shut."

"To forget it?"

"No. Just to wait. That could be the same thing."

"I'm surprised he told you."

Ralph's voice held a smile. "Yeah, well, he's second-generation FBI, and I helped his old man once. You know how it is, Red. You scratch my back, I'll scratch yours."

And since Griffin's family had scratched Ralph Haskins' back to the tune of many hundreds of thousands of dollars over the years, Griffin felt comfortable asking, "What about the other? Anything there?"

Ralph's tone went from smug to humble. "Nothing. She's smart as a whip. Always was. I remember when I was over at the house and she used to sit there hanging on my every word. I'd think of *Moonlighting* or *Remington Steele,* and I'd picture her growing up to do something like that. I figured neither of those women had anything over our Cindy." He made a self-deprecating sound. "She's a clever one. Right from the start, she covered her tracks. Becoming invisible isn't rocket science. A little ingenuity, and it's done. I wouldn't put it past her to be watching me doing the looking all this time."

Griffin thought of Heather Malone, with her lovely life in a bucolic town and no past to speak of. He imagined Cindy living like that somewhere. "So how do we find her?" he asked. His own little searches were coming up empty.

"A tip," Ralph said. "That's the way it works. You get a lucky break, you talk to the right person, you get a tip."

Griffin thought of Randy's case. He was thinking that he didn't want to wait fifteen years to find Cindy, when he heard a car approaching the house. He felt a quickening at the thought of Poppy returning. "I'm impatient, I guess."

"I'll keep on it."

"Thanks, Ralph." He disconnected the call and would have gone to the door if a button hadn't lit up on the panel just then. It was Poppy's private line. Hoping to look thoroughly in control when she walked through the door, he said a lyrical, "Poppy Blake's residence."

"Who is this?" asked an accusing voice.

"Who is *this?*" he asked right back.

"Poppy's sister, Rose."

"Rose, it's Griffin." They had met twice before, once in October and once yesterday. In both instances, he had sensed that Rose was a force to contend with. He would have liked to talk with her and win her over a bit, but this was not the time. Poppy was leaving the Blazer; he heard the door slam. And Rose wasn't in a chatty mood.

"Is Poppy there?" she asked coldly.

"No." And with *that* tone of voice, he wasn't putting her on hold until Poppy came in. He could protect his girl. "May I take a message?"

"Tell her I need to talk with her. Thanks."

The line went dead at the same time the front door opened, but Poppy didn't wheel through. The woman who slipped in, set down a thermal bag, lowered the hood of her parka, and looked hopefully around was twenty-plus years older than Poppy. Her hair was short, dark, and cut stylishly enough so that even after being mussed by the hood, it fell well. Her eyes were gentle and her skin tanned. Below the parka were jeans and tall, Sherpa-lined boots. Her hands were graceful as they emerged from one glove, then the other. If ever there was an indication of how handsomely Poppy would age, Maida Blake was it.

* * *

Driving home, Poppy took several small skids. She blamed them first on the snow, then on the lousy job that someone had done plowing the roads. But the snow had let up well before she reached Lake Henry, and the roads were sanded, which meant—bottom line—that the fault was hers.

She was distracted. She was fighting a panic that came in spurts. With each one, she accelerated. With each skid, she slowed.

It's no mistake. That was what Heather had mouthed. Poppy had been telling her about Griffin's pictures of Lisa, and was remarking on the similarity in their looks. *You can understand why someone made this mistake,* Poppy had said.

It's no mistake, Heather mouthed.

Poppy kept trying to find other words that might have looked the same. She kept telling herself that she had misread Heather's lips. But she kept coming back to, *It's no mistake,* and it left her stunned.

No, not stunned.

Well, maybe yes, stunned—by the enormity of the confession.

But Poppy felt other things, too. She was disappointed. She was frightened. She was heartsick. She was confused. She was *hurt,* though she didn't know why she should be. All these years, Heather hadn't lied. She simply hadn't told the truth.

Well, hell, Poppy hadn't either. But that didn't mean she wasn't a good person now—at least, not if Griffin's theory of growth was to be believed. He claimed people who experienced trauma could learn from it, wise up, and adapt. If so, Heather was a good person now. If she was responsible for Rob DiCenza's death, there must have been justifiable cause.

The only one that came to Poppy's mind was self-defense, and the person she wanted to run it past was Griffin. But when she went down the newly plowed drive to her house, his truck wasn't the only one there. Maida's SUV was parked beside it.

In a split second, Poppy ran through the list of people who might be driving Maida's car while she was in Florida. A little voice inside, though, told her that it was Maida herself. There had been something in Maida's tone the other day—something different, tentative, unsure.

Uneasy on several counts, Poppy pulled up to the house. All the while she was wondering what Maida would be saying to Griffin and vice versa, and thinking that whatever it was, she wasn't up for it.

She quickly maneuvered out of the Blazer. The ramp was damp but free of snow. She was barely at the top when Maida opened the door and said with a grin and the kind of dry wit that Poppy didn't usually see in her, "I'd shout '*Surprise!*' except that isn't my style."

Seeing the grin on her mother's face, Poppy felt pleasure in spite of herself. "You're not here, Mom. You're in Florida."

"Oh, it got boring there," Maida said breezily. "More was happening here, so I packed up and flew home. Someone must have seen me driving through town, though, because Rose just called here. Griffin said she sounded in a snit." She gave an urgent little wave. "Come inside. It's freezing."

"Did you call Rose back?"

"No. She'll hold. I wanted to see you first. Poppy, come *in.* You'll catch *cold.*"

Poppy crossed the porch and entered the house just as Griffin was pulling on his parka. He called out a discreet, "Did you have a good afternoon?"

"Good" was not a word Poppy would use to describe the afternoon's events, but suddenly she didn't even want to *think* about them, much less get into the whole thing with Maida. So she said to him, "Are you leaving?"

"I asked him to dinner," Maida put in, ever the consummate hostess, "but he said he had work to do." Poppy smelled something cooking. It was a familiar smell that brought back memories. She wondered how long Maida had been there.

Griffin stretched the blue band over his head. "You and your mom want time together."

Poppy was thinking that she wasn't sure about that, when a movement on the sofa caught her eye. She had forgotten about Victoria. But what a nice surprise she was. The cat was sitting on Poppy's favorite chenille throw, simultaneously arching her back and stretching her front legs, looking as though she'd just woken up.

"Did you meet my cat?" Poppy asked Maida.

"*Your* cat?" Griffin asked.

The words were barely out of his mouth when Victoria leaped off the sofa. With unerring aim, she approached Poppy. She slowed only for an orienting rub alongside one of the wheels, then she jumped right up. Poppy's heart melted. Wool jacket and all, fingerless gloves and all, she wrapped her arms around the cat and, letting go of Heather's confession in the balm of this warm little creature, buried her face in that soft orange fur. She imagined she smelled her own cologne there, picked up on the chenille throw, no doubt.

A soft purring started. Poppy absorbed it with her face in the fur. Unable to resist, she raised smug eyes to Griffin's.

"Okay," he said, butt against the wall for balance as he put on one boot, then the other. "That's it. A guy can only take so much rejection in one day. I'll leave you three ladies to yourselves." He went out, closing the door behind him.

Poppy stroked the cat's head with the bare finger of one hand and used the other hand to unwind her scarf. "So *did* you meet Victoria?" she asked her mother.

"Oh yes. She woke up for that. Then she went right back to sleep. So now she's awake. She seems to be interested in you, only you." Maida smiled. "And so, my dear, does Griffin." She took the scarf out of Poppy's hand.

"Griffin," Poppy informed her, "is interested in using my shower, my desk space, and my phone. I don't know what he told you, but the truth is no one else in Lake Henry will do that for him."

She might as well have saved her breath, because Maida had already reached her own conclusion. "He seems like a nice person," she mused. "He behaved well enough during Lily's problems last fall. I wish he weren't a reporter. But John's one, and Lily's doing just fine with him. I suppose if I can live with one journalist son-in-law, I can live with a second."

"Don't get used to the idea, Mom." Poppy tucked her gloves in her pocket. "I am not marrying Griffin."

Maida held out a hand for Poppy's coat. "Oh, I know that, Poppy. You aren't getting married at all." She took the coat when Poppy slid out her arms, and hung it on a hook by the door. "You've been saying that since you were five. For the longest time, I worried that it was something your father and I did to turn you off to marriage. Then I realized you just loved *him* that much."

Poppy had. George Blake had been gentle and kind, old-fashioned in the most positive of ways. He believed in wearing overalls, in cooking with fresh butter, fresh cream, and fresh eggs, and in doing the books in longhand in a large leather-bound ledger. When Poppy pictured her father, she could smell warm sun, damp earth, and ripe apples.

When she pictured her mother, she smelled tension. It hung heavy over her memories.

"There's a contradiction here," she challenged. "You know I'm not getting married, but you say you can live with Griffin as a son-in-law."

"Wishful thinking," Maida replied.

Poppy knew she was being humored, but it was odd coming from her mother. Maida was a perfectionist. She liked things just so. More typically, she would have urged Poppy to *encourage* Griffin because, after all, getting married and having children was the ideal. That she didn't argue now—that she had actually been honest enough to acknowledge that she wouldn't necessarily get her way, and to do it with grace, gave Poppy pause.

"Are you all right?" she asked. There had been an issue of headaches the summer and fall before. Poppy didn't want to think that a doctor had diagnosed something dreadful, which had in turn mellowed Maida. Maida certainly seemed healthy enough.

"I'm fine," she confirmed.

"You look rested. You're tanned. But you've never been bored down there before."

Maida grew reflective—and Poppy wasn't used to that, either. She and her mother had never been friends. They had never shared their innermost thoughts. She doubted Maida did that with anyone. Yet, there was a pensiveness now, and a quiet, "This year's different. Lily's back, and she's married. I want to see her happy. Rose is being hard on Hannah, which makes me uneasy, because . . . well, just because. So I was down in Florida thinking that I could be here giving Hannah extra attention. And now there's you and Heather."

"*Me* and Heather?" Poppy countered. "*Heather* and Heather."

"What's happening there?"

Poppy wanted to tell her the latest, but she couldn't. And it wouldn't have mattered had Lily, or John, or Cassie been there instead of Maida. She closed a lid on that particular Pandora's box, locking in the meaning of those three mouthed words. "Nothing's happening. Heather's sitting in jail while the people in California put together enough of a case to get her sent back there."

"*Back* there?"

"There," Poppy corrected.

"Did she come from California?"

"No. I don't want to talk about this, Mom." Leaving a hand on Victoria—her ally—she went to the phone panel. "Oh my."

"What?"

"Griffin left a list of every call he answered. I need to use this man more." He had even switched on the audio, so she would hear if another call came in. He had also left his own papers in a pile at the end of the desk, and his briefcase was on the floor nearby. It was either a statement of trust or an invitation for Poppy to take a look.

Not up for deciding which, she wheeled past the phone bank and followed the scent of bay leaves and sage down the hall. The closer she got to the kitchen, the stronger the smells grew. Once she crossed the threshold, they became positively divine.

She opened the oven to peek. Victoria stirred enough to lift her head and sniff right along with Poppy. "Ahhh," Poppy sighed with satisfaction. "No one does pot roast like you do."

"Nothing's fresh there," Maida cautioned, more like her exacting self now. "I had to get everything from the freezer or the pantry, not that it's the season for Mary Joan's red potatoes anyway, so I had to use canned ones. But I walked in the door, put the meat in the microwave to defrost, and had the whole thing starting to cook before I unpacked."

Poppy was used to Maida's doting. She was forever sending Poppy cooked food, uncooked food, clothes, candy, and books. Still, Poppy was touched by the effort made now. "You didn't have to do this."

"I wanted to." She grew serious. "It was lonely down there, Poppy."

"But you have lots of friends."

"Friends aren't my girls." Seeming embarrassed, she turned to the counter. Opening a bag, she began to put fresh oranges in a large wooden bowl. "You're all good girls."

"Well, *that's* quite a statement," Poppy blurted out. "You wouldn't have said it so long ago. You *hated* what Lily was doing."

"I was frightened," Maida confessed. She didn't look at Poppy, just continued arranging oranges in the bowl.

"What's changed now?"

Maida added an orange to the pile, set it here, set it there, studied the arrangement. "I don't know. At my age, well . . ."

"You're only fifty-seven."

"Almost fifty-eight." She removed that orange and two others, and put them back in different spots. "I used to think that was old, but here I am with three daughters who'll be in their forties before I know it."

"I'm only thirty-two."

"My point is, the three of you are grown up."

"We have been for a while."

"I'm trying to accept that." She looked up from the bowl. "If you're adults, that means I can't control you. I can't tell you what to do. You have to live your own lives. Make your own mistakes."

There it was. That was Maida. Afraid of mistakes. Afraid that her life wouldn't be perfect.

She went on. "But that doesn't mean I don't worry. I worry a lot. You can't change the thinking of a lifetime in a few short months."

"Be glad you're not Heather's mother," Poppy said, and was suddenly curious. "What if you were her, reading about all this in the paper? What would you be thinking?"

"Are we assuming that Heather is not Lisa?"

"Yes," Poppy said with only a glimmer of guilt. They were talking hypotheticals, after all. Still, she tossed in one fact. "Heather's mother left when she was little."

Maida thought about that for a minute, then asked, "What kind of woman does that?"

"I don't know. But let's say there was a reason. Let's say the separation was necessary. So what would you, as Heather's mother, be feeling?"

"Exposed," Maida immediately said. Then she followed it up with a quieter, "Frightened. Worried. Confused. I'd be wondering what she did to bring this on herself."

"Would you go to see her? Would you support her? Would you scrounge up money to help with her defense?"

"That would depend on the nature of the relationship, on why she left all those years ago."

"We're talking mother and daughter," Poppy said impatiently. "Would you *support* her?"

Maida let out a reluctant breath. "Well, that would certainly be the right thing to do."

"But would you *do* it?"

"I'd have to know the truth about what she'd done," Maida said.

Poppy could have screamed, because she didn't want waffling. She didn't want conditions. She wanted an answer. A definitive answer. A positive answer.

What she wanted, she realized, was for Maida to say that if she were Heather's mother, she would love Heather no matter what. Poppy wanted Maida, the perfectionist, to express this kind of unconditional love. *That* would have made Poppy feel better when she had phoned Maida the other day.

But it was asking too much, and that upset her. She was relieved when Victoria chose that moment to jump off her lap and go to her food.

Maida, too, was distracted. "How did she know it was there?"

"We showed her before. She remembers."

They watched in silence while Victoria ate. After a minute, the cat went to the litter box. She didn't enter, just sniffed the lip of the box. Then she returned to her food.

"How does she *do* that?" Maida asked. "Is it by smell?"

"Smell, memory, whiskers. I would think that since she lost her sight, her other senses are heightened."

"I take it she's an indoor cat."

"I certainly wouldn't let her out."

"And Griffin brought her for you? What a sweet thing."

"Well, he didn't bring her for me, exactly. He brought her in to show her to me, and she seemed to like the place, so it made sense to let her stay. But it's just for the time being, until Griffin leaves."

"I think he brought her for you."

"He didn't. Trust me."

Maida went on as though Poppy hadn't spoken. "He knew you needed a pet."

"I don't need a pet."

"You were always good with our cats. Do you remember that tabby?"

"I do. We called her Tabby. But that was then, Mom. My life is pretty busy now. I'm in and out all the time. I have plenty of responsibility. I don't need a pet."

"He saw this one and knew you'd take care of it. He knew you would understand her special needs."

Poppy didn't like the sound of that. "What needs are those?"

"This cat's blind. That takes understanding. You know what it is to have special needs."

Poppy bristled. "The handicapped cat for the handicapped girl?"

"No," Maida replied with care. "The handicapped cat for the girl who understands. That's all I meant, Poppy."

But Poppy couldn't get the other out of her mind. "The handicapped cat for the handicapped girl," she repeated. She wondered if Griffin had thought that, too—and was suddenly furious that Maida had pointed it out. "Did you have to say that?"

"I didn't say it. You did. That wasn't what *I* had in mind."

"I've made a life here, Mom. I've made a life that's good and full. I've gotten used to being in this chair, and part of the reason is that people around me accept that I'm here and don't talk about it or question it or even . . . even *notice* it. I don't know why you have to throw it in my face." She wheeled around and headed out of the kitchen.

"I didn't, Poppy," Maida called, following quickly.

"You did. You took something innocent on Griffin's part and made it into something so . . . so pathetic that it makes me feel like a *cripple*." She wheeled her chair in an abrupt one-eighty and faced Maida. "No one else makes me feel that way. Why do you have to do it? Why can't you accept me as I am? Why can't you treat me like I'm normal? It'd help, y'know. It'd help a whole lot!"

Doing another one-eighty, she wheeled off toward her bedroom. Once in that wing of the house, though, she turned into the weight room and pulled the door closed. For a minute, she sat fuming with her jaw clenched and her hands tight on her wheels. Then she heard a sound at the door.

Had it been Maida's voice there, she might have asked for time alone. Angry as she was—*hurt* as she was—she knew she had overreacted.

But the sound she heard wasn't Maida's voice, just a plaintive, questioning meow.

Poppy slid the door open only enough for Victoria to slip through. The sight of the cat brought a whisper of calm. Sitting back, Poppy watched her explore the room. She walked along two walls first, getting a grasp on the width and length. Then she moved in toward the equipment, finding one piece after another. She walked around each, using her whiskers, nose, and paws to plot height and shape. She rose on her hind legs to explore the weights, and jumped onto the seat of the recumbent bicycle. Seconds later, she was down again. When she reached the parallel bars, she stepped daintily on the thin runner and walked its length. At its end, she sat and turned toward Poppy.

"You're a smart one," Poppy said softly, feeling fully in control again. She came forward, putting her elbows on her thighs. "Tell you what. You can have that one. It's yours. Walk on it all you want. Sit there. Grin. That one's yours, the others are mine. Does that sound like a fair deal?"

*   *   *

Victoria seemed to agree, but it was the only fair deal Poppy felt she struck that day. She had dinner with Maida, but it was a quiet one. She loved having Victoria with her, but if Griffin had been playing matchmaker, come morning, the cat was his. And then there was the issue of Heather. Once Poppy had finished brooding about Maida, and finished brooding about Griffin, she brooded about Heather—and not only about the identity issue. Now, hours later, in the privacy of her own home, she heard Heather's words again and again.

Is it too painful being Poppy?

Chapter Eleven

Though Griffin watched the clock for much of the evening, he wasn't idle. After leaving Poppy's, he picked up sandwiches at Charlie's and shared them with Billy Farraway in the bobhouse. Later, heading back to the cabin, he took his time. With starry skies now and a three-quarter moon shining on a fresh coat of snow, the night was a deep, brilliant blue. He pulled up his collar, stuck his hands in his pockets, and just stood for a while. The light of an occasional airplane crossed the sky, along with a slower-moving satellite or two. Once in a while the sound of a truck echoed across the lake, but for the most part there was silence.

Oh, he heard a loon or two—Billy did love his pipe. Otherwise, though, the lake was beautifully quiet and still.

Then he saw a fox. At least, he guessed it was a fox from its skinny dog size and large bushy tail. Holding its head down in a way that few dogs did, it walked through the snow across the lake. It stopped once to look his way, then continued on toward the shore and disappeared into the trees.

Growing cold, Griffin went inside. He built up the fire and checked his watch. He made coffee and checked his watch. He opened the door, looked out again, and checked his watch.

When it was late enough, he put on his warmest things and walked to shore through the footprints that he'd made on the way to the cabin. He climbed into the truck, let it warm a minute or two, then drove off. When he was at just the right spot, he pulled over, set his blinkers, and called Poppy.

"Hey," he said, feeling a lift at the sound of her voice. "I didn't wake you, did I?" She didn't sound so much sleepy as deep in thought.

"No. I'm awake." She sighed softly. "Lots on my mind. Uh, I thought you didn't have cell reception."

"I don't on the island. I'm sitting here in the truck on the side of the road at the exact spot where I know the reception starts. You learn these things."

"What time is it?" she asked, and must have looked at the clock, because she answered herself. "Nearly eleven. It must have been cold crossing the lake."

"Not as bad as it's been. There's no wind. But I didn't want to do it earlier. I wanted to make sure your mother was gone. How did it go?"

"How did what go?" Poppy asked with a sharpness that reminded him about her visit with Heather. But first things first.

"Dinner with your mother."

There was another pause, then a surprised but gentler, "It was okay. Thank you for asking."

Relieved that he'd hit on something safe, he said, "She was perfectly lovely to me. But I sense that you and she don't always get along. I guess it's a usual mother-daughter thing. You know, competition. Woman versus woman. Generation gap. Pull and tug of who's in charge."

"I guess," Poppy said, but she didn't pick up on anything he'd offered, and her tone suggested something else was on her mind. "Griffin? I have to ask you something."

His heart beat a little faster. He was ready for a personal question, like whether he was seeing anyone in Princeton, or whether he liked Lake Henry, or what he *really* felt about her being in a wheelchair. He could answer these questions. He truly could.

"I'm listening," he said. "Ask me whatever."

"Did you take this cat with me in mind?"

Well, it was a personal question, albeit not one of those he had anticipated. He wondered if the cat was sick and Poppy was trying to break it to him gently. "Is something wrong with her?"

"No. She's sleeping up here on the bed, right beside me. Charlotte was right. She's a lap cat. But she's also blind. So I'm asking whether the in-stant you realized that, you thought of me?"

"As in, thought you'd want this cat?"

"As in," she pushed, "thought it'd be a good *pairing*. She's handi-capped. I'm handicapped. Was that it?"

"No," he answered honestly. "I didn't think that. I didn't take her from Charlotte with you in mind at all. I took her for myself, because she . . . touched me."

"Because she's blind?"

"Because she deserves a good home."

"Because she's blind?" Poppy repeated with some insistence.

"Yes. Maybe that."

"Is that how you feel about me?"

He chuckled. "Looks to me like you have a good home."

"But not a man. Not a relationship. So there you are with the kind of sensitivity that makes you want to give a blind cat a home, and that same kind of sensitivity might be what's bringing you here to me. I just wanted you to know I'm not that hard up. There are lots of men who've been af-ter me since the accident."

"I'm sure there are."

"Have you met Jace Campion? He owns a forge over in Hedgeton."

"A forge?"

"He's a blacksmith. Well, he only does that once in a while now. It was his father's business, but there aren't many people around here with horses anymore. Jace shoes the few that need shoeing, but when he's not doing that, he forges metal into beautiful pieces of art. His stuff is shown in New York. He's been written up in all the magazines. He's rolling in it. I mean, he's really made it."

Griffin didn't respond. He sensed that the way to deal with Poppy was to let her air everything out.

"I'm telling you this," she obliged, "so you'll know that I could be with someone if I wanted. I don't want your pity. I don't *need* your pity. Jace is asking me out all the time, and he isn't the only one. So if you're here because that soft heart of yours is touched by my *situation,* I want you to know that the situation isn't what you think it is. I'm not desperate."

Griffin barked out a protest. "Thanks a lot."

"That came out wrong."

"I'm not desperate either, Poppy. I could be dating lots of other women."

"Why aren't you?"

"Beats me," he exclaimed. "They'd be a hell of a lot less prickly than you are." He thought about that and calmed. "But prickly is fun. It's interesting. Those others don't intrigue me the way you do."

"It's curiosity, then? Wondering what it's like to do it with a paraplegic?"

"Oh, come *off* it, Poppy," he scolded. "If you don't have more faith in me than that, there's no hope for us at all. You intrigue me because you think. You're a leader. You act. You do what you want. I've never aspired to make love to a paraplegic." His voice softened. "I do aspire to make love to you. I spend lots of time wondering what that'd be like. It's making me physically uncomfortable."

"Physically uncomfortable, as in repulsed?"

"As in hard, Poppy. Hard."

She was silent for the longest time.

He wondered if he'd grossed her out. "Are you still there?" he finally asked.

"I'm here," she said, but her voice sounded different. He could swear it had a broken quality to it.

"Are you crying again?" he charged, trying to make a joke of it so that he wouldn't hurt quite so much inside himself.

She sniffled. "It's been a rough day."

"Your visit with Heather?" When he heard something that sounded like a moan, he said, "Are you okay?"

"I guess." But she didn't sound it. He heard a soft hiccuping.

"I'm coming over."

"No." There were more sniffles, and then a half-wailed, "No, I'm okay, it's just that you say amazing things sometimes, and I have my sensitive side, too."

"I can be there in ten minutes."

She gave a nasal laugh. "You can not. You'd kill yourself—skid right off the road into a tree—just like Marcy McCleary—Marcy Smith—Micah's wife—former wife."

"Late wife," Griffin amended. "I get the picture. Now tell me about Heather. Did she say something?"

"I don't know."

"What do you mean?"

"She might have. Or I might be wrong."

Griffin waited. When the silence stood, he said, "You're not gonna leave me hanging like that, are you?"

"I just don't *know*," Poppy cried, and he sensed they'd come full circle. This was where she'd been when he had first called.

Quietly, he asked, "Is she Lisa?"

"I don't know."

"Did she give you any clues?"

Poppy didn't answer. And he didn't want to push. She was independent; he liked that about her. She had lived a long time without him. He had to let her think things through. "Can I come over in the morning and make you breakfast?"

"I can make myself breakfast."

"I know that," he acknowledged, "but I like to cook, and the setup on Little Bear is primitive. So indulge me, Poppy. Either that, or take pity on me. Let me use a real stove. Come on. Be a sport."

"Haven't I heard that one before?"

"Let me make breakfast."

There was a pause, then a hedgy, "What do you make?"

"What do you like?"

"I asked you first."

"Okay. I make omelets. I make pancakes. I make a terrific French toast."

"Baked?"

"Can be. What do you say?"

"That sounds pretty good. I like French toast."

"Is eight too early?"

"No."

"It's a date, then." He instantly regretted his choice of words, half expecting her to object. When she didn't, he was heartened. Very gently, he said, "When we're done, will you tell me what upset you so about Heather?"

There was a pause, then a quiet, "We'll see." And an even quieter, "Griffin?"

"Hmm?"

"Thank you." It was half whispered.

"For what?"

"Calling. To see how things went with my mother. Caring that I was upset. People don't usually do that."

"That, dollface," he quipped, because his heart was beating up a storm and he had to make light of the moment, "is because you put out messages saying that you're entirely independent and self-sufficient—and you *are* those good things. But it's nice to have someone do something for you once in a while, isn't it?"

"Yeah," she drawled, apparently agreeing that a lightening of emotions was needed. "Drive carefully."

"I will. Sleep well."

"You, too."

*   *   *

Cassie was working late, though she had little to show for it. Still, she was absorbed, to the extent that she jumped when Mark put a hand on her shoulder. She put a quick hand over his.

"Come to bed," he said.

She smiled. "Soon."

"You said that an hour ago." He paused, took his hand away, and straightened. "This is not getting better."

No. It wasn't, and it was her fault. The deal that they'd agreed to in couples therapy was that they would go to bed together, at the same time, several times a week, whether it was to talk, to make love, or just to lie close. They hadn't done it now in days.

She pushed a hand through her hair. The blond curls were totally unruly—more so than usual, surely reflecting her own lack of control. "I'm sorry. I just . . . need this thinking time."

He leaned over her shoulder to peer at the papers spread on the desk. "Is this Committee stuff?"

"Some of it is. We really do have to safeguard the lake. We drink that water."

"I thought you finished the cost work on Friday."

"I did. Three police officers, one for each eight-hour shift, plus a cruiser, plus testing equipment—it's not that expensive. It could be covered by a nominal increase in property taxes. I'd say that's a small price to pay for peace of mind."

"Who's saying no?"

"The usual suspects. Alf Buzzell and the lived-here-all-my-life camp say we're imagining a threat, that Lake Henry is as safe as it's ever been. Nathaniel Roy and the live-free-or-die camp say we don't want a police presence. Willie Jake and *his* camp say that they know what it takes to guard this town, and if we *really* want to prevent someone from dumping lethal stuff in the lake, we'd have to hire *nine* guys, so that three can patrol at any given time. That camp says one guy at a time would be so ineffective that it'd be a pure waste of money. And they don't want the property tax going up."

"How does the Town Meeting vote line up?"

"In our favor, I think. But it'll be close, so either way there will be unhappy people."

"You need to do a PR campaign. You need to educate those people about the dangers."

"We are," she said, gesturing toward the papers that a friend in Concord had put together. "Unfortunately, some people are happy burying their heads in the sand. They don't want to know the risks. They like their lives as they are, right now, today."

Mark pulled at the corner of a paper that lay at the bottom of the pile. Not a paper, actually. A photograph. Cassie stared at it right along with him. Even after hours of studying it, she was startled.

"This is either Lisa Matlock or Heather Malone," he said. "Trick question?"

"No trick. It's Lisa."

"Oooh. You have a problem."

"Correct, and Heather isn't helping. So there's the possibility that she's unable to help. I've spoken with two psychiatrists who say she may be suffering from post-traumatic stress disorder. But if we don't know what the trauma is, we haven't a leg to stand on. Either she doesn't understand the risk of silence, or she is so guilty of this and more, that anything she says will condemn her."

Mark drew back to study her. "You're her champion. You're not supposed to think that."

"Maybe not," Cassie said ruefully, "but I don't know how else to think. I've gotten some preliminary stuff from California, and it describes a woman who could easily, easily, easily be Heather. This picture sends the same message as the ones in the newspaper clippings I've seen. Okay, so I have expert witnesses prepared to testify that handwriting analysis can be unreliable. But I have nothing else. Nothing. Heather is a dear friend of mine, but I can't mount a defense." She could feel herself getting worked up. Again. "She won't give me anything to work with. *What* am I supposed to do?"

"Get information on Lisa."

"That won't help Heather."

"It will if she's Lisa. If she's Lisa, and she's also the woman we know, there has to be a good reason why she ran that guy down. The woman we know isn't a murderer. She isn't prone to hysteria or to mad fits of anger. She isn't manic-depressive, and she isn't insane. So there's a reason. Up until now you've been obsessed with proving she's Heather—"

"Not obsessed," Cassie cut in.

"Yes, obsessed, and that's okay, Cass, because you're a loyal friend. But maybe now you need to come at it from a different angle."

Cassie turned to look at him. "And how am I supposed to do that," she said. It was more a statement of frustration than a question. "What funds do I have? None. Micah's up to his ears in loans for his new equipment, and even then he offered to take out another—at least, he offered that at the start, but he's so angry at Heather right now that I'm not sure the offer still stands. So how do I get information on Lisa?"

"Griffin."

"Griffin's an outsider and a journalist."

"He got you this photograph."

"He got it for Poppy. No, Mark. I need an independent person working for Heather, but that means paying costs for transportation, room and board, time by the hour, plus fees for getting the information, because there are always those. I'd use our reserve, but you say it's too low. What am I supposed to do?"

"Use Griffin."

"I can't trust Griffin."

"Is it that? Or is it pride?"

Cassie was stung. "That's not fair."

"You're a prideful person. You admitted it last week."

In therapy. She had. Now she felt defensive. "I said I took pride in what I did and, because of that, I sometimes had trouble letting go of an issue. But that's different from refusing help out of pride."

"How?"

"Taking pride in my work is positive. You can find fault with me when I spend too much time on a case, but that's a good thing for my clients, just like it is for your students. Refusing help out of pride is negative. It suggests that I don't go all-out for my clients. I'm a better lawyer than that."

"Forget lawyer. Think person. Think *woman*. You do take pride in doing things yourself."

"I like getting things done."

"By *you*, and I understand that, Cass," he argued. "You left town after high school when you should have stayed, so you need to make up for the time you were gone."

It had only been eight years, through college and law school. But during that time, her father had died of cancer, her sister of drugs, and her mother of loneliness. Cassie hadn't truly understood what she should have done until she'd married and become a mother herself—and having children had been crucial to her. Creating a family, and doing it right, was one hope for a second chance. Working her tail off as a lawyer was another. And even in spite of these two things, she would live the rest of her life wishing she had been there for her parents and her sister.

Mark went on. "You don't need to prove yourself all the time. Do you honestly think that anyone holds the past against you, after what you've done for the people of this town in the nine years you've been back?"

"Yes," Cassie said. "I do think so. My parents' friends remember what I did. There's always a little dig when Alf makes his lived-here-all-my-life argument to me. Same with Nathaniel Roy. On the surface, he's pleasant enough. But the truth is, he resents what I did those years away, and resents that I came back and took control. If I call in Griffin Hughes, the old guard will have more to resent."

"Do you care?"

"No. Yes." Sighing, she admitted the quandary. "I do care. I want the respect of those people. But then there's Heather. What do I do about Heather? I've never felt so stymied in a case."

"Call Griffin," Mark suggested again and stood. "I'm going to bed."

*　*　*

Poppy lay in the not-quite dark of a night lit by the moon reflecting on snow. She wasn't thinking about Griffin, though she had for a while when she had first turned out the lamp. Nor was she thinking about Heather, because she had done so much of that earlier.

Now she was thinking about Perry Walker. He had been a handsome guy—six feet tall, sandy hair that flowed to his shoulders, laughing eyes and a wide smile—the life of the party until the very moment of his death. He'd been telling her a joke, shouting over the growl of the snowmobile. The joke had likely been either off-color or politically incorrect, because Perry delighted in being irreverent. She couldn't remember the words, though. They had been lost in the horror of what had followed.

Moaning at the memory, she threw an arm over her eyes, then quickly lifted it off when she felt a movement at her side. It was the cat. She had been curled up near Poppy. Now she sat, her head aimed at nothing in particular.

"Why are you awake?" Poppy asked softly.

Victoria yawned. She lifted a paw, licked it, ran it over her eyes.

Poppy wondered what she felt behind those lids, whether there was the same lack of sensation Poppy had in her legs. She wondered whether Victoria remembered seeing things and, if so, whether that helped her function without sight.

Memory didn't help Poppy. It hurt. She started by picturing Perry as he had been those weeks before he'd died, and the next thing she knew, she was trying to picture what he would be like if he had lived. She figured he would have had a whole slew of kids, not because of any major plan or religious conviction, but out of sheer carelessness. He was a randy guy. He had enjoyed sex the way he enjoyed hockey, hunting, and beer. He would no more have considered using a condom than he would have loaded his rifle with blanks.

Poppy had been six weeks late once. To this day, she was sure she'd been pregnant. She had never had it confirmed—was too afraid—hadn't been able to *begin* to consider the ramifications—and then it was a moot point. Her period had come in a rush of blood and cramps.

At the time, she had simply thanked her lucky stars and gone on the pill. After the accident, during those weeks in the hospital when she had nothing to do but think, she decided that divine design was behind the loss. She wouldn't have been able to mother a child. She had no *right* to mother a child.

It was just punishment.

Like being confined to a wheelchair.

Like never skiing again.

Like doing nothing so much as even *kissing* a man.

Then she had a thought. She wondered what it would have been like if the tables had been turned. Wondered what Perry would have done if she had been the one to die. Wondered whether he would have been the one to reform.

Victoria walked to the edge of the bed and, lowering her front paws down the comforter, slipped to the floor. Poppy watched her walk toward the window and sit squarely in a patch of moonshine. There she groomed herself, looking confident and content. At one point, she raised her face toward the window. It was open a notch, as was Poppy's habit. She liked to hear what was happening outside. It made her feel less at a disadvantage.

Approaching the wall beneath it, Victoria put her front paws up. With a graceful little bound, she was up on the narrow sill, making herself narrow to match it and settling in like a duck with her nose to the spot where the cool air came in.

Poppy wondered whether she had always been so deft, or whether it came with blindness. The cat was certainly adventurous. And independent. Once she had food and litter, she was also self-sufficient. Granted, having been unceremoniously passed from Charlotte to Griffin to Poppy, she hadn't had a choice about trying new things, but she had certainly done it with style.

Of course, Victoria wasn't weighed down by guilt.

*   *   *

Micah had barely fallen asleep when he was awakened by a small cry. In an instant, he was out of bed and across the hall. He found Star was sitting up in bed, whimpering.

He hunkered down. "Are you sick?"

She shook her head.

"Bad dream?"

She nodded.

He looked at the other bed. Missy was sound asleep.

"Want milk?" he asked Star.

When she nodded, he scooped her up, settled her on his hip, and left the room. He didn't turn on the light in the kitchen. It would have been too harsh, given how raw he felt. Thanks to the moon, the night was plenty bright. He could see his way.

Setting Star on the counter, he poured her a cup of milk. She held it with both hands and drank slowly—tasting, swallowing, tasting, swallowing. Watching her, he felt a clenching in his chest. Star had been special right from birth, so grown up, as though she had come from the womb knowing what she faced, and was equipped to deal with it. But she was still a child.

With her eyes on the milk, she whispered, "It was just me in the dream."

"Just you? Where was I?"

Solemnly she said, "I dunno."

"Where would I *go?*"

She shrugged.

Taking the cup from her hand, he set it on the counter and pulled her close. The feel of her arms clutching his neck brought tears to his eyes. "I live here," he whispered fiercely. "With you. I'm not going anywhere."

He held her very tightly for another minute, carried her back to bed, and sat with her. Even after she'd rolled to her side and curled her hands under her chin, he felt them around his neck. He hadn't known much touching as a child. He had always guessed that was why being with a woman meant so much to him. Marcy had been a toucher. That was part of her appeal. And then Heather had come into his life. Her touch was so different from Marcy's, so much more honest and sincere.

So. Was that a big fat lie, right along with where she'd come from and who she'd been?

The possibility infuriated him.

And now, here, Star. And in the other bed, Missy. Heather had taught them to reach out, touch, and hold. Star had tried to do just that in her sleep, and was left clutching air.

Looking at her now, still feeling the trust in her arms and the awesome responsibility that went with it—all his now, his alone—he felt an acute resentment toward Heather. By the time Star turned over, sound asleep, he was rip-roaring mad.

Chapter Twelve

Wanting to work out and shower before Griffin arrived, Poppy was up early Monday morning. She went through her usual routine, first with weights for strength, then the bicycle for flexibility. Victoria sat at the foot of the parallel bars, turning toward wherever she was. From time to time, seeming impatient, she rose, lifted a paw, put it down, lifted her tail. In each instance, Poppy said, "The lap isn't free yet, Victoria. Soon, little girl. Soon."

When she finished up, using the standing table last, she settled back in her chair, wheeled over to the parallel bars, and stroked the cat's head. Words were unnecessary. The cat seemed to know. With uncanny accuracy, she jumped up into Poppy's lap, a small orange body that turned, tested one spot, turned a little more and tested another. Poppy couldn't feel the weight on her legs, but once Victoria was settled snug up against her, her belly felt the warmth.

Keeping a hand on the cat and taking comfort from her, Poppy studied the bars. Aside from their being at waist height rather than overhead, they weren't terribly different from the monkey bars she had used on the school playground when she was growing up. Tomboy that she was—*competitor* that she was—she had easily crossed those using the momentum of her swinging body to give a boost to the pull of her arms. Her arms were stronger now than they'd been then. She was also heavier, but not by much. She barely topped 110. That wasn't much weight to hold up.

She could move herself down these bars doing what gymnasts did, shifting her weight from one bar to the other. But traversing the bars wasn't the point. The point was using them for stability while she swung one hip forward, then the next. She could teach her hips to do that. With practice, it would work.

Still with a hand on the cat, she looked across the room. There, on hooks that made them easily accessible, were a pair of leg braces. They weren't pretty. And they were a major hassle to put on. *And* they made noise—she hated that the most. The tiniest little mechanical click made her think of a robot, which, as far as she was concerned, was ample reason not to use the things.

Besides, at best she would need crutches, and, even then, she would lurch. She didn't know why she should do that, when she could wheel herself around ever so smoothly.

Yes, she remembered Star Smith up in the woods while she was back at the door feeling frustrated and impotent, growing panicky when she realized that she couldn't go after the child. But that was an isolated incident.

It would be different if she had kids of her own. Maybe then it would be worth the effort to try to walk.

But she didn't have kids. She probably *shouldn't* have kids. She wasn't the most responsible of people. Not in the long run.

*   *   *

" 'It's no mistake'?" Griffin echoed. "Are you sure that's what she said?"

"Watch my lips." Poppy mouthed the three words. Her lips were licked clean of the syrup she had poured on his oven-baked French toast, which he had to admit was the best he'd ever made.

She mouthed the words a second time.

"That's pretty clear," he agreed. "She's Lisa then?" When Poppy bent over, put her cheek to her knees and her hands on her ankles, he felt a wrenching inside. "You're not going to cry again, are you?" he asked, fearful. It broke his heart when she cried, because she was such a strong woman. Besides, they needed to strategize.

"No," she said quietly. "I just . . . feel . . . weary."

He stroked her head. Her dark hair was short, but it was soft and thick and clean, even lingeringly damp from the shower she just finished when he arrived. He ran his fingers through it, lightly massaging her scalp.

"The question," she said in that same tired voice, "is how the Heather I know could have killed Rob DiCenza—or *anyone*."

Leaving his hand in her hair, he spoke quietly. "That's the direction we take. We assume that Lisa is not the villain the DiCenzas make her out to be, and we try to find the reason she might have run him down. But there's a problem. My friend Ralph is hitting a wall. No one in California is willing to talk, and the only person we have on this end is Heather."

"She wouldn't tell Micah a thing."

"But she mouthed those words to you. So there's an admission."

"She may deny it. She may hate me for telling you."

"She may fry," Griffin said and regretted it when he felt Poppy stiffen. Cupping her head with both hands, he leaned close. "I think we need another opinion. Can you get someone in to cover the phones while we go for a ride?"

* * *

After dropping the girls at school, Micah stopped for gas at the station on the edge of town. He had barely run his credit card through and started the flow of gas when a truck pulled up on the opposite side of the tanks. Three men were inside, all Lake Henryites. He had gone to high school with two of them; the third had moved to town later. They worked for a local builder and, from the looks of them, were on their way to a job.

"Hey, Micah," Skip Houser, the driver, called out as he climbed from the cab. "How's it goin'?"

Micah nodded and focused on what he was doing. He wasn't in the mood to talk.

"Sun's rising higher," Skip said, unscrewing his gas cap and inserting the nozzle. "S'posed to be high thirties today. Are you laying tubing yet?"

Micah was closely monitoring both the Weather Channel and his barometers. High thirties today, and who knew what tomorrow. A spell at forty and the sap could start to flow, which meant that on top of everything else, the season was messing him up by coming early. He planned to start with the tubing that morning and work like the devil was on his tail.

None of this being Skip Houser's business, he just grunted an indifferent, "Nah."

"We're puttin' up this big house other side of West Eames," Skip went on. "Don't know as I'll be able to help any with sugaring this year. I feel bad, your being without Heather and all. She worked good. I liked her."

Micah didn't care for his use of the past tense.

"Is she doing okay in jail?" Skip asked and hitched his head toward the cab of his truck. "Dunfy in there spent a couple weeks locked up for foolin' around with Harry Schwicks' little girl before she admitted she was lying. He says the place isn't so bad."

Dunfy was the one not originally from there, but Micah knew about him. He was a no-good slime who had probably done everything the little girl said and more. He wasn't worth Heather's spit.

Riled that Skip had put Heather and Dunfy in the same category, Micah pulled out the gas nozzle. The tank wasn't full, but he didn't care.

He was screwing on the gas cap when Skip said, "Did you know she was Lisa?"

It was one remark too many, and it just hit him the wrong way. Micah slowly raised his head. "Did you say something?"

Skip, who had never been terribly bright, took that as an invitation. "I asked if you knew who she really was. I mean, man, here you're living with her all this time."

Micah hauled open his door. "Who says she's Lisa?"

"Hey, it isn't just me. Most everyone in town's saying it. I was hearing it again just now at Charlie's. Hell, it's all over the Ridge. We keep waiting to hear something else, only nothing's coming out. It's like Heather just showed up here one day with no past at all—and then we think of her palling around with the son of a senator and maybe even going to Washington if the guy had been—"

"You don't know nothing, Skip," Micah cut him off. "Keep your filthy mouth shut." He put a foot in the cab.

"It isn't just *me*."

"Then tell *them* to keep their filthy mouths shut."

Skip sniffed in a nervous way. "You don't *pay* me enough to do that, bud. I've worked for you, remember?"

"Yeah, I remember," Micah replied. "I remember you bitching and moaning from three in the afternoon on, wanting to go home, get a beer, stuff your face. Well, I don't need you, Skip. I don't need you, and I don't need your buddies." He slid in, started the truck, and pulled out. He didn't look back. He didn't have to. He knew he was being given the finger. Three fingers.

But he meant what he said. He didn't need them around. As far as he was concerned, if they came to help this year, they would give the syrup the same bad taste as if it was too late in the season to be tapping at all.

*   *   *

Poppy and Griffin took separate cars. She insisted that it was easier this way, since the Blazer was fully equipped for her and her chair. Now that she had a sub at the phones, she told Griffin, she might not come straight back. She might stop to see Lily, she told him, or drop in at the bookstore to see Marianne. What she didn't tell him—because she was afraid he'd invite himself along—was that she might stop in at Charlie's for lunch. The sun was bright, quickly melting the new-fallen snow. The café's glassed-in porch was a haven on days like this.

"Baloney," Griffin teased. "You just don't want to be seen with me."

She hesitated for a minute, then admitted, "That, too." He ought to know. Showing up at the café with him would give people something to discuss other than Heather, but at Poppy's expense. She was taking enough of a chance entering the center of town now with Griffin's truck on her tail. John McGillicudy paused in raking snow from his roof to wave. Maddy Harris waved as she walked her dog. Luther Wolfe and Mercedes Levesque waved from the post office porch.

She waved back to all of them—and with some enthusiasm. She felt revived, much better now that she was actually doing something for Heather. And, yes, she had Griffin to thank. She had been spinning her wheels, going nowhere with Heather's confession until she shared it with him.

That didn't mean the town had to know they were working together.

Totally aside from romantic speculation, she didn't know how it would play.

Fortunately, Cassie's office was around a bend and out of sight from the center of town. It was in a small, pale blue house that had white trim, a picket fence artfully capped with snow, and a large oak plaque hanging from the porch. *Cassie Byrnes, Attorney At Law* it said in raised, midnight blue letters.

* * *

Cassie prided herself on being proactive and bold. Ideally, she would have approached Griffin, rather than the other way around. But she wouldn't have done it yet. She wasn't ready. She was still mulling over what Mark had said. Besides, she had a new client coming in that morning, a woman from the Ridge who had finally agreed to seek a restraining order against an abusive boyfriend. She didn't have the *time* to seek out Griffin.

But Poppy had called and requested a meeting, and Cassie trusted Poppy. So there was Griffin, pulling into the driveway right behind Poppy's Blazer.

Watching him jog gallantly up to Poppy's door and give her a hand with the lift—a hand that Poppy didn't need, but that was charming, nonetheless—Cassie tried to put her finger on what bothered her about Griffin. Mark had hit the main point: Griffin was an outsider. Because of that, Cassie couldn't trust him to have Heather's best interests at heart. But there was more. He was a writer, and that made her uneasy. He was well-connected, and that made her uneasy. Mostly what made her uneasy was that he wanted Poppy. Cassie was nearly as protective of Poppy as she was of Lake Henry, as she was of Heather.

But she was getting nowhere with the latter, which was a source of frustration and, yes, embarrassment. Mark was correct there, too. Her pride was wounded. It bothered her that she couldn't help Heather.

It also bothered her that her office was a god-awful mess. Cassie knew the Griffin type; she had gone to college and law school with them. Their image of law firms was of the rich, male variety, with fine art, mahogany, marble, and Oriental rugs. Those firms hired assistants who were paid to type labels and organize files, but Cassie couldn't afford that. Her office was an ecclectic collection of file cabinets, bookcases, and work space, added over the years as the need arose. Her walls were covered with the fine art of three children under the age of seven, and her pens had cartoon characters, pom poms, and other doodads affixed to the ends, gifts from said children. If all that suggested a lack of professionalism, she had never thought twice about it before now.

She loved her office and resented Griffin for making her apologetic. Of course, he must have known that, because he smiled at the chaos of books, papers, and files, and said an amused, "Cool," before taking the seat Cassie had pointed him toward.

Then she forgot about the office, because Poppy told her what Heather had mouthed the afternoon before.

She wasn't ready for that news any more than she was for Griffin, but it explained many things. Feeling a vast sadness, she hung her head. When she raised it, she let out a discouraged breath. "I suppose it makes sense. If it's true, we need to build a defense."

"That's what we have to discuss," Poppy said.

Griffin asked, "Legally, what happens if you admit in court that Heather is Lisa?"

"Immediately?" Cassie had already drawn up a pad and was jotting notes quickly enough to shake the googly eyes of the monster at the tip of the pen. "If we drop our resistance to the charges and waive extradition hearings—she gets shipped back to California."

"Supposing that happens," he said. "What's her chance of bail?"

"For a capital case? None. Zero. Waste of breath."

"Capital case?" Poppy looked horrified. "As in capital punishment?"

"Yes. Not that the prosecutors will necessarily ask for that. They don't have premeditation. But this is still a murder case. There wouldn't be bail, unless we come up with something so strong that it makes everyone think twice."

"Like what?" Poppy asked.

Having focused on the mistaken-identity angle, Cassie was just beginning to open her mind to other possibilities. "Like Heather having reason to fear for her life. Like she was threatened, or battered, or raped. By Rob. Or by his father."

"His father?" Poppy said. "Oh God. I never thought of that."

"The problem is we'd need a witness," Cassie said.

"*Big* problem," Griffin injected. "From what I hear, everyone who might have known Lisa has been reached by the DiCenzas. No one's talking. So if there was a witness to anything, he or she is not coming forward, and then there's the PR war. Lisa's lost it, unless we change something fast."

Cassie sat back. Tossing her pen on the pad, she folded her arms. "What do you suggest?" she challenged.

"A private meeting between Heather and me."

"Private? Poppy and I are her friends. Micah's her lover. Why would she tell you, and not any of us?"

"Why can a wife tell a therapist things she can't tell her husband? Because there's a neutrality to it, an objectivity. There isn't the fear of censure. Heather loves you all. She cares what you think of her. She may be frightened of what you'll say. Me, I'm nothing to her."

Cassie had to admit that there was an element of truth in what he said. But he wasn't saying it all. "You're a writer."

"He's not writing about this," Poppy said.

"Then what's in it for him?"

Poppy smirked. "Me. He wants to impress me." The smirk gave way to entreaty. "Cassie, he has resources that we don't."

"And he'd spend them on Heather? Why?" There had to be a catch.

"Because he has a guilty conscience," Griffin put in, and proceeded to explain his role in Heather's arrest.

Cassie felt momentarily justified in her distrust of Griffin. "That's swell. Just swell."

"It's done, Cassie," Poppy argued. "Water under the bridge. He wants to help. And he has contacts."

"Like his brother?" Cassie was still having trouble taking in what she'd just learned. If Griffin hadn't shot his mouth off while he looked at a picture in his brother's office, none of this would have happened.

"Like private investigators who owe me favors," Griffin said. "Rob DiCenza abused women. Lisa sought medical treatment at least twice."

Cassie arched a brow. "And you can connect those two things? You can tie his battering to her seeking treatment?" She had him there; she could see it in his eyes. "Do you have someone who'll testify to the connection? Because that's what we need. Hearsay is no good, rumor doesn't work, and circumstantial evidence is iffy. I'm telling you"—she widened her gaze to include Poppy—"if you can't get firsthand evidence, Heather would be just as well claiming she isn't Lisa at all."

"Which brings us full circle," Poppy said. "Griffin wants to talk with her. Will you set up a meeting?"

Cassie wasn't sure Griffin would get anything more from Heather than the rest of them had. The psychiatrists she had talked with said that if Heather was suffering from post-traumatic stress disorder, the truth might be buried too deep to be unearthed without significant therapy. Griffin seemed liked a nice enough guy—Cassie had to give him that—but he wasn't a psychiatrist.

So where did that leave them? Micah had no money to give, and Cassie might donate her own time, but she couldn't afford to hire a psychiatrist to dig for Heather's truths. Nor could she afford to hire a private investigator to get those truths another way. If Griffin had a PI friend and a guilty conscience, meaning that he would help out on Heather's case for free, far be it from Cassie to object. If she did, she would be proving Mark right.

Besides, while Griffin grilled Heather, she had plenty to do. Griffin was right about the PR war being nearly lost, and he was smart enough to know it mattered. Before Cassie plotted her legal strategy, she needed to know more about the principals in the case, and that didn't mean Heather or Rob. That meant others who could impact a case—in this instance, the governor, the attorney general, and the assistant attorney general of California, Charles DiCenza and his wife, surely the judge who had been assigned the case. If Cassie knew the personalities she was up against, she could more easily craft an approach.

She had calls to make. Griffin wasn't the only one with contacts. Cassie had law school friends in California who would share what they knew. She had John Kipling, who had a network of newspapermen who would gladly tell John what they knew. And she had Mark, who was right yet again. She needed to call and let him know. There was no room for pride in this, either.

"When do you want to go?" she asked Griffin as she reached for the phone.

*   *   *

Micah drove with the window open, hoping that the cold air would cool his anger, but he was still stewing when he turned off the lake road, came down his drive, and saw the dark sedan at his house. Two agents were on the front porch. They were the same ones that had searched the house the Thursday before. One carried Heather's computer.

Just the sight of them brought back the sense of violation he had felt at the time. Pulling up more sharply than he might have, he stepped from the truck and stood there with a hand on the open door.

"That was fast," he said.

"We figured you needed it."

"Wrong. You searched the thing and found nothing, just like I said. The only stuff in there has to do with my work."

"And Lisa's."

"There's no Lisa here. That's Heather's work."

"You're playin' with words. Where do you want this?"

Micah didn't budge. "I want it where it was when you took it."

"Well now, we went through the whole house. Excuse us if we don't recall exactly where this was sitting."

"Where is the work done?" Micah prompted.

The agents exchanged tempered looks.

Drop it on the porch, Micah goaded. *Drop the fuckin' thing, and I'll sue you for malicious destruction of property.*

He was almost disappointed when they came down the steps and headed around to the back. "Is the door locked?" one called.

"Was it last time?" Micah asked. "Did you even see a lock there?"

When they disappeared around back, he slammed his door and followed only until he could see the sugarhouse. Stopping there, he waited, and as he did that, two things ran through his mind. The first had to do with a fragment of the conversation they'd just had.

There's no Lisa here, Micah had said. *That's Heather's work.* And the agent replied, *You're playin' with words.*

I'm Heather Malone, Heather had insisted during that first meeting at the courthouse. It struck him that she'd been playing with words, too. She might truthfully say she was Heather Malone now, though she might have been someone else fifteen years ago—which led to the second thing that hit him. He felt a sudden, intense desire to see what was in that knapsack.

He stood with his hands on his hips until the agents emerged. They walked past him without a word and slid into their car. He watched them back around and drive off, and would have gone straight to the woodpile in the sugarhouse the instant the car was out of sight, if another car hadn't passed it on the way in. This one was a small Chevy that had to be a dozen years old. It was well kept, though. Everything about Camille Savidge was well kept.

Pulling up on the near side of his truck, she rolled down her window. She shot a quick glance behind and asked, "Is everything all right?"

He grunted. "They returned the computer. Didn't even argue much. My guess? The insides are gone. Wiped clean."

Camille held up a handful of disks. "I can fix that. And I can do whatever accounting you need."

Anyone else, and he would have just turned and walked off. But a man didn't do that with Camille. She was too decent a person. So he said, "I'm okay," and prayed that she would leave.

"Can you restore these yourself?"

"Nah. I'll work the way I used to."

"But if you don't know what's on the disks—"

"I'll manage."

"How?"

Anyone else, and he would say something crude. But a man didn't swear at Camille. As civilly as he could, given the impatience he felt, he said, "I'll *manage,* Camille. Can we talk about this another time? I have to work."

"Did Heather leave a hard copy of what's on these disks?"

"I don't know. I'll find out."

"Let me, Micah. I don't have anything to do until later. I want to help."

"Can you get Heather out of jail?" he threw back, and suddenly more just spilled out. "Can you prove she isn't Lisa? Can you make Heather talk? Can you explain to Missy and Star why someone who says she loves them can hide secrets so bad she can't speak up to save her life? Can you explain it to *me?* I can't deal with this Heather, Camille. I want the one I had before. We had a good life. I want it back."

The stricken look on her face made him regret the outburst. Not that he'd had any control. He had kept too much locked up inside, and he felt like it had been there for years rather than days.

Unable to analyze that or to think about Heather for another second, Micah raised both hands in surrender and strode off. He had tubing to lay. He was good at that. More than anything else right now, he needed the routine.

*   *   *

Poppy's plans were thwarted. Lily was teaching, Marianne was at the dentist, and it was too early for lunch. She might have settled in by the woodstove at the general store and talked to whomever came by, but she wasn't in the mood. Nor was she in the mood to see Maida—or anyone else, she realized. She wanted to be by herself.

So she drove around for a bit, actually drove all the way around the lake, with no radio, only the shush of the tires where melting snow wet the road. When she had made the whole circle and was back in the center of town, she pulled in at the church. The spire was sunlit and gloriously white against a clear blue sky. She studied it awhile, then put the car in gear again and drove onto the narrow road that wound through the town cemetery. She coasted slowly, recalling various people who were buried there. At her father's grave, she felt a catch in her throat.

Pulling past it, she sat for a bit, not knowing what she felt, why she was here, what she wanted. Without conscious intent, she drove on. When she crested a small rise, her breathing grew shallow.

She had been to the cemetery in the years since her accident, mourning not only her father, but others from town who had died. Hadn't it been Gus Kipling, John's father, just a few short months ago? She hadn't had a problem then. She had easily avoided this particular spot. Now, though, for the life of her, she couldn't drive on.

Pulling over onto the snowy berm, she let the Blazer idle. She tried to compose herself by taking deep, slow breaths; she tried to distract herself by thinking about Victoria; she tried looking anywhere else but *there*. Inexorably, though, *there* was where her eye was drawn, up past a dozen granite markers of different sizes and shapes to a simple but handsome one that stood in the back looking very much apart and alone.

Even under sun, the winter landscape felt bleak here. Dogwoods flanking the stone were scrawny and bare. What might have been a bench was now a raised rectangle of snow.

But that wasn't why this particular gravestone seemed so alone. Perry Walker had died young, and though there was space here for others of his family, they were all still alive. His stone was the only one in the whole of the family plot.

Perry's parents lived in Elkland now, forty minutes to the north. Poppy had never known if they left Lake Henry because of the accident. Nor did she know whether any of Perry's siblings were still in New Hampshire. She hadn't asked. Couldn't. Didn't want to know. She might well have heard something over the years and just tuned it out. The mind did things like that when a subject brought threat of pain.

Even now, she felt a great yawing inside, the need to veer off and escape. But her eyes clung to that stone, to the neatly carved letters that were visible even from where she sat, as though they had been designed just for Poppy, as though someone had wanted her to be able to see them from the road, to read and remember and regret. Yes, she wanted to run away. More, though, she wanted to talk to Perry.

But the thought of saying certain things aloud, even to a dead man, terrified her.

So she swallowed hard, shifted gears, and gave the Blazer some gas. When Perry called out to her, she accelerated. In no time she had left his gravestone behind. She exited the cemetery without looking back, but that didn't mean she was done. She and Perry had unfinished business. She had to figure out the best way to approach it.

*   *   *

Griffin had no problems getting into the jail. Cassie had made the necessary calls, so that not only was he expected, he was given the privacy of a lawyer-client meeting room. He doubted that would have happened in New Jersey or New York or California. It was one of the beauties of a small and civil state like New Hampshire.

When the door opened and Heather was let in, he felt as though he knew her well. Hair dark despite its silver threads, eyes a striking gray, skin pale, mouth scarred into a smile—all were familiar, after hours spent studying her pictures.

She, on the other hand, was startled.

As soon as the door was closed, he extended a hand. "I'm Griffin Hughes, Poppy's friend. Poppy and Cassie agreed that I should come. Want to sit?"

She ignored the invitation and simply stood by the door, looking as though she might make a run for it if things went wrong. "Why aren't they here?" she asked unsteadily.

"They thought you'd feel more comfortable with just me."

She didn't look comfortable at all. She looked frightened.

Gently he said, "They figured that it was okay if you hated me. But I don't want you to do that. I'm a friend. I'm not here to cause you harm."

When she continued to look frightened, he took a seat. He figured that if she had a height advantage, she might feel more secure. He had already decided not to confront her about the confession she'd made to Poppy. It was enough that she'd made it. That signaled she was ready to talk. Or getting there. Maybe.

"Here's the thing," he said. "It sounds like you won't talk, which means we don't have any leads about where you were before you came to Lake Henry. You can say that you're Heather Malone all you want, but unless we get proof, it isn't worth anything. Lisa Matlock left California fifteen years ago. We need proof that you were Heather Malone before that time. Paperwork will do it. Same with a witness—a friend, relative, coworker. Lawyers use the word 'corroboration.' That's what we need."

"You're not a lawyer," she said in that same shaky voice.

"No. I'm a writer. But I'm not here to write. I'm here as a friend, because I think I can help. My specialty as a writer is investigative journalism. My stories sell because I dig up facts that other writers don't. I can do that because I have a network of contacts. Some are my own, some are my father's. They'll do favors for me. It won't cost you a cent."

She didn't look any more at ease.

"So what we need," he went on in the same gentle voice, "is corroborative evidence. Ideally, we'd look for evidence on Heather Malone, but you won't talk. You won't give us a lead. My contacts are as good as any, but if they have no place to start, they can't go anywhere. We know that Heather Malone showed up in Lake Henry fourteen years ago. Before that, she worked at a restaurant in Atlanta, but only for a short time, and the trail ends there. So this is what we're going to do. We're going to look at it from the other end—from the Lisa end. We're going to try to figure out why Lisa Matlock ran down Rob DiCenza."

Heather pushed her hands into the pockets of her orange jumpsuit. "Why isn't Cassie here? Does she hate me?"

He smiled to soften his words, but that was the extent of sugarcoating he was willing to do. "She doesn't hate you. She feels frustrated, because you won't help."

"Micah hates me."

"I doubt that. If he did, he wouldn't be as upset as he is."

"He hasn't come."

"He's up to his ears in work. And he has to keep tabs on the girls."

She leaned against the door. "If you're going after Lisa, what do you want from me?"

"Anything you can give us on the Heather end. Anything at all. A name. A date. A place. It's kind of a last-ditch effort. See, the other end is tough. The DiCenza family has gotten to most of the people who knew anything about Rob and Lisa, so no one's talking. What I know is this: I know that Rob was abusive. Lisa made several trips to area ERs under assumed names, and she always denied the abuse. I know that she was smart, that she was headed to college on scholarship, that she had no prior record, not even a speeding ticket. I don't think she meant to kill Rob. My guess? It was dark that night, and he bolted in front of the car. She may not have seen him. Or if she did, she may not have been able to stop. It was a field. There were cars parked all over, and he probably just darted out from between them, which would make the crime negligent homicide, rather than murder. I don't think she planned to hit him. I don't even think she knew he was dead. She probably fled before she knew that. She knew how powerful his family was, so she knew she was in trouble just for hitting him. Once she learned he was dead, she just kept going.

"And I don't blame her," he continued. "The DiCenzas had power, and she had none. She knew—rightly—that her story wouldn't be believed. The thing is"—he grew beseechful—"someone had to have seen something in that relationship. Someone had to have heard something—an argument or a threat. Rob DiCenza was a party boy. There were people around him all the time. The records have statements from witnesses saying that Rob and Lisa were seeing each other, albeit on the sly. Some one of those witnesses had to have seen or heard something to suggest that he was less than a gentleman."

"But you said the family got to the witnesses. If they wouldn't talk then, why will they talk now?"

"Fifteen years have passed. That's a long time for guilt to be eating at someone who may have lied. Or that person may be at a different place in his life. He may have a gripe against the DiCenzas now, one that he didn't have then. Or there may be someone else entirely who wasn't reached during the investigation fifteen years ago. Lisa's father said she had friends, but none of them came forward. One of them may be willing to do it now. Someone back then may have kept quiet out of fear. Maybe he—or she—doesn't have cause for fear now."

She thought about that, then said in a quiet voice, "Being Heather, I wouldn't know about that."

He tried to soften her up with a grin. "Any chance you and Lisa are identical twins separated at birth?"

She didn't grin back. Nor did she speak.

"I know," he said. "There's the scar."

She didn't blink.

"Help me, Heather," he pleaded. "Help *yourself.*"

She slipped down a notch on the door, held there by lightly splayed legs. "What's the use?"

"Are you kidding?" he asked. "The alternative is spending the rest of your life in prison. If you insist that you're Heather but you can't prove it, they'll convict you."

"Maybe they'll think I'm insane."

"If they do, you'll be locked up with insane people. I did a story once on someone who got off, quote unquote, by reason of insanity. I wouldn't call what he got 'getting off.' It was brutal."

Her eyes welled up.

He pressed on. "So maybe that doesn't bother you, but it will bother your friends—and your friends are as good a reason as any to at least *try* to defend yourself. They're in your corner all the way. They love you. The longer you stay silent, the more you let them down."

Her chin trembled. Even with the scar giving her mouth the hint of a smile, she looked profoundly unhappy.

He refused to soften the words, but let them stand in the silence that ensued.

Finally she cried, "What do you *want* from me?"

"Just what I said before: A name. A date. A place. I want something that relates either to Heather or to Lisa, something suggesting that the people in California are wrong."

She covered her face with her hands. The legs of her jumpsuit trembled in the area where her knees would be.

"Hate me, Heather," he challenged, taking a chance that she would turn around and walk out the door, but needing to push her that little bit more. "Hate my guts for saying this, but what you're doing is selfish. It's selfish and self-absorbed and shortsighted. You aren't the only one involved here. If you can't do something for Poppy and Cassie and all the other friends you have in town, do it for Micah and Missy and Star. Your silence is hurting *them.* They took you into their lives and their hearts. Shoot yourself in the foot if you want, but don't shoot them. What you're doing to them is not fair. They deserve an explanation."

She lowered her head, and for a minute he feared she might sink to the floor. But she just stood there with her hands over her face and her legs bracing her body against the door. It took all of Griffin's self-control not to say something that would give her an out. He felt cruel.

But he waited, first one minute, then another, then just one more.

Finally, she pushed herself up against the door and dropped her hands. Her eyes were dry. "Aidan Greene," she said in a monotone, and spelled it out. "A-I-D-A-N. G-R-E-E-N-E."

Griffin didn't have to write down the name; it was instantly burned into his mind. "Where can I find him?"

"Now? I don't know."

"Fifteen years ago?" .

"Sacramento." Her eyes grew woeful with the admission.

He smiled sadly, rose, and went to her. Gently, he squeezed her shoulder. "Thank you, Heather. This is good. It will help."

*   *   *

Micah returned from the sugarbush earlier than he might have, but as the afternoon wore on, as he stretched coil after coil of tubing from one tree to the next, as his body tired, the sun fell low, and the shadows on the snow lengthened, the issue of the knapsack loomed large.

Inside the sugarhouse, he went to the pile of wood, uncovered the worn canvas pack, and set it on the worktable. For a minute, only a minute, he was held back by the same old fears. This time, though, his need to know what was inside was greater than his fear of what he would find.

Undoing the buckles, he opened the sack. There were three envelopes inside. He pulled them out.

One was smaller than the others and contained three photographs. They were black-and-white shots, the same two young women in each. They couldn't have been more than teenagers, though it was hard to be sure. Clothing, hair, even the narrow street in which they stood, looked foreign. There was something familiar about their faces. Micah imagined he saw traces of Heather. Mother and aunt? Grandmother and great-aunt? There was no writing anywhere, no date, no notation of any sort.

Replacing the photographs, he turned to the larger envelopes. The thinner of the two bore the return address of a law firm in Chicago and was addressed to Heather at a post office box in that city. He took out the letter it held and read it once, then again. Then he opened the last envelope. It had the return address of a hospital, but there was no addressee, no stamp, no postmark. Inside were two plastic ID bracelets of the kind that hospitals used. Each had been neatly cut near the metal clasp that had held it on. The larger had Heather's name on it, the smaller that of Baby Girl Malone.

That was it, then. Heather had had a baby six months before coming to Lake Henry, and had given it up for adoption through a Chicago law firm.

Micah let out a long pent-up breath. He should have been angry. Heather hadn't been willing to have *his* baby, though she knew he wanted it. Now he could only figure that she had left part of her heart with this child, who, for whatever reason, she had to give up.

He was trying to think what that reason might be and how it played in her silence now, when he heard the crunch of boots on packed-down snow that was starting to soften. He looked up as Griffin came through the door.

It didn't occur to him to hide the knapsack. Along with his anger went pride. Griffin might be an outsider, but there was something about him that put Micah at ease. Maybe it was just that being an outsider made Griffin more objective about the situation. Or maybe it was the fact that Poppy trusted him, and Micah trusted Poppy. Or the fact that the guy had passed a trial by fire on Little Bear, and seemed to be taking it all in stride. Micah needed help.

Griffin spoke first. "Do you know a man by the name of Aidan Greene?"

"No." Micah pushed the envelopes toward Griffin. "These were inside the knapsack. She's had it hidden since she moved in with me."

Griffin looked at the photographs first, just as Micah had. "Relatives?"

"Must be."

Then he read the law firm letter and examined the ID bracelets. When his eyes rose to Micah's, they were eager. "Looks like both of us hit pay dirt today." He told Micah about his talk with Heather. "A law firm can be called. Hospital records can be examined. This is a start."

Micah tried to share his eagerness, but the fear was back. He didn't know the Heather who had been in a Chicago hospital. He didn't know any child. He didn't know the women in the photographs. And he didn't know Aidan Greene.

A door had opened on Heather's past. He was terrified to learn where it would lead.

Chapter Thirteen

Early Tuesday morning, Griffin awoke to the sun slanting in through the cabin window. He hadn't pulled the café curtains the night before; he rarely did. Privacy was a city need. Here, no one looked in. No one even walked by. On Little Bear, he had his own tiny corner of the world. He had lights, though he found himself using candles as often as not. Having mastered the art of keeping the woodstove going, cooking rudimentary meals, and doing his business in a latrine in the woods, he was surprisingly comfortable. His cell phone still didn't work here, but there was an advantage in that. For every wanted call that he had to wait to access until he reached the mainland, there were three calls that he was happy to miss. He had lots of friends, and they called often. He had lots of brothers, and they called often, too. Looking back, Griffin guessed that, totally aside from work, he had been spending two hours a day on the phone— and he hadn't minded it then. It was a way of life.

Here, the phone was an adjunct, not a focus. Here, he saw people face-to-face, and if they remained wary of him, they weren't as wary now as they had been at first. They knew who he was. They greeted him by name. They were getting used to seeing him at the post office, the general store, the laundromat, the gas station. They let him eavesdrop on conversations, which was a remarkable concession.

He didn't need the phone to fill his time here. He was with people— even for breakfast, because when he wasn't at Poppy's, he was with Billy Farraway. The old man had taken to dropping by for fried eggs and toast, and presented such a lean and hungry figure, in the broadest sense of the word, that Griffin made him breakfast even when he himself was going to wait to have breakfast later with Poppy. Billy was a relic of the Lake Henry that had existed when Charlie's Café was one wall of the general store and served little more than ham and beans. He never said much, but what he did say had charm.

This morning, it was barely seven when Billy came by—and that was another thing Griffin had noticed. Waking up early. It came naturally here. Of course, there was no night life to speak of, but Griffin didn't miss it. He felt good. The bruise on his face had healed. His muscles weren't sore anymore. He felt stronger than he had in ages, more energetic.

That was one of the reasons he set off for town as soon as Billy was gone. Another was the Farraway bon mot for the day. *'Round here,* the old man said in his crusty voice, *you gotta look up to live right. Look up for the sun, look up for the crow, look up for the crown of the tree. Good crown, good sap. Loud crow, loud tap.*

Griffin stopped by the general store long enough to fill his mug with coffee and catch the pulse of the town before heading for Micah's. He arrived just as Micah was returning home from dropping the girls at school.

Draining the mug, Griffin climbed from the cab of his truck. "I gave the information to my investigator," he said as he fell into step beside the taller man. "He's the expert. He'll call when he learns something. Need any help here?"

Micah shot him a look that perfectly reflected the general sentiment at Charlie's. Sugaring season was coming on fast. With the sun strong for a second day in a row, snow was melting off the cupola, icicles were dripping from eaves, the air was gentler on the lungs, and the world smelled promising—all of which created a sense of anticipation in the rest of the townsfolk, and a sense of urgency for Micah, who now needed to lay tubing through the sugarbush in a handful of days. The race was on; everyone knew that the first run was the best. They all also knew that Micah was putting people off right and left. He didn't want them there, he claimed. He could manage himself. He didn't need favors.

Truth be told, Griffin was doing himself the favor by coming. He had suffered through another tedious talk with Prentiss Hayden the evening

before, and on principle alone wasn't working on the politician's bio today. He wanted to be outside in the fresh air, the sun, and the snow.

Micah went in the back door of the house to pull on a hat and gloves.
He handed Griffin a pair of showshoes, and tossed a pair for himself in
the bed of the truck. At the sugarhouse, they loaded the truck with coils
of piping. Then they headed up the hill.

The first part of the road was already cleared. When that part ended,
Micah lowered the plow and drove on, pushing snow aside with a speed
that had Griffin staring out the windshield in amazement. Had they been
going around the lake, he might have feared they'd end up off the side of
the road. Here, the only danger was in hitting trees, and he knew Micah
wouldn't do that. Instead, they sped up a succession of snow-covered
hills, climbing steadily toward a point high above the lake.

"Sugar maple loves steep slopes," Micah said.

Just then, Griffin didn't care what the sugar maple loved. "How do you
know where the *road* is?" he asked as they barreled on up.

"I know the trees. I know which side of the road each one is on."

Griffin saw thin trees and fat trees. The thin trees looked alike. The fat
trees looked alike. He couldn't make out a pattern. *"How?"*

"They're my life. Besides, I know where the road is. I put it in myself."
He shifted and slowed a bit.

Griffin relaxed commensurately. "When did you do that?"

"A dozen years back. I kept buying land, adding to the sugarbush until it got too big to do on foot. Before that, we used a horse."

Griffin smiled. "A horse? As recently as a dozen years ago?"

"And buckets. Some people still use them. Know what it's like to haul
buckets of sap from two, three thousand trees?" He pulled up on the
snow, set the brake, and left the truck.

Griffin was outside in time to strap on snowshoes, as Micah was doing, and shoulder several coils of the blue plastic tubing. After strapping
on a waist pack with tools, Micah loaded up with coils himself and led
the way.

Griffin had used snowshoes at his grandfather's cabin, but they were
the old-fashioned wood kind. These were smaller and made of alu-
minum. Once past the first few awkward steps, he was able to walk with

surprising ease. Staying on the surface was a decided improvement over his last attempt to help here, when he had sunk in with each step.

Micah was all business. "See that black tubing?" he asked.

Griffin did. It was roughly an inch in diameter and skirted the area in which they were headed.

"That's the mainline," Micah explained. "It's wider than what we're bringing in now, and it stays up year-round. Leaving it here takes some care, but it's easier than taking it down."

Griffin could understand why. The mainline was held in place by a system of steel posts, cable wires, and small plastic ties, the latter affixed every foot. Every foot. In a fifty-acre spread? He couldn't begin to count the number of ties used in all.

"End of season," Micah went on, "after I've flushed the thing out, I cover the openings with tape. Otherwise, insects get inside and nest. The last few weeks, I went over every inch of mainline. I had to replace a couple of parts that squirrels and deer chewed away. What we're putting in now is the lateral line. It carries sap from trees to mainline. Mainline takes it down the hill to the sugarhouse."

Griffin was intrigued by the process. He was also intrigued by how much Micah had said at once and without the slightest edge. Clearly sugarmaking was a good thing for him.

Now he was silent, but his actions spoke for themselves. After tying one end of the thin blue tubing around the tree farthest from the mainline, he stretched it to the next closer tree, then the next. He worked around alternating sides of successive trees—right side, left side, right side, left side—maximizing the tension to hold the tubing in place.

From time to time, he indicated that Griffin should brace a section until the tension picked up, but words weren't necessary here, either. Griffin caught on; he began to anticipate a need and be there.

"DTS," Micah said at one point. "Downhill, tight, and straight."

That was self-explanatory, too.

Not that Griffin was minimizing the job. There was clearly an art to it, and Micah was a master. He knew how high to wrap the tubing, how tight to pull it, how to eliminate slack when it occurred. He knew how to connect it to the mainline using small fittings and other little gadgets that he pulled from the pouch at his waist. Moreover, he seemed to have a mental map of the entire sugarbush, such that with only a glance at the code on the tiny tin tag on each coil, he knew exactly which trees matched which coil.

"You're skipping these?" Griffin asked when Micah completely by-passed several trees.

"They're too small," he explained. "In another couple of years, those ones'll be sap givers, while these two big ones here will be retired. It's a theory of sugarbush management." As he spoke, he pointed at the trees with his eyes. His hands weren't taking the time off. They worked steadily—wrapping, stretching, connecting, clipping.

Tying no more than four trees to each mainline connection, he fin-ished one area, moved to the next, finished that one and drove on. The truck was nearly empty when a cell phone rang.

Feeling a quick anticipation, the hope that Ralph might have located Aidan Greene, Griffin reached into his pocket. But Micah's hand was the one that came up with the ringer.

"Yeah," he said into it. "Nothing . . . no . . . twenty minutes." He dropped the phone back in his pocket and set off with the last coil. "Poppy has lunch at the house."

Griffin felt anticipation again. This time it lasted not only for the twenty minutes—on the nose—that it took to finish laying the last coil and drive back down to the house, but through lunch. All he had to do was look at Poppy, and he felt a lift. Her eyes were a warm brown, her cheeks pink, her hair adorably messy. She smiled easily, insisted that Griffin eat the half of her tuna sandwich that she claimed she couldn't finish, and repeatedly reassured Micah that Aidan Greene was their lead. She was also wonderful when the school called to say that Star was sick.

"I'm on my way," she said and pulled on her jacket. Then she paused.

*   *   *

There was something Poppy needed to say. It was hovering there in the kitchen, between Heather's fingerprints and Micah's brooding. He stood by the phone now, with his brow furrowed and his eyes on the floor. She wheeled over to him.

"We didn't talk about the baby thing," she said quietly. "Are you okay with that?"

He raised somber eyes. "No. She should've told me."

Poppy agreed. But she could see Heather's side, too. "It was part of her past, and that past involved another man. Maybe she felt you didn't want to hear that."

"I knew she'd been with a man before me. I'm not stupid. She wasn't a virgin. And she wasn't in love with another man when she came here. No lingering thing. I knew that. So why couldn't she tell me about the baby?"

"Maybe she associated the baby with the man."

"A baby's a baby. If she'd been pregnant when we first got involved, I'd have taken the baby. I wouldn't have cared about the man if she didn't."

"But it was part of her past," Poppy repeated, needing to make this point. "It was over and done. Why did she have to tell you that?"

"Because she loved me," Micah answered. "At least, she said she did. You don't keep secrets like that from someone you say you love. Having a baby is a big thing for a woman. How could she never say a single word about it?"

"Maybe she just couldn't."

"I can't buy 'couldn't.' "

But Poppy knew it was possible. "You said it yourself," she pleaded. "Having a baby is a big thing for a woman. Having to give it up could be even bigger. There are all sorts of emotions tied up with that."

Micah grunted. "Well, I'm getting tired of it. I have emotions, too. I have feelings. I have two little girls, and I don't know what to say. These things are starting to come out, and all I can think is that I don't know the half."

Poppy might have said the same thing herself. She hadn't expected all this. Nor had she expected to feel guilty on Heather's behalf, but that did explain why she felt such a need to defend her. "About the baby, I'm sure she thought you'd be hurt."

Micah obviously had considered that. Silent as he usually was, he was eloquent now. "She could have said it was a hard pregnancy and that she couldn't survive another one. She could have said that after giving one baby up she couldn't bear to have another. I wouldn't have agreed with her, but it would have been better than her saying nothing. And you—you were her friend, Poppy. Woman to woman, she couldn't tell you? Doesn't that bother you?"

"Yes," Poppy said. It bothered her a lot. "But I don't know the circumstances surrounding that baby's birth."

"Because she won't say."

Poppy sat back. She didn't know where to go with the discussion, particularly with Griffin sitting right there. He was staying out of it, and wisely so, but she knew he was listening.

So she felt she couldn't say more, certainly couldn't make the kinds of arguments that might convince Micah. Besides, defending Heather was one thing; moving ahead was another. And they did need to move ahead.

Facing Micah with a new resolve, she said, "Maybe she needs help. Maybe we need to say the words for her. Break the ice. Let her know it's okay."

Micah went to the table and gathered sandwich wrappers. "I don't know if I can say it's okay," he confessed, but more quietly.

The statement disturbed Poppy. She turned her chair to follow him. "You can't forgive her?"

He crumpled up the wrappers.

Micah was a good person. He was honest and decent and loyal. Poppy needed to believe that he was capable of forgiveness—and if he wasn't, she didn't want to know. Besides, Star was waiting. "Can we talk about this again another time?" she asked.

He pushed the crumpled wrappers into the trash can. Straightening, he frowned. Finally, he gave a short nod.

She gave his arm a squeeze, then turned and wheeled out the door.

Griffin followed her to the Blazer. He didn't push the argument, didn't ask how she understood Heather so well, didn't mention Poppy's accident, though she knew that he knew there was a connection. Seconds before she was on the lift, he cupped her head from behind, tipped it back, and kissed her forehead. "You're a very kind person," he said.

She didn't say a word. She couldn't. Her throat was too tight.

* * *

Star wasn't terribly sick. She was tired and said that her head hurt, but she wasn't feverish, and she revived the instant Poppy belted her into the passenger's seat. Sensing that she needed TLC more than Tylenol, Poppy took her home to see Victoria. Leaving Annie at the phones, the three of them burrowed in bed with the television on and the sound very low.

Star was more interested in the cat than the TV. "Does she sleep with you?" she asked.

"Uh-huh," Poppy said. "Every night. I think she likes the down comforter. See how it makes a little nest around her?"

"If her eyes are closed all the time, how do you know she's sleeping?"

"See the way she's curled up with her head on her paws? It's a safe bet she's napping."

"Her ears are moving."

"She's listening to us talk."

Star whispered a dramatic, "Shhhhhhh," and lightly, very lightly, stroked the cat's orange fur. She giggled when Victoria nosed around to her palm. Moments later, the cat was up, wading across the comforter to the foot of the bed. "Nap's done," the little girl sang, then gasped when the cat seemed to fall off the end. Star scrambled up on all fours, crawled to the edge of the bed, and looked over.

"She's okay," she reported to Poppy. "I think she wants to be closer to the TV."

Victoria went up on her hind legs against the bureau. Seconds later, she tried to jump up. Her claws missed by a fraction of an inch. She missed a second time, but made it the third. Leading with her whiskers, she explored the TV.

Star snuggled up against Poppy again and, considerately, whispered, "Does she know she's blind?"

"Not like we would," Poppy whispered back. "Not consciously."

"So she doesn't feel bad about it?"

"What's to feel bad about? It looks to me like there isn't much she can't do."

"She can't see birds."

"But she can hear them, better than we can. I watched her yesterday. She was at the window listening to a big old crow outside."

"Daddy hears the crows. That's how he knows the sap's coming. Poppy, the kitty's eyes are always closed. Does she have eyes—I mean, *real* eyes—inside?"

"I think so," Poppy said, though she doubted it. She assumed that Victoria's lids had been sewn shut precisely because there was nothing behind them, but she feared the starkness of that would upset the child.

"If her lids are down," Star mused, "everything's dark all the time. That would scare me. I don't like the dark. But she doesn't seem scared. She just keeps trying things." Star squealed then. "Look, she's up on *top* of the TV. She isn't scared *at all*."

"Cats are curious—more curious than scared."

Star tipped her head back in the hollow of Poppy's shoulder, so that her eyes met Poppy's. They had lost all humor. "Momma says I shouldn't be afraid, but I can't help it sometimes."

"What are you afraid of?"

"The dark."

"What else?"

"Daddy leaving."

Poppy was about to assure her that Micah wouldn't leave, when Star went on. "I'm afraid of Missy locking me in the bathroom and no one knowing I'm there. If I was a cat, I could climb out the window and jump down and then go around the front and come in the front door and scare Missy. I wish I was a cat."

Poppy gave her a hug and held on, because Star was the most beautiful child in the world, making this moment sweet when so much else was sour. *Not sour,* Poppy reminded herself. *Scary.* If Poppy were a cat, she might be handling things better. She might be confronting Heather, or telling Maida the truth. Or kissing Griffin.

Star gave her an excuse to put off these thoughts. The child was warm. She demanded nothing but Poppy's arms—gave Poppy the same kind of unconditional love that Victoria did. Just then, she seemed perfectly content, and that was important to Poppy. She needed to know that she could do this right, if only for a little while. She needed to focus on Star so she didn't fixate on Griffin or Maida, or Perry, or Heather, or the baby that had been given up for adoption. Especially not on that.

Had things been different, Poppy might have liked to have a baby. She could admit that to herself. It would have been nice, had things been different.

* * *

Had things been different, Poppy might have invited Griffin to stay for dinner. Missy and Star were home with Micah, all three well fed by the beef stew that Maida had brought Poppy, which Poppy had quickly divvied up and delivered to Micah along with the girls, and there was Griffin, who had helped Micah all day and was now badly in need of a shower and food.

But Tuesday nights were for the Lake Henry Hospitality Committee, which meant that Marianne, Sigrid, and Cassie were coming. Poppy half wished it wasn't so. She knew they would be talking about Heather, rehashing old stuff, imagining new, getting nowhere. She half wished she could spend the evening with Griffin.

Instead, she gave him a rain check for Wednesday night, though when the time came around she was having second thoughts. She had showered in advance, had put on a silk shirt, black jeans, and boots, had fiddled with her hair and her eyes and her cheeks—all things that she absolutely should not have done, lest he think this was a date.

But she owed him for helping Micah, which he continued to do, and he was coming here each day to shower anyway, with or without news to report about Heather, and he had a right to see his cat, though Poppy had absolutely no intention of letting him take the cat to Princeton.

Besides, Poppy liked him.

So she set two places in the kitchen, using the brick red placemats, napkins, and coasters that Sigrid had woven for her at Christmas, and had just finished checking on the Rock Cornish hen in the oven when he showed up fresh from the shower. He looked delightfully damp, smelled decidedly good, produced a bottle of wine that was definitely a grade above her usual, and promptly uncorked it.

"We're celebrating," he announced, filling two glasses. "Aidan Greene's been found."

Poppy's eyes opened wide. There were so many things to ask, along with the fear of asking *any* of them. So she settled for a simple, "Oh my."

Griffin smiled as he handed her a glass. "Micah had the exact same ambivalence on his face, like finding Aidan Greene is at the same time the best news and the worst."

Quietly, Poppy explained, "I feel an affinity for Heather." She didn't want to hear anything bad. But there might be something good. So she asked a cautious, "Is Aidan Greene someone we want to acknowledge?"

"My guess is yes. He was Rob DiCenza's best friend."

Poppy's heart sank. A best friend would take Rob's side. "Well then, he *won't* help."

"He wouldn't at the time of the accident." Griffin opened the oven and peered inside. "Did you make this?"

"My mom did. I just put it in the oven."

"It smells incredible." He closed the door and straightened. "At the time, Aidan Greene said he was in the men's room that night and nowhere near the field of cars when the accident happened. Later, when the police questioned him about the relationship between Rob and Lisa, he gave the party line. Less than a year after that, though, he pretty much disappeared."

"Disappeared," Poppy asked, "as in *he* had something to do with Heather's baby?" The baby remained foremost in her mind.

"Disappeared," Griffin corrected, "as in left Sacramento and slipped off the radar screen. He had a great job with the DiCenza Foundation, but he quit it, moved away, let friendships die. That's why we had a hard time finding him. People suggested he might be in different places, but no one knew for sure."

"So where is he?"

"Minneapolis. He's a school counselor there. He has a wife and two kids, and lives the kind of quiet, careful life that keeps his name out of newspapers, social circles, police blotters. Ralph tracked him down through a cousin who accidentally bumped into him in an airport."

Poppy took a drink of her wine. She didn't want to know. But she *had* to know. "What did he say?"

"Nothing. Ralph hasn't approached him yet. He thought I might want to do it myself, but I can't—at least, not for another two or three days, until the tubing's all up. So he'll approach the guy himself tomorrow."

Poppy remained cautious. "Why do we think he'll say anything different now from what he said then?"

Griffin opened the oven again. This time he reached for mitts and pulled out the pan. "This is done," he decided. Setting aside the mitts, he took up the serving pieces lying nearby and started filling each plate with half a hen, roasted potatoes, and an array of vegetables. "We think he'll say something different now, because fifteen years have passed and the man's done an about-face. Back then, he had a great job, lots of friends, and a private line to the DiCenzas. He has none of that now. He's settled into total obscurity. People don't usually go from one extreme to the other like that unless there's a reason for it."

"Maybe he was tired of California," Poppy offered. "Maybe moving was part of his master plan."

"Maybe. But maybe he couldn't live with the DiCenza restraints. Maybe he didn't like being told to keep quiet."

"If that's so, and if he had a different story to tell now, wouldn't he have already gone to the police? He must read the papers. He must know that Heather's been arrested."

Griffin put a plate at each of the table settings. "He may need a push. Ralph'll try. If he strikes out, I'll go." He gestured her to the table. "I'm sorry to be so impatient, but my body is saying that it earned its keep today. I am starved, this smells divine, and we aren't waiting a second longer. May I help you with your chair, madam?"

Poppy couldn't help but smile.

*   *   *

She was still smiling later that evening. The hen, potatoes, and veggies were gone. The wine was gone. The table was gone, or more aptly, they were gone from it and had settled into the sofa by the fire. Even Poppy's chair was gone, off to the side where she couldn't see it, so that she could pretend she was as physically able as the next. Harry Connick Jr. crooned softly. The fire blazed and popped around the bark of each birch log that Griffin added. Griffin himself was sprawled on the sofa, within arm's reach, but not touching.

Close, but no cigar, Poppy thought and studied his profile. It felt familiar in ways that her fantasies hadn't imagined. She felt absurdly close to him, absurdly content. "I shouldn't be this relaxed," she told him. "Not with everything that's going on."

Griffin turned his head against the sofa back. With the absence of incandescent light, his hair was more auburn and his eyes a darker blue. "You sound like you feel guilty."

"I do."

"What Heather did or didn't do isn't your fault."

"I know. Still. She's my friend."

When Griffin didn't respond, Poppy looked back at the fire. Seconds later, he caught up her hand. He didn't do anything with it, just laced his fingers through hers. It felt nice enough, safe enough. So she didn't pull away.

"Want a kiss?" he asked and dug into his pocket with a free hand.

"No. No kiss. I'm stuffed."

He settled in again. "Tell me about the accident."

Her eyes flew to his. She didn't pretend to think he was talking about the Sacramento accident. There was an intimacy in his face, an intimacy in the moment. In her dreams, she could pour out the whole thing and still be loved.

"It was a long time ago," she said with a sad smile.

"Tell me anyway."

She returned a dry, "Tell me what you already know."

He smiled so sweetly that her heart turned over. "I won't apologize for that. It's part of who I am. After I met you last fall, I wanted to know what happened."

"Tell me what you know," she repeated.

"There was a party—an outdoor affair in the middle of December, with a big bonfire in a clearing up in the hills. You'd all gone by snowmobile, and there was lots of booze. You and Perry left. The snowmobile took a turn too fast and hit a boulder. You were both thrown off. Perry was killed. You lived."

Staring into the fire, Poppy allowed herself to recall it. "I didn't want to at first. Didn't want to live."

"Because of Perry?"

"Yes. And my legs. It was one of those awful things that so easily could have been different. If we'd only been a few feet to one side or the other, we'd both be whole."

"You're whole."

She didn't reply.

He took her hand to his chest. "Were you and Perry in love?"

"I don't think so. We were lovers. But it wouldn't have lasted. We were too different." She rethought that. "Actually, we weren't. We were too alike. That was the problem. We had the same wild streak, the same need to rebel. Neither one of us could temper the other, but I think that good relationships need partners who do that—a head and a tail, yin and yang."

"Do you think about him often?"

"I try not to."

"That didn't answer my question."

Looking at him then, she found his eyes level with hers. "I think about him more since you've come."

"Why?"

She gave him a crooked smile. "You know."

"Not for sure. I want to think it's because I'm the first man you've let come close since him."

She didn't say anything.

"So where's it going, Poppy? I'm sitting here wanting to kiss you and not daring, because you could as easily chew me out as kiss me back."

She wouldn't chew him out, she decided. The thought of responding to his kiss held appeal. It was part of good wine, good company, a good fire. It was part of the dream.

"Say something," he whispered.

She didn't know what to say.

"You told Micah," he began softly, "that he might have to break the ice and say the things that Heather couldn't. If I were to do that with you, I'd say that you do like me—you like me more than any other man who's come along—but you don't feel you have a right to do some of the things that you want. It's a kind of punishment. For Perry."

Poppy didn't deny it. "He's dead, and I'm alive."

"Do you have to punish yourself for that? How long does the punishment go on? When is it done? When do you get to go for the gold?"

Poppy didn't know.

"Am I all wrong?" Griffin asked unsurely.

She took her hand back, still laced with his, and studied their fingers; his were more masculine than hers, but they were woven together as neatly as the threads of Sigrid's mats.

"You're not all wrong," she said softly. It was easier not looking at him. "I may be punishing myself."

"It was an accident."

"It could have been prevented. If we'd been going slower, if we'd had less to drink, if it hadn't been so late at night and we hadn't been so tired. We thought we were immortal."

"We all feel immortal at that age. And it's not like you punish yourself in everything, Poppy. You've made a good life. You're productive. You're comfortable. You just won't allow yourself to go beyond a certain point."

Her eyes met his. "What point?"

"Adventure. Skiing. Snowmobiling. Taking risks. Having a husband and kids."

"My sister Rose says I'm unfit to be a mother."

"Your sister Rose is full of shit."

"Griffin, I do have limitations. The fact is that I'll never be able to walk."

"Maybe not the way I do."

"Or dance. Even if I got past all that guilt, there'd be the guilt of knowing that if I get involved with a guy, I'd be holding him back."

Griffin made a face. "That's a crock of it too, Poppy." In a second, he was up off the sofa, going to the stereo, switching CDs. By the time he was back, the opening bars of Collin Raye's "In This Life" were filling the room.

He hunkered down in front of her. "I want to show you how we can dance, but you have to trust me."

Poppy did trust him. But she was frightened.

Before she could say so, he slipped his hands under her and lifted her. "Put your arms around my neck," he said, but they were already there, gone up naturally, only in part to fight the fear. Holding her against him, he began to sway to the music, but it wasn't just any old swaying. His upper body moved in soothing ways, rhythmic ways, ways that she could feel, and he kept going, moving gently around the room while his upper body conveyed the beat.

"Relax," he whispered after the first turn, and how could Poppy not? Yes, she was frightened. She was frightened of failing. She loved the music, loved the beat, loved the confident way Griffin held her—and she loved to dance. The accident hadn't killed that urge. She often sat in her chair, swaying to the music. But she hadn't tried it again with a man.

A few more bars, though, and, ever so easily, it happened. Her upper spine loosened, and her arms circled his neck more out of volition than need. She let her body feel the beat, let it slide through her shoulders and her chest. Dropping her cheek to his shoulder, she moved with him, and that, too, was so very easy. Their bodies were totally in sync.

Poppy was just getting started when the song ended. "Replay it," she ordered giddily and did the button pressing herself when he danced them to the machine. This time, she was into the song from start to finish, raising her head at the end, meeting his eyes, smiling in delight.

He kissed that smile and took her breath away, right along with the fear that she couldn't do it, that it wouldn't work, that something would go wrong and spoil the dream. She was feeling dizzy when he drew back.

"Don't stop," she whispered and, sliding her hands into his hair, she returned his kiss. Nothing went wrong this time either, not the mating of lips or tongue or breath—until his arms began to shake. She didn't protest when he lowered her to the sofa and kissed her there, or when he lowered his mouth to her throat, or when he cupped her breasts with his hands. Her moan had nothing to do with protest.

"Do you feel that?" he whispered.

"Oh yeah," she whispered back.

"Is it good?"

"Very." She felt incredibly alive. After being twelve years without, she was stunned. The sensation was stronger than she had imagined. Perhaps she had forgotten. Perhaps memory had been replaced by a new reality. Perhaps, like Victoria hearing more without sight, her breasts had become more sensitive to make up for a numbness below. The thing was, below didn't feel numb. Oh, it wasn't the same as she remembered. But it felt incredibly full.

She was thinking that the fullness was special and that she wanted to see where it led, when Griffin drew back. His cheeks were flushed, his forehead damp, his eyes the deepest blue she'd ever seen. She started to laugh.

Those eyes went wide. "This is not a laughing matter."

She cupped his cheek and ran her thumb over the barest shadow of the bruise he had gotten his first day in town. He was totally dear. "I'm sorry. It's just that you warned me back in October. You said your eyes were dark blue during sex. I mean, this isn't sex, not really, not in that sense, but they are."

"Why isn't this sex?" he asked.

"Because it isn't—you know"—she gestured down their bodies—"it isn't—you know—the whole thing and all."

Griffin drew in a long and slightly uneven breath. Letting a bit of it out, he said, "That is through no lack of desire on my part."

"I can't feel that," she whispered in reminder.

He reached for her hand and would have shown her, if she hadn't pulled it back. She didn't want to feel it wither, didn't want to know when his interest died.

Hitching himself up on his elbows, he said in the lowest, gentlest, most sensual voice, "Then you'll have to take my word for it, Poppy. But I want you to take my word on something else. If you don't want to do this now, I'm fine without. I won't push you beyond what you want to give. This is too important."

Absurdly, she felt tears in her eyes.

"Is that okay?" he asked.

Unable to speak, she nodded.

"There's a price, though," he said. "I know about Thursdays at Charlie's Back Room. I want to go. Be my date?"

Chapter Fourteen

Charlie's Back Room had been a Lake Henry tradition for more years than anyone but the oldest of the old-timers could count. After taking it over from Charlie Senior, who had taken it over from his dad, Charlie Joe, the current Charlie had changed only what his wife, Annette, absolutely insisted upon, namely café tables and chairs to replace rows of benches, and a new sound system. Other than a shoring up, the small, raised stage hadn't changed, nor had the potbelly stove that exuded a welcome warmth in the cold. The place still smelled of old barn board, now mixed with the aroma of coffee in every modern form. Best of all, in Poppy's opinion, was the wafting scent of chocolate chip cookies baked from Charlie's grandmother's recipe and served warm from the oven.

Whereas Saturday nights in the Back Room meant listening to established groups, Thursday nights were for novel ones. Tonight's opener was a boy from the North Woods who played acoustic guitar, but the evening's headliner was a string quartet of fifty-something players who did the Beatles on violin, viola, cello, and bass.

Poppy loved the Beatles. Apparently Griffin did, too. For every opening line she quoted as they drove there, he had the name of the song. So she used that excuse in explaining his presence with her that night.

"He's a die-hard Beatles fan," she told everyone they met as they made their way into the Back Room. "He's been helping Micah all week. I figured we owe him this."

Poppy figured she owed him more than thanks for helping Micah. She owed him for bringing her Victoria, whom she adored, and for cooking oven-baked French toast, which had been salivatingly good. She owed him for respecting her need for caution when it came to romantic issues. On that score, conversely, she owed him for dancing with her. In doing that, he had given her one of the best times she'd had since the accident.

She also owed him for Heather. The whole town did, she decided with no sarcasm at all. If Griffin hadn't been the one to remark on the similarity between Heather and Lisa, someone else would have done it. But Poppy doubted that anyone else would be as compassionate and involved in the aftermath as Griffin was. She doubted anyone would have called in the resources he had. Yes, the town owed him thanks for that.

But old habits died hard. Though Poppy's bringing Griffin to the Back Room was a stamp of approval, the fact remained that he had been in town little more than a week. Poppy found that astounding, given how close she felt to him, but the rest of the town didn't see him as much as she did. Yes, he had survived a trial by fire on Little Bear. But he was still an outsider to them.

That said, he played them well. If he was itching to go with his natural inclination and ask questions, he showed restraint. He remained at Poppy's side, quiet and amiable, letting her make the introductions, ask the questions, take the lead in conversation. After a bit, she actually felt he was being excluded, and began directing the conversation his way.

It was an easy transition, because the talk turned to sugaring. Since Micah wasn't there, and since Griffin had worked with Micah, he was a natural to fill in. He gave a status report on the tubing, an update on the washing, even an endorsement of the new labels. He said that Micah could use help in the sugarbush—and Poppy hoped that the invitation would bring offers. But there were only sad smiles and sympathetic nods. Micah had offended one too many of the townsfolk.

The crowd quieted when the boy from the North Woods began to play, but his repertoire was limited. Within fifteen minutes, he was done and the talk resumed. Griffin seemed comfortable—increasingly so, Poppy realized. He was the kind who could find something to talk about with anyone who approached. With Cassie's husband, Mark, it was Princeton, from which it turned out they had both graduated. With Charlie it was

Little Bear, now that Griffin had a few stories to add to the Owens' collection. With John, it was mutual friends in Boston.

On Poppy's side, there was inevitable speculation. Cassie began by scolding her in a whisper, "You didn't *tell* me you were coming with him."

"I didn't know," Poppy whispered back. "It was a last-minute thing. He loves the Beatles."

"Yeah, yeah, yeah," Cassie teased. "But I'm glad he's here. The Heather situation is up in the air. I was worried there'd be nothing but talk of that, and I'm feeling on the hot seat."

"You're doing your best."

"My best isn't getting us far. Your being here with your guy gives them something to talk about besides that."

"He's not my guy."

Cassie smiled a bit smugly. "Well, you look really pretty anyway. I like your hair. Is it longer?"

"Two days' worth, since I last saw you," Poppy replied with an eloquent stare.

She couldn't joke as easily with Annette, who pulled up a chair as soon as Charlie and Griffin started talking. "He's adorable, Poppy. Charlie wants to be cautious, but look at him, he's failing dismally. There's something about Griffin that he likes. I'm glad he's here. And he's truly gone over you."

Poppy had to deny it for the record alone. Though Annette had neither a mean nor an irresponsible bone in her body, she was a fulcrum for town talk. Anything she said aloud made the rounds, regardless of how lightly it was spoken.

"He is not 'gone' over me," Poppy corrected, "and even if he was, I am not 'gone' over him."

"He's certainly persistent enough. You gave him the boot in October, but he's back, game for the chase." She studied Griffin. "A guy who looks like that must have lots of women to choose from."

"Yup," Poppy said matter-of-factly. "Satisfying him in ways that I can't." The words dared Annette to probe into the sexuality of a paraplegic, which, being old-world in that sense, Annette would not do.

Lily—with the brashness, perhaps *love* of a sister—wasn't as prudent.

When Griffin and John began to talk, she pulled a chair close. "You're wearing mascara. What does that mean?"

Poppy laughed. It was an easy diversionary tactic. "Mom said that when I turned sixteen—those exact same words. Remember, when I was going out with that guy who was the head of the Dartmouth ski team?"

"Oh, I do. I was already away at school, but I heard about him—*and* about one infamous pot-smoking night. So it was experimentation then. You were playing at being grown-up and in charge. What is it now?"

"Wait a second," Poppy chided. "Look at you. You're wearing mascara—and lipstick—and blusher."

"No blusher," Lily said, though Poppy could have sworn she was. Lily had always been the beauty of the family, but she positively glowed now. "Mascara and lipstick," she specified, "and I do it to look extra nice for John. What's your excuse?"

"Survival," Poppy declared, albeit as quietly as the rest of their talk. "I need a pick-me-up. It's been a bad week, worrying about Heather. But if you're thinking I did it for Griffin, think again. He's a friend, Lily. That's all."

"Too bad. I like him."

"I do, too. That's what being friends is about."

"I'm sorry it isn't more. It should be, with a guy like that. You should be thinking indecent things."

Poppy was, but she couldn't get herself to say so. She didn't know if the relationship would go anywhere, didn't know if she wanted it to. At sixteen, eighteen, or twenty, she had lived for the moment. She couldn't do that now, not at thirty-two. In many respects, she was no different from other women her age who couldn't bear to get their hopes up that Prince Charming had arrived. Except, Poppy *was* different. She had a major handicap. That raised the stakes.

"Friends don't think indecent things about each other," she told Lily.

"Well, you should. He's perfect for you."

"Not. He's Ivy League. He's media. He's *rich*, for God's sake."

"Oh, Poppy," Lily scolded under her breath, "so are we."

"Not like he is. He's city. He's society. Can you see me ironing my pretty white linen napkins and tying them up with my sweet little berry rings that match my adorable little centerpieces on each of eight lovely rented tables for the sixth annual New Year's Day dinner at my very vertical and wholly unmanageable townhouse in the wealthiest section of Philly?"

"Griffin doesn't live in Philly."

"New Jersey's close, but you get my point. The fact is, I'm perfect for *me*," Poppy insisted. She was starting to feel peeved. "I knew there'd be talk if I came here with him. Why does everyone think I *need* someone? Am I not functioning well enough alone?"

"You're functioning very well," Lily said in a way that, given Poppy's current mood, would have been patronizing coming from anyone else. But Lily was sensitive. She knew what it was to have a handicap. Granted, the stutter seemed to have gone the way of her single status, but that was on the outside. Lily did have moments of lingering insecurity. They were close enough as sisters for Poppy to know that.

This was not one of those moments, though. Lily leaned closer, sounding as sure of herself as she'd ever been before. "I've been watching the two of you since you got here. You may think he's totally absorbed, talking with John or Charlie or Mark, but he keeps looking back at you, like you're his center . . . his *anchor*. He wants to be near you, Poppy."

"Well, of course he does. I'm his entrée here. I'm his protection."

Lily shook her head with slow conviction. "That's not what I see."

"Well, it's what *I* see," Poppy insisted and, on the verge of a snit, glanced around. "Is there a reason why everyone is harping on this?"

Lily smiled. "I can't speak for other people."

"Then speak for yourself. Tell me something that doesn't have to do with Griffin."

"I'm pregnant."

Poppy caught in a breath.

Incredibly, so did Lily. Her eyes were suddenly open wide, like she couldn't believe what she'd just said. She seemed totally, comically shocked.

"Close your *mouth*," Poppy chided in a whisper, and, grinning, gave her a hug. "What incredible news!"

"No one else knows," Lily said against her ear, "I mean, other than John. I'm barely six weeks along. I wasn't going to tell you yet."

Poppy held her back. "I am *so* happy for you."

Lily's eyes held worry. "Are you? I wasn't sure."

"Why wouldn't I be? Because I can't have kids myself? I can, Lily. I just choose not to."

"Okay, then. But I've had so many good things come my way in the last few months. I feel guilty sometimes."

"Oh, Lily, you deserve it all," Poppy said, meaning every word. "You've suffered through ugly times. It's your turn."

"And you?" Lily asked ever so gently. "When's yours?"

* * *

"Excuse me?"

Griffin looked around as a woman emerged from the shadows. He was in a corner of the general store, which was closed now, and quiet in contrast to the Back Room. He had to come here to call in his flight arrangements. Aidan Greene was refusing to talk. Griffin wanted to have a go at him himself.

Now he smiled and put out his hand. "I'm Griffin. And you're Camille."

Camille Savidge was an attractive woman in her fifties, with chocolate-colored eyes, fair skin that remained dewy and smooth, and a head of gray hair that should have made her look older, but was so thick, long, and shiny with waves that it did not. She dressed simply—slacks, a blouse, a shawl—and in muted colors, but there was an elegance to her that set her apart, something in the dignified way she held herself, the measured way she spoke, the fact that she was a loner and preferred the background to center stage. In her own quiet way, as bookkeeper, accountant, and computer person, she was involved in the lives of half of Lake Henry.

That was what Charlie had told Griffin several mornings before, when Camille had whisked past them emerging from the office, heading down an aisle filled with cheeses, dips, and other appetizer-type goodies, and out the front door. Tonight was the first time Griffin and she had formally met.

"Do you have a minute?" Camille asked him.

Distant chatter came from the Back Room. Griffin had a few minutes yet. "Of course."

"It's about Heather. I know that Cassie is donating her time, and they say that you're not charging either, but Micah is strapped. I have a kitty. If you need something, please let me know."

Griffin wouldn't accept her offer, but he was touched. "That's very generous."

"I've always liked Heather."

"You already do a lot for Micah. He said you were going to work there tonight."

"I did. We were checking the inventory—labels, bottles, jugs, and such—and trying to prioritize the bills, but he kept zoning out."

"Oh, I've seen him do that," Griffin confirmed, "not in the bush—he's all business out there—but when we're taking breaks for coffee or lunch. He's worried about Heather."

"And exhausted. I don't think he sleeps." She grew hesitant. "Does Heather have a chance of beating this?"

"I'll know more in a few days. I'm heading out tomorrow morning. There may be someone with new information."

Camille seemed to want to ask more. After several seconds, though, she simply pressed her lips together and nodded.

Griffin, of course, was curious about Camille's involvement. "Did you know Micah's family?"

She raised both brows and smiled. "Oh yes. They were good people."

"And his first wife?"

Camille reflected on that, then gave an eloquent one-shouldered shrug. "But Heather is a good person, too. I worked with her when she first came to town. I was happy when she and Micah got together. It was the right thing for both of them."

Up to that point, Griffin had assumed that if Heather confided in anyone, it would be in Micah, or in Poppy or Cassie. It struck him now that he might have been wrong. "Are you close to Heather?"

Camille smiled. "We're good friends."

"Do you know about her past?"

"She doesn't talk about that."

"Were you surprised when all this happened?"

"Very. We didn't expect it. Micah certainly didn't. Now he feels so much pressure. If I can lighten that any by helping you find something to help Heather, I want to do it. Will you let me know?"

Griffin nodded.

"Thank you," she said and went off as quietly as she had come.

* * *

Poppy kept a nonchalant eye on the door, and was relieved when Griffin finally appeared. She wanted him there for the main event, didn't want him missing a single song. If they were a pair in loving this, she wanted him beside her through it all.

Flashing her an eager smile, he slipped into his chair just as the violin, viola, cello, and bass finished warming up. Then the fun began. Songs like "Yesterday," "Norwegian Wood," and "Strawberry Fields Forever" seemed made for strings, and this group played them well.

Poppy lost herself in the music. When they moved on to faster songs—"Here Comes the Sun," "Eight Days a Week," and "All You Need Is Love"—she kept time with a hand on the arm of her chair. And how not to sing along with the chorus of "Yellow Submarine"? She exchanged grins with Griffin any number of times, pleased to see him as involved as she was.

At the end of the first set, the quartet took a break, and chocolate chip cookies came around, warm, gooey, and sweet. Cassie and Mark went off to visit on the other side of the room, and the empty chairs must have been too much of a lure—that, or the townsfolk were feeling mellow, or they were just too curious to resist—because people started coming by to talk with Griffin.

Poppy wasn't surprised by the first of the questions. They reflected the ones she'd been getting on the phone. In a matter of days, Heather had gone from being wrongly accused, to being curiously silent, to being Lisa.

"Will she have to go back to California?" asked Amy Kreuger, who had gone to college in Santa Barbara before returning to run the family's poultry farm.

"Will she serve time?" asked Leila Higgins, who relied on Heather's presence at the library and wanted her back.

"Any chance she can beat it?" asked Charlie Owens' oldest son, Seth.

Then the discussion took a subtle shift, and the group around Poppy and Griffin grew, talking among themselves as much as to Poppy and Griffin. It was particularly true when Allison Quimby, head of the local realty office, got going with Anna Winslow, head of the textile mill.

"Heather's been nothing but honest and hardworking since she came here," Anna said. "We all think that."

"Not think it," Allison amended. "Know it. We each have our Heather stories. She's gone out of her way to help all of us at one time or another."

"Do you think she did that deliberately?" Anna asked. "Was she making up for what she did back in California?"

Allison waved an impatient hand. "I don't care what she did there."

"That boy's family does."

"But what about *now*? She's a different person. She's been living an upstanding life for fourteen years."

"A *model* life for fourteen years," Anna insisted. "So does a woman get credit for having reformed?"

"If you ask me," Allison put in archly, "the crime would be wasting taxpayers' money to lock her up, when she's become a productive citizen. Is she a danger to society? I think not."

Poppy *knew* not. Heather was everything good that they'd said—and yes, it ought to count for something. She had often wondered that about her own life, wondered whether the kind of responsible person she had been since the accident counted for something. She wanted to believe it did. She was more generous, more patient, more thoughtful. Was this a change in her basic nature, or simply a reaction to an accident? It didn't matter, she realized. The end result was the same. And for Heather, too. Poppy wondered whether the authorities in California would consider that.

She was about to ask Cassie's opinion, when the music started again. The tunes were more mellow now. "The Fool on the Hill" segued into "Eleanor Rigby," which segued into "Hey Jude." By popular demand, as so often happened in the Back Room, Lily was shouted up to the stage. She sang "Strawberry Fields Forever" and "Yesterday." When, despite raucous applause and Poppy's own wolf whistle, she refused to do another, the quartet launched into the more upbeat "Hello Goodbye" and several couples began to dance in the perimeter of the room. Others followed them during "Here Comes the Sun," with even more of the audience singing along.

Poppy sang. So did Griffin. When he caught her eye, though, she wasn't thinking about singing. She was remembering the way they had danced the night before. His look said he was game.

But she couldn't do it. Not here. Not in front of everyone. Once upon a time, she would have been front and center, leading the pack, dancing with whomever could keep up, but she couldn't do it now. She was different now. She couldn't escape that fact.

There was something else, though—something that was larger in her mind the longer Griffin held her gaze. What they had done together was private. It was sensual and arousing. She wanted to do it again. Very much. But not here.

The show ended with a prolonged version of "Let It Be," and a particularly strong rendition it was. Before the song was halfway done, the better part of the audience was on its feet, swaying. By the time the last note had sounded, the applause was deafening.

Poppy applauded. So did Griffin. They waved to those who left first, said their own goodbyes, and went out to the Blazer. They didn't say much as Poppy drove home, and when they got there, he asked simply, "Can I come in?"

She was terrified. But she couldn't have kept him out if her life had depended on it.

He must have sensed her apprehension and known where they were headed, because by the time he came to her side to help her out, he said, "Let's go down to the lake first."

She didn't ask how she would get there. Having danced with Griffin, she understood the mechanics. "It'll be cold," she warned, but she figured that the cold was the point. There had been heat in that car, far beyond what the Blazer produced. He was slowing things down. She was grateful for that.

Reaching in, he tied her scarf around the collar of her jacket, then zipped his own and pulled on his earband. She pulled on gloves. He pulled on gloves. Then he picked her up and carried her through the snow down to the lake.

It wasn't a smooth trip. The daytime sun had softened the snow, but the chill in the air now had refrozen the surface, so that with each step, his boot stayed flat for a second or two, then broke through and sank.

Poppy didn't complain. She hadn't been out on the lakeshore at night since the first snow of the season had come. "Any other season," she said, "and I do this by myself. There's a dock and a system of ramps. I wheel myself down into the water, slip out of my chair, and swim off."

"I bet you love doing that."

"I love doing that."

"I bet you're a good swimmer."

"I'm a good swimmer."

They reached the edge of the lake. Without shelter here, there was a light breeze. The moon peered through gnarled fingers of clouds, but, even at its dimmest, cast enough light for him to see. "Want to go out a little?"

She nodded vigorously. "You have to go down over some rocks. Here. That's it."

He took the rocks like the pro he'd apparently become since staying on Little Bear, and once he was on the lake, the walking was easier. "I guess you'd have to be a good swimmer, growing up on a lake like this," he remarked.

"Do you swim?"

"Sure do."

"Where'd you learn?"

His mouth twitched. "At a club." He looked at her as he walked. "I'd apologize for that, except it was a really nice club. Dining room, grill room, golf course, tennis courts, two swimming pools—"

"Two?"

"One for Pampers, one for Speedos."

She grinned. "I can't picture you in a Speedo."

He stopped walking. "I was really fast. I used to swim for the team there. Haven't done that in a while."

"Did you like it?"

"Loved it," he said and met her gaze.

"I feel free in the water. My upper body compensates for what my lower body can't do."

"I'm surprised you don't go south for the winter so that you can swim year-round."

"Like the loons?" she asked.

"Like the loons. When'll they be back?"

"In April. Within hours of ice-out. It's uncanny, really. Ice-out itself is something to see. For days you watch the ice getting thinner and thinner, until it's black. Then it gets porous, and, within hours it seems, it just breaks up and goes away. The loons land—I'm telling you—within *hours* of that."

"How do they know?"

"They scout. The males come first—leave the ocean and fly north as soon as some inner voice tells them the seasons are changing. They must come right up the coast, then turn inland and fly reconnaissance missions. They can't land unless there's open water, because they need open water to find fish *and* to take off again. If they were to land on ice, not only would they not have food, but they'd be stuck there until it melted. The first time you hear them in spring . . ." She felt a sudden yearning for that. "It's so nice." She looked up at the sky. "So is this."

The moon was behind one of those fingers of clouds, but that didn't take anything from the charm of the night. There were stars; with a slow scan of the sky, she took them in. Yes, it was cold, but she was sheltered against Griffin. Besides, the cold was half the fun.

"Another week," she mused, "and the moon will be full. This time of year, it's the maple moon. Sugar moon, is what Native Americans called it. Do you know that they were the first sugarmakers?"

"Micah told me that," Griffin said with a grin. "And about sugarmaking being done without slaves."

"Did I tell you about sugar on snow?"

His grin didn't budge. "I don't believe you did."

"If you take hot, new syrup and drizzle it on snow, it hardens into chewy strings. We make a party of it during sugaring. Chewy syrup, raised donuts, and a sour pickle. One taste works off the other to en-

hance all three." Smiling, she tucked her nose in the warm spot just below his ear.

"Cold?"

She shook her head. "Can't feel my toes, though," she joked.

"Well, then." He didn't miss a beat. "We'll have to do something about
that."

He started back across the lake. She left her nose where it was. He
smelled of her aloe soap. She had always thought it had a light, female
freshness. It was still light and fresh, but on him, it was masculine.

Climbing up over the rocks from lake to land, he began the short trek
to the house. Poppy moved her nose up to the very edge of his earband,
and pressed a kiss where her nose had been. Even outside, with the
breeze stirring up a rustle of evergreen limbs, she heard the catch of his
breath. She put her tongue to the very same spot, which was behind the
shadow of his beard. The skin was surprisingly smooth.

He didn't say a word. *That* was a challenge, and Poppy knew about
challenges. Meeting them had been her specialty before the accident.
What she felt like doing, she did. What she wanted, she took. What
tempted her, she chased.

With her chair still in the Blazer and Griffin heading for the steps, it
was easy to forget the twelve years between then and now. It was like she
was able to walk but chose not to—and whyever should she, with a gorgeous guy carrying her off in his arms?

He went in the door, kicked it shut behind him, and carried her down
the hall to her bedroom. She was too absorbed nuzzling his jaw to
protest, and when she had to stop, simply because in laying her on the
bed their bodies came apart, she was equally absorbed by his eyes.

She hadn't seen a hunger like that in more than a dozen years. She
hadn't expected to see it again at all, but there it was. If there were
inklings of fear in the back of her mind, that hunger held them at bay. He
pulled off her gloves, untied her scarf, and unzipped her jacket, and all
the while his eyes held that hunger. His cheeks were ruddy, his breathing
unsteady. Tossing his own gloves aside, he quickly followed with his earband and jacket. Then he crossed his arms, reached for the hem of his
sweater, and whipped it off right along with the shirt underneath.

Poppy wasn't prepared for that. She felt a jolt and, quite helplessly, put a hand out. She had never *seen* his bare chest, much less felt it. It was warm and perfectly shaped, with a smattering of auburn hair in the shape of a T. Fingers spread, she slid her palm over lean muscle and ribs.

He drew in a sharp breath. She looked up quickly, half fearing that he was done, turned off, wanting out—because she was, after all, a paraplegic, and little touches notwithstanding, she didn't know how far she could go, didn't know how far *he* could go.

A little farther, he seemed to say, because he took her mouth then with the same hunger she had seen in his eyes, and how could she not answer it? She definitely felt the hunger. She hadn't been sure that she would. Technically, her sexual organs functioned; she had known that. But sex wasn't just a physical thing. Thanks to her disability, it was wrapped up in a mess of emotional issues. Not wanting to deal with those, she had always before chosen to ignore the possibilities.

But those possibilities were suddenly heady. She felt a tingling, and could have sworn it was in her lower body as well. The brain was able to compensate that way, receiving a message from one place and assigning it to another. She hoped that this wasn't compensation alone. It certainly felt real.

His mouth stroked hers, again and again, deepening the kiss slowly, steadily, until it was very mutual, very open, very intimate—little more than the exchange of a breath or the touch of a tongue. It was unbelievably arousing. Poppy arched her back—so nice to be able to do that—and suddenly he had her sweater up.

"Lift, baby," he whispered, and when the sweater went over her head and she wore only her bra, he took that off as well.

He looked. He touched. She had never felt overly endowed, certainly not compared to her sisters. When she had done this before the accident, breasts had always been incidental. She had never seen them as crucial to her identity, because femininity itself had never been a major issue. Sex was sex—she was a girl, the guy was a guy—girls and guys did it together—it was fun. It was also naughty, because it was not what her mother wanted her to do, and that increased the fun.

So this was new. Griffin's mouth made her breasts feel feminine indeed. Not only did they swell and peak, but the ripples of heat that he caused traveled deep, so deep that she would have writhed had she had the mobility.

That thought was brief. She must have done something, though— taken a sudden breath, pulled back a tad, *something*—because Griffin raised his head.

"Are you okay?" he whispered.

By way of answer, she took his face and brought it down. She initiated the kiss this time, and drove it deeper, because that was one way to stave off scary little thoughts. She loved the feel of his jaw, which was just the least bit stubbly now, several hours after a shave. She loved the thickness of his wavy hair, loved the strength of his neck, loved the way his muscles bunched—back, shoulders, chest—when she touched them. Needing to feel his belly, she pushed her fingers down under the waist band of his jeans.

When he made a choked sound, she stopped short.

"Don't," he said hoarsely.

Horrified, she pulled her hands up and away.

"Don't *stop*," he pleaded, but the words seemed forced, or so her appalled mind heard.

She tucked her hands under the pillows—lots of pillows—more pillows than a normal person would have—pillows that a paraplegic needed to hold one position or another.

He slid to his side and drew her over to face him. He did it gently, pulling one of those pillows to support her back. His breathing was rough, but he seemed in full control.

"What happened?" he asked.

"I don't know." But she did. Of course she did.

"Did I hurt you?"

"No."

"But you stopped."

"Because you did. You made a sound, like more was happening than you wanted."

He took her chin. "That sound was because not *enough* was happening."

Tears welled. "I know. I can't do more. I'm sorry. I can't help what I am."

"That's not what I meant," he scolded, moving his thumb to her mouth. "Not enough was happening, because we were just getting going, and I'm impatient. I wanted it faster, that's all, faster, but that's me being a man and has nothing to do with anything except your being a woman and turning me on." He paused. "What *are* you?" His hand was at her nape now.

"A paraplegic."

"Could've fooled me. I didn't feel anything disabled about what we were doing. It felt like you were enjoying yourself."

"I was until something . . . reminded you."

"You're the one who was reminded. What did it?"

You groaned. Or choked. Or whatever. You'd had enough.

"Tell me, Poppy. Did I do something wrong? Did something not feel good? Not feel right? Did something not feel—not *feel*—at all?"

"I felt," she confessed, because she could be truthful in this. "I felt like a woman. I haven't felt that way in so long."

He caught her mouth and kissed her once, slowly, then again. That fast, she began to feel the warmth of it.

He drew back again, this time resting his ear on the pillow. "Tell me what you're thinking."

"You're a good kisser."

"Not about that. About doing it. I want to do it, Poppy. Do you want to?"

She did. She didn't.

"Are you afraid?" he asked.

She was terrified, but how could she say that? Sex had never terrified her before. Strong women weren't frightened of sex. Rebels certainly weren't.

His smile was exquisitely gentle. "I think you are. I think you're afraid you won't feel what you want to feel. You're afraid it won't work. You're afraid I'll be turned off by something and that I won't be able to get it up or keep it there. Is that it?"

He did understand after all. Her chin wobbled, but she nodded.

"I won't have that problem," he said in a voice that had grown raspy again. "Trust me, I won't have that problem." His eyes fell to her breasts. "You are just so beautiful."

"Maybe there," she cried, "but not—"

"Not where? Your legs?" He ran a hand down. "You can't feel that, Poppy, but I do, and they feel just right." The backs of his fingers brushed their way up her body until they grazed her breasts.

The sensation was so strong that she closed her eyes, put her head back, drew in a breath.

"Your body's working," he whispered against her throat, "so I'm thinking that the problem is emotional. I'm thinking that you feel guilty doing this."

She did, indeed, but his knuckles were lightly chafing her breasts, taking away her breath in the process, and suddenly she didn't care about the other. She might die of guilt in the morning, but she wanted this now.

Taking his face in her hands, she kissed him. Immersing herself in the novelty of it and the pleasure it brought, she pushed guilt away, pushed fear away, until all that remained was the feeling. She focused on that— on the heat, the tingling, the sense of being feminine. She kept it up while he removed the rest of her clothes—focused on the feeling—and it was so intense that she was suddenly the impatient one, pushing away his clothes just to get him closer.

If he was unusually slow or gentle or careful, she didn't know it, because she loved what he did. It had been so long, and she had been so frightened. But the fullness was there, the rising inside, and if the orgasm she had was different from the ones she'd had before the accident, she couldn't say that it was any less satisfying. It was a miracle.

And even if she hadn't climaxed, she would have reveled in his. His entire body shook with the force of it. It was the best thing that had happened to her since wheelchairs with mag wheels—which was what she told Griffin when his wristwatch beeped at five the next morning.

Griffin was not pleased.

Chapter Fifteen

Griffin didn't like the hour, didn't like the darkness, didn't like Victoria butting in between his leg and Poppy's. He didn't like the fact that he was booked on a six-thirty flight to Minneapolis. What really bothered him, though, was the word "thing." "The best *thing* since mag wheels? I don't call what we did a *thing*."

"What would you call it?"

"The best experience of my life," Griffin said. They were lying face-to-face, now, though they hadn't been for long. She had spent most of the night on her stomach, with pillows comfortably arranged. *Stretches the muscles,* she announced in the way she had of needing to remind him that she was disabled. He didn't care how she slept, as long as it was with him, and in truth, he found her backside as exciting as her front. Of course, now he could see her breasts. They had an immediate impact on him. He reached out to touch, thought twice about it, pulled back. "Can't do this now. Gotta get up."

Defying him, she touched his chest.

He held her hand still. "I have a plane to catch."

She pulled her hand free, wrapped it around his neck, and brought him close for a kiss, and it fired him up all over again. He was as hard as he had been the night before—as hard as he had ever been. He whispered her name in a last attempt to stop, but she wouldn't allow it—and how could he stop? She wanted him. If she wanted to call it sex, fine. If she wanted to call it a *thing*, that was fine, too. Yes, he had to catch a plane, but satisfying her was more important.

And so pleasurable for him. And so easy. She might not be able to move her legs, but he could move them. He brought one up over his hip, opening her, and he quickly filled that space. He loved how tight she was, loved the sensual way she moved her upper body. He loved the catch of her breath, the shuddering sighs, the guttural little sounds she made when the heat rose in her. It was all he could do not to come a dozen times in response, but he waited, waited, held back until she peaked first, before letting go himself.

He wanted to lie there with her and enjoy the afterglow, but he did have a plane to catch. So he scooped her up and took her into the shower. Doing this was important to him. *I can't stand in the shower,* she had said, another of those roadblocks she had tried to throw in his way, but he knocked it down like he had the issue of dancing. The grab bars that lined the shower stall offered a perfect little ledge for propping her up while he soaped her, while she soaped him, while they kissed and touched and, incredibly, made love again. Then he wrapped her in a towel, set her out of the stall in the displaced shower chair, and let her watch while he hurriedly dressed.

"I am so late," he said, hopping on one leg to put a sock on the other, "but it was worth every second."

She looked flushed, sated and pleased.

He tugged on his jeans. "I guessed it would be that way the first time I laid eyes on you—no, even before that. I felt it on the phone."

"You did not," she chided, but she was smiling widely.

"I did. There was something between us right from the start. You are unique, Poppy."

She patted the arm of her chair. "I am that."

He wasn't going to deny that part of it. Pushing his arms into the sleeves of his shirt, he fastened two buttons while he chose his words. Then he put his own hands on the arms of the chair and put his face level with hers. "This chair is part of who you are. I have no problem with that. I don't see that it interferes with anything I want in a woman." He kissed her nose. "I love you, Poppy."

He wouldn't have minded if she had cried then. As helpless as he had felt when discouragement made her cry, tears of happiness were okay.

They were appropriate, along with a smile, a hug, and a kiss, not to mention a return of those three words.

There was none of that, though. Her smile faded. Her eyes grew sad.

He steeled himself. If she planned to say something about her disability, he would clobber her. "Poppy . . ."

Tears did come to her eyes, but they weren't tears of happiness. She shook her head slowly and pleaded in a whisper, "Don't say that. Don't spoil this."

"I was hoping to make it even better," he teased, desperate at least for a smile. "I haven't ever said those words to a woman before. It's momentous, don't you think?"

Still she didn't smile.

Pushing up, he finished buttoning his shirt. He brushed his teeth, scrubbed his hair with a towel, combed it first with his hands, then a brush. All the while, she was silent.

"Don't feel you have to say anything," he remarked. "Telling a person you love him is big stuff. I wouldn't want you saying it unless you felt it, which clearly you don't right now. I just wanted you to know how I felt." He glanced at his watch and swore softly. "I gotta go."

*　*　*

Griffin had never had his heart broken. He had always been the one who was less involved, and though he tried to be gentle about moving on, he knew he had caused pain. Now he felt it himself.

It wasn't that he and Poppy had broken up, just that he had wanted her to say those words. Okay, he knew she had hang-ups about the accident. But as a couple, they had something good going, something special. And he was human. He wanted to be loved, too.

She might love him. Or she might not.

Needing to protect himself in that very dark early morning—needing to reclaim the Griffin he had been before he had ever heard Poppy's voice—he drove Buck's truck to the marina where the Porsche was stashed. He greeted Sage with an enthusiasm she had probably never known, and once he was on the highway, he put his foot to the floor.

He was pulled over going eighty-five, and though the state trooper wasn't much older than he was and might have appreciated love-life problems, Griffin took his ticket like a man. When he returned to the road, he drove sanely.

* * *

Poppy picked up the girls and brought them back to her house for breakfast. She knew that Micah would welcome the extra hour to work, and she welcomed the distraction. She tested Missy on her spelling words and baked up a quick batch of cookies when Star mentioned a bake sale. By the time she dropped the girls at school, she was feeling comfortable with her life again. Very comfortable. *Pleased,* actually.

She had satisfied Griffin. The thought of that brought relief. Brought a sense of *triumph.*

On the other issue, the issue of taking care of two little girls, well, she wasn't Heather. Not many surrogate mothers could be as good as that. But she was doing okay at it, for a paraplegic.

On her way home, she stopped by the cemetery and told that to Perry Walker.

He didn't answer.

But then, he was there and she was here.

* * *

Micah was putting in spiles. He remembered the old days, when holes were hand-cranked by a brace and bit, metal spouts were hammered into the trees, and buckets hung directly below. His spiles were plastic now. Each had two feet of thin plastic tubing already attached and hanging down, thanks to the work he'd done late nights for the last few weeks.

Sleep? He didn't need sleep. His bed was lonely and cold. Sleep only caused him to lose focus, and when he lost focus, he thought of Heather, and then his heart positively ached. He couldn't explain the yearning he felt—couldn't explain the sadness that threatened to turn him inside out. Anger was easier to bear than the sadness, so he hid behind that. Heather had kept secrets. She had kept him in the dark. She had betrayed him. That was cause enough for anger.

This—this focus on tapping—was therapeutic. Flatlanders assumed it was mindless work—make a hole, stick in a spout, hang a pail, get syrup.

Mindless work? They had no idea. First off, you had to know where to make a hole. If it was too close to an old hole, you wouldn't get anything worth boiling. If it was drilled straight in, you wouldn't get the force of gravity. And if you agonized over it, you'd take so long that you wouldn't have half the trees tapped by first run.

Micah worked fast. One look and he knew whether a tree needed one tap or two, and he knew just where those taps should be. Using a power drill, he made a hole that angled slightly up as it went in, so that the sap would drip down. He knew how deep to drill and not come out with the darker shavings that meant he'd hit heartwood. Heartwood was no good. Sap came from sapwood, and the shavings from that were light.

Once the hole was made, he inserted the spile and tapped it in. He knew how hard to tap and did it with an economy of motion. He used a fitting-assembly tool to quickly and efficiently attach the drop line to the lateral line, and he didn't linger at it. Once the connection was made, he moved on to the next tree.

For the past three years, he had done this with Heather. He drilled, and she tapped while he made the fitting to the lateral line. They had worked well as a team, moving from grid to grid with remarkable speed. Her enthusiasm matched his. He had never thought of tapping as a chore, because having her there made it fun.

There was no fun this year. What he felt instead was out-and-out anxiety. The sun was high, the snow was thinning, and the crows were cawing up a storm. These were the signs. He could see them, could feel the sap rising. Another couple of days and it would flow. He would bet money on that. And here he was, just putting in the first of the spiles.

A gruff voice startled him with a loud, "Hey."

He looked around fast. Billy Farraway stood not a dozen feet off. His boots were unlaced and planted wide in snowshoes of the ancient wood type. His jacket was undone, but at least he'd had the sense to wear a hat. Granted it was his hunter's hat and cocked far back on his head. The old man would catch his death one of these days, Micah knew. Then again, he was a hardy old nut. He must have gotten the longevity in the family, along with the height. For a man who bent over most of the time, he was surprisingly tall.

"Hey," Billy repeated.

"What're you doing up here?" Micah asked gently.

"Just taking a look."

"You should be down at the lake."

"I heard you were alone. You won't finish in time if you're alone."

Micah turned back to his tree. He drilled a second hole, well to the side and higher than the first, and tapped in the spile. He reached into his tool belt for fittings. "You shouldn't be here, Billy."

"Because my brother forbid it? That was lots of years ago. Isn't it time to let go of the past?"

Micah snorted and muttered a facetious, "Maybe I could, if I knew what it was."

"You don't know? You don't *know?*"

Micah didn't—not about Heather, not about Billy.

"Well, I'll tell you," Billy said, "because it's time, it's time. Your father imagined I was coveting his wife, and there was never any truth to it; we were just friends, but he was a jealous man. Know what set him off? I cried at her funeral. Hell, someone had to. You were in shock and Dale was angry—angry she had the gall to leave him, like she asked for that cancer. Once she was gone, he needed someone to blame, and there I was, her friend, like I'd conspired to disrupt his life. So he blamed me for that and for every other little dream he'd ever had that wasn't about to come true. He blamed me, said I was no good, said he didn't need me, said he'd shoot me on sight if I came up here again, so I didn't. How long's he been dead now?"

"Eleven years," Micah managed to say, though he was startled. He hadn't heard this story. His father hadn't been a talker.

"And we're still listening to him, you and me?" Billy asked. "Well, hell, you're not. You bring me wood. You bring me clothes. You bring me food. And you say I can't help here?"

Micah did all those things. He had a soft spot in his heart for his uncle. Part of it had to do with Billy's daughters, who saw their father as an old man who was backwoods simple and, as such, an embarrassment. Both women lived in the city and rarely returned. But Micah's soft spot came from personal experience, as well. Billy had taught him much of what he knew—had taught him quietly and gently, behind the back of the big boss, the tough boss, Billy's older brother. Micah could remember laughing with Billy. He had never laughed with his father. Dale Smith had been a stern, impatient man with a need for domination.

Micah had been grateful that the man hadn't talked much, because what he said was dark. He hadn't only been jealous of Billy. He'd been jealous of Micah as well.

And Micah's mother? If Billy had helped make her life more pleasant, then that was something Micah and Billy shared. Perhaps Micah had known of this bond on some unconscious level. Perhaps that explained the pleasure he took in providing for Billy.

Now Billy wanted to do some sugaring. "I didn't say you couldn't help here," Micah explained. "*He* did. He said it over and over again."

"Ay-uh. On his deathbed. I did hear that. But he's dead, Micah. This all's yours now, and you'd've done fine if your woman had been here, but she isn't. You've told everyone in town that you don't need help, just like Dale did. Only I know different. You're never gonna get it done in time for first run if you don't let someone help. Well, I'm not just someone. In case you've forgotten, nephew, I've done this before."

"Not with tubing."

"So show me. I can learn. You won't find anyone in town more eager for that than me."

Micah knew he was right. But it was like his father was still *there*, like Micah would be breaking a law, somehow desecrating his father's memory.

"Cripes, boy," Billy finally said, "if you can't do it because you need help, do it for me. Sugaring was my life for more years than I can count, and the maple moon brings it all back. I get this . . . thing in my blood, like it's heating right up before the sap does. I've been here before, y'know. I come up every season and look around. Old Dale, he used to put four taps in a tree, and you're right doing just two. You're also right thinning things out. He resisted doing that, but I'd warrant your output is up. So, okay, you don't want anyone in town knowing I'm here, I won't tell.

Wouldn't want to spoil your image as a gruff guy like your dad. But let me help. I don't have many years left. I want to do it again before I die."

* * *

While Micah let one part of the past go and Griffin chased down another, Cassie called the Chicago office of Weymarr, Higgins, and Hack and asked for Jonathan Fitzgerald. His name was the one on the letter that Heather had stashed in her knapsack.

Mr. Fitzgerald wasn't in yet, she was told, and when she called back thirty minutes later, he was on another line. She didn't want to leave a message, because she knew how some lawyers worked. Leave a name, leave the reason for a call, and at the end of the day they picked and chose which calls to return. For all Cassie knew, the DiCenzas had already gotten to Jonathan Fitzgerald.

So, saying simply that she had a legal problem and doing it in the same secretive way that her own clients did all the time, she held the line.

Ten minutes later, all business, he picked up the phone. "Yes. This is Jonathan Fitzgerald. Who is this?"

"Mr. Fitzgerald, my name is Cassandra Byrnes. I'm a lawyer, and I'm calling on behalf of a client who needs your help."

Either he was a truly decent man or professional collegiality kicked in, because he asked in a pleasant tone, "What's the problem?"

"She had a baby a while back. You helped arrange a private adoption."

"I haven't done that kind of work in a long time. I can recommend someone else, if she's looking to place another child."

"No. There isn't another child. She wants to locate the first. We're wondering if you've kept records and would have that information."

"It's a moot point. I can't give out adoption information. There are strict laws governing confidentiality. You would have to file a petition stating a pressing reason for wanting the information—such as a medical condition."

"My client has been accused of murder. It could be that DNA tests on the child will show a relationship between my client and the deceased that may be denied by the prosecution. Establishing the relationship could be key to my client's defense." Cassie didn't know if this was true at all, but in the absence of anything else, it sounded reasonable. "And I did know before I called that you couldn't give me the information. I'm just wondering whether you do still have it. We're short on time on this end. I would hate to file a petition and wait however long, only to find out that you haven't kept files that far back."

"How far are we talking?"

"Fourteen and a half years."

"The client's name?"

"Heather Malone," Cassie said, because she didn't see any way around it.

There was a pause on the other end, then a surprised, "The same Heather Malone?"

Cassie breathed a sigh of relief. His surprise was genuine. "The same."

"I was wondering, when I heard it on the news."

"I was afraid the DiCenza family reached you before I did."

"I doubt they know about me."

"Then you must have a very good memory."

"Not always. I used to handle a lot of these cases, and most of them were easy. Heather had more trouble than some of the others."

"Trouble?"

"Giving up the child."

"Did she tell you anything about her life, anything about the child's conception?"

"No. She wouldn't. And I did ask, because I felt bad for her. Most of the girls who come to me have someone with them—friend, parent, probation officer—but she was alone."

"Would you have thought she was capable of murder?"

"No, nor extortion." Before Cassie could ask, he explained, "I read about that in the paper. No, the Heather Malone who came to me had trouble taking money at all. Living expenses, hospital costs—she would have paid for everything herself, if I hadn't told her that this was how private adoptions worked. I gave her money to rent a room. When the child was born a week early, Heather returned the rent money she didn't use. Doesn't sound like a gold digger to me."

"Would you testify to that?"

"I would."

"But you won't help me locate the child?"

"I do have those records, Ms. Byrnes, and I'm sorely tempted. But I can't. The law forbids it. On the other hand, if you can come up with ev-idence—*anything*—to show the need for it, I'll go to the judge myself."

*   *   *

Griffin got lost finding Aidan Greene's house, which was precisely why he had Sage in the Porsche. He wasn't good at reading maps. But the Porsche was back at the Manchester Airport, and his rental car here had nothing but a rental car map, which was more attuned to getting the car back to the airport at the end of the day than to helping him find his way between now and then. So he stopped to ask for directions, and was therefore later than he wanted to be. But not too late. The sight of two cars in the driveway of the small brick home on a modest, tree-lined street told him that Aidan hadn't yet left for work.

Griffin parked. The snow was deeper here than in New Hampshire, and the air had no hint of maple sugar warmth. Grateful that he was wearing his Lake Henry layers, he went up the front steps and knocked on the door. It was opened by a woman close to his age. Totally un-adorned, she had dirty blond hair, a young child on her hip, and another in her belly, to judge from the bulge under the oversized shirt she wore. She seemed friendly, trusting, not wary at all.

"I'm looking for Aidan Greene," he said with his most amiable smile. "My name is Griffin Hughes. We have a mutual friend."

She smiled. "You do?" She turned her head. "*Aidan?*" She faced Griffin again. "Are you from California?"

"No, but my friend is." He glanced at her belly. "Is this your second?"

"Third." She gave an affectionate jiggle to the child on her hip. "This one's the second. The first one just got on the school bus. He's Thomas, and he's five. This one's Jessica, and she's two. The one inside here is Brooke."

"Is that a boy or a girl?"

"We'll know soon," she sang good-naturedly as her husband came up from behind. She tipped her head back. "Honey, this is Griffin Hughes. He knows friends of yours in California."

Aidan Greene was Griffin's height, though a bit heavier. Beneath short, straight blond hair that would probably be white in another dozen years, he had fair skin and a furrowed brow. One look at Griffin, and the furrows deepened. Aidan was as wary as his wife was open.

"The bath's ready for Jessie," he told her. "Want to take her in while Griffin and I talk?"

His wife smiled at Griffin and left. Aidan's amiability left with her.

"Who's our mutual friend?" he asked coldly.

"Lisa."

He started to close the door.

Putting a foot in the way, Griffin kept his voice low and urgent. "Please hear me out. My friend is actually Heather—no, my friend is actually Heather's best friend, but only one of many she has in New Hampshire. She's made a good life for herself there. Something doesn't add up."

"Is Haskins your man?"

"Yes."

"I told him I had nothing to say. The same goes for you." He pushed at the door. When Griffin's foot held it, he said, "You're trespassing. Get your goddamned foot out of the way, or I'll call the cops."

"If you do that, I'll have to tell why I'm here. I'll have to tell the papers why I'm here, and if the *Sacramento Bee* gets wind of it, they may come running up here themselves. It took us a while to find you. Someone went to the effort of erasing tracks in the snow, so to speak."

Aidan wasn't amused. "Why are you here? How'd you get my name? What do you want from me?"

"Heather gave me your name, which is why I'm here, and as for what I want from you, I have no idea. She wouldn't say. She won't say much of anything, which means that she'll be returned to Sacramento and put on trial for murder. Think she can get a fair trial there, with all the publicity surrounding this case?"

"That's not my worry."

"Is that why you moved out here and dropped out of the DiCenza scene, so you wouldn't have to worry? I can understand that. Heather's case is definitely cause for worry. Right now, there are a whole lot of people in New Hampshire who are worried." He pulled photos from his pocket and showed Aidan the first. "Here's Heather. This was taken last summer. That's Micah with her. Big smiles here? None lately. She's worried that Micah won't love her if he knows the truth, and he's worried, because he needs her in his life and now she's gone."

Griffin turned to the second photo. "Here's Heather with the girls. That's Missy on the left and Star on the right. Missy's seven, Star is five, like your Thomas. The girls aren't Heather's by birth. Their biological mother died when Star was two months old. Heather came into their lives a few months after that, and at this point she's the only mother they know. They're sweet little girls, *vulnerable* little girls. *They're* worried right now, because they don't know why Heather's in jail or when she'll be back. Having lost their biological mother, you can bet they're wondering whether there's something about them that makes mothers leave. Heather's a good mother, Aidan."

"I don't know Heather," Aidan said, but more weary now than wary.

Griffin brought up the last photo. "She's a gentle, quiet sort. Here she is with her friends. They meet every Tuesday night." He pointed. "Cassie's a lawyer, Marianne sells books, Sigrid's a weaver, and Poppy runs an answering service for the town. Poppy's my girl. She's been in a wheelchair since a snowmobile accident twelve years ago. Heather was a major source of support during her recovery. She's a major source of support for a lot of the town, and these four sophisticated, smart, successful women adore her. She's also an involved mom, always doing things with the girls, always upbeat, always smiling. She reminds me of your wife, which raises the issue of your relationship with Heather. She gave us your name. What were you to her?"

"I don't know Heather."

"Lisa, then. Were you her lover?"

Aidan shook his head. "I was not involved with Lisa."

"But Rob was, and you were his best friend. Tell me something, Aidan."

The man sighed. With the expulsion of breath, the whole of him seemed to sink inward. "Tell you what? That she didn't do it? I didn't see anything."

"That's what you told the police. But then you left Sacramento and severed ties with the DiCenzas, and I'm thinking that you didn't want to have to remember them."

"Didn't want to have to be *beholden* to them, is more like it," Aidan scoffed. "Do you know what that family's like? Do you know the kind of power they wield? Charlie DiCenza can make you or break you, even today. One phone call, and he can get you fired from your job and blacklisted for sins you never considered, much less committed."

"Is that what he did to Lisa?" Griffin asked.

"I don't know what he did to Lisa."

"Do you know what Rob did to Lisa? Do you know that he beat her?"

Aidan said nothing.

"We have doctors who'll testify to it," Griffin said. "And people who'll tell us how dark it was that night, so dark that even if they'd been on that field where the cars were parked, they wouldn't have seen much. So the question becomes if it was so dark that they couldn't see, how could Lisa see Rob? Do you think she deliberately ran him down?"

"I have no idea."

"Was she extorting him?"

Aidan snorted.

Griffin waited. When Aidan said nothing, he asked, "What does that mean?" Still nothing. "Did you know she was pregnant?" Still nothing. "Was it your baby?"

"No."

"Then Rob's? Or even Charlie DiCenza's? A family tie can be proven. If we find the child, tests can be done. Heather put it up for adoption. Did you help her do that?"

"I told you. I wasn't involved. Listen, I gotta get to work."

"I know. I got here as early as I could. By the way, I think it's pretty neat, what you do. Did you get the counseling degree after you left California?"

Aidan nodded.

"And before that, you worked for the DiCenza Foundation. Put those two things together, and I'd say you're a decent person. I'm surprised that what happened with Rob and Lisa isn't eating you alive."

Aidan suddenly looked like it was.

Griffin asked, "Was she the conniving little nasty thing they've made her out to be?"

Aidan looked away.

"Was it first-degree murder?" Griffin prodded. "Premeditated? No one will tell us. No one will talk. So here's a woman who has made something of her life, and all that is about to go down the tubes because a family wants revenge. When does it end? With her execution, for God's sake?"

"It wasn't premeditated," Aidan said and closed his mouth.

"Don't stop there," Griffin warned, "unless they have their claws in you still. Is that it? Did they get you your current job?"

"No." He put a hand high on the edge of the door. Griffin saw a tremor there, but the rest of him—eyes, voice, back—was suddenly solid. Griffin had pushed the right button. It had PRIDE written all over it. "They have *nothing* to do with my job, or my home, or my wife or my kids or my car. Everything I have now I've earned myself, and I've done it even in spite of having to live with the memories of that night. Do you know how memories can haunt? I don't need a shrink to tell me that I became a school counselor to help kids because I couldn't help her. She got a raw deal."

"You say it in the past tense," Griffin said, grateful for an admission of sorts but needing far, far more. "It's not over. It may be just starting for her. We need a story, Aidan. She won't talk, possibly because she's even more frightened of the DiCenzas than you are, but we need to know what happened that night. Your name is the only piece of information she's given us. She hasn't even admitted to being Lisa. You're the connection. So here's your chance for redemption. Talk to me, Aidan."

* * *

Griffin hated failure. Perhaps it had been arrogant of him to think he could get through to Aidan when neither Ralph nor Aidan's own conscience could. Aidan hadn't responded to the pitch he'd made there at the door, nor the one he'd made later in the school corridor, nor the one he'd made in the parking lot when Aidan returned to his car after work.

Granted, Aidan hadn't called the cops. He hadn't even threatened it after the first time. Rather, he waged a war of attrition, holding firm to his silence, letting Griffin make his case again and again, until he finally ran out of steam.

Griffin knew that Aidan could be subpoenaed. He could be questioned on the witness stand, under oath. But that would be at a trial. Griffin didn't want it to get that far.

Discouraged, he took an evening plane back to Manchester. Retrieving the Porsche, he drove back to the marina, retrieved the truck, and went directly back to Poppy's.

* * *

Poppy heard Victoria first. The cat was sitting on the bed facing the door, meowing in the dark. Seconds later, stockinged feet padded down the hall. Seconds after that, Griffin was sitting on the side of the bed.

Poppy stared at him in the dark, cautious on several scores. There was sex. There was love. There was Aidan.

Griffin didn't give her a clue, simply stared back at her. After a minute, he whispered, "Your door wasn't locked."

"It never is. What time is it?"

"Two."

She waited, wondering which of the three biggies was foremost on his mind. When she couldn't bear the suspense, she asked, "How did it go?"

"Lousy. I'm exhausted, so if you want sex, babe, you're out of luck. It's been a long, totally frustrating day. I just want to sleep with you, Poppy. Can I do that?"

She did want sex. She had been thinking about it all day, wanting to know that what they'd done was real and not just another of her dreams, wanting to hear him *say* that he had been satisfied in spite of her limitations and that he wanted more.

But life was about more than sex, and he was clearly upset. The fact that he had come to her touched her. It touched her deeply. And he hadn't said those three words again. He was respecting her feelings on that point.

Feeling oddly satisfied, nearly as pleased as if he had fallen on her in lust, she maneuvered herself back and raised the quilt.

*   *   *

Griffin didn't sleep for more than four hours. His mind was filled with wayward little thoughts that gave him a buzz. The nervous energy he had would have made a mockery even of sex. He needed to be up, on his feet, doing something distracting.

Leaving Poppy in bed, he plugged in his computer, accessed his e-mail, then ran a quick search of Cindy pseudonyms. He had last done it six days before, but with the approach of March, new publications would be posted.

His heart skipped a beat when a finding came up for one of the names on his list. Following the link with a shaky hand, he found a poem. It spoke of dreams as the first step in overcoming regret. There were barely a dozen lines, some of only one or two words, but the poem was powerful. As far as he was concerned, it had Cindy's fingerprints on it.

Hurriedly, he jotted down the name of the poem, the author, the publication and page. There was no clue as to the poet's whereabouts, but a call to the magazine's editorial department might help. Unfortunately, it was Saturday. His hands were tied until Monday.

Frustrated, he tore off the slip of paper and stuffed it in his pocket. By the time he logged off, he was more restless than ever. He needed to do something that was physical, practical, and positive.

He arrived at Micah's just as the girls were going off with Camille for the day. Micah was tapping. Griffin wanted in.

Billy Farraway was already there. He sat on the tailgate of Micah's truck with his hunter's cap perched on the back of his head and his legs hanging down, looking for all the world like he was going to work. Griffin might have asked about that, if another truck hadn't come down the drive. Pete Duffy emerged from its cab at the same time that Micah came out of the house.

Both men stopped. They stared at one another.

Micah said, "I thought I told you not to come."

"That was last weekend," Pete replied. "This is this weekend. Time's running short. My guess is the sap'll be running Monday or Tuesday."

"Tuesday. It'll be running Tuesday."

"Tuesday." Billy echoed.

Pete said, "I'm off work for three days. I want to help."

"Do the Feds know you're here?"

"No," Pete snapped. "This is my business, not theirs. I don't work for them. I never did. The only reason I came here with them that morning was because Willie Jake told me to, and I do work for him."

"Does he know you're here?" Micah asked.

Pete didn't blink. "Sure does. He has no problem with it. You're the only one who has a problem. So you can stand there and call me a traitor, or you can take me up on my offer. If you have Billy and Griffin, my being here makes four. That's two teams. It means twice as much work gets done."

"How do I know you won't sabotage the operation?"

Pete looked away for an angry moment. When he looked back, he said, "I always liked you because you were smart. You knew what you wanted. You knew what you needed to do. You learned what you had to in order to broaden this operation—and you can say Heather did it all you want, but she wasn't the one going to maple school over in Vermont all the time to learn the newest this and that. You did it, Micah. She helped, but you did it, and you did it because you take pride in this place. So why are you going stupid now? Use me, man. *Use* me."

"He's right, Micah," Billy said.

Micah shot the old man a dark look. Flippantly, he turned that dark look on Griffin. "You want to put in your two bits, too?"

Griffin considered it for a minute, then shook his head. "I just need to work."

* * *

They worked through Saturday and Sunday, twelve hours each day, well into the darkness, lit by strobes on the bed of the truck. Griffin had never been more tired in his life, but there was satisfaction along with the fatigue. By Monday noon, every south-facing slope had been tapped and was ready to go. Given that these slopes comprised two-thirds of the sugarbush, and that south-facing trees gave up their sap first, it was an achievement.

In another world, Griffin might have taken the rest of the day off. But Micah was in charge—more to the point, Mother Nature was, and she was closing in fast. There were still more than a dozen acres to tap.

But he needed an hour to himself, he told Micah. No. Two hours. He promised to be back then.

While he drove, he accessed calls from Prentiss Hayden, his editor, his brother Alex, and a pair of friends. When a message came from the magazine where he had seen what might have been Cindy's poem, he pulled over. That was the only call he returned. The editor was agreeable; she had recognized his name from his own work, hence had returned his call this quickly, but she had no name for the poet other than the one printed in the magazine. She had a post office box and a phone number, neither of which she wanted to give out, but Griffin could be persuasive when he set his mind to it. Within minutes, he had the phone number. He promptly stuffed it in his pocket.

With three minutes left in the truck, he called Aidan Greene's office and left a message on the answering machine. Mother Nature wasn't the only one closing in fast; so, Cassie said, was the attorney general of California.

"Aidan, it's Griffin Hughes. I'm hoping you've given some thought to what we discussed. California had a month to deliver a governor's warrant, and nearly half of that's gone. If you're ever going to help, now's the time. You have my number. Call any time."

He punched off just as he pulled up at Poppy's.

*   *   *

Poppy was at her phone bank, looking out at the lake, thinking that she ought to be enjoying the silence, because in another hour she would be picking up the girls at school. They had been sleeping here with her since Saturday night, which she and Camille had agreed was the easiest thing, what with Micah off in the woods all day long. Once the sap began to run and the sugarhouse came alive, the girls would go home again. They could help there, each in her own little way. Micah would want that.

Poppy would miss them. She had enjoyed the noise, the busywork, the company, and she had managed well. She had managed *quite* well.

Rose would have been pleased. Actually, Poppy decided with some satisfaction, Rose would have been *appalled*. She would have imagined the problems that might have arisen, and she would have focused on those.

Poppy's satisfaction ended with the sound of a truck—not just any truck, but Buck's old rattletrap. A minute later, the front door opened, and Griffin came in. His cheeks were ruddy, his eyes excited.

"We're nearly done," he said. "Another day, and that's it."

Poppy smiled. "That's nice."

"What's going on here?"

She looked at the quiet phone bank, looked at the book she'd been reading before getting lost in her thoughts, looked at Victoria sleeping in a ball on the desk. She shrugged. "Not much."

"When do you go for the girls?"

"In an hour."

He raised both brows.

"What?" she asked.

He looked down the hall toward the bedroom. "I thought maybe . . ."

"Maybe what?" She wasn't making it easy. She had too many fears to just coast along with this. She couldn't take anything for granted.

He sighed. "I thought maybe you'd let me hold you."

Her heart fell. "You did that last Friday night for all of four hours, and you haven't been here since then. That doesn't say much for what we had."

"What did we have?"

"Great sex."

"Great sex? I'd say there was more. I'd say there was love, because you haven't done that with another guy, not like we did it. I said I loved you. You didn't want to hear that. Tell me why."

"I'm not ready. It's too soon. You haven't known me long enough to think you love me."

"Are we eighteen?" he asked gently. "Are we naive? Are we inexperienced?"

"You know what I mean."

"No, honestly I don't," he replied, looking hurt. "I just turned thirty-one. I've spent a long time looking for the right woman. I think I know what I want. I think you do, too, only you're afraid to go after it."

"Why am I afraid?" she asked, unable to say the words herself and wondering if he would come up with the same ones.

"Because you're disabled. Because you think that has to matter to me, and you're afraid of rejection."

"Everyone is. Aren't you?"

"Oh no. We're not talking about me. We're talking about you. You're afraid that I'll get tired of being with someone who can't do the things I can, so I'm trying to go through that list of yours. We danced, didn't we?"

"Yes."

"And showered together?"

"Yes."

"One of these days, I'll get you on a snowmobile, too."

She couldn't rule it out. But keeping up with him wasn't her greatest worry. "There's still a lot that you don't know."

"Well, that would be the accident," he said. Tossing his jacket on the sofa, he pulled up a chair. "So tell me about it."

"I have."

He didn't blink. Patiently, he repeated, "So tell me about it."

She didn't want to. She had meant what she'd told Micah, that some things brought too much pain to think about. But Griffin wasn't about to let this go, so she took the easiest tack.

"I was in the hospital for eight weeks. I was in a coma for the first one, not bad for me but a nightmare for my parents. Then I woke up and learned what had happened. It was difficult."

He frowned. *Not being able to move?* she imagined him thinking.

"Knowing Perry was dead," she corrected. "He'd been buried by then, and everyone tried to gloss over it and tell me how lucky I was, but it took me a while to see that. They got me up and around as fast as they could. The last few weeks of the eight, I was in a rehab center. I really am lucky. Money wasn't an issue. My parents adapted one wing of their house so that I could get around, then they built me this one. It's a good thing you're not six six. You'd have to stoop to use the stove."

"Tell me about the accident."

"I thought I did once already."

He was as patient as he'd been before and every bit as stubborn. "What do you remember of it?"

"Not much."

"By design? Not *wanting* to remember?"

"Would that be so bad?" she asked in self-defense. "It was a horrible night."

"There was a party. There was drinking." His tone urged her to go on.

"There was an accident."

He waited, but she was done. She didn't want to think about this, certainly didn't want to talk about it. She was paying the price of irresponsibility by living in a wheelchair. She didn't owe Griffin further penance.

But he was looking her in the eye. "When I first got back here after Heather's arrest, I said that you trusted me on some level. You argued, but I believed it then, and I believe it now. Only, that level doesn't reach as deep as I thought. I think you have a problem with trust." He rose from the chair and went for his jacket. "You and Heather are two peas in a pod. Neither one of you trust that someone can know everything about you and still love you."

"That's a lot of trust," she argued. "Many people have trouble with that."

"I'm not talking about many people," he said, "and I'm not really talking about Heather, either. I'm talking about you."

"What do you want me to *say*?" she cried.

He shrugged and pulled on his earband. "I have to get back," he said, and left.

Chapter Sixteen

Had Micah bet on Tuesday, he would have won a bundle. First thing that morning, the sun rose high and strong, and in a matter of hours the air went from subfreezing to well above. The snow dripped from notches of trees, bare earth at the foot of evergreens emitted a fertile scent, and the sap started to flow.

Had he been asked, he might have pinned the start of the run down to the hour, and that, without actually seeing the telltale slide of liquid down the tubing—first a drop, then several, then enough to half fill the tubing, then all the way. He spent the morning tapping trees on the north-facing slopes, and there was no sap flow there, probably wouldn't be for a week, but he could feel the other. It was as if the pulse of boyhood memory kicked in, and he heard those first *pings* of sap dripping from the spile into the bucket. He had grown up with that excitement. Though there were no buckets now, the sound still echoed in his blood. Spring was on its way. This first crop of the year marked a rebirth.

He wished Heather were there. She had loved this. He wished the girls were there right then, too, so that they could share the excitement. Later, they would come. Poppy would bring them from school, and they would help. It used to be that school came second to sugaring. He had been younger than Star when he had first been involved. Sugarmaking was a family affair.

At least, it used to be. And now? He and Billy were family, but Griffin was not. Nor was Pete, though he had surely proven himself a friend. He had put in the energy and the hours, and had put up with Micah's pique.

At some point, Micah would thank him. At some point, perhaps, when the resentment was gone.

He figured he had four, maybe five hours to tap. It would take that long for enough sap to run from tree through lateral line to mainline to sugarhouse, to warrant firing up the evaporator. With Pete back being a cop today, Billy and Griffin were a team, while Micah worked alone.

He would have liked to team up with a son. He had told Heather that. One of the girls might marry a fellow who would be interested, but it wouldn't be the same. Micah couldn't expect a son-in-law to feel the excitement in the same way.

He didn't have a son. But he did have his trees. They would be here for him whether the girls married, Heather was convicted, or old Billy died. They were his issue, in that most archaic sense. He had raised them and nurtured them. He had protected them from others that would have stolen their sun, had let them grow until they were mature enough to tap, had trimmed them back when they got greedy and staked them when they needed support. He had relieved them of excess sugar one year, so that they might thrive to produce more the next.

They were his children. He took pride in their performance now.

* * *

Poppy got the call shortly after noon and began making calls of her own. She didn't have to identify herself, didn't have to mince words. "Sap's running," was all she had to say and the townsfolk took it from there. They hung up the phone, finished what they were doing, and rushed to the sugarhouse laden with enough food and drink to feed the sugarmaker, his assistants, and as many visitors as chose to drop by.

At least, that was the way it had been in the past. This time, the reception Poppy got was only lukewarm.

"Oh?" one said. "Well, it's time, I guess."

From another there was a mildly concerned, "Is Micah ready? I heard he still had tapping to do."

And from a third, "I hope it's a good year for him. He's had a rough spell."

Indeed, Poppy's mother was the only one who expressed any of the usual excitement. But then, Maida was a cidermaker. She knew what it was to approach the finish line with the fruit of one's labor. She also loved to cook.

"I'm already in the kitchen," she told Poppy. "Let me make a few more things. Midafternoon, I'll be at Micah's."

"Why don't I pick you up?" Poppy suggested.

Maida sounded surprised, and rightfully so. Poppy wasn't often the initiator in their relationship. She didn't have to be. Maida jumped in first, pampering ad nauseum. If anything, Poppy usually ran in the other direction to avoid being smothered.

She didn't know why she didn't now. Perhaps it was that Maida was back from her vacation early, or that she was in the big house all alone, or that Poppy wanted a chance to talk with her. Whatever, she felt an odd reward when Maida seemed pleased with her offer.

"Oh, Poppy. That's a *nice* idea. But aren't you getting the girls?"

"I'll pick you up on the way. Can you be ready by three?"

"I surely can," Maida promised, and she was. Poppy had barely pulled up under the porte cochere in front of her mother's handsome fieldstone home, when Maida came out for the first time. She deposited one wicker basket of foil packs in the back of the Blazer, ran back in for a second, then a third. Breathless, she slipped into the passenger's seat and gave Poppy a satisfied smile. "There. That'll go a little way toward feeding the hungry."

"You must have emptied your freezer," Poppy remarked as she put the Blazer in gear and drove off.

"Not entirely. I've been at it since you called. I learned how to cook while cooking for large groups."

"You mean us?"

"Before you. Before Lake Henry, even. Back in Maine. My mother was working, and there were all of my uncles to feed."

"Three uncles." Poppy had seen a picture. Lily had shown it to her, having found it among their grandmother's things when Celia died. Up to that point, none of them had known there was any family at all back in Maine. It was not a subject that Maida usually discussed.

"Four uncles," she said now in an offhanded way. She was looking out the front windshield as Poppy negotiated the ups, downs, and turns of the road into town. "Celia had four brothers, and she raised them all. They were younger than she was, the youngest, Phillip, by twenty years. He was more my age than hers. He was my best friend."

Poppy continued to drive, but she was unsettled. Not only didn't Maida usually talk about her childhood, she rarely used that breezy tone. It should have connoted nonchalance, but that wasn't what came through to Poppy.

But Maida kept at it, stayed focused on the road, while the tires hissed on the melt from the hillside snow. "We used to go everywhere together. We'd talk for hours." She glanced at Poppy. "Was that the kind of relationship you had with Perry?"

"No," Poppy replied with caution. She didn't know where her mother was headed.

"Then with Griffin?"

"That's still very new."

"Well, Phillip was family," her mother went on. "He's right there in my earliest memories. My father was a hard man, and we didn't have much money. Phillip and I gave each other comfort through that. We grew up together. Then we were lovers."

Poppy's hands twitched on the wheel—not a muscle spasm as much as shock. She darted Maida a glance before pulling her eyes quickly back to the road. They were approaching town. She had to take care. "Lovers?"

"Yes," Maida said, but the breeziness in her tone was gone, as though this was the point of her talk all along. "He was sent away when people found out, but he didn't know where to turn, and he felt lost. He killed himself."

Poppy drew in a sharp breath. "How awful. I'm so sorry."

"Sorry that we were lovers?" Maida asked, sounding nervous.

"Sorry that he died."

"And the lover part?"

Poppy sent her mother another fast glance. Maida appeared almost frightened, which made a statement about how times had changed. It wasn't that Poppy thought incest was more common now, just that it was discussed more openly. Indeed, Poppy's shock had more to do with the unexpectedness of Maida making a confession than with its content. Poppy hadn't known her great-uncle, hadn't known any of the four. Nor did she know the woman who had lived in Maine, but she was intrigued. The Maida whom Poppy did know wouldn't have mentioned having sex with her own husband, much less an uncle.

The center of town sparkled with sun that shimmered off the melting snow. Poppy distractedly raised a hand to acknowledge one of Charlie's sons, who was sweeping melt off the general store walk. "I think," she said, feeling a kind of release, "that . . . it's a hoot."

"A hoot?"

"Well, immoral. But emotional. And very human. *And* a long time ago. I wouldn't exactly call the life you've lived since then debauched."

"Your father never knew," Maida challenged, seeming to invite Poppy's censure. "I lived with the guilt of that. And the fear."

Poppy wasn't about to censure her mother. The pot didn't call the kettle black. "Fear that he would find out?"

"Yes. It was not a fun way to live. I worked twice as hard to make everything in our lives twice as good."

"I think you succeeded," Poppy said.

"It was not a fun way to live," Maida repeated. Slipping down in her seat, she turned her face to the window, effectively ending the conversation.

Poppy couldn't let that happen. She sensed there was a message here for her. She wanted to know more. "What brought this on?" she asked as they passed Cassie's office.

"I saw someone in Florida."

"A man?" Poppy asked. It was the first thing that popped into her mind. George Blake had been dead three years. If Maida had met someone new, it would follow that she might view the old from a different place.

"A therapist."

Poppy was shocked again. "You did?"

"Yes. I was starting to feel old. Then I got down there in January and realized that I was younger than many of the people around me. I'm only fifty-seven. That isn't old by today's standards. So I started asking myself why I felt so old, and when I couldn't find an answer, I got a name."

"Of a therapist?"

"Yes. She's helping me see what I want."

"Which is?"

Maida turned to her. "Happiness. Enjoyment. Lily said she told you that she's pregnant."

Excited at the mention of Lily's baby, Poppy nodded.

"Well, I want to enjoy that baby," Maida said. "I want to do things for that baby that I didn't do for Lily. I wasn't a good mother to her."

"You *were* a good mother," Poppy corrected as she turned onto the road that led to the school. She was directly behind a Suburban driven by a friend who was there to pick up her four kids. "You just weren't always . . . understanding."

"You're being very kind, Poppy, and I won't argue with you. But the truth is that I was obsessed with where I'd come from and what I'd done back there. I was obsessed with compensating for the guilt I felt, and I overdid it when my first child was born. Lily, being that child, took the brunt of all that I was trying to hide. But trying to hide things like that just doesn't work. You think that you've tucked your dirty laundry away in a safe place, but after a while, inevitably, the smell escapes."

"That's a disgusting analogy."

"But it's true," Maida insisted. "Or think about Micah's sugaring. I've been here in town more than thirty years, so I've been watching sugaring that long, and things have changed. Dale Smith used to use a single large pan for the boiling. When the syrup started to sheet, he'd pour that off and add fresh sap to the pan, but there was always a little of the old left, and it would keep boiling, just keep boiling, and the finished product was never quite as pure or sweet, with that faint taste of old sap. Micah uses three pans. Sap moves from one to the next as it condenses, and when it starts to sheet, the whole of that batch comes off. It's fresh. It isn't tainted by old boil."

This one was a prettier analogy. Poppy certainly got the point. Again, though, she started imagining. "Why are you telling me this?"

Maida didn't speak for a minute. Then she said quietly, "I just want you to know."

Poppy might have pressed the point if she hadn't pulled up at the school and seen the girls already racing down the walk, eager to hear about the sap and to enthuse about going home. Then the moment was gone.

* * *

Steam billowed from the cupola of the sugarhouse, drifting up through the tops of the trees and into the sky over town. Even more than Poppy's phone calls, the steam should have been a rallying cry. Cars should have been coming down Micah's drive, disgorging townsfolk intent on sampling the first of the season's syrup.

This year, there were no cars arriving other than Poppy's. She pulled up to the sugarhouse, parked beside Griffin's truck, and let the girls out. They bolted inside.

"Where is everyone?" Maida muttered in dismay, but it was a rhetorical question. Without awaiting an answer, she left the car and went around to the back.

Poppy would have liked to follow the girls into the sugarhouse. She loved the sweet smell inside when the sap was boiling. But she figured that Maida might want to add something further to their conversation— a question, an observation, even an accusation. Poppy wanted to be there for that.

Maida did have an accusation to make, but it had nothing to do with Poppy. "This is not right," she muttered as she hauled out one of the baskets. "They know he's going through a hard time. So he lost his temper."

"More than once."

"Fine. But they know he meant no ill will. They should be here."

Poppy pulled out another of the baskets, set it on her lap, and wheeled to the porch. The going was rougher than it had been even the day before, bare patches mingling with snow-packed ones. In another few weeks, the whole thing would be mud. By then, Micah would lay out long wood planks, not so much for Poppy as for Heather and the girls. Mud season was an unholy mess.

Heather might miss it this year, Poppy thought, wheeling back toward the Blazer. Wood planks or no wood planks, if she wanted to go into the house she would have to drive around to the front. That was where the ramp was.

Maida shooed her off before she could get on the lift. "Go into the sugar shack, Poppy. They need an audience. I'll organize these things, then I'll be over."

Poppy put her hands to her wheels, then pulled them back. Maida seemed calm. She seemed comfortable now. "What you told me on the way here—do the others know?"

"Your sisters? Lily does. I told her last fall, when she was having such a bad time. She didn't understand why I was so frightened about having the press here. It was the only way I could explain my . . . fear of exposure. It helped both of us, I think. I haven't told Rose. I should." She sighed. "That'll take more courage. But I'm working on it."

*   *   *

Griffin was the grunt man. His job was to fire up the arch under the evaporator pan and to restack wood as the pile was depleted. Missy and Star helped with the stacking, running one log at a time from the wood-pile to the pallet by the arch. They didn't mind the back and forth; they had all the energy in the world. They were excited to be home and ex-cited to be helping. Early on they threw their jackets aside, because the sugarhouse was warm. It was also moist; Missy's hair grew curlier and curlier.

Griffin teased her, as he often did with his two curly-haired nieces. "You are just growing more and more and more hair," he said. "Did you eat something special for breakfast?"

Missy shook her head and did a little dance around the side of the room. Star was quieter, staying close to his side. From time to time, she reached into his coat pocket, pulled out a chocolate kiss, and unwrapped it. He had made sure that the ones in his pockets had nuts. This was not the pocket that held the phone number that could be Cindy's. That was in his back pocket, transferred from one pair of jeans to the other, but not called yet. He hadn't drummed up the nerve. The way he figured it, as long as Ralph was off looking in other places, Cindy would stay put—assuming this really was Cindy, and he did want to assume that. The reality was that after all these years it could be another dead end. He was giving himself just a little longer to pretend that wasn't so.

Keeping busy helped. When he wasn't adding wood to the fire, Griffin was content to keep an eye on the girls, especially since Micah couldn't do it. He was the sugarmaker. He was the maestro, and the process wasn't simple at all. This was no boil-it-in-kettles-out-back-in-the-woods stuff. Griffin had sensed that, when he had first seen the equipment in the sugarhouse. The reality of it was more apparent now that the equipment was running.

Micah explained the process in a quiet voice as he monitored, shifted, directed, and scooped. Griffin didn't know whether the narration was for him, for Billy, or for the girls, but he was grateful for it.

"This valve allows sap to flow in from the tank outside. I keep it there as long as I can, because the cold lessens the chance of bacteria developing. Once it comes in, it goes first through the reverse osmosis machine. That takes out a lot of the water. From there, it goes to the back flue, where the steam from what's already boiling gives it a start heating up. Then it comes into the back pan and is brought to a boil." He moved the liquid forward with a large metal scoop. "This next pan, the middle one of the three, is smaller than the back one because the sap's already starting to condense."

"How sweet is it straight from the tree?" Griffin asked.

"Sap from the tree is two percent sugar. Half an hour in these pans, and it's syrup. That's sixty-seven percent sugar."

He worked for a bit, alternately moving the sap and leaving it alone to bubble. "Used to be you burned at least one pan every season. Not only did you have to throw out that batch of sap, but the pan was often ruined, too. Now I've got a gauge on each pan to monitor the level of the sap. When it gets low, it lets me know."

"Can I taste?" Missy asked.

"Not yet," Micah said. "But soon."

He moved more sap along. "The front pan, here, is where things get tricky. This is the last stage. This is where sap turns into syrup."

"How do you know when that happens?" Griffin asked.

"You hear it," Billy put in.

Micah explained, "There's a subtle change in the bubbling. If you don't hear it, you can tell from the thermometer in here. Sap changes to syrup when it reaches seven degrees above boiling. If you want to be sure, you test it with that little thing over there. It's a sugar hydrometer."

"Something smells wonderful," came a voice from the door. It was Lily Kipling, followed closely by her husband and Charlie Owens. When they took off their coats and looked ready to stay, Griffin left the girls in their care and went down to the house.

*   *   *

Micah liked talking about what he did. He felt competent and strong. With the arrival of guests, though, his attention was thrown off. Friends and neighbors stopping by at the first sign of sugar steam was the way in Lake Henry. This year, he would rather have done without their visit. Oh, he needed Billy and Griffin—they did the peripherals while he handled the sap. He also didn't mind it when Maida brought food and drink up from the house. And he surely didn't mind Poppy coming up. The girls loved her. She was practically family. He didn't know what he would have done without her these past days.

He could have done without Lily, John, and Charlie, though. They reminded him of the crowds that used to come with the first sap and how different it was this year. Worse, Charlie knew it too, and tried to be solicitous.

"What needs to be done?" he asked, rubbing his hands together. "I can work."

"I'm set," Micah answered, eyes fixed on the bubbling gold in the pan.

"Did you finish puttin' in spiles?"

"No. I'll do it mornings. Can't start boiling until afternoon, anyway," he said, thinking that Charlie knew that—and if he didn't, why the hell would Micah want him around? Anyone who knew anything about sugaring knew that sap ran during the height of the day's warmth and stopped when the sun went down and the temperature fell again. Micah might boil sap well into the night to finish up what had come down from the trees that day, because the best syrup came from fresh sap. Inevitably, though, he had to stop and wait until the sap flowed again.

"I can spare a boy or two, if you can use extra hands," Charlie offered.

"I'm fine," Micah said, setting his jaw. Truth was, he felt like a fool in the eyes of the town, what with Heather turning out to be someone else and his not knowing a thing. She might as well have cheated on him. He felt humiliated.

"Hey," Billy said with a nudge.

Refocusing on the sap, Micah heard that deeper bubbling and felt anticipation in spite of himself. He carefully swept his metal scoop through the pan and lifted it clear. He had syrup. It dripped from the edge of the scoop in a sheet.

Flipping a valve, he let the syrup empty out of the pan into a vat. While it sat there, he scooped the next batch of syrup into the front pan, moved the sap in the back pan to the middle pan, opened the valve way in back and let in another seven inches of raw sap. It wasn't until he was pouring the hot new syrup from the vat into an even larger vat lined with filters that he thought about Billy's timely nudge. Without it, he might have scorched the sap. He prided himself on being a better sugarmaker than that.

Who to blame? He could blame Lily, John, and Charlie for distracting him, or Heather for haunting him. In the end, though, the fault was his. It behooved him to pay attention, or the season would be doomed.

*   *   *

Poppy was sitting in a cozy corner of Micah's old sofa when Griffin came down the hall from the kitchen. She wasn't reading. She wasn't watching television or listening to music. She couldn't say she was doing much of anything—and yet that seemed to take all the strength she had.

She smiled when he came in, but didn't speak.

He smiled back. "Your mom's busy as a bee back there. I thought you'd be helping. Are you okay?"

She wasn't sure. She felt . . . blue. It wasn't something she was used to feeling.

But she nodded anyway and gestured for Griffin to come close. When he hunkered down, she bent forward and put her nose to his flannel shirt. "Mmmm. Maple sugar. It's an insidious smell. How's it going up there?"

"Your sister came."

Lily. *Mommy-to-be Lily,* Poppy thought, and felt a sudden need to share this news with Griffin. "She's pregnant, only no one's supposed to know yet, so don't say anything."

"I won't. Thank you for telling me. A new baby's always exciting."

Poppy nodded. She laced her fingers in her lap.

"Something is wrong," he said, still on his haunches.

She shrugged. But he was right, and she needed to vent. "I feel . . . like . . . a spectator. Like I'm just sitting here watching things happen."

"Like Lily having a baby? Or Heather being locked up? We're doing what we can. I'm hounding Aidan. Cassie is hounding the California A.A.G. To some extent, we're all spectators."

"But you're busy with other things."

His eyes lit. "Do you want to go back up to the sugarhouse with me?"

"And watch?" she asked crossly. She knew that she sounded like a moody child, but she couldn't help herself. "No. I don't want to watch."

"You could help with the wood."

She shook her head. The frustration she felt had nothing to do with sugaring.

"Are you still angry at me for what I said?" he asked.

"I should be. For that and more."

"What more?"

"Coming here. Making me think of everything I can't do. I used to feel like I could do anything I wanted."

"Can't you?"

Rather than answering, she said, "I sit at home and watch Victoria. She tries things. Nothing stands in her way. She is fearless."

"She's a cat. Cats don't think the way we do. They don't analyze things. They don't feel guilt or regret. Or fear."

"Well, I do," she muttered. "I'm afraid of *lots* of things."

"Name one."

"You." Embarrassed by the confession, she rushed on. "My mom is seeing a shrink. I think I should, too."

"You don't need one," he said. "A good friend can serve the same purpose. It's not like you have deep-seated anxieties. Sometimes it's just a matter of having a forum to air out your thoughts. A friend can provide that."

"So can a shrink."

"A friend is cheaper. Besides, you don't need a shrink. You have me."

Taking a side of his collar in each hand, she moaned, "You're the *problem.*"

"Because I love you? That's crazy, Poppy."

"That's why I need a shrink," she said.

"A shrink would sit here with you until you hated the silence enough to blurt out your fears. I could show you how it works. We could do some role-playing, you and I—only I don't have very long. Not right now. I have to be back helping Micah. So let's cut to the chase." Everything about him gentled then, from his eyes to his voice to the hands that he placed on either side of her face. "I know about the accident, Poppy. I *know* about it. Imagine the very worst, and I know it. If you're thinking that I'll find out about it later and hate you, you're wrong. There's nothing you can say that can turn me off."

Poppy could barely breathe. She didn't speak. Couldn't speak. He was calling her bluff, purely and simply.

"If it's a matter of forgiveness," Griffin went on in that same gentle voice, "you have it, but it's not even needed. Shit happens. Want to hear about shit? Shit is when your oldest brother supplies drugs for your teenage sister, and everyone looks the other way."

Poppy gasped. "Cindy?"

He nodded sadly. "So we acknowledge it years later, but only in whispers, two of us at a time, and only after the damage is done. James is living with his wife and three kids in Green Bay, Wisconsin, and Cindy's long gone. He says she begged him for it, and, yeah, she was a rebel—yeah, she started with pot, and he had nothing to do with that—but then she got into the hard stuff, and he *was* involved."

"He was *dealing?*" Poppy asked.

"No. But he had access. When she asked him for it, he got it. She kept asking, he kept getting. Things got worse and worse between her and the folks, worse and worse in her life until she was hooked, really messed up. Then all hell broke loose. She couldn't take it, so she ran. Who was at fault? My dad, for being so rigid and judgmental that none of us would approach him—me and the others for not doing something anyway—James, obviously, for giving her the stuff just to tweak the old man." Griffin took a breath. "What James did involved malice. You?" With a quick shake of his head he returned to the subject at hand. "Even when I dream up the *worst*-case scenario, I don't see any malice on your part."

Poppy was silent as she returned from the nightmare of Cindy Hughes's story to her own. No, no malice, she thought, just a gross irresponsibility that had caused a person's death.

"So that raises something else, says Griffin the shrink," he teased in a way that told Poppy he was trying to make the truth easier to swallow. "That suggests the problem isn't really about me. You don't need me to forgive you for what happened that night. You need to forgive yourself."

A thud of boots sounded on the front porch. Seconds later, Camille came through the door, arms laden with foil packs. Unaware that she was interrupting, she toed off her boots.

Then again, Poppy realized, Camille was fully aware of interrupting, just being tactfully nonchalant, as only she did so well. "They'll need help through the evening," she said, heading for the kitchen. "I'm here for the duration."

Poppy watched until she was out of sight and involved in distant conversation with Maida. Looking back at Griffin, she saw a surprising vulnerability.

"Tell me more about Cindy."

He shook his head. He pointed at her. And he waited, waited until she couldn't stand the silence.

It took her all of two seconds. "What do you want me to do?" she whispered. But he wasn't giving her the answer she needed. He couldn't. She knew that.

Instead, quietly, he said, "Let me come home to you at night. I'll work here with Micah as long as he needs me—and, for the record, it isn't about his forgiving me as much as me forgiving me, so I know whence I speak. But I don't want Little Bear late at night. I want you."

She put her fingers to his mouth. Assuming everything he said was true—about the accident, about malice, about forgiveness—he definitely made things worse. He was a remarkable man, seemingly hers for the taking, but she didn't deserve him.

That said, she wasn't about to deny his request. She might be guilty of things she hadn't ever spoken aloud. But she wasn't stupid.

*   *   *

Griffin was at the sugarhouse until nearly midnight that night, until past eleven on Wednesday, and midnight again on Thursday. For all those years of opening pretty little tins of pure maple syrup and carelessly pouring it on pancakes, he had never imagined the work that went into the making. Micah was a stickler, but it all made sense. Once the sap became syrup, it had to be filtered to remove even the tiniest specks of grit. Bottling immediately followed, while the syrup was hot enough both to be sterilized and to create a vacuum in the tin as it cooled—and as if that wasn't enough work for one day, everything that had been used in the sugarhouse had to be cleaned.

By the time he got to Poppy's each night, he was exhausted. Thursday night, he was also chilled. A light rain had fallen on and off during the day, no problem while they were tapping because the air remained warm, but come nighttime, when the temperature dropped, he felt even the small amount of dampness in his clothing. A hot shower was a must. Since he couldn't get that on Little Bear, he was particularly grateful that Poppy had agreed to his request.

Truth be told, he couldn't have made it to Little Bear if his life had depended on it. The days were just too exhausting. That also meant he wasn't much good for anything when he climbed in beside Poppy. He was bone-tired, and he was up with first light to go back and help Micah tap the rest of the trees.

But nice things happened between first light and Micah. Griffin had never felt as compatible with a woman as he did, physically, with Poppy.

He didn't ask about the accident anymore. She had to work that out for herself. Nor did he talk about Cindy. He wanted to make better use of their little time together.

The drizzle continued on Friday, often little more than a mist. It didn't fall hard enough to stop the tapping, nor was the air cold enough to stop the sap flow. The moisture simply made the snow on the ground more dense and their clothing more uncomfortable.

Come Saturday morning, when they woke up to more of the same, he would have given anything just to stay in bed with Poppy. But sugar maples knew nothing about weekends. Nor did they care about rain. When the sap ran, it ran, and it had to be processed. Griffin was invested enough in the season by now—and trained solely by Micah—not to want sap sitting in a storage tank any longer than necessary. Besides, there were still trees to tap. With a little luck, they would finish the last of the slopes before noon. That, in itself, was cause for showing up to work.

An even better cause presented itself that day. They arrived down from the sugarbush for lunch, ready to fire up the evaporator for an afternoon of sugarmaking, when a nondescript car pulled in. One look at it, and Micah swore under his breath. But Griffin knew the car wasn't FBI. He recognized the man behind the wheel as Aidan Greene.

Chapter Seventeen

Micah might have preferred the FBI to Aidan Greene. He could criticize
FBI agents. He could accuse them of ignorance, overzealousness, roboti-
cism, or indifference. Aidan Greene was a real-life figure from Heather's
past, and though Micah's brain knew now that she was Lisa, his heart
continued to resist, continued to hope that there was another reason why
she couldn't tell him the truth.

I don't have time for this, the sugarmaker thought. *I gotta work.* But the
man who had been head over heels in love with Heather didn't move.

His heart pounded as Aidan approached, though he wasn't what
Micah had expected. Micah had expected power. He had expected arro-
gance and savvy. This man was dressed well enough; he looked comfortably citified and clean. But nothing about him suggested privilege. He
looked tired and wan. Hollow. Even apprehensive.

Griffin met him halfway and extended a hand. "I'd have picked you up
at the airport if you'd called."

"I didn't know I was coming," Aidan said. "Didn't know I'd make it all
the way here. A guy in the general store in town told me where you
were." He shot Micah a glance.

Micah couldn't get himself to go forward. If he acknowledged Aidan's
existence, he had to detest the fact that the man had taken this long to
speak up.

"That surly guy is Micah," Griffin advised. "He's having trouble with
all this, so if he lacks graciousness, we have to forgive him. Can we go inside?" he asked Micah.

I don't have time for this, the sugarmaker thought again. *I have sap to boil.* But Micah nodded. He would rather they talk in his own house than somewhere else. Here, at least, he had a semblance of control.

He went in through the kitchen, thinking that the back door was just fine for Aidan Greene; besides, the man ought to see how they lived. This home wasn't a mansion in Sacramento. There was no butler, no maid, no cook. If there was drip from their clothes, it would dry on the floor.

Poppy, with her short hair, bare face, and fleece vest, was at the table with the girls. They had just finished lunch. A platter of sandwiches awaited the men.

Micah couldn't eat a thing, and told Poppy as much with a look.

Griffin and Aidan followed him through the kitchen. He heard Poppy offer them food, heard them refuse everything but coffee, heard her say something to the girls, but by this time he was hearing too many other little voices to make out what she said. He was hearing all the things that had been spoken in the days since Heather's arrest—all the speculation, the wondering, the supposing, the guessing. He wasn't sure he was ready for the answers. He wasn't sure he ever would be.

He didn't offer anyone a seat in the living room, and graciousness had nothing to do with it. This wasn't a tea party. It was a moment of reckoning. He looked out the front window, trying to find comfort in the land that he owned, trying to take a full, deep breath, failing on both counts. His breathing remained shallow, and his heart continued to pound.

Turning to face the room, he leaned against the wall by the window, folded his arms, stared at Aidan, and waited.

Aidan was draping his coat on a ladder-back chair. He looked up, seeming relieved when Poppy wheeled in with coffee. "Headache," he murmured under his breath as he reached for the coffee and took several desperate sips.

Poppy parked near the sofa, clearly staying. Micah figured she had a right. After the girls and him, she was the one most deeply affected by Heather's secret past.

When Micah was thinking he didn't know where to begin, Griffin said to Aidan, "You were determined not to talk when I was in Minneapolis. What changed your mind?"

Aidan put his mug to his mouth for another sip. When he lowered the cup, he stared at the coffee. "You made a remark about my becoming a counselor, and you were right. I am a do-gooder—always was, even as a kid. That was why Rob loved having me around. I did and felt all the things he was supposed to do and feel. Teaming up with me helped his image."

"Why did he need help?" Griffin asked. "He was a DiCenza. The family is famously charitable."

Aidan shot him a dry look. "When you have as much money as the DiCenzas, you have to do something with it or you end up giving it all to Uncle Sam. Charlie DiCenza would choke to death before he did that. All his talk about being against big government? He didn't mind big government, per se. It was a great place to get jobs for his friends. He just didn't want to be the one to pay for it. The DiCenza Foundation was created primarily as a tax deduction. The charitable image was a side benefit. In that sense, the Foundation killed two birds with one stone."

"Did you know all this back then?"

"Yes. We all did. But when you're young, you think you can jump on the bandwagon of a powerful entity and use it for your own ends. You don't realize that they've sunk their teeth into you until it's too late to shake them off. By then, they own you."

"You shook them off."

Aidan ran his tongue up on his teeth in a sign of distaste. "Not back then. I have a law degree. I got it straight from college. I had it the whole time the business with Rob and Lisa was going on. Rob was my friend, so I felt a loyalty to him, and the old man had that power. I really thought he was going to be elected vice president, in which case there might be a nice position for me in either the White House or as legal counsel to a congressional committee. I had this illusion that I could milk him for that, and then use the position to do some good." He made a self-denigrating sound. "I was naive."

"How so?" Griffin asked.

"Because I kept my mouth shut about Lisa and Rob, because I told the cops one thing when the truth was something else, I'd in essence perjured myself." He waved a hand. "Oh, it wasn't official, but it was there in

my mind. I'd sold out. I was doing small-time legal stuff for the Foundation and suddenly I couldn't stomach it. I felt like a fraud. So I dropped
out. Resurfacing as a counselor felt better, and the law degree didn't go to
waste. The kids I work with have legal hassles. I plot their defense and
feed it to their lawyer, who picks it up and follows through like it was his
idea in the first place."

Micah was feeling antsy. He had work to do. "Well, you're just a model
citizen," he said mockingly, "a bad guy gone good."

Aidan stared at him. "I try."

He stared back. "Now try something for Heather's sake. Try the truth."

"She was a nice person."

"She still is. Say something new."

"She loved Rob DiCenza," Aidan said.

That hurt. Micah knew Aidan had meant for it to. He backed off.

Griffin asked Aidan, "Did Rob love her?"

It was a minute before Aidan let out a breath and refocused on Griffin.
"Rob wasn't capable of love as you and I know it. He was raised in a family where love was bartered—you do this for me, I do this for you. Most
everything had a political purpose. Nothing was pure. Lisa's love was
pure."

"Did she set her sights on him, like the papers said?" Griffin asked.

"No. She wouldn't have done that. She wasn't sophisticated or self-
confident enough. He was the one who went after her, not the other way
around. She worked for the caterer that the DiCenza family used. They
were always having parties, so she was over there twice a month. Rob
was probably initially attracted to her *because* she tried to be distant, and
he *loved* that she was poor. It drove old Charlie nuts. He liked the illusion
of being a man of the people, but he was a social climber. He'd come from
poor. He milked that fact for all it was worth—the old rags-to-riches-
helps-rags story—but he didn't want his kids socializing with poor."

"Did you know that Rob knocked her around?" Griffin asked.

Aidan studied his coffee again. "He said she mouthed off. That she deserved what she got."

"Over and over again?"

Aidan shrugged. It was an admission.

"And you didn't do anything?" Micah asked tightly and held his ground when Aidan's eyes met his.

"Yes, I did something. I told him not to hurt her. I told him that some-day one of his girls was going to go to the cops, and that once one talked, the others would follow suit. I told him he could see prison time. He laughed at me. He thought I was crazy."

"What about the pregnancy?" Griffin asked.

Aidan looked away. "When she told him about it, he said that she was trying to trap him, that it wasn't his, that he'd pay for an abortion out of the goodness of his heart, but only because he liked her."

"Was it his?" Micah asked. His Heather was a one-man woman. She didn't run around.

"How the hell should I know?" Aidan asked.

"Guess," Griffin coaxed.

"It was his. She wasn't seeing anyone else. Like I said, she was in love."

"Did she agree to get the abortion?"

"No. That was the problem."

"Problem, as in source of dissension?"

"Yes."

"Was she shaking him down for money, like the family says?"

"No. I doubt the thought of that ever entered her mind. She was too gentle, and also naive. Besides, she wouldn't have done anything to irri-tate him. She knew what his fists felt like. She kept hoping he'd soften and decide that he wanted the baby, too."

"How do you know what she was hoping?" Micah asked.

Aidan held his gaze. "She told me."

"She called you on the phone and just poured it all out?"

"She didn't have to call me on the phone. I was always around. I'd drive them on dates."

"You were his chauffeur."

"I prefer to say I was his designated driver. I was also his best friend. She thought I could convince him that it wouldn't be so bad having the baby and her."

"Did you try?"

"There was no point. I knew how he felt. Like I said, Rob was incapable of love. So I told her she could do better. I told her to just leave town, have the baby, and find another guy."

Poppy spoke, her voice quiet, "In some regards, that's what she did."

"Except that something happened in the 'just leave town' stage," Griffin said. "We're missing a page." He looked at Aidan. "Were you there that night?"

Aidan stood straighter. "I was. That's in the record. But I wasn't in the men's room."

"Did you see what happened?"

"It was dark."

Micah reached the end of his leash. "Is that what you flew out here to tell us, that it was dark? This is my busy season, man. I've been at it since eight this morning, and I'll be at it until midnight. I can't waste my time pulling teeth. If you have something to say, now's the time. Otherwise, get out of my house."

*   *   *

The telling took five minutes and left Micah with two problems. The first was that he wouldn't believe Aidan until Heather confirmed what the man said, and Heather wasn't speaking. The second was more immediate. Aidan had no sooner finished speaking when a movement caught Micah's eye. It was only a ripple in the cloth that covered the table and reached the floor, possibly a draft. Barely breathing, Micah watched the fabric. When it moved a second time, he crossed the room, raised it, and lifted out Star.

"You were not supposed to be here," he scolded, but totally without anger. She was his baby. She was his responsibility. She had suffered more loss in her short life than she deserved. If he never provided her with another thing, he wanted to give her a childhood.

"Momma's a good driver," the little girl told him. "She doesn't drive fast."

"I know, baby. We were talking about another place and another time."

"But about Momma?"

"About someone named Lisa."

"I want Momma."

He held her cheek to his shoulder. "We're working on getting her back. That's what this is about." He looked around the room, searching out other little hiding places. "Where's your sister?"

"In the clubhouse. She doesn't want him here."

Micah headed for the hall. "Call Cassie," he told Griffin and, holding Star, went to the girls' bedroom. The closet door was ajar.

"Come out here, Missy."

"No," said a muted voice.

He opened the door. Blankets were draped off hooks, so that he couldn't see Missy, but he heard her again.

"*You* can come in," she said, "but not that man, and not Heather."

Micah squatted down where the voice indicated she was, settling Star on his knee. "Why not Heather?"

"She isn't in our family anymore."

"Why not?"

"Because I don't like that man."

Micah knew what she was trying to say. Aidan represented a part of Heather that was frightening to them. Missy was reacting to that fear.

How to comfort her, he wondered, when he felt no comfort himself?

"Come out here," he coaxed.

"No."

"It's just me. Me and Star."

"And Poppy and Griffin. I don't like him, either."

"I do," said Star.

Missy stuck her head out from between the blankets. "That's because you like chocolate, but you're too *little* to see what I see."

"What do you see?" Micah asked.

"That he's trying to take Poppy away from us, just like someone took Heather and someone took Mommy."

"He's not doing that, Missy. What's going on here isn't about taking away. It's about adding. Adding Griffin to Poppy. Adding Heather to us."

Missy's eyes were stormy, her voice the little female version of what he feared his had been in the other room. "I don't need Heather."

"I thought you loved her," Micah said.

Star looked up at him. "*I* do. You do too, don't you?"

"Micah," Poppy called softly from the door. "Cassie wants us to come."

He rose, taking Star up again. "I can't go. The girls and I have sap to boil." Skirting the wheelchair, he set off for the kitchen with Star on his hip. Billy was there, eating a sandwich. Passing by, he said, "I'm firing up the evaporator." He went through the back hall and had a hand on the door when Griffin's voice stopped him.

"We have to meet with Heather."

Micah looked back. "Be my guest."

"Aidan's coming."

"Good."

Poppy wheeled around Griffin. "You have to be there, Micah. It's important."

Micah wished Poppy was right. But he'd been there before, and Heather hadn't talked. So what good was he on that score?

On this score, in the sugarhouse, with the girls, he had a purpose, a reason. "I have to work, Poppy. I can't go racing up to West Eames. Sap's running, sun's shining. If I don't do this, who will?"

"Me," said Billy, coming up from behind Griffin. Standing now, he seemed taller than ever. "I can get it started. Let me use your phone, and I'll get help. I'm not without friends in this town."

Poppy wheeled close and said with quiet urgency, "How can you be angry, after what Aidan said?"

Micah didn't have an answer, but he was certainly angry.

"We're so close, so close," she begged. "Cassie wants corroboration. She needs to hear the story from Heather. Don't you?"

He did. That was all he'd wanted for days.

"Seeing Aidan could make it happen," Poppy went on in that same pleading tone. "Cassie is counting on that. But if you're not there, Heather might not care. She loves you, Micah. If ever she needed you, now's the time." She paused for a breath, then whispered, "She's already afraid she's lost you because you haven't been to see her. Can't you forgive her?"

He was spared having to answer by Star, who took his face with two little hands and turned it her way. "I helped Poppy make the sandwiches, and there's tuna there. Momma loves tuna. Maybe if you bring her one, she'll think of me?"

* * *

The room was small for five people, but Cassie insisted that all five were vital to Heather's defense, so the guard showed them in. Micah stayed in the background, leaning against the wall, telling himself that he was only there for Star's sake—until the door opened and Heather came in. When her silver eyes went right to his, he knew he was lying to himself. His heart ached the same way it had when she had first been taken away.

Then she saw Aidan, and what little color she had drained away. She looked frantically at Cassie, who went to her, took her hands, and spoke softly.

* * *

Cassie was determined to succeed. Mark might accuse her of becoming too involved with her work to the exclusion of those she loved, but Heather was one of the latter. If there was ever a time when she could make a difference in a life, it was now.

"I finally have a workable argument," she told Heather. "With Aidan testifying about the abuse, we can make a case that you feared for your life."

Heather sent Aidan a skeptical look, then whispered to Cassie, "There are other charges."

"Flight to avoid prosecution? We can deal. Literally. I've done my homework. The DiCenza family prides itself on its image. They've spoken up long and loud about how terrible you are, and their words have gone unchallenged because you haven't been there to speak for yourself. Things will be different if you decide to talk. They'll hate what you say and, more important, they won't want you quoted in the press. They'll direct the assistant attorney general to plea bargain. Once they hear your side, they'll want this settled quickly and quietly."

"They have power. They can convict an innocent person."

"Not this time. We have medical records. We have adoption records. We have Aidan."

Heather glanced at him again, and, once more, whispered to Cassie, "Why now?"

The room was small. Her whisper carried.

Aidan answered. "Because they're abusers, and not only physically. They abuse power, and that's not right. Rob is dead. You have a good life. I don't see what purpose they have in going after you now. You suffered. I know. I drove you to the hospital. Twice. And I did tell the old man. He said he was going to forget I said it and that I'd be best to do the same."

"And you did!" Micah charged. "You kept your goddamned mouth shut when they accused her of murder!"

"She was gone," Aidan argued. "There was no trial. She escaped. She made a better life. My crime wasn't in keeping quiet then; it was in letting things go so far now. I'll have to live with that. But it's not too late to change the outcome."

Heather seemed to be holding her breath.

Cassie pressed her case. "Rob's mother is the point of vulnerability. Rob was her baby; she won't want his name dragged through the mud. And then there's the child." When Heather's eyes flew to Micah, Cassie gave her hands a shake to bring her gaze back. "Rob's mother is devout. She won't want word coming out that her son wanted to abort his own child."

"He said it wasn't his," Heather said in little more than a whisper.

"Tests can prove that it was."

"How? Without the baby? I don't know where she is."

"We can find her, Heather. Trust me on this."

"She'll hate me for what I did."

"*No* one hates you for what you did then. We just hate you for what you're doing *now*," Cassie said, but with a smile to soften the words. "The Heather we know is strong. She is able. She is dedicated and determined, but this Heather, the one in this jail, hasn't been like that. We want our old Heather back. She's the one we love."

"But—"

"None of us is perfect. Your silence—this silence—is inexcusable. Anything else, we can forgive."

Again, Heather's eyes went to Micah. This time they stayed.

* * *

Poppy was listening to every word, focusing on Heather without blinking, sending the strongest message she could that Heather should speak, tell all, defend herself. When Heather looked at Micah, though, Poppy glanced at Griffin.

His eyes were waiting.

Do you really know? she asked.

He gave a tiny nod.

And forgive?

He nodded again, then raised both brows. *What about you? Do you forgive?*

Poppy could forgive Heather. She could forgive Micah for being angry and Griffin for causing the whole mess in the first place. She could forgive her mother for being a perfectionist and Lily for being too beautiful for her own good and Rose for being a prig. Forgiving herself was harder.

* * *

Micah didn't hear much of what Cassie said at the end. He was too busy remembering all that had been good about his life with Heather, all that he still wanted. Yes, he did want it, especially when she looked at him the way she was looking now, as though he was the center of her universe, as though what he said mattered more than anything anyone else said, as though his love was the only thing she had ever truly wanted.

Anger? What was anger but a passing emotion, a misunderstanding, a failure to communicate? It had no lasting place in a long, full life, a life spent with someone you love.

"This is what we need," Cassie was saying, "but Aidan's word alone won't do it. You were the only one in the car that night. You have to tell us what happened."

All the while Cassie talked, Heather looked at Micah. Her eyes were filled with fear, intensifying the ache he felt inside. Suddenly the wall he leaned against was cold and hard. Moving away from it, he wrapped his hands around her neck and tipped her chin up with both thumbs.

"Tell me," he said quietly, "in your words."

She lingered for a last minute, searching his face. Everything about him screamed, *Tell me. I need to know. I love you. That won't change.* She must have heard, because she closed her hands on his wrists and held tight.

The words came in a woeful rush. "I didn't want to date him. I mean, I *did,* because someone like me dating someone like him was a dream come true, but it couldn't work. I knew that. We were too different. When I told him so, he kept saying that it was all right, that he loved me, that we needed to keep our relationship secret until just the right time, and then he'd tell the world. 'Tell the world.' Those were the words he used, like he really was proud of us."

"But he hit you," Micah said with his thumb on the scar at the corner of her mouth.

"When he drank. He always apologized for the drink, and for the hitting, and I loved him, or loved the dream. Then I got pregnant and things fell apart. He was furious. He said the baby couldn't be his. He said he always used a condom."

"Did he?"

"When he was sober. But it was his. I wasn't with anyone else. And I didn't demand that he marry me. I just wanted him to help me keep the baby." Her voice fell to a whisper. Her eyes welled with longing. "I wanted her. I wanted her so much."

"Were you arguing about the baby that night?"

"Not me. I wasn't going to say anything. I was working. But he kept seeking me out and following me around, and he kept drinking. He started calling me names, loudly, so I finally went off with him to try to calm him down. He wanted to know if I'd aborted the baby yet, and when I said I hadn't, he said he'd do it for me."

Micah felt sick. "Do it?"

"Kick me. He said he could kick the baby out, and he started pushing me, pushing me back away from other people. When I turned and ran, he followed."

Micah could see the pain in her eyes and wanted to end it, stop her. She was only saying what Aidan had. Still she needed to go on. They had to get it all out, because Aidan's story only went so far.

"Then what happened?"

Her eyes filled with tears, as words that had been locked inside for so long poured out. "I believed him. I believed that he would kick me and kill the baby. I couldn't let that happen. So I ran between the cars on the field and got to my own, because the only thing I could think was that I had to get away. I started to drive, and it was dark. I got to an open part of the field, and I remember thinking I was almost there, almost free, so I went faster. I had no idea he'd race out in front of the car." She had started to shake. "I didn't know he was dead. I figured that he was protected because he was loosey-goosey drunk. And because he was a DiCenza. DiCenzas didn't die. They didn't even get hurt."

"But you ran."

"He was a *DiCenza*. He could have ended up with a concussion, and they'd have come after me. They'd have sent me to prison and taken my baby. Yes, I ran, and when I learned that he was dead, I kept running. It nearly killed me to give the baby up, but I wanted her to be safe. Then I came to Lake Henry, and I found you and the girls, and I just . . . just pushed all of that unhappiness out of my mind. When you do that, when you push it all out, you can pretend it never happened. Ninety percent of the time, that was how I felt."

"And the other ten percent?" Micah asked.

"That was when you talked about marriage and kids, and I heard it."

"Heard it?"

"The thud of his body against the car. I hear it sometimes, so loud and relentless, and then I realize it's my heart. I'll never forget that sound. It's an awful sound, Micah, and then when you find out that it represents the end of a life . . . if it hadn't been for the baby I might have ended my own. I can't conceive of killing someone."

"There's our argument," Cassie announced.

"They won't believe me," Heather told Micah.

He looked at Aidan. "Is what she said consistent with what you wit-nessed?"

Aidan nodded. "He was drunk. He threatened her."

Cassie asked, "And you'll testify to that?"

"Yes."

Heather's hands tightened on Micah's wrists. "I don't want to go back there. You don't know the power they have."

No, Micah didn't. He had been privileged to spend his life with more decent people than the DiCenzas. He had a feeling that if he could mend a few bridges, those decent people would rally around Heather once they heard all this, which wasn't to say that things would be easy. There would be headlines now. Heather would have to return to California, and God knew what faced her there.

He did know one thing, though. When she went, she wouldn't be alone.

*   *   *

Poppy wanted to celebrate. She knew that Cassie still had a lot of work to do if she was to get Heather the best possible deal before she returned to California, and then there was the matter of the child. They had to locate her if the threat of DNA testing was to hold water. But in that afternoon, they had come so much further than they previously had been, that Poppy felt giddy. She felt optimistic. She felt *brave.*

That was what she told Victoria when she returned to the house, after she had taken over the phones, answered a few curious calls, made a few exuberant ones of her own. She still had energy to spare, so she went to the exercise room.

"I do feel brave," she told the cat, and promptly picked the orange bundle of fur up off her lap, set her gently on the floor, and went to the wall. She took the braces down, held them, turned them. She even went so far as to bend over and place one against her leg.

Then she heard the sound of a snowmobile on the lake and went to the wall of windows. A headlight cut through the fast-fading day. She watched the machine with its helmeted driver, knowing exactly who it was. Dropping the brace, she wheeled out to the main room and opened the deck door just as he parked the machine. She moved aside to let him in.

Removing the helmet, he grinned. "Hey."

She grinned back, helpless to resist. He was adorable with his auburn hair all mussed and his cheeks red. He was enjoying the lake in winter; that pleased her. "Hey, yourself."

"We did good today."

She nodded.

"So I'm here to take you for a ride."

"Micah dismissed you early?"

His grin widened. "Billy had his friend, Amos, there. You know, old guy from Cotter Cove, grew up working a sugarbush there? They didn't need us. Micah hung around fueling the fire with the girls, but I was superfluous."

"Superfluous?"

"Couldn't have been happier. So come on. Let's go for a ride."

She did know what he was feeling. There was a light-headedness that came with the sudden easing of a weight. But she didn't do snowmobiles anymore. "It's getting dark."

"Do you know the visibility on those things, once the headlight reflects on the snow?"

She did. She knew everything about "those things."

"Maybe another time," she said.

"I want to take you to Little Bear."

"It's raining," she tried, but he had an answer for that, too.

"Not now, it isn't. It's barely misting. Billy told me to use his snowmobile, so I thought we'd do dinner out there. I picked up chili at Charlie's. You love Charlie's chili."

Poppy eyed the machine. "I can't go on that."

"Is it a matter of distrust?"

"No. Bad memories."

"Maybe it's time we made some new ones."

On principle, she could buy that. But the timing was off. She wasn't ready.

"Come on, Poppy," Griffin coaxed. "It was stormy that night. What happened had nothing to do with booze. It could have happened to the best of drivers."

The last of Poppy's smile, the last of her indulgence faded away. She sat back in her chair. "How did you learn about this? Who did you talk with?"

"If I tell, will you come for a ride?"

"Yes."

"I read the police file. It's a matter of public record."

"Who'd you talk with?"

"You. Just you."

"I don't talk about the accident."

"That's right. I put two and two together, and you confirmed it."

She had failed to deny it, that was what she had done. Feeling trapped, she wheeled around and returned to the weight room. She heard the thud of his boots as he kicked them off, then the sound of stockinged feet following her in. With her back to him, she said, "I don't have any more right to go out on a snowmobile than I have to walk or get married or have kids."

"So sin again," he said, and before she knew what he was up to, he had one of her arms after the other in her parka. Seconds before he lifted her in his arms, he dropped her hat in her lap. "Put it on," he directed as he strode toward the other room.

"I don't want to do this, Griffin," she said, feeling more than a little unease as he stepped back into his boots. "It's getting dark. Snowmobiles scare me. I want my chair." The cold hit her face when he opened the door, but it was eased moments later when he slid a helmet over her head.

Straddling the snowmobile, he set her sidesaddle before him and pulled on his own helmet. Only then did he pause. He raised both faceplates. His eyes gentled. "Tell me you don't want to do this. If you truly don't, I'll take you back inside."

If he hadn't given her the choice, Poppy might have refused him. She was an adult. She was her own person. She saw no reason why she should be railroaded into *anything,* let alone something that was emotionally disturbing for her. But emotions ran two ways. Yes, being on a snowmobile for the first time since the accident brought back memories—but, oddly, the bad ones were vague. Far clearer were the good ones—the excitement, the sense of daring, even the nip of the cold.

She didn't want to go back inside. It was a night to celebrate. This was fitting.

*   *   *

Fitting barely described it. The ride out over the lake was exhilarating, dinner in front of the fire was charming, lovemaking in the afterglow was divine. She wasn't wild about the bathroom facilities, but Griffin had thought that through and managed with commendable grace. The air was damp but surprisingly mild, so they stayed out a bit, wrapped in blankets under the porch overhang. There weren't any stars and the moon was totally obscured. When the mist turned into a drizzle, and the drizzle turned into large, loose flakes of snow, the lake was stellar.

There was a quiet intimacy as they sat there on the porch. Cushioned by it, Poppy wanted to ask when he was returning to Princeton. He would go, she knew. He would get tired of this.

She couldn't go to Princeton. Well, she could, but she didn't want to. She loved Lake Henry. She loved her life here. She loved the people, the smallness, the sense of control. Here she was, on an island, totally dependent for mobility on Griffin, yet she didn't mind. She couldn't imagine feeling as comfortable in the city.

In the end, that intimacy notwithstanding, she didn't ask him when he was returning, because she didn't want to hear the answer. But she thought about it when she woke up in the middle of the night as he tossed a log on the fire, and she thought about it a few hours after that, woken this time by sleet on the roof.

"Red squirrels," Griffin murmured sleepily as he pulled her into the curve of his body.

"Sleet," she whispered, wondering if he'd deliberately pulled her that way to support her when she couldn't do it herself. She didn't mind, actually. It was a totally natural, totally comfortable, totally pleasurable way to sleep.

Only she didn't sleep, not for a while. As she lay there trying not to think about why she still felt guilty being with him, she listened to the sleet. She could tell from its resonance when it turned into freezing rain, and knew that it picked up force as morning approached. However, since monitoring freezing rain was akin to counting sheep, she eventually fell asleep.

*   *   *

With wet snow clumped like shades on the windows, the cabin was dark, so it was a while before they realized that they had overslept.

Then Griffin bolted up and checked his watch. "Omigod. It's ten-thirty."

"It's Sunday, and it's cold," Poppy murmured. "I need your warmth here."

Twisting at the waist, he looked down at her. "I was supposed to be at Micah's."

"I don't think you'll make it. Look outside."

Swearing softly because the woodstove was out and it was cold, he hurried naked to the door, inched it open, peered out. When he finally spoke, his voice held awe. "Everything is frozen. Good thing we finished tapping yesterday. We'd have had to chip away ice to do it today." He shut the door tight and returned to the layers of quilts and pillows that they called a bed.

Poppy felt the chill on his body and rubbed at it to warm him up. "You're not going over there today."

"Don't know as I'd make it," he said, pulling the covers higher. "Don't know as we'll make it back to shore, period."

Poppy grinned.

*   *   *

By noon, a freezing rain was falling, making the thought of a snowmobile ride even more unappealing. So they ate soup from the pot and peanut butter from a jar, and fell back to sleep. By one, they were awake again and looking outside. Ice was thick on everything in sight, and a freezing rain continued to fall. Figuring that it had to be better in another hour, they closed the door and returned to the fire.

"What's your first memory?" Poppy asked.

Griffin smiled. "First ever? That's going back a ways." He thought for a minute. "Randy going to school, so I guess I was three. He was my playmate. I hated him for leaving. I remember standing at the screen door watching him get on that school bus. What's yours?"

"My dad holding me. Reading a story. I wish you could have met him. He was a gentle man. What's your best memory?"

"Best? Thanksgivings, right up through college. We used to have more than thirty people. I loved it. By the time I was done with college, Cindy was gone. It was never the same. What's yours?"

She would have liked to hear more about Cindy, but her own best memory came right out in front of that thought. "It's a new one. Maida hugging Lily in the meeting house last October. It was symbolic." Moments after that, she had seen Griffin for the very first time, making it a best memory and a new beginning, all in one. Then she scolded herself for being unduly imaginative, and asked, "Worst memory?"

"The night my mom died. Yours?"

"You know." The accident.

"One wish," he said. "If you could make just one, what would it be?"

"You first."

"Five kids, three dogs, and a cat, the cat to keep the others in line. Your turn."

"Two. I'd settle for two kids," she said and looked at him in surprise.

He didn't say anything—didn't tease her for blurting it out, or remind her about the odd ways in which the subconscious worked—which made her love him all the more. Given her druthers, she'd have stayed at the cabin for a week.

Then came the *craa-aack* and thud of a pine limb breaking from its trunk and hitting the ground, and Poppy felt a glimmer of worry. Griffin, not being a native, took a little longer to understand, but when the worry hit, it hit harder.

"If there's damage to the sugarbush in a storm like this, what happens?" he asked.

When Poppy refused to say the words, he began gathering their things.

* * *

The ride back was slow. As they crossed open ice fields, the signs of damage mounted before their eyes. Trees bent and cracked; lean-tos collapsed. As they neared Poppy's, they saw a tree fall across her deck.

Seconds later, the deck door opened and Maida, Lily, and Rose came out. When Maida slipped and nearly fell on the ice, Lily and Rose caught her. All three stopped then and stared—not at the tree, but at Poppy and Griffin.

Chapter Eighteen

Maida looked terrified, which, in turn, frightened Poppy, who started thinking that someone they knew had been hurt, or worse.

Griffin pulled up as close as he could behind the fallen tree, turned off the snowmobile, and lifted her, and it wasn't as fast or as fun as it had been the day before. What had been snow then was now a thick coat of ice. Twice he slipped and nearly fell. By the time he had her inside, she was grateful to be there.

"Thank God," Maida cried, following along as Griffin carried her through to the weight room. She had a hand to her chest and was taking deep breaths. "Thank *God*. Do you know how frightened I've been?"

"About me?" Poppy asked.

"Of course, about you. I came over first thing this morning to make sure you were all right, and you were gone. Your chair was here—your chair and your car—but no you. Do you know what went through my mind?"

"She thought you were kidnapped," Rose said, materializing beside Maida as Griffin settled Poppy in her chair. "Kidnapped, raped, and murdered. Didn't it occur to you to call one of us and let us know where you were?"

It hadn't. Poppy felt instant remorse. She reached for Victoria, who was on her hind legs wanting up, but putting the cat in her lap brought only a modicum of comfort. She shot Griffin a helpless look.

"There's no phone on the island," he said. "We would have been back this morning, but I thought the going would be too rough. I'm sorry. It was my fault."

He had been addressing Maida, but Rose was the one to reply. "Poppy should have known better. She should have known we would worry. How could you *not* know that, Poppy? You don't take off overnight. You never do that. And without your chair?"

"Rose," Lily said quietly. "She's back. It was a misunderstanding."

"It was selfishness," Rose corrected. "The chair was sitting here, empty except for the cat. What did she think we would think?"

"I didn't know you would come," Poppy said.

"Not when it started to storm?" There was a thud outside. Rose's eyes flew to the ceiling. Seeming validated, she said with satisfaction, "There. That's perfect reason to worry. God knows what can happen in a storm like this, and here you are, insisting on living alone, which is selfish in and of itself, though that's a whole other story. Mom *always* checks on you. You've aged her ten years."

"I'm all right," Maida murmured.

"She has," Rose argued. "You were absolutely panicked. You're not as young as you used to be."

"And I'm not as *old* as you make me out to be, Rose. I'm all *right*," Maida insisted, but Rose turned back to Poppy.

"It was one thing when we were kids and you had to do your own thing. The wilder the better—you didn't care what Mom and Dad thought. You didn't care that they worried. Well, I'm a mom myself now, and I know what it feels like when a child is irresponsible. Only you're not a child. I thought the accident gave you some sense of responsibility."

"Apparently not," Poppy said, because it was the only way to quiet Rose. "Life's events come and go. I'm an adult, and I'm still irresponsible. You're a mom, and you're still small-minded."

"Poppy," Maida begged.

But Poppy was annoyed. "She's right about one thing. I don't take off overnight, and without my chair? I haven't done that in twelve years, but I did it this time, because there was something I wanted to do badly enough to get past the idea . . . the idea," she struggled to articulate it, struggled to say it *aloud*, "that I didn't have a right to do it. I've lived that way for twelve years, while Rose had a good time at college and married sweet Art and had three wonderful children, and that's fine, because she deserves all those things, and I don't."

"Poppy—" Lily whispered, moving toward her.

"I don't," Poppy said, but she didn't look at Lily or at Rose, only at Maida. "I was driving that night. Griffin guessed it. You must have, too."

Rose gasped. "*You* were driving?"

Poppy's eyes didn't leave her mother. She had been needing to say this for twelve years, solely to see Maida's reaction. Back in the cabin, when Griffin had asked about her dream, she had nearly said that she wanted her mother's love. Now, vigilant, she watched.

"We were up there drinking and laughing," she said, "and when it came time to go home, Perry was tanked, so I drove. I wasn't drunk. But I went too fast and lost control. We were both thrown off. I hit the ground, so I'm in a chair. Perry hit a tree, so he's in a grave."

"Do the police know this?" Rose asked, sounding horrified.

"*Rose,*" Lily scolded and put a reassuring hand on Poppy's shoulder.

Poppy faced Rose. "I never told them. You can if you want."

"I didn't say that— I just— I didn't mean—"

"She won't," Maida told Poppy. "There's absolutely no point."

"Maida's right," Griffin said, standing behind Poppy's shoulder. He didn't touch her, but Poppy felt his presence. "What law was broken? Reckless driving? Well, maybe there was that, but it can't be proven one way or another. Negligent homicide? Maybe, but how would you punish her, Rose? What would you do?"

Rose waved a hand. "I wouldn't— I didn't say—"

"Would you put her in prison?" Griffin asked. Poppy sensed his anger and loved him for it. "Would you sentence her to life in a wheelchair— oops, she's already sentenced to that, so you can't get her that way. Would you sentence her to guilt? To self-flagellation? To a public flogging?"

"I am not the bad guy here," Rose protested.

"Am *I?*" Poppy asked her mother.

Maida's face held pain, though not surprise. Then a sadness took over, and, through it, incredibly, she smiled. "No, Poppy. You're no more the bad guy than any of the rest of us."

Tears came to Poppy's eyes, and in that instant, she remembered the game she and Griffin had played. Best memory? Maida hugging Lily. Best memory to replace that one? Maida hugging Poppy.

Before it could happen, though, another tree fell, this one with a louder crash and a tremor that sent Victoria flying off Poppy's lap and running for cover with unerring aim. Then the lights went out, leaving the room in the late afternoon darkness.

"Oh dear," said Maida.

"Lanterns?" Lily asked Poppy.

"In the kitchen." She headed that way herself.

"I have to get home," Rose announced and caught up her coat as they passed the living room. "Art's with the girls, but if other lines are down in town and the mill is out, he'll have to get over there."

The phone rang. It was Poppy's private line. She picked up in the kitchen. "Hello?"

"It's Micah. Is Griffin with you?"

"He is." Her eyes found Griffin's. "What's wrong?"

"You name it. Lights out, trees down, mainline split. I need help."

*   *   *

A sheet of ice covered the road, making the driving treacherous. Poppy watched Rose and Lily slide around in the Suburban on their way out. Maida would have done the same in her van had Griffin not been at the wheel. He was far more cautious than a native Lake Henryite would be.

Poppy was able to spend an hour making calls before the phone lines went down, and though she switched to her cell phone then, other town phone lines were down as well. Fortunately, an increasing number of locals used cell phones when they were in their trucks or at work, and Poppy, being Poppy, had their numbers. She reached the people she wanted to reach, and this time she wasn't deferential. She wasn't settling for sympathetic murmurings about tough luck. Nor did she want to hear meteorological talk about layers of cold air sandwiching one of warm. She had been around Lake Henry long enough to know how ice storms worked. Precipitation fell through the top cold layer, melted through the middle warmer layer, chilled again in the cold air above the ground and then froze on contact with trees, wires, and tubing, not to mention roads—on which issue she had no patience at all. She didn't want to hear that getting to Micah's might be too difficult. Everyone she called had trucks, sand, and chains like those under Buck Kipling's seat.

"Here's the scoop," she said time and again. "Trees are down in the sugarbush, and the mainline is split. It can't be repaired until the trees are *off*. We need chainsaws and manpower, as much and as early as possible tomorrow at Micah's. Can you be there?" When she heard hemming and hawing, she said, "It's do-or-die for Micah. Without the mainline, he has no sap to boil. Sugarmakers have been wiped out by storms like this." When she heard buts, she said, "I seem to recall Micah fixing the leak in your roof on Christmas day two years ago," or reminded them of his replacing a broken window, hauling a sunken boat from the lake, even building a treehouse—he was always doing something. "He didn't charge you then, so you can pay him now with this."

She wasn't taking no for an answer.

* * *

Cassie was thwarted by the lights, the phone, and her middle child Ethan, who had croup and wanted nothing more than to be held by his mother. So she held him on her lap, letting him sleep with his head on her shoulder, while she sat at her desk, making notes on a yellow pad in the light of an oil lamp. She wanted to be prepared, wanted to have her thoughts organized. It was the least she could do, given that she was making calls on a Sunday rather than waiting until the work week began. Actually, she would have made them Saturday night, if Mark hadn't shamed her out of it. Shamed her? More like sweet-talked her. She was a sucker for candlelight dinners, made for her with all the kids in bed and a husband whom she did desire.

But this was Sunday. If it was the Lord's day, He would surely excuse her, because her mission was a humanitarian one. The clock was running down; the court order keeping Heather in New Hampshire expired in twelve days. Given the way some jurisdictions worked, that wasn't much. Her first call would therefore be to Jonathan Fitzgerald. Given the story that Heather had told, finding the child was a must. The DiCenza family maintained that she hadn't been carrying Rob's child. If it could be proven that she was, there would be a major hole poked in their case.

She waited until the time difference made her call a late afternoon one in Chicago. Then, turning in her chair, Ethan and all—and refusing to think about the absurdity of it—she angled herself in a way that gave her cell phone the best reception. Directory assistance provided Jonathan Fitzgerald's home number. Feeling so close to success, not to mention restricted by her sleeping son, who was nowhere near as light as he used to be, she splurged and allowed the call to be automatically placed.

After a single ring, a woman's voice said a fast, "Hello?"

"Jonathan Fitzgerald, please."

There was a release of breath and a quieter, "Who is this?"

"Cassie Byrnes. I'm a colleague. I'm calling from New Hampshire. We've been working on something together." It was a stretch of the truth, but a harmless one, she figured. "I'm sorry to be calling on a Sunday—"

"He's in the hospital. He had a heart attack on Friday. I thought you might be the doctor. We don't know whether he'll pull through."

For a stunned minute, Cassie was silent. She had chosen her words, had been prepared to launch into them as soon as Jonathan came on the line. She had run through various scenarios, including one in which he had rethought his offer to help. She hadn't anticipated this.

"Oh my," she finally said. "I'm sorry."

"He's in intensive care. We're telling people not to come to the hospital, because he's not allowed visitors, other than us, of course."

Cassie thought fast. "I understand, and you're totally right. The most important thing is that he have a chance to recover."

"The next few days are crucial."

As indeed they are here, Cassie thought. "And after that, he'll need to take it easy, get back to work slowly. I don't want to bother him during that time. Is one of his partners covering for him?"

"You know that the firm disbanded."

Cassie's heart fell. "No."

"Well, he's still with it, he and another partner, but the rest left a few months back. That's been a source of strain for him. You can certainly call his partner. He's young, but he's good."

Cassie jotted down the name, thanked the woman, wished her husband a speedy recovery, then ended the call and punched out the partner's number. Alex Fireman might have been both young and good, but he was not pleased to be called on a Sunday.

Cassie explained the urgency, then said, "Jonathan offered to go to bat for us on this."

"I'm already swamped covering for him. If you call again on Tuesday or Wednesday, I may be able to get a name of someone else who can help."

"You have the records there, I believe."

"Not me. Jonathan. I won't go into his records unless he directs me to. I've only been with him two years."

"He felt strongly about this case."

"I can't bother him now. I'm sorry."

The call lasted less than a minute longer, at which point Cassie rifled one-handed through her papers. Her second call was to have been to the assistant attorney general in charge of the case in Sacramento. Given this newest glitch, though, she went over his head to the attorney general himself. One of her law school friends worked for the A.G. from Washington state, who was a good friend of the A.G. from California, which meant that Cassie's friend knew something of the man—although not his home phone number. She got that from the sister of another friend, who worked on numerous committees with the attorney general's wife.

What Cassie learned from the first friend was that the attorney general of California had been adopted at birth and then, in his early twenties, had gone looking for his biological parents on the premise that children needed to connect to their roots. Cassie was hoping that she would find him to be a man whose own life experience might make him more sympathetic to Heather and her cause.

What she got was a man who was beholden either to the DiCenzas or to the letter of the law. "I don't know what you want from me, Ms. Byrnes," he said after she quietly and efficiently laid out her case. "Are you admitting that Heather Malone is Lisa Matlock?"

"I can't do that until I find the child."

"Then find the child."

"That's easier said than done, given what I told you about the situation in Chicago."

The man sighed. "There are certain accepted avenues here, Ms. Byrnes. Calling me at home isn't one. Have you talked with Mr. Grinelle about this?"

Bud Grinelle was the assistant officially leading the charge. "Mr. Grinelle has been agreeable," Cassie said. "He hears me out and promises to get back to me. You and I both know that he is checking with you at every step. With a case like this, he would have to. You're too good a lawyer—too responsible an attorney general—not to have him do that. I haven't mentioned the child to him. Did you know about her before?"

"There were allegations at the time. The family denied them."

"Tests can prove a connection. I'd like the existence of the child brought into the equation."

"Find the child, and we'll do it."

"She exists. We know where and when she was born. Unfortunately, with the lawyer who handled the adoption sidelined, it will take longer to find her."

"Whenever is fine."

"Not from the point of view of my client. My own resources are limited. Yours are less so. Quite frankly, I'm thinking of the child, too. If she's to be found, it should be done quickly and cleanly. This is a child who was adopted at birth. She's fourteen now. That's a vulnerable age. I'd hate to see the press ferreting her out before I'm able to. You have resources that could make it happen before harm is done to the girl." If there was any chance that his own experience as an adopted child would enhance his empathy for this one, she had laid the groundwork. She couldn't be more obvious.

But the man was dogmatic and impersonal. He wasn't thinking about the case in human terms. "You don't seem to understand, Ms. Byrnes," he said, and she knew right then that she'd struck out. "We don't need the child. You're the one who does. Our case is solid."

"What about justice? Wouldn't you like to know what really happened between Lisa and Rob?"

"We already know. We have a dozen different statements, all pointing to the theory that a scorned and conniving woman ran down a good man. We have a thorough case. The core of it will be part of the governor's warrant that we present to the judge there. We're ahead of schedule. You can expect it at the end of the week."

Cassie was dismayed. At the rate she was going, she would need every one of those thirty days. Playing the game, though, she said, "I was hoping we could talk turkey before then."

"We'll do that once Lisa's back here, and in any event, *I* don't talk turkey. You'd have to do that with Mr. Grinelle."

"Thank you," Cassie said politely. "I will. I'm sorry to have bothered you. Enjoy the rest of your weekend."

She ended the call and set down the phone. Where to go now? There was only one place. Lifting the phone again, she called Griffin.

* * *

Griffin didn't get the message until the wee hours of Monday morning, which was how late he and Micah were in the sugarbush. They had taken the tractor up, because it was the only thing that would hold ground on the ice, and they supplemented its headlights with handhelds. Even then, assessing the damage at night was hard.

Micah, of course, knew what he was looking for and therefore saw more than Griffin. As soon as they returned to the house, he sat with paper and pencil, listing the parts that he needed to buy for immediate repairs. His first concern was the lowest portion of mainline that had split under a fallen tree. Its proximity to the sugarhouse would make it easier to repair. Conversely, its proximity to the sugarhouse made it a final destination for the rest of the lines, which meant that it was crucial. No sap at all would make it to the sugarhouse tanks until it was fixed.

While Micah made his list, Griffin accessed his messages. He smiled at the ones from Poppy, which had come in hourly until eleven and were amusing monologues that passed on the good news that help would be at Micah's come morning. Griffin's smile faded, though, when he listened to Cassie's. Moments later, he left another message for Ralph.

"It's crunch time on Lisa Matlock's baby," he said, meeting Micah's gaze when the man looked up. "The lawyer we thought would help is in the hospital in intensive care, nothing related to this, but out of the picture, and the A.G. in California would be happiest if the child wasn't found at all. Also, time is shorter than we thought. The governor's warrant will be on its way by the end of the week. Do what you can. Thanks." He ended the call and was lowering the phone when, with the scrape of his chair, Micah rose, but he did it with a fatigue that Griffin had never seen in him, but totally understood. They had come so far and were so close. It didn't seem fair that when they knew what they needed, they couldn't *seize* it.

"Think your man can find her?" Micah asked.

"Yes. In time to keep Heather from going back to California? I don't know."

"Micah?" Camille was at the door. She had been staying with the girls while Micah and Griffin were in the woods and, as of ten minutes before, had been asleep on the living room sofa herself. "Star just woke up. Should I go in?"

"No," he said quietly. "I'll go." As he passed her, he said softly, "Thanks."

When his footsteps faded, Camille looked at Griffin. She was alert in a way that belied the hour. Clearly, she had heard the message to Ralph. "If the child is found," she asked, "would that keep Heather here?"

Griffin suddenly felt as tired as Micah looked. Pushing a hand through his hair, he let out a breath. "I don't know, Camille. The child is a smoking gun. She's proof that Rob lied, and that he lied about an innocent child. The family may not want that coming out. My guess? Heather will have to go back to face the charges at some point, but if we can find the child, the deal will be better."

Camille considered that. Frowning, she looked at the table. Then she approached it, took Micah's pencil, tore off a piece of paper from the bottom of the pad, and wrote down something. She handed the paper to Griffin. "That's the child you want."

Griffin studied the paper, then Camille, and suddenly it made sense—the quiet concern, the surrogate grandmotherhood here, the offer of money. "What are you to Heather?"

Camille smiled sadly. "Not her mother. That would have been too easy. If I'd been her mother, I'd never have left her. I'm her aunt. Her mother was my sister."

"Was?"

"She died years ago. She was a tortured soul."

"Because of Heather's father?"

"No. He was just another by-product of her problems, like drugs."

"Why was she so tortured?"

Pondering that, Camille studied her hands. "I don't know. I never did." Her eyes came up. "Would you like some tea?" She answered herself. "I'd like some tea." She went to the stove and put a kettle on to boil.

"Were you the older or the younger?" Griffin asked, one of dozens of questions he suddenly had.

"Older. By four years. We aren't native-born Americans."

Griffin knew that about Lisa's mother. Now it explained the feeling he'd often had that Camille spoke too well, too carefully, as though loath to make the slightest verbal slip.

"We were born in eastern Europe, in a small town that doesn't exist anymore, at least, not as we know it," she said. "After our parents died, we came here looking for a better life. I wanted to settle in a small town like the one we had left. Stacia—short for Anastasia, her given name and very theatrical, very fitting—Stacia wanted excitement and glamour."

"Hollywood?"

Camille nodded, then turned the nod into a slow headshake. "She had no acting ability. None at all. I could never tell her that, of course. She had her dream. Somewhere along the line she met Harlan Matlock. Now, there was another tortured soul." The kettle whistled; she took tea bags from the cupboard. "They went north to Sacramento and settled down, at least as much as my sister ever could. She was pregnant, but that didn't seem to help. She had a restlessness. She needed to be on the move, only she didn't have the slightest idea where she wanted to go. She disappeared when Lisa was five. She left a note saying that since Lisa was in school, there would be teachers looking after her and doing a better job of it than she could ever do." Camille poured the tea.

"Were there?" Griffin asked.

"There must have been. Lisa certainly did well in school. Someone had

to have inspired her, and it surely wasn't Harlan. Oh, she was smart to begin with, but that doesn't always translate into academic success. It didn't
with her mother."

"Where did you come in?"

"Lemon? Milk?"

"Black, please."

She set an eathenware mug in front of him. "The more appropriate
question would be *when* did I come in, and the answer is, too late. My sister stopped calling me somewhere between Hollywood and Sacramento.
I'd write, thinking someone would forward my letters, but they always
came back marked 'addressee unknown.' I used to dial information from
time to time to see if there was a phone listing. Whenever I got one, I
called it. Harlan would answer and say Stacia was out. He would give me
a little tidbit of information about what she was doing or how the baby
was, tempting me, letting me know what he had and I did not. Then he
would tell me not to call again or write or try to visit. He said Stacia
didn't want it." Profoundly sad, she added, "It was probably true."

"Why is that?"

Camille took up her own mug, and sipped from it as she leaned
against the counter. When she answered, her voice held an element of
defeat. "When we first came to this country, we had lofty dreams. Hers
were always more so than mine, which meant that she had more at stake.
I found a lovely place here in Lake Henry. I found work and friends.
There is nothing lofty about my life here. I certainly didn't find the
wealth Stacia and I dreamed about, but I've been happy. Stacia was never
happy. Her life was a disappointment to her. She would have been embarrassed to have me see it."

"Why didn't you go after her?" Griffin asked.

Her eyes flew to his. "Didn't I just answer that?"

She had. Indirectly. Dismayed, he realized that he was voicing his own
frustration, which had to do with his own sister, not with Stacia.

While this realization registered, Camille continued. "The truth is I
was afraid of her. She was always temperamental. I reasoned that she
knew where to find me, and that if she wanted to see me or wanted me to
come to visit, she would call. I didn't want to impose myself on her. Then

she died. I didn't learn of it until months afterward, when I made one of those chance calls and got through. Lisa was eight at the time. He said she was fine." Her spine seemed to stiffen. "No, I did not believe him. I wanted to see for myself. So I flew out there. I waited at the schoolyard." She chuckled softly, sadly. "Like in the movies. Just like that. I was prepared to ask a teacher who she was, but I recognized her right away. She was the image of Stacia. She recognized me, too. She'd seen pictures, but it was more like there was a mystical connection." She smiled, shrugged, said in a self-mocking way, "I always imagined there was that, because I needed it. It was probably more a case of her looking at me because I was staring at her."

"Did you talk?" Griffin asked.

"For a bit," Camille said, and took another sip of her tea. When she spoke again, it was from the distance of years. "I do think there was a connection. I told her who I was. I told her a few of the things Stacia and I used to do when we were children. I gave her pictures that I had. I gave her my address and my phone number. I told her that if she ever wanted to call me, she should. I told her that if she ever needed help—with *any-thing*—she should call me."

"Did she ever call?"

"Not until after the accident."

"Were you the one who gave her the name of the lawyer in Chicago?"

"No. She got that herself. She was a resourceful young woman. She had to be, raising herself. She did tell me about the arrangements, so I knew where the baby was born, and we talked about her coming to Lake Henry. I didn't know she would actually do it until she arrived. It was really quite seamless. She showed up one day and signed on with Char-lie. He found her a room to rent. We led our own lives. We both knew it was safer that way."

"You never met secretly?"

"Never as aunt and niece. She was Heather by then. My niece was Lisa. I talked with Heather the same way I would any lovely young woman who had newly come to town. We became friends, and visited as friends do. I do Micah's bookkeeping, though Heather's taken over most of that. I've helped her with the computer. I do take comfort in her being here, and I believe she feels the same. But our relationship has evolved naturally, as one between friends might. No one in town suspects anything more."

More quietly, Griffin asked, "Not even Micah?"

She answered in kind, little more than a whisper. "No. Not even Micah. If he's going to know, she'll be the one to tell him."

Griffin studied the name on the paper. "How did you get this?"

"That baby was my grand-niece. I was at the hospital the day she was picked up by her adoptive family. If you're in the right place at the right time, you hear the right things. I was, and I did. I interpreted that to mean that I was meant to keep an eye on the child."

"Have you?"

"Covertly. I'm good at that," she added. "The adoptive mother was initially from Chicago, hence the lawyer there handling the adoption. She had an illness that precluded her ever having children of her own. As it happened, she died when the child was eight, the same age Lisa was when her mother died. Is that eerie?"

"Very," Griffin said. "What happened after that?"

"All good things, relatively speaking. Obviously, there were never any other children, and the father hasn't remarried. But he's been successful at what he does. They live in Florida, in a luxury condo. He appears to adore the child. He spends time with her. She wants for nothing. She's fourteen now, not so little a girl."

"What will she feel about Heather?"

"I don't know."

"Will she cooperate with us?"

"I don't know. I've never talked with her."

He held up the paper. "Does Heather have this?"

Camille thought about that a moment. Then she took in a deep breath. "No. She does not. There were times when I was tempted to share it, but I thought that giving the child an identity might make it harder for her. For the most part, she doesn't think about the child, any more than she thinks about that night in Sacramento. There's too much pain involved. Far easier just to push it from her mind. But then there's the anniversary of the child's birth, and Heather gets melancholy. She never says why. But

I can tell. That's the day when she seeks me out, even just for a cup of tea. She needs to be with family that day."

* * *

Driving back to Poppy's in those wee morning hours, Griffin punched in Ralph Haskins' number twice. Each time, he cleared it and set the cell phone on the seat. Poppy was asleep when he came in. He undressed, climbed into bed, and drew her close.

She whispered a smiling hi against his throat. He didn't know if she was awake enough to take in what he had to say, but he told her anyway.

Chapter Nineteen

Poppy wanted to go to Florida. She knew it the minute Griffin told her about Heather's child, and lay awake beside him for a long time thinking about it. She couldn't explain the compulsion she felt. Lord knew, she didn't travel easily; she hadn't been on a plane since before the accident. But something told her if Heather couldn't be there to talk with the child, she had to do it for her.

Cassie, whom they called at first light with the news, wasn't sure that a trip was necessary. She had a friend with a law firm in Miami whom she felt would gladly meet with the family and do the asking. After all, what did they need? A mouth swab? A strand of hair? It seemed a simple enough request.

But Poppy wasn't thinking about physical evidence. She was worried about the emotional impact on a fourteen-year-old child having her biological mother suddenly reenter her life. That was heavy enough under normal circumstances, but Heather wasn't just any old biological mother. She was one who was charged with the murder of that child's biological father. It would be a double whammy for an unsuspecting child.

*   *   *

Had it not been for the ice storm, Griffin would have flown to Miami himself. After protecting Camille's identity by crediting Ralph with finding the child, he felt that he had a right to take the investigation to this next step. He was good with people. He was also just enough of a Lake Henry outsider to be a credible messenger.

But there was work to be done in Lake Henry, and it wouldn't wait. He had promised to help Micah, and so he would. Fallen limbs had to be cleared, and not only from the section of mainline they had focused on the night before. The entire sugarbush had to be scoured, downed wood removed, and damaged tubing repaired, and it had to be done fast. Loss of one day's sap wouldn't break the season; loss of many more than that might.

Having no choice but to let Cassie handle the Florida arrangements, he drove to the sugarbush early Monday morning. Poppy was behind him in the Blazer—significantly behind, for safety's sake. Though the road had been sanded, pure ice lay beneath. Indeed, Poppy's chair skidded down the entire length of the ramp outside her house before they realized that without electricity, the coils didn't work. She had whooped through the skid and laughed at the end, as she might have done taking a wild slalom run, but it was a sobering moment for Griffin, who felt he should have anticipated the problem.

The day was gray and cold, but dry and so beautiful that it was hard to believe the sugar season was in doubt. Everything on the roadside wore a coating of ice that held it perfectly still in the headlights' beam, frozen in time, gloriously delineated, highlighted, and framed. It was a crystalline world marred only by fallen trees, and those came in bunches, slain giants that had been on the wrong side of the hill. Smoke rose from each chimney he passed, the fires within providing the only source of heat. Windows were dark; lights were out all over town. There were no shovelers, only the occasional Lake Henryite holding an ice pick, gazing in bewilderment at what looked like a world of glass.

This time, Griffin and Poppy weren't the only ones coming down Micah's drive. Pete Duffy was already there, quickly joined by Charlie Owens and his two oldest boys, John Kipling and his cousin Buck, Art Winslow and three burly men from the mill, Leila Higgins' husband, and half a dozen men from the Ridge. All had chainsaws, crampons, and thermoses of coffee.

Griffin was as gratified that they'd come as he was by the humble look Micah wore each time another truck pulled up. There was a sense of community here. Hard feelings could be set aside when more important things came to the fore.

Micah didn't say much. None of the men did. It was too early and their task too urgent. Working with maps that showed the grids of the sugarbush, they broke into teams of four each and set off up the hill.

* * *

Poppy watched from the back door. She could see branches down in the woods abutting the sugarhouse, but the men were seeking out places where the flow of sap had been cut. Each foursome had two chainsaws, coils of tubing and someone who knew how to lay it. One group rode the tractor; the rest were on foot. Those following the John Deere walked in its tracks, but those heading for other parts of the sugarbush had to struggle up a slope of sheer ice. Even with crampons notching the surface, there were slips.

The last of the men and their white puffs of breath had disappeared when the women began to arrive, and none came empty-handed. The kitchen quickly filled with food and the kind of quiet talk that Poppy found to be as soothing as the lake on a warm summer night. With oil lamps burning in place of lights, and the fireplace ablaze with logs, there was an air of gentle camaraderie that even Missy and Star seemed to feel. Though Poppy kept a close eye on them, they were content to wander about, lean against a thigh or sit on a lap, and tune in and out of the talk.

The kitchen table was piled with sandwiches and the counter held bowls of soup when the men returned for lunch. As they ate, they huddled together, giving Micah reports of what damage they'd found and what repair was needed. On the positive side, Micah's team had finished removing debris from the crucial portion of mainline that had split, and could have the line repaired by the end of the day. On the negative side, there was enough other damage, both to trees and to tubing, to warrant two more days of work in the woods.

* * *

Micah didn't have two more days to work in the woods. He could spend mornings at it, but prime sap was running. Its color was lighter, its taste more delicate, its open-market price higher. Once the mainline was repaired and sap flowed down the hillside again, he had to boil it.

If all of the same men showed up for the next two days, he could recover with a minimum of loss. If not, he was in trouble.

He wanted to ask them. Wanted to *beg* them. But there was that last breath of pride.

* * *

Cassie spent a good part of Monday afternoon in her car, talking on her cell phone while the engine charged it up. She went back and forth between the assistant attorney general in Sacramento and her law school friend in Miami. In the end, she struck out with both.

Bud Grinelle insisted that it was absurd to discuss any child possibly fathered by Rob DiCenza until Heather Malone admitted that she was Lisa Matlock—which Cassie couldn't have Heather do until they had the firepower of a child willing to submit to DNA testing.

On that score, what she learned from her law school friend suggested that willingness might be harder to achieve than she had thought. She fully expected that the DiCenzas would fight the release of blood samples from Rob's clothing, but she had hoped to speed things up by cooperation on the Florida end.

"Norman Anderson may be a problem," she explained to the few of them remaining at Micah's that evening. "My friend spent a while talking with one of her partners who's had dealings with him. Norman is a decent man who has made a great deal of money over the years as the president and chairman of the board of a group of banks in the southern U.S. He isn't lavish with his money. He isn't showy. He's a quiet, private person who values that privacy above everything else—except his daughter. He adores her. Apparently, they were always close but became even more so when his wife died, which, I'm told, was also handled in a quiet, decent, private manner. He absolutely will not want the publicity from something like this."

"Neither did I," Micah charged, "but I didn't have a choice. Neither will he, if this goes to court."

"The problem is that he may beat us there," Cassie explained. "If we don't win him over now, he's apt to file for an injunction to keep a lid on things until his lawyers can present a case saying why the rights of this child need to be protected."

"No one's trying to violate her rights."

"He may hope that if he slows things down, we'll cave in and just plead guilty, and it will be over and done without his daughter having to be involved. It's a delay tactic."

"How long can it go on?"

"Months, Micah."

"But if Anderson works with us," Griffin argued, "won't he be able to control the publicity? His daughter's confidentiality will be guaranteed, won't it?"

Cassie nodded. "That's what we'll argue. My friend has a meeting with him set up for tomorrow. She wants to assure him on the confidentiality angle, but she also wants to tell him about Heather. She feels that if they lay things out for him, there's a chance he'll be sympathetic to our position."

* * *

Poppy had trouble picturing a group of people who had never met Heather sitting around a table discussing something that intimately affected her. "What kind of chance do we have?" she asked Cassie.

"Fifty-fifty, maybe."

"That's lousy. What if you were there? Would it help?"

"I offered. My friend asked her partner, but he felt too many lawyers would turn Anderson off. He said I'd be better off staying here by the phone."

"What about me, then?" Poppy asked. Her stomach started to jump, but it was the opening she wanted. "I'm not a lawyer. I'm just an ordinary person. What if I was there representing our side?"

Maida stirred from the background. "Poppy, you don't travel that way."

"But what if I did?" Poppy turned back to Cassie. "What if I was there to give Heather a personal face? Would it help?"

Cassie smiled crookedly. "It wouldn't hurt. You're certainly not threatening."

"I evoke sympathy."

"I did not say that."

"Well, I *do*," Poppy insisted. "I've never used my disability before, but in this instance, I don't care. If my traveling that distance in a wheelchair makes him take notice and think, really think, about my friend Heather as a human being, I'll do it."

Griffin put a hand on her shoulder. "Wait a few days. Once the sugar-bush is cleared, I'll go with you."

"This won't wait."

"Then I'll go with you," Maida offered. "I'm an old hand at the Florida route."

But Poppy shook her head, very sure of what she wanted. Her stomach was still jumping. She figured it would do that the entire time she was away from Lake Henry, and it had nothing to do with homesickness. Before the accident, she had traveled at the drop of a hat. She had traveled since—to Cape Cod, to Boston, even as far afield as Pennsylvania—but always by car and never alone. She hadn't had to worry about the mechanics of wheelchair travel, or about finding herself in a strange place with no one to help. Now she thought about both of those things, and they frightened her. But just because she was frightened of something didn't mean she shouldn't try.

"I need to do this," she said with quiet confidence. Her eyes were on Maida.

Micah may have said something. Or Cassie. Poppy heard a little bit of a buzz. But Griffin was silent. He understood. And Maida?

She studied her daughter for a long moment, then crossed the short distance, bent down, and gave Poppy the hug she had been wanting for so very long.

*   *   *

Griffin drove her to Manchester early Tuesday morning for the 6:45 flight to Miami. Along the way, there were more than a few moments of insecurity when she might have begged that he come along on the plane. He could lift her; he could handle her chair. He could help her making trips to the bathroom, without embarrassment on either of their parts. He could entertain her. He knew when to talk and when to be quiet. He was perfect.

But she kept her doubts to herself. She needed to do this alone.

"It's not like I haven't gone places since the accident," she reasoned, talking in spurts to calm herself. "My dad felt strongly that the accident shouldn't keep me tied to Lake Henry. He tried to plan a trip a year. He had a Blake Orchard van adapted for me, kind of like my Blazer is, except rather than my driving, I was a passenger. We'd go for four, five days sometimes, but we did day trips all over New England. We had our favorite places, my dad and me. He was a special man. Do you think Norman Anderson is like that?"

"If he is, we have a chance. I get uneasy when I think of the legal teams that wealthy people have at the ready. My father used to represent those kinds of people on the corporate side. He had a roster of defense attorneys set to jump in at a moment's notice." Darting her a glance in the early morning darkness, Griffin reached for her hand. "I'm glad you're going. If anyone can make a strong case, you're the one."

He *was* perfect. And Poppy did love him. She could admit to that. She still had moments of doubt, but they weren't about her own feelings. They were about his. It was hard for her to believe that he wouldn't tire of her limitations.

He certainly wasn't tired yet. Once they got to the airport, he set her in her chair, put her carry-on over his own shoulder, and wheeled her inside. When they reached the security point that he couldn't pass, he hunkered down with his hands framing her chair.

"Do you have money?"

"Yes."

"Credit card? Picture ID? Cell phone?"

"Yes."

"Change of underwear? Meds?"

"Yes, but only because you hounded me into it. I'm coming back tonight."

"Just in case."

"I'm coming back tonight," she insisted. Thinking that made her feel better. "I land in Miami at eleven forty-two. The meeting at the law firm is set for one-thirty. If I don't make the four-nineteen flight back, there's another at six-thirty. That gets me here—right here—at eleven fifty-four. Can't I just take a taxi back to Lake Henry?"

"No," he said in a way that brooked no argument. Then he smiled and stood back, taking all of her in. "You look so pretty."

She was wearing the most sedate clothing she owned—a pair of tapered wool slacks over leather boots, a silk blouse, a smart black blazer. "Not too conservative?"

"I'd have voted for the leather pants, but you're right to wear these—they're far more appropriate." His eyes found hers. "Do me a favor? If you have any trouble getting on or off the plane, in or out of the airport, ask for help? I love that you're doing this, but you don't need to do it all alone. Are you nervous about the connecting flights?"

"I'm nervous about the whole thing." When he leaned toward her, she hung a hand around his neck. "But I'm doing something, Griffin. I'm not watching." She knew he understood, could see it in his eyes. "Please leave now," she said. "I have to get in line, and you have to be at the sugarbush."

"I can wait with you."

"You can't. You don't have time. I'm okay, Griffin. I really am."

He rose, kissing her halfway up. "I know you are, dollface. That's the problem. I'm worried you'll find out just how okay you are and forget that I'm waiting for you here." Smiling, he straightened and put the carry-on in her lap. He backed off, turned and walked away, turned again and walked backward for a bit with his eyes on her, only her, and all the while she watched.

* * *

Poppy's fears were unfounded. She didn't set off a cacophony of alarms going through security—wasn't stopped in front of everyone and made to shift in her chair before boarding the plane so that flight personnel could see if she was sitting on something lethal. More than twelve years had passed since she had last flown out of Manchester. Back then, boarding had taken place outside after a short walk across the tarmac and a climb up stairs into the aircraft. This time there was a jetway, which was easily handled in her chair. She didn't have to rely on a lift at any stage, didn't fall in the aisle transferring from her wheelchair to her assigned seat, didn't weep when the flight attendant folded her chair and stowed it at the front of the craft—which didn't mean she liked having the chair out of reach. Her wheelchair was vital to her self-sufficiency; without it, she couldn't move very far or very fast. She shuddered to think what would happen if there was an emergency, and she had to exit the plane.

But there was no emergency. In fact, the flight was smoother than she remembered flying to be. She had planned well—had limited her intake of fluid and used the airport bathroom prior to boarding, so that she didn't have to use the lav on board. Once she was in her seat and strapped in like everyone else, she *felt* like everyone else. When a businessman type, one of the last to board, slid across into the window seat beside her and proceeded to flirt with her all the way to Pittsburgh, she fancied that he had no idea she couldn't walk. By the time they landed, she was tired enough of hearing about his life that, when the flight attendant approached with her chair, she felt a perverse satisfaction.

She didn't look at the man's face again, though, because the flight attendant explained, "Normally, we'd let the others deplane first, but we're cutting it close with your connecting flight," and suddenly there was a rush.

She made the second flight with minutes to spare, unfortunately without time for the bathroom. Fearful that it would be a serious problem before she reached Miami, she explained the situation as soon as she boarded. Unable to let her back into the terminal, one of the flight attendants helped her in and out of the tiny lavatory. Totally embarrassed, Poppy then found her assigned seat, gave up her wheelchair, and spent the next half hour imagining that everyone around her had watched the show.

Then she heard a tiny meow. The woman beside her pulled up a carrying case, inserted a hand, and cooed softly to the kitten inside. To Poppy, she explained, "I'm a breeder. This one's just ten weeks old. I'm delivering him to his new home. He's scared."

Poppy thought of a small kitten seeing its mother for the very last time, being tucked into a carrier, and flown off to a totally strange place.

That was scary, she decided, certainly worse than any embarrassment she felt herself. Another little meow, and she thought of Victoria trying once, then twice to reach the top of the bureau, finally making it on the third try. At that point, Poppy put the embarrassment aside.

It didn't return. Somewhere in the airspace between West Virginia and Florida, she decided that embarrassment was a wasted emotion at a time when there were too many more important ones to confront. She spent the rest of the trip focusing on those.

When the plane taxied up to the jetport in Miami, Cassie's friend, Susan McDermott, was waiting at the gate. She came forward with a smile as soon as Poppy wheeled into the terminal, and, alerting her that the meeting had been moved up an hour, led her out to a waiting car. They were quickly on their way into the city.

Poppy took it all in—warm air, snowless streets, palm trees, a skyline of buildings rather than hills—but what she felt most was the satisfaction of having gotten this far. She let that pleasure buoy her as she wheeled into the elevator in the law firm's building, but it dwindled as she disembarked on the fifth floor, went through the glass double door, and followed Susan down the hall to a mahogany-appointed conference room.

Norman Anderson was older than Poppy had pictured, close to Maida's age, she guessed, but he looked every bit as down-to-earth and decent as she had been led to expect. He also looked vulnerable, which would have surprised her if she hadn't been even more surprised by his companion.

*   *   *

Micah struggled not to think about what was taking place in Florida, because too much was at stake, and he had no control over any of it—not the least of it being this fourteen-year-old daughter of Heather's. He couldn't help but resent the fact that a child whom Heather had given up at birth should now hold such complete power, and not only over Heather's life, but over his and his daughters' lives as well. That didn't seem right.

But the world was full of "didn't-seem-rights," not the least of which were Rob DiCenza's mistreatment of Heather, her arrest for his murder, and an ice storm that threatened to ruin Micah's crop. Unable to do anything about the first two that Tuesday, he focused on the sugarbush. Another dozen men from town had shown up, and they spent the morning working different sections of the woods. With the mainline repaired and carrying sap enough to boil, and the lines deeper in the bush being cleared of debris one by one and fixed, he was feeling more optimistic by lunchtime. While Griffin led the teams back up to the sugarbush that afternoon, he stayed behind to boil what was trickling down.

He fired up the arch. He got the sap moving through reverse osmosis and into the evaporator, got it boiling from the back pan, through the front pan, into the finish pan. When it was nearly syrup, he turned on the filter press. That was when he ran into the latest "didn't-seem-right." The filter press was the only piece of machinery that relied on electricity, and there still was no electricity today. He hadn't been concerned, however, because he had a backup generator. Now, just when he needed it, the generator wouldn't start.

*   *   *

One look at Heather's daughter, and Poppy lost her breath. She didn't need an introduction; Althea Anderson didn't have her mother's silver eyes, certainly not that telltale scar, but the resemblance was everywhere else. Mother and daughter had the same long, thick hair, the same heart-shaped face, straight eyebrows, and slight build.

Poppy put a hand to her heart. She couldn't take her eyes off the child. Child? Thea was fourteen going on twenty-two. She was gently developed, sweetly curved, and dressed in a miniskirt and sweater that were very possibly Italian and surprisingly discreet. Her whole manner was refined. Calling her a teenager seemed wrong. She was very much a young woman.

Disciplining herself, Poppy tried to focus on the other introductions, but there were eight people in the room. Had it not been for a natural division in the seating arrangement around the large conference table, she wouldn't have been able to keep straight whose lawyers were whose. But she nodded in acknowledgment as each name was given, did the same with Norman Anderson, then with Thea. And there her eyes stayed, and stayed, and *stayed.*

"I'm sorry," she finally said, but in a breathy way, because she was feeling choked up. "You are just so much like your mother. You're very beautiful."

"Thank you," Thea whispered, seeming unsure despite a tentative smile.

As Susan gave a bare-bones description of the case Cassie was hoping to make on behalf of Heather with the people in California, Poppy tried to imagine what she would be feeling if she were in Thea's shoes. By virtue of the biological reality, a mother-child relationship was intrinsically intimate. If Poppy had been adopted, she would want to know about her birth mother—not necessarily live with her or love her, but know about her.

The lawyers went back and forth then—about legalities, about confidentiality, about constitutional guarantees and juvenile rights. Poppy listened, but her eyes kept returning to Thea, and Thea's met them every time. She didn't seem as interested in what the lawyers were saying as Poppy thought she would be. Then she realized that Thea had heard it all before. There was no surprise here. What there was, was curiosity. If Poppy were to guess, the girl wanted to know about Heather.

Her father was quiet, leaving it to his lawyer to counter Susan McDermott's plea for immediate cooperation, and it was much as Cassie had said it would be. The Andersons' lawyer talked about the visibility of the case. He talked about the potential sordidness as details emerged, certainly about the tragedy of it. He argued against rushing, when it came to involving a child like Thea.

Involving a child like Thea? Poppy couldn't let the statement go unchallenged. "I'm surprised she's here now. I would have thought you would want to shield her even from this."

Norman Anderson answered in a patient but firm way. "My daughter has a mind of her own. She's been following this case in the news. She wanted to be here."

"Has she always known who her biological parents are?"

"She's always known she was adopted," her father said. "I hadn't realized she knew the identity of her birth mother until a few days ago."

When Thea slid him a guilty look, Poppy decided against asking the details of that. It didn't matter how Thea had learned that Heather was her birth mother. What mattered was that she didn't seem traumatized by what had happened.

"Heather has a mind of her own, too," Poppy told the girl. "She wouldn't tell any of us that she'd had a child, because she didn't want to involve you in this. We had to get your name from someone else, because she doesn't know it. She doesn't feel she has a right to, since she gave you up. She knew you had parents who loved you, and she's grateful for that. She came to Lake Henry with nothing of her past except a little backpack with a letter from the law firm that handled the adoption, and this." She dug the tiny plastic ID bracelet from her bag and held it out over the table.

"I don't think that's appropriate," the Andersons' lawyer began. It became a moot point when Thea reached across the table and took the bracelet.

Good for you! Poppy wanted to tell the girl, because if letting her see her own baby bracelet wasn't appropriate, Poppy didn't know what was. Clearly, the lawyer didn't want the bracelet introduced because it was a personal connection that just might get Thea identifying with Heather, which was precisely why Poppy had brought the bracelet along.

Thea studied it closely.

The lawyer went back to his initial argument. "The issue is time. Let's be frank. We all understand that Althea may have to be involved at some point. We simply want to make sure that, prior to that, every safeguard is in place to protect her."

Susan McDermott reiterated the reasons why speed was needed, and they went back and forth. When it appeared that neither side would budge, Susan suggested that they take a short break.

Frustrated, Poppy wheeled herself down the hall to the ladies' room. She had just emerged from the largest stall and was approaching the sink when Thea slipped into the room and eased the door closed.

Her eyes were large, filled with a curiosity. "Is she beautiful?" she whispered.

Poppy nodded. "She is. Wait." She washed and dried her hands, then pulled pictures from her bag. They were the ones Griffin had taken with him to Minneapolis. Watching Thea's face as she turned from one to the next was a sight in itself.

"I've seen pictures in the news," the girl said, "but it isn't the same. She's happy in these."

"She has a happy life. She's a lovely person, Thea, beautiful inside and out, and she would do absolutely nothing to hurt you. For the record, she doesn't know I'm here."

"Why did you come?"

"She's my best friend. There were times when I'd have given up after the accident that put me in this chair, but she wouldn't let me do that."

"What kind of accident?"

"Snowmobile."

"Was she there when it happened?"

"She came minutes later."

"You said she didn't know my name. Doesn't she want to?"

Poppy knew Heather well enough to answer. "She wants to, but she knows it's not smart. Letting you go was too painful. Knowing your name would make you real, and then she would want to know more, maybe want to meet you and get to know you. But you have your own life. She won't intrude on that."

"Does she know my mother died?"

"No."

Suddenly sounding more her age, Thea said, "I snuck the adoption papers from Mom's drawer right after she died, and, like, I didn't want to *do* anything with them, I just wanted to have them, y'know? I thought my dad would be upset, so I didn't say anything until this week, but I knew he was following the news, and I wanted him to know I was, too."

"What grade are you in?"

"Ninth. I go to a private school."

Poppy figured she was young for the grade. "I'll bet you're smart."

Thea gave a modest shrug. "Is she? Heather? What does she do?"

"You name it. She cooks. She's good with her hands—she knits and sews. She decorates the house."

"I can't do those things. What's her best school subject?"

"I didn't know her when she was in school, but she uses her computer a lot, and she's kind of the business manager for Micah, so math is definitely a strong suit."

"Mine, too," Thea said eagerly, then frowned. "My mom died of cancer. Does Heather have anything like that?"

"No. She gets bad colds, but that's all."

"Me, *too*. That's so incredible. My dad never gets colds."

"He seems like a wonderful man."

"He is. He's so cool. Like letting me come here today. That's why he made the meeting earlier, so I could do it during lunch hour. A lot of parents wouldn't do that. I watched all the stuff about your town. It looks incredible."

"We're in the middle of a crisis right now. We had an ice storm that may ruin the sugar season."

"Sugar season?"

"Maple sap, maple sugar, maple syrup."

Thea singled out the photograph of Heather and Micah. "His business?"

"Hers, too. She's his muse."

Thea leaned against the sink, seeming to settle in for a while. "Tell me about a day in her life—like, what time she gets up, what she has for breakfast, what she does after that, you know."

Susan opened the ladies' room door and murmured a discreet, "There's a little concern out here."

Poppy could have gone on for a while. She felt the same rapport with Thea that she had always felt with Heather. But the girl was fourteen, and the current meeting was supposed to be protecting her from the past. Though Poppy didn't think she needed protecting, she didn't want to create tension between Thea and her father.

"Okay. I'd better start back," she said, and wheeled out.

*   *   *

Thea still had the pictures. Slipping them into the little leather pouch that hung by her hip, she pushed a hand up through her hair, waited a minute longer, then went out the door. Her father was waiting down the hall, looking worried.

"Are you okay, pumpkin?" he asked in the gentle, soft-spoken way she loved.

She nodded as she came alongside him. "Are you?"

He smiled sadly and waggled a hand. "It's odd hearing about her, different from reading the paper."

"Does it bother you?" She knew he might be feeling threatened; she had been in enough Internet chat rooms on the subject of adoption to be aware of that. She wouldn't hurt him for the world. "If it does," she assured him, "I won't ask anything more. I love you. You're my dad."

"I know, sweetie. I know."

"But it's kind of exciting, don't you think?" she asked, because the idea of it all was bubbling up inside her. "It's like discovering a long-lost relative—and for you, too, because you're my dad, so in a way, she's related to you, too."

He looked unsure, worried again.

"I don't think she killed him," Thea said.

"But he died. I'm sorry you have to think about that."

"He's been dead so long, he isn't real to me. It could be a movie, like he's a character in someone else's life." Her mother, on the other hand, was alive and very real.

"Still," Norman said, "I'd rather your birth parents had gone on to lead happy and healthy lives."

Thea took his hand. "That's because you're a good person, and because you love me. No one could be a better dad for me than you."

Drawing in a breath, he threw an arm around her shoulder and gave her a squeeze. Then, with the same let's-go-get-'em look that he used when he was heading off to a meeting of the shareholders of the bank, he cocked his head toward the conference room.

Chapter Twenty

While Susan called Cassie with the good news, Poppy left the firm with the Andersons.

"Would you like to see where I live?" Thea had asked at the end of the meeting, and Poppy couldn't have possibly said no. Thea hadn't asked out of politeness; there was genuine eagerness there. Poppy shared the eagerness. She wanted to see as much as she could, so that she would have answers if Heather asked.

Norman Anderson had a uniformed driver, but he drove a town car rather than a limo. Poppy and Thea sat in back, with Poppy's chair and carry-on in the trunk. The car was no sooner away from the curb, when Norman put an arm back over the seat and said to his daughter, "You're supposed to be going back to school."

"For a French review, but I'm okay, Dad. I know enough for the test. I really don't need to review, and if I find that I do, I'll call Tiffany. She's smarter than I am."

Norman gave her a dubious look and turned to Poppy. "That last is questionable. But how do you argue with your daughter on something like this when she's going into the exam with an A average in an honors course?"

That was how Poppy learned that math wasn't Thea's only strong subject. She learned that Thea's school was an international one, when they drove past the stucco complex and Thea stuck her head out the window to exchange enthusiastic waves with a markedly diverse group on the steps. Poppy saw the house where Thea had spent her youngest years, saw the park where Thea's mother had taken her to play, saw the stores where they had shopped. She saw the club where Norman played golf and Thea played tennis. She saw the movie theater, restaurant, and record store that Thea favored, because Thea was directing the tour. The girl gave Poppy a running narration, as she instructed the driver where to turn.

Poppy decided that if extroversion was inherited, Thea took hers from her birth father, since Heather was more quiet. Poppy might have resented it, if the girl hadn't been so adorable.

Then the car turned in at the gates of the community where Thea and her father lived now, and there was no way Poppy could protest. She had already given up on making the 4:19 flight, and there was time before she had to be at the airport for the 6:30 one.

"I think I need to call my guy," Poppy said and dug into her bag for the phone. *My guy*. It was so cool to say that. So easy. So normal.

"What's his name?" Thea asked with enthusiasm.

"Griffin. Griffin Hughes."

Norman glanced back. "Griffin Hughes? Any relation to Piper?"

"His son. Do you know Piper?"

"Our paths have crossed," he said in a way that suggested a positive force. "I didn't know he had a son living in Lake Henry."

"Griffin actually lives in New Jersey, but he's been in Lake Henry helping Micah out with sugaring, what with Heather not there and all." She punched out the number. "The ice storm's been a nightmare. Griffin dropped me at the airport this morning and was heading back to clear more debris from the sugarbush." Griffin's line began to ring. "Once the fallen limbs are cleared, the tubing can be repaired, and once that's done, sap will start flowing to the sugarhouse again."

"Hey," Griffin said.

Poppy grinned, looked down, and lowered her voice for a little privacy. "Hey yourself. Did you hear?"

"Sure did. Congratulations, honey. You did good."

"It wasn't me," she said softly. "Is Micah pleased?"

"You bet. He's holding his breath that Cassie can make a deal. She's working on it as we speak. Meantime, Micah's making syrup again."

"Did the lights come back on?"

"No, and his generator is on the fritz, so he's doing the filtering by hand. He's apt to drop from exhaustion, but at least the sap isn't lost. Are you at the airport?"

Thea touched her elbow and pointed as they pulled in at a low, sprawling house.

"No. I'll take the later plane. The Andersons are giving me the cook's tour of their lives. We've just pulled up at their house. It's even on one level," she added with a wink for Thea.

"You'll be on the six-thirty then?"

"Uh-huh. Are you sure it isn't too late for you? You were up early."

"So were you. Are you tired?"

"A little."

"Did you manage everything okay?"

"Totally. I have to run, Griffin. I'll call again on my way to the airport."

"Please. I love you."

She paused for only half a second. "Me, too." Before he could respond to that, she pushed the end button and dropped the phone in her bag.

Moments later, from the comfort of her wheelchair, Poppy toured Thea's home. She saw the girl's bedroom, which was green, gold, and tasteful, and the adjoining bathroom, which was twice the size of Poppy's. She saw the kitchen, the dining room, the living room, and the den. Thea was the guide here, too, introducing her to a maid and a cook along the way. When the tour was done, they went out to the patio and sat by the pool.

Poppy would have loved to sit silently and enjoy the warm air and summery scents, if there hadn't been so much to say. Thea wanted to know anything and everything about Lake Henry, and Poppy wanted to know about Thea's favorite foods, favorite bands, favorite sports. The cook brought lemonade. Norman was in and out.

When it was time for Poppy to head for the airport, Thea wouldn't hear of it. "We have to take Poppy to the club for dinner," she begged her father. "It's so nice there."

"What about your exam?" Norman asked.

"I'll study. I'll study for an hour now, then more when we get back. You can stay over, Poppy, can't you? I heard you tell Griffin that you'd be getting in very late, and why should you do that, when you can just as easily fly out tomorrow morning? We have a gorgeous guest room. Our travel agent can change your reservations. I have to be at school by eight, anyway. We can drop you at the airport, then go on to school."

"That'll mean a very early morning for you," Norman cautioned his daughter.

Thea shot him a look of dismay. "It's okay. I can't let Poppy go to the airport alone." She turned to Poppy. "Will you stay?"

* * *

Cassie couldn't accomplish all she had to do without electricity and phones. That meant packing up her files and her assistant, and driving over to Center Sayfield, which did have electricity and phones, to use the copying machine and fax at the office of a friend. From there, she called the attorney general of California. In the hour it took before she actually had him on the phone, she fine-tuned her notes.

"There's been a new development on my end," she told him. "I know that you'd rather I work through Bud Grinelle, but since he's only going to have to check with you, I thought maybe we could bypass the middle man. So I FedExed the package directly to you for delivery tomorrow morning. It contains letters of agreement and affidavits that lay out our case."

"Which is?" the man asked politely.

Cassie would have done almost anything to avoid full disclosure. Unfortunately, plea bargaining entailed showing the other side how strong one's case was. This maneuver involved risk. If the plea bargain failed and they went to trial, the prosecution would know her case in advance and be fully prepared. But it couldn't be helped. She did have a strong case. Now she had to convince the attorney general of that.

"We found the child," she said. "We have a signed agreement from her father allowing her to participate in DNA tests. Heather will submit to the tests, also, so we'll be able to prove that she is the child's mother.

We'll be petitioning to have tests done from blood on the clothing Rob DiCenza wore that night. I understand your state police have it. Our lawyer out there—"

"What lawyer?"

"J. C. Beckett," she said with some satisfaction. It had been a coup getting J. C. to work on the case. He was a renegade who headed his own firm and had a history of courtroom wins. The prosecution detested him. He, on the other hand, loved to tweak the noses of people in power, and since the DiCenzas were the epitome of that, he was willing to work on the case pro bono. "He's writing up the petition. He doesn't see any reason why it won't be granted, since the evidence is already there. It's a win-win proposition. If it turns out the child isn't Rob's, that's the end of it. If it turns out the other way, we have a whole other ball game."

"I take it you think the child is his."

"I *know* the child is his. Heather—Lisa—was not with anyone else. No one, out of all those people your guys interviewed after the accident, even remotely suggested that she was. They made lots of other allegations, but never that. Oh, I know. Rob said that it wasn't his baby. But there's been no other man. No one's come forward to claim that child— not back then and not now."

There was a brief silence. Then he said quietly, "Go on."

Pleased that he wasn't fobbing her off on Bud Grinelle but was listening to her himself, Cassie grew bolder. "If the paternity issue falls into place, it gives credence to other arguments we've made that the DiCenzas have refuted. And then there's Aidan Greene."

"Ahh. So it was you nosing around about him?"

"Yes. And we found him. He was Rob's best friend. He was right there through much of what went on in that relationship, and since he never testified under oath, he can't be charged with perjury."

"He can be charged with giving misleading information in an investigation."

"He didn't. We have the transcripts to show it. They're in the pack you'll be receiving. You'll see that Aidan answered every question that he was asked. If the investigators didn't ask the right ones, he can't be held liable for that. Actually," she said, because she sensed that the DiCenzas had influenced the investigation, "if your guys didn't ask the right questions, I'd like to know if possibly they were instructed not to look too deeply into Rob's side of this."

"Let's get something straight. These were not 'my' guys. I wasn't in office then."

Cassie liked his defensiveness. "Then it might be in your best interest to take your predecessor to task."

"That's neither here nor there. What's your argument? Spell it out, please. I don't have all day."

"We contend that Lisa Matlock was impregnated by Rob DiCenza. When she refused to get the abortion that he wanted, he threatened her life and that of the child, and he did it at the party that night. When she got into her car, her only thought was to get away from him. He came out of the dark and jumped in front of the car. She couldn't stop."

"She left the scene."

"She had no idea Rob was dead. She was terrified of him. The fact is, sir, that we have a strong case, should this go to a jury. We have a dark night, lots of cars, and a drunk man running between them. We have a poor, powerless young woman taken advantage of by a privileged, politically powerful man who was older than her. We have a relationship with a history of physical abuse, to which doctors from two different clinics will attest. Those papers are in your pack, too. We have a pregnancy, a demand for an abortion, a threat of physical harm, with an independent witness willing to testify to all three. We have an attempt at a cover-up by the family."

"Hold on. You have nothing of the sort."

"We may, by the time we're done. Do all those people who said they saw nothing still love Charlie DiCenza? All we need is one disenchanted soul to admit that he was asked to be kind to their boy. Aidan Greene says it; that's in the sworn statement that he gave to me last week, and a copy of that statement is in your pack. But there's more. If this case goes to trial, we'll put people on the stand testifying that Lisa Matlock wasn't the only woman Rob DiCenza beat."

"Oh, for heaven's sake. What's the point of that? The boy is dead."

Cassie couldn't believe he'd said that. The remark was totally biased, totally unprofessional. Livid now, she didn't need to look at her notes. Everything she wanted to say was on the tip of her tongue. "You're right. He's dead. This whole *case* should be dead, because Rob's death was nothing more than a tragic accident. That's what a jury will find, only to prove it, we'll have to bring up all the rest. Will the family like that? I doubt it. But that's their problem. They've brought this on themselves. They certainly didn't have any trouble bad-mouthing Lisa Matlock—or now, Heather Malone—in a very public way. They've looked for the lime-light in this case, and that's exactly where this new information will come out if we don't settle it within the next day, in a quiet and fair way."

"The next *day?*"

"Okay, I'll give you two. Forty-eight hours. After that, I'll have to go to the press."

"I can prevent that with a gag order."

"Do that, and you'll *really* have the charge of a cover-up in your lap, only it'll have nothing to do with your predecessor and everything to do with you. Let's talk about free speech and freedom of the press. Let's talk about my client's civil rights. Thanks to the DiCenzas, there's no way that Heather can get a fair trial. Only one side has come out. The other side needs an airing."

"In court. Before a jury."

Cassie refused to buckle. "If it doesn't come out now, it'll come out then. And in open court, with all the hoopla that the DiCenzas were hoping to use to get a conviction. You need to talk to them. Ask if they want their son dragged through the mud. Ask if they want a financial claim made on them by a fourteen-year-old child who may be proven to be their grandchild. If we don't get a deal by Thursday afternoon, that's what'll happen."

"Okay," the attorney general said, clearly humoring her, "what kind of deal do you want?"

Cassie aimed high. She had nothing to lose. "I want the case dropped."

"*Dropped?*"

"Dropped."

"*I* can't do that. Not with a *murder* case."

"Of course you can." She had thought this through. "You can either say that after reviewing the case, given the amount of time that's passed since that night and the potential for fuzzy memories, there isn't enough evidence to convict. Or you can say that new evidence has emerged that casts doubt on any murder charge."

"The press will want to know what that 'new evidence' is, which does all the dirtying, anyway. The family will never go for that."

"Then take the first option. You, as attorney general, advise the family that it's in their best interest to let this case die. You save face by coming forward as the compassionate arbiter of the situation. The family saves face by taking the lead and *requesting* that the charges be dropped. They can say that it is simply too painful for them to have to relive this tragedy."

"You want her to go scot-*free?*"

"I want the charges dropped," Cassie insisted. "All of them. It wasn't murder. She was fleeing for her life, and he ran in front of her car on a dark night in a crowded, unlit parking lot. Drop those charges, and if there's no crime, there's no charge of flight to avoid prosecution."

"Christ, you don't budge. Give me a crumb, here. What about vehicular homicide?"

"It wasn't that. He was drunk, and he ran out from between parked cars. There's no vehicular homicide here. My client has paid dearly for knowing Rob DiCenza. If she weren't as quiet and gentle as she is, and if she didn't have a quiet and gentle life here, I'd have her turn around and sue the DiCenza family for defamation of character. But she *is* quiet and gentle. All she wants is to return to her family here. I don't even want her going to California to appear in court for dismissal of the charges. There's no need for that."

"Give me something, Ms. Byrnes."

"Agree to all of the above, and my client will agree not to divulge anything related to Rob DiCenza or this case, but I want her released from prison as soon as we make our deal. She isn't a danger to society. She shouldn't have to spend even one more day in jail. That's why I want this

done fast. I want every part of it done fast. You can make that happen."
He might be a lousy lawyer, but he surely knew about political expediency.

"You give me too much credit," the man muttered. "I don't have the final say here."

Cassie understood that. "The DiCenzas are in town. I've checked this out and know they are. I also know that you can be very persuasive when you want to. If you want," she added, knowing that he was an adoptee himself, "you can make the argument that a fourteen-year-old who has a loving adoptive family shouldn't have to relive the sins of her birth parents. I'll look forward to hearing from you."

*   *   *

After calling Micah with a report, Cassie packed up everything at her friend's office and drove back to Lake Henry. She dropped her assistant at home along the way and stopped at the office only to close up the place for the night. Then she headed home. As she drove, she planned dinner, which she would be able to cook since she had a gas stove. She decided on games that she wanted to play with each of the kids, youngest first so that one went to bed as she moved on to the next. She mentally located every candle she had in the house, intent on lighting at least a dozen for games to play with Mark when the house settled down.

She arrived home to find a note on the kitchen table saying that he had taken the kids to Concord for fast food and a movie.

Feeling a letdown, and the irrational sense that her family was moving on without her, she made herself macaroni and cheese from a box, built up the fire in the living room, and settled in on the sofa to wait. In less than twenty minutes, she was asleep.

*   *   *

Micah was sweating. He was so hot he thought he would die of it, as he poured off the latest batch of syrup and carted the tank toward the filtering system he had rigged up. Granted, the heat in the sugarhouse was a good thing, what with the girls playing with dolls in a corner of the room. The house was cold, and now that everyone had gone home, there was no one to stoke the fire there. Missy and Star had their sleeping bags here and would stay as long as Micah did.

"How's this depth?" Griffin asked. He was standing over the finish pan, which was newly replenished with sap that was nearing the syrup stage. Skimmer in hand, he was at the ready should anything start to foam.

Micah glanced over and nodded that it was fine, but quickly returned to the task at hand. The sweat that trickled down his body wasn't only from work. Much of it was the product of fear. He was behind in the process. Having to filter everything by hand was slowing up the works. Even with Griffin helping, he would be working past midnight. He wouldn't mind that, if it wore him out enough so that he could sleep for five hours straight, something he hadn't done in a while. Niggling problems kept waking him up.

One problem was solved. As of late afternoon, all of the tubing was clear and running.

That created another problem. If he was backed up now, after a day's sap flow from barely half his trees, with everything running tomorrow he would be twice as backed up. He needed the electricity back on for the filter press, but the power company wasn't promising help for another two or three days.

By then he would be dead on his feet, and maybe that was okay, too. If he was too tired to think, he couldn't think about Heather, and if he didn't think about Heather, he wouldn't have trouble breathing. He took a breath now and tried to relax, but the tightness was still there. It was the product of fear—fear of Heather returning, fear of her not returning, fear of his not knowing the person she was when and if she did return.

Cassie said they had to wait. He was in purgatory.

The sugarhouse door barreled open, and Skip Houser backed in. Micah hadn't seen Skip since that day at the gas pumps, and was about to ask what in the *hell* he was doing, when he saw that Skip and another man were struggling to carry in something that looked familiar enough.

Micah continued pouring syrup through the filters.

Glancing behind him, Skip backed up to the nonfunctioning electric filter. He squatted to put his end of the small generator on the floor.

When his partner had done the same, Skip straightened. He pulled off his gloves and stared at Micah.

"This was s'posed to go up to the job site. I figured no one'd notice if it was a couple days late. You didn't see *me* bring it, though," he warned and set to hooking it up to the machine. In less than fifteen minutes, the filter press was running and he was headed out the door.

"Hey," Micah said. "Thanks, man."

Raising a hand in acknowledgment, Skip disappeared.

* * *

Two hours later, after the last of the day's sap had been boiled into syrup, passed through the filter press, poured into quart tins, and sealed, Micah sent Griffin home. He finished up the washing himself, rather enjoying the cleansing, thinking that this year he would give gallons of syrup to all the people in town who had helped. He wouldn't have thought Skip would be one of them, which went to show how little Micah knew.

Wiping down the sink, he hung the rags to dry, then knelt by the little lumps buried in sleeping bags and gently shook the girls awake. "Time for bed," he whispered, and started gathering the sleeping bags as soon as they crawled out. "Boots on," he prompted. When it was done, Star put her arms up. He set her on his hip. "Get the lantern, Missy, and stay close."

There was an instant then—just an instant—when the warmth lingered, the scent of sugar wafted from the rafters, and the three of them stood so very close that he felt a fullness near his heart. Right here, right now, his past, present, and future coalesced. Only one thing could have made it better.

Guiding Missy along, he closed the sugarhouse door on shelves that were neatly lined with new tins of syrup. "Quick, quick," he whispered once they were outside, because though the moon lit the path, it was cold. The house wasn't much better, but the sleeping bags retained warmth. Missy went right to bed and was asleep in minutes. Star left an arm around his neck when he would have tucked her into bed.

"Daddy?" she whispered.

He sat, pulling the sleeping bag around her to keep her warm.

"Does Momma have a baby?"

He had a flash of that instant back at the sugarhouse, when the only thing that could have deepened the fullness he felt would have been Heather and a baby of their own. Of course, that wasn't what Star meant.

"She did once," he told her, because he knew that if the women had talked of this at the house, Star would have picked up on it.

"What happened to it?"

"She couldn't take care of it, so she gave it to some people who could."

"Why couldn't she take care of it?"

"She was too young."

"Did the baby cry when she gave it away?"

"I think the baby was too little to know."

"I'd cry if you gave me away."

He tightened his hold of her. "Well, I would never do that. So you don't have to worry."

"Does Heather's baby miss her now?"

Micah didn't know that. He didn't know what Poppy had found. Nor did he know what Heather felt about it all. "The baby isn't a baby anymore. She's almost grown up, and she has her own daddy."

"Me, too, but I miss Momma. If she had to choose, would she choose that baby instead of us?"

"She'd choose us," Micah said. But he wasn't sure, and therein lay the crux of his fear. Heather had a past now. Regardless of the outcome of Cassie's dealings, she was free to be Lisa again. He couldn't imagine her choosing to return to California. But how could he know for sure?

He loved Heather. If she became Lisa again, he and the girls would be on their own.

*   *   *

Griffin had been on his own for so long that he rarely thought twice about coming home to an empty place. Coming back to Poppy's, though, he felt lonely. Despite his insistence that she take an overnight bag, he had really wanted her home, had been counting the hours, while he worked at Micah's. But she wouldn't be back until morning. She had left a message to that extent on his phone, with no mention of those two little words.

Me, too. She had said it and then hung up.

He wanted to know if she meant it. Assuming that she would call back, certainly on her way to the airport as she had promised, he kept the phone in his pocket the whole time he'd been at Micah's—only to pull it out when he returned to the truck and find it stone cold and blank. The thing had gotten turned off somehow. He must have bumped it in just a certain way. When he turned it on and called her back, the messaging system picked up.

Her house was quiet now, dark and cold. He lit candles, built a fire, poured himself a glass of wine. A lengthy search turned up Victoria sleeping on a pile of spare blankets in Poppy's closet, but the cat had no desire to come out and visit, not with him, at least.

With a candle in one hand and his wineglass in the other, he wandered around the house. He would have thought that after being with other people so much lately, he would welcome the solitude. But being with Poppy wasn't like being with "other people." She was easy and, aside from the occasional venting, totally agreeable. She was fun, smart, caring. She was certainly brave.

He had thought he was the brave one, surviving Little Bear, weathering the isolation of being an outsider in an insider town. But there was Poppy, wheelchair-bound in Florida, getting around on her own and no doubt doing it well—while here he sat, afraid to call the phone number on the scrap of paper in his pocket.

Disgusted with himself, he pulled out the paper, turned on his cell phone, and punched in the number. Heart pounding, he listened through four long rings. He was fully expecting an answering machine to come on, when a groggy female voice murmured, "This had better be good."

Griffin swallowed. "Is Cynthia Hughes there?"

There was silence for several seconds—muffled sounds to suggest the transfer of the phone—then a different voice. This one was gentler, more cautious, familiar even after seven years. "Yes?"

Griffin had trouble breathing. "Cindy?"

There was such utter silence on the other end that he feared she'd hung up.

"Stay with me," he begged. "Please don't hang up. I've looked for you for so long." Still she said nothing. His heart positively thundered. "Cindy?"

"Yes," she whispered. "How did you find me?"

"Your poem. The one in *Yankee* magazine. Robin Chris. Christopher Robin. You always loved Winnie-the-Pooh. Remember I used to read the books to you?"

There was a pause, then a quiet, "That was a long time ago."

"Your poem was beautiful—but sad. Is that how you are?"

"I'm okay."

"I get your notes, but they don't say much about you."

"I know."

"When you just disappeared, we didn't know if you'd make it."

"Neither did I," she said, and he imagined he heard the trace of a smile.

"I know why you left," he went on. "It was an untenable situation. There was no give from Mom and Dad, and none of *us* helped. You know that Mom's gone." He figured Cindy knew everything that had happened since she had left.

"Yes," she whispered.

"And that we've all kind of . . . separated."

"Yes. I feel guilty about that."

"It wasn't your fault. It was us."

"I caused it."

"You were a kid. Kids rebel. We were older and should have been more responsible. But we each stayed in our own little lives and kept our mouths shut—like if we ignored the trouble at home, it didn't exist. We were wrong. We were *wrong*."

She didn't respond.

"Cindy?"

"I ran away," she said, "because I couldn't deal with the mess of everything. I wanted to leave it all behind, start fresh, y'know? And I have. But you don't forget. Not with family. You don't stop feeling."

Had they been carrying on a casual conversation, Griffin might have told her about Heather, because there were analogies there. But this was no casual conversation. It was a groundbreaking one. The focus had to be on the here and now. "Are you . . . okay?"

"I don't do drugs, if that's what you mean. I haven't since soon after I left. I wrote that in my note. I wanted you to know."

Griffin also knew that addicts sometimes had setbacks. He was relieved that Cindy had stayed clean. "You're not married?"

"No. I don't trust myself enough for that."

It was the guilt thing, he knew. She blamed herself for destroying a family. "Are you seeing someone for it?"

"Yes."

"Do you need help paying?"

"No."

"Are you sure?" When she didn't answer, he asked, "Are there good things for you there?" He needed to know that there were. "Who was that who answered the phone?"

"A friend. We share the rent. And yes, there are good things. My friends are . . . offbeat, but I love them. To hear the stories some of them tell, our family's dysfunctionality was mild. But we've kind of formed a family ourselves. And I get pleasure from my work."

"You should. It's incredibly good. Tell me more about your life."

"It's . . . fluid."

That was a warning. She meant she could go anywhere—as in, disappear—on a moment's notice. "Are you happy?" he asked.

"Often."

That was something. "Do you need anything?"

"No."

"Can I see you?"

"No."

"I'll come to wherever."

"You *know* wherever," she said with a bit of the spirit he remembered. "You dialed an area code that tells you exactly where I am. Are you going to show up here? Or tell the others?"

"If you say no, I won't."

"I say no. If anyone else finds me, I'm out of here."

"Even if it's Peter or Alex?" Griffin asked. They were the gentlest of his brothers.

"I'm not steady enough on my own, Griffin. Just the mention of their names takes me back to the person I was, and I don't want to go there."

Griffin suspected she had too solid a grasp of what she wanted to do much backsliding now, but she had to realize that herself. "You've always stayed one step ahead of us. When I saw that pseudonym, I was afraid to believe. A tiny part of me hoped you were sending me a message."

She didn't deny it. Quietly, she said, "I have to go now, Griffin. Give me your number."

He gave her his cell phone, along with his Princeton address and phone number, along with Poppy's address and phone number.

When he gave her the last, she asked, "Is Poppy Blake related to Lily Blake from last fall?"

"Sister. She's an incredible woman—spunky like you, which is probably why I felt an immediate connection. She's dealing with a lot of past stuff, too."

"And you're helping her because you can't help me?"

"I'm not sure I'm helping her. She's doing that herself. I just love her."

"Oh my," Cindy said, again with the kind of spirit Griffin remembered. "You'll have to keep me apprised."

"Will you stay at this number?"

"As long as no one comes. I keep tabs on Ralph. But you knew that."

"Yes. If you move, will you let me know?"

"That depends on why I have to move. I know what Ralph is up to. Randy's more roundabout. He broke the Matlock case. Is he up there in New Hampshire with you?"

"No. His role in it ended with the arrest." Griffin paused. "Dad would want to know you're okay. Can I tell him we've talked?"

"No. He'd subpoena your phone record, get my number, and be here in no time, judging . . . me again. I'm not ready for that. Maybe someday. But not yet."

Griffin knew that "someday" would come. If he had learned anything from Poppy and Heather, it was that. For now, he understood what his sister was feeling. As long as she stayed in touch with him, there was hope.

* * *

Wednesday morning, for the first time in more than a week, Griffin didn't go to Micah's. Instead, buoyed by talking with Cindy and looking forward to seeing Poppy, he cleaned up her place, had breakfast at the café, then went to the marina, switched the truck for his Porsche, and headed for Manchester. He was there earlier than he needed to be, but he wasn't good for much else. Waiting for Poppy felt right.

Her plane was late. He had another cup of coffee and stood alternately watching the arrivals board and asking the airline agent for the latest news. The agent was female, and old enough to be his mother, which was probably why she took pity on him. Once he had shown identification, submitted to a search, and satisfactorily answered every one of her questions, she assisted him in getting through the security checkpoints to meet "the woman in the wheelchair" at the gate.

Griffin's eyes were on the board when the ETA changed to IN. He watched the plane taxi to the terminal and connect to the jetport. Eyes on the jetway, he waited for Poppy to come out. She was the very last one to emerge, but the wait was worth it. The sight of her made his heart swell.

He started forward as soon as there was room, shifted her carry-on from her lap to his shoulder, and bent over to hug her. When her arms went tight around his neck, he scooped her up and whirled her around. He didn't care who was watching, didn't care if the whole world saw his girl and him. He was so proud of her, so proud to be with her.

She was laughing by the time he set her back in her seat.

He rested his hands on the arms of the chair. "Did you mean it?" He was talking about the words, of course.

She nodded. "Don't know what I'm going to do with it yet," she said, but she was smiling.

"We'll figure that out," he said, feeling giddy. "Come on. I want to introduce you to someone."

He pushed her chair through the terminal, out the door, and into the short-term parking lot. She spotted the Porsche well before they reached it, and looked up at him.

"Someone?"

"She's inside."

"There's no way we're all fitting in—your mystery person, me, my carry-on, and my chair."

"Have faith," Griffin said. He had done the figuring. He had thought it all out. There was no way he was knowingly subjecting the love of his life to failure. What he wanted—what he would always want—was to open doors for her.

He steadied her wheels while she shifted into the passenger seat of the Porsche. Then he folded the chair and brought it to the trunk. He had a moment's panic when it didn't quite fit. With a bit of thought and a tiny turn, though, it slid in. The carry-on was flexible. A push here and a squeeze there, and it, too, was stowed. Pleased with himself, he closed the hood and slid in behind the wheel.

Beside him, Poppy was moving a hand over the leather upholstery. "This is a handsome car." She pointed to the GPS monitor. "Turn it on. Is this her?"

There went his surprise. "How did *you* know?"

She grinned. "We use these things on the lake. It helps finding our way through the islands at night. Charlie calls his Amelia."

Griffin sighed. "Mine's Sage. You just know too much, Poppy Blake. I can't surprise you with anything." As he turned the key in the ignition, Poppy closed a hand on his arm.

"You surprise me," she said, very serious now and vulnerable. "You're here."

Heart clenching, he nearly went for his pocket. He had something there, and it wasn't a kiss. But the timing wasn't right yet. She admitted that she loved him. *Don't know what I'm going to do with it yet,* she had said. He couldn't push her too far too fast.

So instead of forcing a commitment, he told her about Cindy.

* * *

One of the things Poppy loved about Griffin was his sense of loyalty, in this instance embodied by his call to his sister. If a woman wanted to know the kind of man she was thinking of spending her life with, Griffin's diligent search for Cindy was as good an endorsement as any. He cared about family. It was an important way to be.

So she was feeling ebullient as they headed back to Lake Henry. Her outlook on life today was totally different from what it had been barely three weeks ago. The Porsche was a perfect example of that. It was sleek and racy. It spoke of possibilities, which was so much of what her trip to Florida had been. Three weeks before, she wouldn't have dreamed that she would have been able to make that trip, much less be loved by Griffin.

Heather's fate was still up in the air. Like with Cindy, though, there was hope.

She thought about that as they drove north. As they approached Lake Henry, though, her ebullience faded. Lake Henry was real, as were certain other realities. The deal with the California authorities could fall through and Heather might have to stand trial. Cindy Hughes could pack up, take off, and be unheard from for another seven years. Griffin could realize that Buck Kipling's old truck wasn't worth another minute, that the Porsche represented his life, and that being in love with Poppy was fine while he was in town, but with a resolution to the Heather situation in hand, New Jersey called.

The next few days were crucial.

Chapter Twenty-one

Cassie agonized. She always did when she was waiting for a legal decision, whether it was that of a judge, a jury, or a prosecutor with whom she was trying to deal. With the power still out, she didn't go to the office, but stayed at home with the kids near the warmth of the living room fire. She could just as easily agonize from there.

Should I have told him more about Rob? Less about Heather? Did I make my case strongly enough? Did I make it too strongly? Was I too greedy? Should I have given him options? Should I have given him more time?

She second-guessed everything she'd done. Heather's future hung in the balance of her dealings with California; this morning, she felt the full weight of that responsibility.

There was always Plan B. If the deal she proposed was turned down, she had a wonderful case for the press. She planned that out while she waited, listing possible revelations in the order of their priority using a pencil with a rubber pom-pom on the top. The pom-pom pencil was from her home stash, others of which were being used by Ethan and his older brother, Brad, who had the hardwood floor covered with paper and were drawing pictures. Their younger brother, Jamie, had caught Ethan's croup and was asleep against Cassie's shoulder much as Ethan had been four days earlier. It was actually a comfortable way to contemplate Plan B.

John Kipling must have felt the vibes coming from her home, because he called shortly before noon. Since it was Wednesday, he was putting the finishing touches on *Lake News* before driving up to the printer.

"Okay," he told her. "I've covered the ice storm. I've covered the schools closing and the crisis at Micah's. I've covered the efforts of our heroes at the electric company and the phone company. Now give me something interesting, Cassie."

She sighed and smiled. "I can't do that in time for this edition, but if I had something at dinnertime tomorrow, what would you do with it?"

"Dinnertime tomorrow?" John asked. "I'd do a *Lake News* supplement. But first, I'd write up a press release and go through my list of major media outlets across the country. Between you, me, and Lily, we'd be able to phone or e-mail everyone on that list in a few hours. If our electricity's still out, we'll do it from Center Sayfield."

Cassie was gratified. John was a good one to have on her side. His efforts would be effective. She wished she had as much faith in her own.

Grumpy, she asked, "Why *does* Center Sayfield have electricity when we don't?"

Ever the repository for interesting little tidbits that only one who covered the neighboring towns for the local paper might know, John didn't disappoint her now. "Because as of two years ago, the single largest employer—translate, taxpayer—in Center Sayfield is a computer company that can't risk losing power even for a day, so there's been significant upgrading of lines, which doesn't mean that the lights don't go out, simply that problems are easier to pinpoint and, hence, fix. Think that's something for the Lake Henry Committee to take up?"

Cassie guessed it was a matter for Town Meeting first, but she knew that it would end up with her committee. So she put her mind to thinking about that. It was one way to pass the time while she waited for a call from California.

* * *

Micah spent his waiting time first in the sugarbush with a chainsaw and two of Charlie's sons, cutting and splitting wood that had been moved aside during the cleanup. They brought three tractorloads down to replenish what had already been used, and stacked it all before Micah had to fire up the arch, and then his afternoon was filled with sugarmaking. That kept his mind busy, but not totally. There were still in-between times when he wondered what was happening in California and what the outcome would be, wondered how Heather would react once she was free to be Lisa, wondered where that would leave him.

Lake Henry was a special place, but it wasn't California. He couldn't go to California. If that was her choice, he was out of luck.

* * *

Griffin's dilemma was different. As Wednesday afternoon settled into Wednesday evening and no call came from California, he began to think more about how people in town would deal with a less than satisfactory outcome in Heather's case. He had done the best he could in helping to put together a case, always hoping that she would return to the life she had lived before he had given the inadvertent tip-off to her whereabouts. If the California authorities rejected a deal and she had to face a nightmare of a trial, the goodwill he had established in Lake Henry could be reversed.

But he liked it here. He felt safe here. If he was to suggest that his sister come anywhere, it was here. Lake Henry was the first place where the thought of raising children appealed to him. It was the first place where he'd been in love—with a woman, a lake, a way of life.

He could continue his freelancing from here, could work out of Poppy's house or rent space at the *Lake News* office. He didn't lack intellectual stimulation here. People like Cassie, John and Lily, Charlie and Annette—they were as sophisticated as people anywhere. And Poppy? She was everything he'd always wanted.

He didn't want to think that her love was contingent on the outcome of Heather's case, but he was a realist. Things . . . lingered. Bad stuff eroded good stuff. If Heather's case went on and on, and if it ended in a less than satisfactory way, Poppy might always remember that he had been the one responsible.

It was rather like her accident. Shift a few inches to the right or the left, and things might never be the same.

* * *

Thursday morning, the lights went back on. By midday, the phones were also back. Their return provided Poppy a distraction, what with people calling all afternoon to check in. It wasn't as if she hadn't seen them. Charlie's was packed each time she stopped by, and if people weren't at Charlie's, they were chatting at the post office or outside the Town Hall. When storms hit and life slowed, people were left with the basics—oil lamps, woodstoves, and each other.

After four days without, phones were more a novelty than anything else.

Except, of course, for long-distance calls. And the one she wanted didn't come.

* * *

Cassie kept an eye on the clock. She had given the attorney general of California forty-eight hours. As that time approached without a call, she felt a sinking in her stomach. Yes, she had Plan B. But she'd been hoping she wouldn't have to resort to that. She had wanted Heather's situation handled quickly and quietly. No one here wanted the publicity. But publicity was preferable to losing Heather.

So she gathered her notes and began thinking along that line, all the more so when Griffin and John arrived. Then the phone rang.

"I'm making progress," the attorney general said, "but I need more time."

Cassie was wary. She didn't trust that the DiCenzas were not playing a game. "You need more time," she repeated for the benefit of Griffin and John. "What does 'making progress' mean?"

She heard a sigh. "It means that I've met resistance and need more time."

"The DiCenzas don't want to agree to the deal?"

"They're having trouble with the idea that the woman who ran down their son will walk away free."

Breezily, Cassie said, "Okay, then. If they don't want to deal, we'll go to the press. Do they understand what we have to say?"

"I'm trying to make them understand it," the attorney general said. He sounded frustrated enough so that Cassie believed him.

"How much more time did you have in mind?" she asked.

"Another forty-eight hours."

"If that was their suggestion," Cassie remarked, "I'd say what they're doing is trying to push this off so that nothing will hit the papers over the weekend, when more people are at home and reading all the fine print. I'm sorry. I can't do forty-eight hours. I can do twenty-four. I'll give you until Friday at five, your time. If they haven't agreed by then, I'll have to hold a news conference. There will be plenty of time for complete coverage in Sunday's paper."

"You're tough."

"With due respect, sir, I'm only doing what you would do if you were representing a client who has already been punished ten times over for what was truly a tragic accident."

*　*　*

Griffin had barely set off from Cassie's office in the truck when his cell phone rang. Thinking it would be Poppy, he said a discouraged, "Hey."

"What's going on there?" Prentiss Hayden asked. "I'm hearing a buzz down here, and it's ugly."

Griffin passed the general store as Charlie put the last of several bags into Alice Bayburr's car. When he lifted a hand, Griffin waved back. "A buzz?"

"Phone calls from mutual DiCenza friends. What's brewing?"

Griffin was disgusted enough with the whole situation to say, "Nothing that most normal people would be surprised at. You people in power just think you're immune."

Impatiently, Prentiss asked, "What's happening with the DiCenzas?"

He glanced in his rearview mirror and saw John turn off the main road, heading toward the *Lake News* office. "Their past is coming back to haunt them."

"Rob was a good boy, and he's dead. Why go after a dead boy?"

"I won't comment on that," Griffin said as he passed the town beach. "It's not my place. But it's what I've been telling you for weeks now. If you draw attention to yourself by writing a bio, and then you choose to hide things, those things will come out. Sooner or later, they will. You won't know when, you won't know where, you won't know how." He left the center of town behind and, shifting gears, set off on the lake road. "On the other hand, if you come clean in your bio, no one has anything on you. You've picked the time, the place, and the method. You've taken control, rather than letting someone else do it."

"I don't want headlines. Not on this. The existence of my son is between him and me."

"Normally, that'd be true. But you're a public figure. There are perks that go with that, and there are liabilities. This is one of the liabilities. If you don't mention your son in this book, even in passing, someone else will."

"You?" the senator asked. "Is that what this has been about—your giving me ample warning so that when you follow this book up with a tell-all of your own, I can't say you didn't warn me?"

Griffin bristled. "I signed a contract guaranteeing confidentiality. If you think I'd break that, then we have a problem with trust, and if we have a problem with trust, there's no way you're going to be happy with this book. Maybe you need another ghostwriter."

"Wait. Wait. Griffin, I did *not* say that I didn't trust you. It was a hypothetical remark."

"It was an *offensive* remark."

"Yes. Well, I'm sorry. I've spent a lifetime being offensive. But I like what you've done so far. I do not want another ghostwriter. It's just that I . . . well, how would *you* feel if you'd led a successful and productive life and then someone wants to focus on a foolish little thing you did in your youth?"

"I don't think your son is foolish. He's a husband and a father. He's a pediatrician. And you helped him get there. I'd think you would be proud of that."

"I am. But it's such an intimate thing."

Griffin sighed. "Let's be honest here. Most people know he exists. All you'd be doing is acknowledging a fine man. His mother's dead, so she wouldn't be hurt, and your wife knows about him. She has no problem discussing him. She's perfectly confident with the four children you had with her. He wouldn't be the focus of the book. We might be talking about one chapter out of twenty—just one chapter, but it would send a message that this is an honest book. They aren't all, you know."

There was a grumbled, "Yes, I know."

"He wasn't planned, but you handled it well. You made the most of it. That would be inspiring for people."

"Do you think?"

"Definitely. People look up to you. This will only add to that."

There was a silence on the other end, then a sigh. "Your daddy was a powerful player in the courtroom. You inherited his silver tongue."

Griffin waited.

After what seemed an eternity, Prentiss Hayden muttered a begrudging, "Oh, do it," and hung up the phone.

*   *   *

Griffin decided to try out that silver tongue on Poppy, but he wasn't relying on words alone, and he wasn't rushing things. He cooked dinner for her, then took her to Charlie's Back Room, where the entertainment was homegrown in the form of a local barbershop quartet. When they got home, he rebuilt the fire, settled her on the sofa in his arms. He told her about Prentiss, and talked about Cindy. Then he said, "You're one of the lucky ones. The past is out there on the table now. The people who would judge you know the truth, and they still love you, so what do you say? Marry me, Poppy?"

Poppy put her fingers over his mouth. "Don't ask that. Not yet."

"I love you."

"Shhhhh."

"I do."

"Now. But what about next week? Or next month?"

"What about next year? Or five years from now? Or *ten* years from now? Will I still love you then? Will you still love me then? Come on, Poppy. That's not the way it works. If people put their lives on hold while they waited to see if love lasted, they'd miss out on it completely. I want to marry you. I want to have kids with you. Two's fine. I can live with two."

"I don't know if I can get pregnant."

"No woman does. No *couple* does."

"You know what I mean."

"No, I don't," he said gently. "You've done things in the last few weeks that you didn't think you'd ever do. What's to stop you from doing this?"

"I can't leave Lake Henry."

"You can. But you don't want to, and neither do I. I'm very happy living here. I love the town, and I love your house."

"It's too small."

"I have money. We'll build on. There's plenty of land here. We could build to the right, the left, or the back. It's called an addition."

"I know. I know. This has just happened so fast."

"Good things do. Do you love me, Poppy?"

She nodded.

"Then why wait?"

"I don't know. There's still something . . ."

"Heather. But we'll know about that soon."

"There's still something . . ."

"Forgiving yourself? I meant what I said about that, Poppy. You need to do it, but why can't we be married while you work on it? What better person to help than your husband?"

"My husband? That is just such a dream."

"Make it come true." He couldn't say the words, couldn't ask her again.

She laced her fingers through his, studied all ten for a minute, then looked up. "Give me a little more time? Just a little more? There's still something . . . I need to do."

*   *   *

There were several somethings Poppy needed to do. She spent Friday morning thinking about those things, because the pace of Lake Henry had slowed to a crawl in ways that it hadn't even during the ice storm. It was an emotional thing—waiting and wondering—and it was reflected in an unusual quiet at Charlie's, at the post office, at Poppy's phone bank.

People weren't in the mood to talk.

Neither was she. She sat alternately at the console staring at the buttons and in the exercise room staring at the equipment. She did her upper-body workout, sat there a while, then returned to the phones. An hour later, she went back into the exercise room and used the recumbent bike. When she was done, she moved to the parallel bars. Victoria sat in her lap when it was free and, when it wasn't, went into the other room. She didn't go near her usual spot under the parallel bars. Poppy wondered if that was a sign.

*　*　*

Griffin spent the morning at Charlie's Café. He figured that Poppy needed time and space, and he had to work. So he staked out a table with a forest view, plugged in his computer, spread out his notes, and nodded yes each time Annette came by with the coffee carafe. Other people came by, but their greetings were short. He didn't take it personally. Shortness was the prevalent mood. Lake Henry was in waiting mode.

He certainly was. He was waiting for news about Heather, hoping that positive word would shorten his wait for Poppy.

*　*　*

Cassie wasn't a pacer, but that was what she was up to by the time Friday afternoon arrived. She had other cases that needed attention, but she couldn't concentrate on those. She had Committee business that needed attention, but she couldn't concentrate on that, either. She kept thinking about Heather and the number of lives that would be affected if the DiCenzas decided to dig in their heels.

Since her office was too small, she paced up and down the hallway, turning first at the window overlooking the street then at the one overlooking the woods. When the hallway closed in, she took both her cell phone and the cordless extension of her office line and paced outside. When she got chilled, she came back inside, where she sat until the need to pace returned.

*　*　*

Micah made sugar. He boiled, he skimmed foam, he scooped syrup. He monitored levels, bubbles, and sugar content. He put new syrup through the filter press, which was running on electricity again, and as afternoon waned and evening began, he packed his containers. The collection was impressive, shelves filled with growing layers of gallon, quart, and pint tins, all with the newly upgraded Smithson Sugarhouse label on the front.

He had Billy and Amos working, and Griffin was there for a time. The girls camped out after dinner in their corner. It was all very comfortable and cozy.

He told himself that he could do this forever. He could make syrup. He could do what had to be done. He could survive, whether Heather returned or not.

But he wanted her back, wanted her to see those neat labels on the neat rows of tins. Cassie hadn't called, which meant that California hadn't called, and the deadline approached.

*   *   *

Cassie's phone rang at eight on the nose. It was her office line, which Poppy had rerouted to the house. Jamie was already asleep; Mark had Ethan and Brad in the bath. She had been cleaning up the mess in the kitchen from the snickerdoodles she had baked up for a bedtime snack. She wanted to think she had done it solely for the kids, but baking was a way to pass the time.

Heart racing, she picked up the phone. "Yes?" she asked guardedly.

"They've agreed," said the attorney general, sounding tired.

Cassie closed her eyes and let out a breath. Smiling, she put a hand on her chest to calm her heart.

"They've agreed to dropping the charges," the attorney general went on, "but they want a nondisclosure agreement, and they want her back here to face the judge for the dismissal."

"Why back there?" Cassie asked, still smiling. She knew what they planned. Of course she did, but she was holding the cards.

"They need closure," he said in the same tired voice. "They feel that if the case disappears from the radar screen without any public explanation, it will raise questions. If there's a public hearing at which Mr. Grinelle explains that we do not have the evidence to convict, the family can follow it up with a press conference honoring the memory of their son, taking the high road, explaining that vengeance won't bring him back and that it's time to put the case to rest. It's a face-saving thing, Ms. Byrnes. Give them this."

Between "evidence to convict" and "press conference," Mark had appeared at the door holding two dripping children in a single large towel. Grinning, Cassie danced to the door and gave the three of them a hug. She backed off only enough to play the tough lawyer again.

"The problem I have," she said into the phone, holding Mark's gaze, finding as much pleasure in his excitement as in the news itself, "is that if there's a press conference, someone will inevitably ask about your not having the evidence to convict. The implication will be that my client is guilty, but that since you can't make a case, she'll go free. You're asking us to sign a nondisclosure agreement. I'm afraid, we'll need the same. I won't have my client returning to a hostile place where she'll be talked about as a killer who beat the system. I'd rather go to trial and have the whole story come out."

Mark stuck a so-*there* fist in the air, then wrapped his arm around her neck and pulled her close again. He was wonderful, she realized. She was a workaholic who too often neglected her man, and he loved her anyway.

From the other end of the line came an exasperated, "I can't control what the press does. Talk shows love this kind of thing. I may be able to keep the DiCenzas from saying anything derogatory, but I can't do anything about public opinion."

"Yes, you can. You can settle this quietly. Heather can appear before a magistrate here in New Hampshire. The charges can be dropped, and that's that. She'll sign away the right to talk about Rob, in exchange for the DiCenzas signing away the right to talk about her. That's a fair deal."

"The boy's dead."

"He was a man," she corrected, "and he abused a woman to the extent that she gave up a name, a history, and a child she wanted. But I'll tell you what. I'll be the good guy here. If the DiCenzas insist, she'll return to California. She'll even sign a nondisclosure agreement. I won't, though. If pot shots are taken at Heather by anyone, I'll answer them in kind."

There was a short pause, then an almost admiring, "You *are* tough."

"Yup," Cassie said with a grin and slipped an arm around her husband's waist.

*   *   *

Ten minutes later, she got the call she wanted. She promptly called Micah, then Poppy and Griffin, then Marianne, Sigrid, Charlie and Annette. And Camille. She called Camille, because she knew that something was special there. She didn't know what it was—didn't want to know. It was enough that this was one more person who cared about Heather.

Chapter Twenty-two

Saturday dawned glorious, though Poppy would have thought it even if the sky had been gray. As it happened, the sun rose a pale yellow and grew bolder as it climbed. She watched it with Griffin first from bed, then from the kitchen. He made omelets this time, quite creatively, and she was game. She didn't mind having raisins in an omelet, particularly when he drizzled maple syrup on the top. *Drizzled.* He was emphatic about that. This was early-season syrup, he stressed. Its delicate flavor was not to be overdone.

Poppy prided herself in being self-sufficient, but she had to admit that having a man dote on her was nice.

Oh, she knew what he was doing. He was showing her what he could bring to her life. And doting wasn't all; he respected her needs. He was patient and encouraging. Take sex. He didn't just make love to her while she lay back and enjoyed it. He knew her disabilities—but he also knew her abilities, and he egged her on. Where there was potential, he urged her to meet it, which meant that she was as often the aggressor as the recipient. From the start, he had made her feel like a woman. In this, he made her feel like a consummate one.

She was fine as long as he didn't start talking about marriage again.

Mercifully, he didn't—not at any time during the impromptu party at Charlie's Café the night before, not when they returned to the house and made love, not when they woke up together knowing that Heather was coming home.

"One way to look at this," Griffin proposed as they got ready to leave the house, "is that my tipping Randy off was actually good. Heather is free now. She isn't haunted by the fear of discovery."

Poppy agreed with him, but only in part. "Legally, she's okay now. Emotionally? We'll have to see. She'll have to reconcile who she *was* with who she *is.*"

"No problem there. Micah loves her. That won't change."

"She pushed the past out of her mind. Now she'll have to deal with it."

"No problem there," Griffin repeated, holding her gaze. "Micah loves her. That won't change."

The message was for Poppy, of course. And she loved Griffin for sending it. But there was something she still had to work out, a reconciliation of her own.

Not today, though. Today was for celebrating.

* * *

Micah had stopped by the café the night before, but only because Camille came to sit with the girls and practically kicked him out. He only stayed in town long enough to thank the people who had done so much for him, though, before heading home. At such an unsure time, he wanted to be with his daughters.

They were his life—the girls and sugarmaking. The girls gave him love, and his trees gave him their sweetness. He was a lucky man, having both. It was more than some people had.

That was what he told himself, because thinking about Heather terrified him. He spent most of the night lying awake in bed, feeling her beside him, remembering the wholeness of it, and when he wasn't doing that, he was drifting in and out of an uneasy sleep.

He hadn't told the girls about Cassie's deal. It was cowardly of him, perhaps irresponsible, but he hadn't wanted to deal with the questions about when she would be home. He didn't know when, because Cassie didn't know when. She had mentioned magistrates, paperwork, and hearings. She had mentioned a confidentiality agreement to be drawn up and signed. She had mentioned a possible return to California.

Besides, Heather coming home was one thing. Her staying there was another. Micah wouldn't know which she would choose until the moment arrived. He didn't want to get the girls' hopes up.

Star wanted Momma back. She was frightened of being abandoned again, frightened that Heather would choose another life and another child. Missy, conversely, didn't know if she wanted Heather back at all. She was angry that Heather had left, and she had put up walls to protect herself. Micah knew how that was. He had done it himself earlier on. Missy was his daughter in that sense. And Star? Star was Heather's in so many ways that it was eerie. If Heather chose to leave, Star would be devastated.

And so Micah's thoughts churned through the night. When morning came, he gave the girls breakfast, dressed them warmly, loaded them in the tractor and took them up the hill into the sugarbush. There was no phone here, no television, no chance of unwanted guests. There was nothing foreign here. He knew every inch of this land. It was safe. It was eternal. That was what he wanted the girls to see and feel.

Stopping the tractor, he lifted them down and led them through the snow to a boulder. It was one he had gone to as a child when he wanted to be alone. Glimpses of blue tubing could be seen through the trees, but this was evergreen territory. It was quiet, untouched, peaceful land.

He lifted the girls onto the boulder one at a time. Then he climbed up between them. He didn't say anything, just sat, looked, and listened. The trees were tall here—mossy pines, deep green hemlocks, and blue firs— and the snow more sparse where their limbs sheltered the ground. A startling number of limbs lay fallen under the weight of ice, but the trees didn't look any worse for it.

"God's pruning?" Missy asked, and he nodded.

Star whispered, "Shhhhh. Listen." The woods were alive with snowmelt, a gentle dripping that came from different directions, different sections of nature's orchestra, each with its own tempo and tone, all harmonizing. Head cocked as she continued to listen, she looked up at him. Her eyes were as large as ever, but rather than being haunted now, they held the light of excitement. "Snow songs."

God's pruning. Nature's orchestra. Snow songs. They were all Heather's expressions. She put into words what Micah felt but couldn't say. Her words would live on in all of them this way, regardless of what she did herself.

He didn't say anything then, though not through any desire for silence so much as sheer inability. His throat was tight with emotions that he couldn't begin to deal with. So he swallowed them away, breathed deeply of the fertile March air, and focused on the moment.

They sat that way for a long time, the girls seemingly as content as he was. Finally climbing down from their rock, they walked through the woods for a while. Missy ran from one fallen log to the next, balancing her way down each, while Star crouched to peer into nooks and crannies for glimpses of tiny forest creatures.

Micah alternately watched them, and watched the blue tubing that was bit by bit filling with liquid as the sap started to flow. Eventually, he herded the girls back to the tractor and drove them down the hill. By the time they reached the sugarhouse, the storage tanks had filled with sap enough to boil, and the driveway was lined with trucks.

Lake Henry had come to make sugar.

* * *

Poppy arrived at Micah's well after the first of the other trucks had pulled in. Squeezing past them, she drove up to the house. Once she had parked, she and Griffin unloaded the huge pot of chili that they'd picked up at Charlie's. The problem was finding room in the kitchen, which was even more packed with food and people than it had been after the ice storm.

Taking it all in, she felt an intense pride. This was her town; these were her people. They did this each year to celebrate the sap harvest— picked a day when the sun was out, the air was clear, and the children had no school, because, like Christmas, sugar on snow was best with kids. The settling of Heather's case only made it better.

Micah surely felt that way. He smiled more in the ten minutes he spared for lunch than he had in all of the last twenty-four days. Then he headed for the sugarhouse with dozens of people in tow. This was the fun part. A packed sugarhouse made the syrup sweeter faster.

A packed sugarhouse makes the syrup sweeter faster.

Heather had said that, Poppy realized as she whipped out the front door and down the ramp. Griffin was already at the sugarhouse, bringing wood in from the shed on the old iron flatcar. She pushed her wheels through the last of the ice that was melting on the gravel drive, and reached the back of the house in time to join the procession.

Far ahead of her, at the foot of the hill, Micah opened the sugarhouse door and turned to hold it for those behind him. In the process, he glanced toward the road.

His body went still. Only his eyes moved, following something down the drive.

Heart pounding, Poppy looked that way. It was a dark red car, late model, not from Lake Henry, rather sedate for its color. She doubted it would be Heather so soon, and it didn't look like FBI. This looked like a rental car, perhaps a reporter coming straight from the airport?

Poppy shot a look back at the sugarhouse door just as Griffin joined Micah. John was nearby as well. Media could be handled.

The red car moved slowly, making its way past the long line of larger vehicles. It pulled up just shy of the house. Even before the driver opened his door, the pounding of Poppy's heart increased.

"Oh God," she whispered. She pushed herself forward, separating from the others just as Norman Anderson straightened. He caught her eye right away and did a little something with his own while he let out a burst of air. The look said that he wouldn't have shown up here unannounced if his headstrong fourteen-year-old daughter hadn't forced the issue.

Sure enough, Thea had left the passenger's seat and was rounding the front of the car. She wore jeans, boots, a camel hair pea coat and a matching beret that was striking against the long, shiny waves of her hair. Her hands were in her pockets. Her face spoke of both excitement and terror. When she caught sight of Poppy, she seemed relieved.

Not so Poppy. She had been proud of herself to have instantly connected with Heather's daughter. It struck her now, though, that the connection might well have been responsible for bringing Thea here at such a bad, bad time.

She wheeled quickly forward. She couldn't begin to think of what would happen if Heather arrived just then. It was enough trying to gauge the impact that Thea alone would have on the town.

Norman met Poppy halfway. "I'm sorry," he said in a low voice. "If I'd said no, Thea would have come here on her own. I couldn't let her do that. She wanted to meet Micah. She wanted to take a look at the town. I thought we could do it without anyone knowing who we are." He shot a dubious look at the crowd. "I guess not."

Thea put an arm around Poppy's shoulder and kissed her cheek. While she was there, she murmured, "Did I do an awful thing?"

They didn't know about the plea agreement, Poppy realized with a start.

"Don't know that yet," she said in a high singsong. "Let's see." She was thinking that it was going to be the three of them—Norman, Thea, and her—against Lake Henry, when Griffin materialized beside her and offered a hand.

"Mr. Anderson, I'm Griffin Hughes. Welcome."

"Thank you," Norman said.

Poppy imagined that he was as relieved to see Griffin as she was.

*   *   *

"Relieved" wasn't a word Micah would have used. He felt just the opposite. He wanted Heather back there and choosing this life before any child of hers appeared, but he could tell it was too late for that. He didn't need an introduction to know that the young woman with Poppy was Heather's daughter. She was a young, elegant version of Heather. Micah imagined that Heather would look every bit as elegant if she lived in California instead of Lake Henry.

The thought, of course, gave him no comfort.

Needing to hold what was his, he looked around for Missy and Star. He saw Missy first—saw the back of a dark, wavy head of hair as she headed for the house. When Maida went after her, he looked around for Star. It was a frightened minute before he saw her emerge on the far side of the crowd from him and walk slowly toward Poppy.

"Star?" he called.

She kept going.

Swearing under his breath, unable to think of anything but that he was losing everything that mattered to him, he followed.

* * *

Poppy didn't see Star at first. Thea was talking, taking the blame for the trip, saying that they wouldn't stay long, insisting that she had only wanted a little look—Norman was trying to explain to her that they couldn't have come at a worse time, perhaps ought to leave, could drive west to ski in Vermont for the weekend—and all the while Griffin was giving Poppy looks that said he didn't know whether to acknowledge the Andersons by introducing them to Micah, or ignore them by getting on with the sugaring.

The first Poppy was aware of anyone else nearby was when Star leaned against her chair. "Oh! Star!"

Star wasn't looking at her. Those big, dark, solemn eyes were focused on Thea.

"Uh," Thea said in surprise. "Okay." She smiled and stuck out her hand toward Star. "Hi. I'm Thea. You're Star, aren't you?"

Star nodded.

"I saw your picture," Thea explained. "You look just the same."

"You look like Momma," Star said.

Micah emerged from the crowd and was beside them in a few long strides. He stopped behind Star, with challenging eyes on Norman, and Poppy had a sudden fear that he would lash out. That would mean back-tracking at a later point, making amends and mending rifts, because the fact was that Thea had been found. She was here. She was strong-willed. She wanted to connect with her roots.

Poppy gave his arm a squeeze through his flannel sleeve, then another until he looked at her. "The timing may be off," she said quietly, "but the sentiment is right." Still holding Micah's arm, she turned to Thea. "This is Micah. It's an emotional day for him, because we don't know when Heather will be getting back. So we're keeping ourselves busy by cele-brating the sugar season. Micah has sap to boil. Maybe you'd like to watch?" When Micah's arm tensed, she tightened her grip.

Thea's eyes widened. She smiled at Micah and said softly, almost timidly, "I would really like that."

Poppy looked up at Micah. This was his house, his land, his sap. Heather might be the one to decide whether she wanted an ongoing relationship with Thea, but he was the one to decide, here and now, whether the girl and her father stayed.

Before he could say anything, Star slipped out from in front of him. She moved around the wheelchair, looked up at Thea, and slowly, carefully, put a hand in hers. Seeming utterly sure of what she was doing, she raised her eyes to Micah.

*   *   *

After that, of course, Micah had no more say in the matter than Norman had when Thea had threatened to fly to Lake Henry by herself. Micah did not want Thea there. He did not want Thea to *exist*. But she was and she did—and he understood what Star felt. Thea exuded the same basic goodness that Heather always had. Even if Star hadn't led the way, he doubted he would have been able to ask her to leave. She was part of Heather, whom he loved.

He also loved Missy, and Missy was upset. Needing to see to her, he motioned the others on to the sugarhouse while he went back into the house. He found Missy in her bedroom with Maida, the two of them sitting side by side on the edge of the bed.

"We were just talking about things," Maida said with a little smile. "Missy needs to vent."

"She kept secrets," Missy charged, scowling.

Micah squatted in front of her. "She had no choice."

"She had another family."

"No. Not really."

"Then who's that out there? She didn't tell us about her. And if she didn't tell us about *her*, what *else* didn't she tell us about?"

Micah didn't know what to say. Missy had a point. But there was another side to all of the things Heather had kept to herself. The fact was, he hadn't asked about them. He hadn't wanted to know. He had built a life with Heather and had gone right along with the idea that the past didn't matter. He had let it happen. So maybe he was at fault, too.

Feeling the weight of that knowledge, he pushed himself up. "We'll talk about it once she's back."

"I don't want her back."

"I do. I love her. We all make mistakes—you, me, Star. If Heather's made some, we have to forgive her."

Missy's chin trembled. "I don't."

"Then you lose her. Is that what you want?"

Missy didn't answer.

He went to the door. "We're doing sugar on snow. Don't you want some?"

That eased her pout a bit. "I don't know. Maybe."

"Well, I'm going to go make it." He held out a hand. When she simply stared at him, he dropped it. It struck him that she would be a handful when she got older, and that he needed Heather's help here, too. For now, he did his best, which was to be nonchalant, which was probably cowardly, because he was avoiding the issue, but the sap called. "Okay. Come over when you're ready."

*   *   *

Micah began boiling the syrup that had just run, and it took concentration. He didn't think about Heather. He didn't think about Thea. He knew that the sugarhouse was packed with people, and that others—kids and parents—were outside packing snow in plastic soup bowls, pie plates, and foil pans. Totally aside from the feast in the house, there was coffee. There was hot chocolate. There was hot cider. There was a buzz of conversation that had a festive feel, and Micah couldn't help but catch it.

The first batch of sap quickly became syrup. Taking it from the finish pan, he poured it through the filter press. He filled pitchers directly from that and had no sooner put them on the canning table by a stack of paper cups when people started to pour and drink. Returning to the evaporator, he focused on the second batch of sap. This time, though, he didn't take it off when it reached the crucial seven degrees above boiling point that would render it syrup. Rather, he let it boil, constantly stirring and scraping so that it wouldn't scorch as the temperature rose. Shortly before it reached the point where it would be high and dry enough to beat into granular sugar, he poured it off into buckets—two for him, two for Griffin. Leaving Billy and Amos at the evaporator, they went outside.

How not to feel good then? Most everyone he cared about was here—Poppy and Lily and John, Cassie and her family, Charlie and Annette and those of their kids who weren't at the store, Camille, the Winslows, Heather's friends—Sigrid, Marianne, Leila Higgins—along with folks from the other side of the lake and from the Ridge, even Willie Jake, who had laid low after his role in Heather's arrest. Micah felt no animosity toward him, nor toward Norman Anderson, who was being shown proper Lake Henry hospitality by Maida, who looked charmed.

The midafternoon sun made everything golden, from jackets and hats that would have otherwise looked late-in-the-season shabby, to eager faces, to the hillside itself. Nearby, a long table held boxes of doughnuts, a barrel of sour pickles, and paper plates, napkins, and forks.

Micah had barely set down his buckets when he was surrounded by children, each holding a container of snow. Taking one at a time, he ladled hot syrup on the snow in a swirling design, handed the container back, and went on to the next. He didn't have to watch to know what happened then. When the syrup hit the snow, it cooled instantly and became chewy enough to be picked up with fingers or a fork. "Maple wax" was its earliest name, but "sugar on snow" was prettier. Eaten alone, it was delicious. Eaten between bites of doughnut and pickle, it was *the* best.

Sugar on snow was one of a few happy childhood memories he had. Caught up in it, he found himself drizzling first-name initials with his ladle just to see the children smile. Star giggled when he put an elaborate "S" on her snow. When she produced a second dish and then shot a sudden, adorably questioning look back at Thea, who was waiting off at the side, he took pity and drew a swirling "T" with the sap. Star rewarded him with a big kiss.

When she started to run off, he caught the back of her jacket. "Where's your sister?"

"I dunno." Clearly, she didn't care. She was in love with this person who was part of Heather.

Griffin, who was ladling syrup beside him, said, "She came by my pail with Rose Winslow's daughters. They're over on the hillside."

Micah checked. Missy was sitting on the snow with Emma, Ruth, and a handful of other little girls. She was picking at the things on her plate, and seemed happy enough.

Relieved by that, he went back to work. Once the children had their fill, the adults came by, and then there were seconds until his buckets ran dry. He was thinking that he ought to go back inside when, far down the drive, a Lake Henry police cruiser appeared.

He set the buckets down. He told himself it would be Pete stopping by to see how things were going, but he felt a chill on the back of his neck—a premonition—much as he had that morning more than three weeks before. He figured it wasn't just him, because around him the laughter seemed to fade and the crowd quieted.

He started forward. Cassie appeared in his periphery, but he kept walking. The cruiser slowed suddenly, though it was still a distance from the house. It had barely come to a halt when the passenger door opened.

Micah did stop then, but only until he saw Heather round the front of the car, pause for a single heart-stopping instant, then break into a run. Her coat flapped open; her hair flew to both sides. Even from the distance, he could see that she was crying, but her eyes were a sparkling silver, her face alive with happiness—and she was coming to him, *running* to him. Suddenly, he had no doubts. He didn't know why he ever had. What he and Heather shared didn't just go away. The mesh of their daily lives, the fit of their personalities, the passion—it hadn't been one-sided, and it *didn't* just go away.

He started to run, faster the closer she came, and then she was in his arms, sobbing his name, holding his neck so tightly that another man might have been strangled to death. Micah? After struggling with it for so many days, he could finally breathe.

"I love you," she whispered. She drew back, hesitant at the last moment. "Can I come back? I want to come back."

He wiped the tears from her cheeks with his thumbs and kissed her with all his strength, all his passion. Then he crushed her to him, closed his eyes to enjoy the pleasure of it, lifted her right off the ground and around. He felt dizzy, but it was part of the transition—that life to this. Good things were going to happen. He could feel it.

When he set her down, he couldn't stop smiling. Nor could she, with that badge-of-honor scar at the corner of her mouth, not even when she whispered that she wanted a shower, wanted to smell like herself, wanted shampoo and honeysuckle soap—and him. She touched his cheek in the gentle way she had, the way that said he meant more to her than anyone else in the world. Then she whispered, "I need to see my girls."

Incredibly, her eyes held his, asking permission.

He glanced back at the crowd to see Star slipping through legs. She ran to Heather, who caught her up off the ground and hugged her nearly as hard as she had hugged Micah.

"Where's Missy?" Heather asked Star, who looked back toward the crowd. Missy was there on its edge, looking as though she could as easily run, stay, or cry.

Come over here this minute, Micah wanted to scold, but caught himself. Those were his father's words, first scolding, then demanding, finally punishing if his will wasn't met. Micah had always wanted to be different from Dale. Heather had helped him.

She did it now. Passing Star to his arms, she crossed to where Missy stood. Micah didn't know if she spoke, he was too far away to hear, but he saw her tip her head and stroke Missy's hair.

Missy's chin trembled. She shot a look at Micah, but couldn't hold it there. When her eyes returned to Heather, they filled with tears. In a matter of seconds, her face crumbled and she went forward, slipping her arms around Heather's waist, locking her hands behind.

Others closed in then, hugging Heather in turns, though Heather kept Missy pressed close through it all.

Pete put a hand on Micah's shoulder. "We pulled strings to get her today. It was the least we could do. She's a good woman. You two need to be together."

Micah shook his hand. Still holding Star, but needing to be near Heather, he joined the crowd. As soon as he was close enough, Heather slid an arm around him. It was the four of them then, standing on the land they owned, surrounded by the people they loved. Right then, if Micah had been offered a million dollars for the land, five million for the business, and a bonus of another ten just for kicks, he would have refused it. He had the richest life any man could want.

Taking a long, deep, easy breath, he looked up. There, standing distant and apart, respectful of Heather and Micah and the life they had, were the Andersons.

Feeling confident now, Micah took Heather's hand. "There's someone I want you to meet." While he held Star, and Heather held Missy, he led her through the crowd. When they emerged on the sugarhouse side, Heather took in a sharp breath and stopped walking.

Micah tightened his hold of her hand.

Thea didn't move. She looked terrified. It occurred to him that while he was frightened of losing Heather to this child, Thea was frightened that her birth mother wouldn't even want to *see* her.

He gave Heather's hand a little forward tug. Quietly, he said, "That's her dad with her. They adore each other, and they have a good life. But she wants to meet you."

Heather looked up at him. Her silver eyes were shimmering with tears again. And again—incredibly—she was asking permission.

She could have asked for anything just then, and he'd have given it, he was that in love with her.

She must have seen it in his eyes, because she drew in a shaky breath and seemed to calm some. Then, taking Missy along with her, she approached Thea.

*   *   *

After a long, full, emotional day, Poppy knew what she needed to do. She didn't know whether it came from watching Micah and seeing growth, from watching Heather and seeing growth, or from watching Maida and seeing growth. All she knew was that she needed to grow, too.

Remarkably, Micah let sugaring go for the day. He had never done that before—at least, not in anyone's memory—but he wanted to be with Heather. That meant Poppy had Griffin with her now. He built a fire and manned the phones, while she changed and went into the exercise room. Victoria followed her in but stayed close by the door. Poppy imagined she was making sure Poppy didn't chicken out.

Poppy wasn't about to do that. It was time.

She did an upper-body workout, then used the recumbent bike for a bit. When she felt that she was sufficiently warmed up, she went to the wall where the leg braces hung. She hated everything about them—hated the sight, the feel, the sound. But they were the means to an end, and that end was the means to a beginning.

With the braces on her lap, she wheeled back to the parallel bars. She looked at them for a final moment, took a breath, and called out for Griffin.

He came to the door smiling. When he saw what she held, his smile faded. His eyes found hers. She saw a question there. She imagined that she also saw hope. Buoyed by that, she held out the braces. "Strapping them on takes a little effort. Will you help?"

*   *   *

Four weeks later, she set off on her own. She didn't say where she was going. She left Griffin writing the final pages of the Hayden biography, pre-occupied enough to assume she was just running into town for a bit. She didn't mind his preoccupation. She had been preoccupied in the last day or two herself.

Driving off in the Blazer, she rolled down her window. April had come, bringing warm rains that turned every unpaved road in town to mud. Sugaring was done for the year. Buds were starting to pop on the trees. Despite the mess underfoot, the air was earthy and full of promise.

Ice-out had occurred at two o'clock the afternoon before. Poppy had watched it from her deck, calling Griffin at the last minute when the ice just seemed to dissolve. Nathaniel Roy won the town pool, coming within an hour of the day and time, and by dusk, Poppy had calls of two separate loon sightings. She had listened from her deck after that, but hadn't heard a thing. She guessed that with only a handful of loons back, the territorial wars hadn't yet begun.

She might have kept a watch out for loons now as she drove around the lake, had her mind not been focused on another spot. Entering the center of town, she passed the town beach, the post office, the yellow Victorian that housed *Lake News*. Her palms were clammy on the steering wheel. As nervous as she was, she refused to turn back.

Turning into the parking lot at the very center of town, she went to the right of the church and started up the narrow cemetery road. It was paved, although only barely, and heavily puddled. Off the road, the snow was gone in all but the most shaded of spots, but the grass was still a winter brown, soggy at places, outright muddy at others.

She drove slowly on. She passed her father's grave and kept going. She passed Gus Kipling's grave and kept going. She crested the small rise that led to Perry's grave, drove to a spot directly opposite, and parked.

Giving herself no time to think, she took the lift to the ground and reached back into the Blazer for her things. The left brace went on, then the right one. She was adept at it now, slowed only by nervous fingers. She might have been going out on her first date, taking her first jump on water skis, waking up from a week's coma to learn that she was paralyzed. The apprehension was the same.

Perry was there, and she was here. The twenty yards separating them was a muddy chasm.

Quickly, lest she lose her nerve, she pulled her crutches from the Blazer and slid her forearms into place. Calculating the hardness of the ground, choosing her spots, she set the crutches, pulled herself forward in the wheelchair, took a deep breath, and levered herself up.

She had done this many times in the last month, practicing the motion and building her strength. In recent days, she had even done it without Griffin. But she had never done it outside the house. Moist earth alone was a challenge. Add to that the distance and the fact that if she fell, she was in trouble, and it was a very daunting challenge.

Determinedly, she shifted her weight onto her left leg, used her right hip to throw the right leg forward, shifted her weight onto that leg, drew the back leg forward, and let both share the weight. Taking a breath, she repeated the motion—shift onto the left, throw the right forward with the hip, drag the back leg up.

She did it again. And again. And again. She refused to look back, refused to think of the distance she was from her wheelchair. Nor did she look at the gravestones on either side. She kept her eyes on the ground ahead, trying to measure its firmness and avoid the muddiest of spots, as she concentrated on the motion of her lower half.

She took one step at a time—punctuating each with a little puff of breath—one clichéd step at a time—but it worked. Slowly, doggedly, she crossed the graveyard. She faltered a time or two when her crutch sank more deeply into the mud than she'd expected, but she remained upright.

What had been a raised slab of snow in February was now a stone bench. That was her goal. When she felt herself tiring—shoulders trembling, arms aching, hips threatening to spasm—she steadied herself, took a breath or two, looked at the bench. Then she plodded on, putting her weight on one leg, throwing the other forward, dragging the rear one up. The farther she went, the harder she breathed, and she was sweating now. But close. She was close. The closer she got, the more determined she grew.

Once upon a time, she would have run for the center of the bench, jumped right over it, and sat down with a grin. Now, with painstaking slowness, she advanced to the left, where the ground looked more solid. Breathing fast and loud, she came abreast of the bench and might easily have settled herself there. But she didn't want to be on the end. She wanted to be smack in the middle, facing Perry.

The last few steps were the hardest. She was tired—and increasingly emotional. As victorious as she felt in reaching this point, she also felt a keen sense of loss.

Nearly there, she took one hitching step, then a second. A third step took her to the center of the bench. Carefully, she turned. Using her crutches for leverage, she lowered herself to the bench and set them down. It was a minute before she recovered from the exertion and caught her breath.

Then, with a breath that shuddered for a whole other reason, she looked at the headstone. *Perry Walker,* it read. *Beloved Son and Friend, Here Too Short a Time.* Below were the dates of his birth and death.

As she stared at the inscription—read and reread it—her throat grew tight. When her eyes filled with tears that blurred the words, she imagined she saw Perry's face in the granite. This was where she had needed to be for so long.

"I'm sorry," she whispered brokenly. "I am so very sorry." Tears came then, and she didn't fight them. Grasping the edge of the bench, she cried for Perry and his family and all they had lost. She cried for her own family and all she had put them through. And she cried for herself—for the loss of her childhood and her athleticism, for the loss of a certain innocence and daring after that night twelve years before. She cried for things she knew she shouldn't—self-pitying things, like mobility and speed and smoothness—but she didn't fight the emotion either. It was a time for cleansing.

She cried until she ran out of tears. And still she sat with Perry. Without speaking aloud, she told him where she'd been and what she'd done since she had seen him last, knowing that he would hear somehow.

Finally, she closed her eyes, bowed her head, and recalled a prayer. She didn't know where she had heard it—actually, didn't know whether she had heard it at all or was simply making it up. It had to do with forgiveness.

A sound came. Eyes opening, she raised her head and listened. It was another minute before it came again, but the wait was worth it. She sat straighter and took a deep breath of the moist spring air. She did feel cleansed. Along with that feeling came a certain calm.

With a last look at Perry's grave, she picked up the crutches and slid her forearms in. Turning on the bench to gauge the return walk, she glanced back at the Blazer.

Griffin stood beside it.

She should have been surprised, but she wasn't. He was attuned to her needs. He must have known why she had wanted to walk. He had probably known why she had been preoccupied lately—and where she was headed today.

Seeing him there, she was struck by the rightness of it. He had been with her through this period of growth. More. He had been its catalyst, its inspiration in so many regards. Indeed, seeing him there in his jeans, sweater, and the same royal blue fleece jacket he had been wearing the first time they had met—a blue that picked up the blue in his eyes and was a perfect foil for hair that, in the sun, looked redder—she was struck by the idea that this moment was destined.

Seeing him there, she was nearly as overcome with emotion as she had been facing Perry. For Perry, it had been sorrow she felt. For Griffin, it was love. Seeing him there, she was so full of joy that she thought her heart might burst.

He didn't move. He didn't rush forward to take her arm or pick her up or express concern, though she did see concern on his face. But he was telling her that he had faith in her. He knew she could do this. He knew she could do most anything she set her mind to. And in that instant, she thought he might be right.

Smiling, she began to walk forward. Her gait was as faltering as it had been on the way out, but the awkwardness was irrelevant now, because she wasn't looking at a gravestone. She wasn't looking at a memory. She wasn't looking at the past. This time she was looking at the present and the future, and that was Griffin.

Only when she was under way did he begin to walk toward her, and then he did it slowly, matching his pace to hers in the most relaxed, most nonchalant of ways. She loved him more with every single uneven step she took.

He met her halfway. Then stood there, not touching her. "I am so in love with you I can't stand it," he said.

She started to laugh. He couldn't have said anything better.

He grinned, but the concern lingered in his eyes. It struck her then that the concern didn't have to do with whether she could walk through the mud on her own.

"I have something in my pocket," he said, and she knew he wasn't talking about a kiss.

"Can I see?" she asked, suddenly *dying* to see.

He stepped closer. "Reach in."

Adjusting her crutches, she put a hand in his pocket. There was only one thing there. She caught her breath.

"Take it out," he whispered.

Her hand emerged with the ring on the tip of her finger. He slid it on the rest of the way, then let her look, and she gasped. The diamond was emerald-cut and exquisite, flanked by single baguettes, the whole of it set in platinum.

"The center stone was my mother's," he said softly. "I would be honored if you would wear it."

Poppy could barely breathe. "Omigod," she whispered. "It's *gorgeous.*" And suddenly she was tired of standing. She threw her arms around Griffin's neck as the crutches fell to the ground. He picked her right up in his arms.

"Gorgeous isn't yes or no," he said against her hair.

"Yes. *Yes!*" she cried, but another cry echoed it. It was one she had heard a short time before, risen from the lake to mark a rebirth.

The loons had returned to Lake Henry.